SHADOWS & FLAMES

TWIN BLADES

BOOK TWO

NOELLE UPTON

Reader Note and Content Warnings

Hello, Dear Reader!

Twin Blades was my first novel, and Shadows and Flames is a continuation of Em and El's story. It is best you familiarize yourself with the events of Twin Blades before embarking on this story.

In this novel, please be aware of the following content:

I've left out the specifics of these, but if you'd like a more specific description of content you want to be aware of, please don't hesitate to reach out to me!

- Mature and explicit sexual content
- Suicidal ideation
- Mention of self-harm
- Mention of sexual assault
- Grief process as a central theme
- Prejudice
- Death of a child (not on-page)
- Explicit violence
- Gore

• Explicit language

• Mental health struggles including depression and PTSD

Lastly, if you are so inclined, I LOVE real-time reactions (makes it a lil easier to deal with the silence while people are reading the book haha).

Thank you again for reading Shadows and Flames!

x Noelle

For my husband.

And for the love of broody boys.

I
DEATH

CHAPTER ONE
ELIÁN

THREE MONTHS AFTER HER

"Why am *I* being punished?" I gritted through my teeth. It was taking all of my strength to not let the depth of my anger show. But I managed. Barely.

"You're being punished, Master Elián, because you've taken it upon yourself to settle a score with your Shadow brother after your Elders have already decided his sentence," Master Varus drawled from his end of the table.

My chin raised, and I didn't remove my eyes from his. Friend of my father's or not, Varus hadn't been much of a fan of me. "I did not agree with the sentence."

"Be that as it may. You are prohibited from securing contracts in the name of The Shadows for the next six months." Both of my brows rose, but when my gaze landed on Noruh at her place at the table of seven, I wiped all expression from my face.

I pressed my fist to my chest and bowed my head.

"You are dismissed." Varus waved his hand toward the door, and I wasted no time. I spun on my heel and pivoted out of the Elder Chambers on silent steps.

I kept my hands behind my back and eyes forward while I

prowled through the Shadow Well halls. Hunting and killing Jones had been irritatingly easy. Once I returned to the Well and discovered that he had never came back after… I left immediately to track him down. He'd been hiding out at his *mother's* home for goddess's sake.

When I'd dragged him back for sentencing, for justice, I pled my case to be the one to punish him. Death, and a painful one, was my request. Smoke nearly blew out of my ears when the Elders were even more lenient on him than they had just been on me.

I turned around the corners of the dimly lit corridors, boots slipping across black stone, and then up a set of stairs. It had been even easier to follow behind him as he left on his first contract. My need to work off that rage kept me focused, careful. And Jones feeling safe and cleared left him unguarded. He routinely stuck to his training while he sought out his mark, creeping into their home in one of the southern Trylas villages.

I watched from the trees as he slit the target's throat and collected the silver locket he was to take back to his contract's employer. My fingers had reached up to grasp my medallion until I remembered it was gone. I'd given it to *her*.

Jones and I had been raised in the Well together, along with Leandro, Tomás, and Noruh. And he'd always been greedy. His mark had an extensive wine collection, it turned out, and I found Jones in the dead male's cellar, sampling at his leisure.

Now, the Master's wing of the Well was quiet, and it was another surprising blessing. My steps slowed to a stop as I unlocked the door and slipped into my room at the end of the last corridor. I had never thought much about decorating my space here, but the darkness now seemed empty where before I'd seen it as simple. Sparse now when it had been organized before.

I stripped off my leathers and weapons and collapsed in my undershorts onto the bed, large and dressed in a simple deep blue blanket. My arms dug into my thighs while I sat, thinking.

That ruined king offered him a hefty payment to do his bidding—that was why Jones had followed the order to attack his brother Shadow. And his own prejudiced views made him sympathetic to *her* brother's plans. We had been raised at the Well, yes, but the traditions and views of our homelands still had a hold. Jones was from Krisla and saw the Vyrkos as the reason for all our race's problems.

Even after traveling the realm, when I finally tracked down Jones, the cold of Trylas offended my body on a base level while I sliced into him, torturing out every piece of information he had.

I scoffed aloud, and ran my hand through my hair. My fingernails were blunt and could never scratch my scalp like she could. The thought of it sent a phantom ripple down my neck.

After he'd given me all he had, burning Jones had done little to satisfy my bloodlust. Though usually stoic, Jones had screamed as I let all my rage out onto him.

The Elder Shadows found out what I did soon after, as I had not tried to hide it. If they were content to let Jones off with barely a slap on his greedy wrist, I would do what they wouldn't. Damn the consequences. I had a sneaking suspicion that Noruh had convinced them to make said consequences less severe than they should have been. I killed another Shadow for revenge, and six months without working was *less* than a slap on the wrist.

A lick of flame bloomed in my palm, and I skated it along the edges of my hand, rolled it over my knuckles. But this release of the Fire, even in this small way, was hollow. I'd come back to deal with Jones and see that the Shadows were all right. To see that Noruh had left her contract safely.

I punished the one who betrayed me, ensured my siblings were safe—so why did I feel as though I made a mistake returning to the Well? And I could not help but wonder—where was *she*?

Another flame lit on my other hand, and I concentrated on juggling the fire to clear my mind. There was no reason to feel guilty. I was a Shadow, and she had been right—I would always return to the Well at one point or another.

But without her here, without the cool darkness she provided… the fire in my hands felt dull. When I closed my eyes, I saw her above me, unclothed and head thrown back in ecstasy. But it wasn't just the feeling of being inside her that left my mouth dry, my heart swelling and cracking at the same time. It was the flames I conjured, dancing around her face like the rays of the sun that she was.

I had never felt anything like it. Like her. When our gifts from the sister Goddesses met, it was like a homecoming. In her Death, I felt settled and at home while still bright—*alive*.

But she would not *listen* to me. She would not hear me. And now it was done. There was no—I snuffed out the fire on my hands and was descended into the darkness of my room once more. There was no point in thinking about her anymore. It was done.

"Open up, mate, or I'm breaking down the door!" My jaw ground, and I scrubbed my hand over my face. The beard I'd grown in these months itched my skin, but I could not be bothered to shave it off.

I stood and made my way to the door, opening it a sliver for my Shadow brother. "I'm not in the mood for company."

Before I could shut the door completely, Tomás stuck his boot in the threshold and pushed back. "I heard about the Elders' decision. Thought you could use some cheering up." Another push against the door had me relenting to his intrusion. I didn't have the energy to resist his persistence.

I stepped back and made my way to the bottle on my bedside table. Sleep was elusive these days, but when my mind was swimming, it was a bit easier to grasp. When I extended the half-full bottle to Tomás, he took a small sip before handing it back to me.

His lanky form slumped into one of the chairs before the small, unlit hearth opposite my bed. The mattress dipped as I sat once again, and I downed almost all that was left in the bottle. Tomás's eyes were filled with judgement, but I didn't have the energy to be embarrassed in my own room. The alcohol didn't even burn anymore.

"Still stuck on that queen?" He lounged back in the leather armchair and crossed an ankle over his knee. When I returned, I hadn't told anyone what happened between her and I, but Tomás guessed after hearing my recounting of Jones's betrayal at the Elder hearing.

I didn't grace him with an answer, though. Instead, I took another swig from the bottle and wiped my mouth with the back of my hand. There was nothing to say.

"So, now what? What are you going to do?" I narrowed my eyes at his question. What was there to do? Wait out my sentence. Perhaps direct my attention to training the acolytes until my six months were up. Then, the same as always. Contract after contract until… another contract.

My teeth clenched when the memory of glowing waves flashed behind my eyes. She had asked what I did for fun that night. It wasn't until that moment that I realized there wasn't much.

"Aeras really got to you with this one, didn't They?"

I glared over the space between us. The fire in my blood throbbed. I felt like I could almost still taste her on my tongue. "Do not make me tell the Elders about *your* run-in with her."

Third on my list of priorities in returning to the Well was confronting Tomás about his teaching her some of our ways. When I saw her in that ring, silently and fluidly maneuvering around her opponent, I'd wanted to drag her past the barrier by her braids and plunge my sword into her gut. Our techniques were sacred. A petty pickpocket mimicking such a thing felt like the deepest insult. And when I took her money, it had only seemed fair after she insulted me again by disrupting my contract.

But after my time at her side, I'd all but forgotten the reason we'd first met. When she told me of Tomás teaching her to settle a debt, I could see that she had felt guilty for not telling me sooner. Unlocking the answer felt just as hollow as I was now.

Tomás rolled his eyes and waved a dark hand in the air. "I know you won't say anything. Although I hate to admit it, she saved my arse that day. Seemed like a fair enough trade."

"It was a fair trade to betray our ways?" But my question had no conviction. It hardly mattered anymore. I drained the rest of the bottle.

He shrugged. "At the time, I suppose." He pointed at my hands. "You know, drinking yourself sick isn't going to make you feel any better."

I put the bottle back on the side table and grumbled, "And talking is? Leave."

Tomás ran a hand through his long, loced hair and looked me over contemplatively. His eyes landed on my lap. "Could give you a distraction."

Now I was the one to roll my eyes. "Is that what you came in here for?"

He shrugged again. "It was just an offer. Seeing as how you don't want to talk. I know Danner's been trying to get your attention again. He was in the common room earlier."

My hands scrubbed my face. I had no desire to take pleasure in Tomás or Danner or Noruh after experiencing *her*. I'd already had to swat Danner's hands away thrice now. Before, I had let his body take my frustration, allowed him to bring me to release. But the thought of touching anyone else right now made my skin crawl.

"No."

Tomás heaved a heavy sigh and began to stand. "Well, if you're content to rotting away in your own misery, I will leave you to it. But if not, we could go spar or run to take the edge off."

If there was ever a time to miss Leandro, it was now. He wasn't like me. He and Tomás could go on for hours talking about anything and everything, and he had never been one to dwell for very long. And he would also know just how to make me feel better. He would find the words I couldn't and speak for the both of us.

I looked down at his name in my hand and scratched at my beard with the other.

"Fine." I stood and crossed to the wardrobe that held my lighter training clothes. If I couldn't go out and make coin, the only thing I *could* do was train. The trousers and tunic were looser than my usual leathers, and once I pulled both on, I turned back to Tomás who had taken post beside the door.

His lips pulled to the side, as if he was trying to decide what to say. I'd heard the whispers after killing Jones. Some of my siblings thought something was wrong with me, that I'd gotten too emotionally involved in my last contract. I could not deny it. What was worse was that I did it all for nothing.

"Mate, why don't you just go find her?"

I tried to push past him toward the door. "Find who."

Tomás shoved my chest, and I glared at him. I'd agreed to training with him so that we *didn't* have to talk. "Just go find her and talk to her. Godyx knows that it would give us all a bit of peace."

I shoved back on his chest and got my hand around the doorknob. Before I opened it, I ground out the words, "She made it clear that I couldn't be a Shadow and choose her."

He scoffed, "Don't blame her." My head whirled around, incredulous. Tomás chuckled as we made our way out to the corridor. "Jones helped her brother try to kill her? I wouldn't want anything to do with us either. But it's been six months." He shrugged and cracked his knuckles. "She might be more willing to hear you out, now."

He didn't think I'd thought of that? Every day, I drank or trained away the thought of finding her and getting on my knees, trying to convince her that we could have both things. But the way she'd looked at me, tears running down her cheeks because of *my* words—I hadn't been heartbroken like that in over a century.

Tomás continued on under his breath. "If I were you, I'd stop your wallowing and track her down. What else do you have to do?"

We went down the steps and headed toward the courtyard while I turned over his words. She'd said that they were leaving everything behind. She could be anywhere. There had been no sign of her during open contract bids, no talk of her from other blades for hire. I did not even know where to start.

I pushed open the door that led to outside, and the gray sky was a blanket over the mid-afternoon sun. The forest surrounding the Shadow Well was dense, expansive, and my muscles hummed in anticipation of weaving through the trees and leaping over the brush.

"Ready?" Tomás jutted his head toward the darkened wood.

A soft breeze swept the small courtyard. It rustled my hair that had grown too long in these months. I tucked the frontmost strands away from my face and angled toward where he indicated. "Ready."

Chapter Two

Elián

Ten months after her

I do not even know why I let them drag me in here.

I clutched my glass in my hand, and I was halfway toward needing to refill it for the fourth time. This common room was unofficially designated for the more seasoned Shadows staying at the Well, and though they didn't live here as much as I did, it seemed that Tomás and Noruh were determined to embarrass me. They said I'd been punishing myself enough, which was completely incorrect—I just had no desire to be around my siblings when we weren't training.

In my other hand, I held a set of old, peeling cards. "Your turn, *Nogón*," Tomás drawled across the table. He'd roped me into playing a game, but I hadn't been paying attention when he explained the rules. I plucked a card at random from my hand and threw it down at the middle of the table.

Noruh sat to my right, hunched over and staring at her hand intently. She threw her pale blonde hair over her shoulder before sighing and throwing down two cards atop mine. She crossed her arms and slumped back in her seat.

Tomás grinned evilly over his cards and placed one on the table. "I win."

"Bullshit," Noruh hissed and glared down at the pile of cards. I rolled my eyes and drained the rest of my drink.

"No bullshit, love. Believe you both will be working my acolyte training shifts this next moon. Split them amongst yourselves." He fluttered his deep brown fingers at us, and I shrugged as I stood. There wasn't much else for me to do anyway. I still had two months left of my punishment for killing Jones, and there were far worse things than training the potential Shadows. My brother, though, despised that part of our responsibilities.

The common room was particularly busy tonight, what with the swearing in of a new Shadow upon us tomorrow. We didn't replenish our ranks very often, as The Killings had definitely taken a toll on our numbers. There were seven in this room, and it already felt like a quarter of us.

The Well was primarily a quiet place, one of solitude and purpose. I reached the long table at the far wall of the dim room that was stocked with multiple kinds of drink. A large hearth sat beside it, and the heat settled some of the tightness in my lungs. Once my glass was full again, I turned back to retake my seat.

A few of my Shadow siblings eyed me warily, but I paid them no mind. The Elder Shadows didn't often have to reprimand us. We were trained assassins—our moral compass allowed for many deeds. But killing another member wasn't something that occurred frequently. We were widespread and mostly respected one another, even if we didn't always get along. Still, I had no regrets about hunting Jones down and killing him. I would do it again if I could.

Danner was sitting with Zafina on one of the low leather sofas, and he tried to make eye contact with me as I sat back down with Tomás and Noruh.

"Up for another game?" Tomás winked at us, and the glint in

his light brown eyes was reflected by the shining silver hoop through his right nostril and his bright, white teeth.

Noruh snorted into her own glass of wine. "You must be joking." She pointed a finger at him. "I know you and your trickster ways. We barely even know the rules of the game!"

He scoffed and clutched a hand to his chest. "You wound me! I am just trying to have a fun evening with my oldest and dearest friends." But I knew that look in his eye just as well as Noruh did. His nimble fingers, also dressed in silver rings, shuffled the old card deck with an expert quickness. Tomás had been hustling and stealing long before he'd become a Shadow. If he wanted to, Noruh and I would be tricked into shouldering his duties until the end of time.

"You are a dirty cheat, that's what you are." Noruh looked at me expectantly when Tomás scoffed and feigned more offense. I just cocked a brow at her and threw back more of my drink.

"All right, *fine*. We don't have to play another game. Wouldn't want you to punish me, too." His eyes cut toward her.

Noruh's blue-green stare narrowed at Tomás, then at me. She'd been chosen by the last group of Elders to take over another's seat when their term ended. She was the first of us to serve the position, as we had just reached the seniority threshold to be chosen. Though I'd told Tomás I suspected Noruh had argued for me to have a lesser punishment for my offense, he hadn't relented in teasing her about it.

"And you think that's my fault?" she shot at him.

He shrugged. "Well, it's one-seventh your fault. Look at him!" Tomás shot his hand out at me, but I just scratched at my bearded cheek. "He's been stuck at the Well for months getting *worse*, and he's even quieter than before."

She rolled her eyes. "And you think saying that and making him do your chores are what's going to get him to speak to you more? Besides, not everyone dislikes living here or training the acolytes. Did you ever think that some of us like it?" I hadn't asked her to defend me, and I knew it was likely guilt about being part of my punishment that motivated her. But she was right. I did enjoy teaching the acolytes. It wasn't one of my few duties that I disliked, anyway. And though I had homes in a few of the busier cities throughout the realm—it made it easier to take contracts when I had a residence to stay in—I was one of the few that stayed at the Well for the majority of the year.

Noruh and Tomás were the opposite—they mostly came here for the few Shadow ceremonies we were all called to attend or when they had to train or meet with the others.

"Nor, you cannot be serious." He lowered his voice since we were drawing the eyes of the others in the room. "You know that Jones deserved it."

Noruh snorted. "I know. *That's* why I did the best I could to talk the rest of them down from a harsher sentence, you lout."

"Ugh." He turned back to me and looked at my empty glass. "And you? Want to play another round?"

It took me a moment to follow my brother's bouncing train of thought. "No. Like she said, I barely know the rules. And I teach the acolytes enough." I took another sip of the liquor and felt the slight warming of it in my chest.

"Then what, we drink ourselves into a stupor?"

I glared over the table at him. "Exactly," I said as I threw back the rest and slammed the empty glass on the table. Tomás didn't abstain from alcohol, but he barely ever drank to excess. I could count on one hand the amount of times I'd seen him drunk in the past two hundred and thirty years.

"Back me up, here!" He looked back to Noruh, apparently wanting her on his side again.

My gaze cut to her, daring her to speak, and the concern on her face made my eyes narrow even more.

"I'm leaving," I said quietly and stood. Neither of them tried to follow me, but I felt their eyes on my back as I grabbed one of the bottles at the back of the room and left.

My steps were silent and steady—it would take a lot more for my mind to descend into a stupor—as I made my way down the dark corridor. The black walls were bare aside from the lamps placed intermittently so that the place wasn't in total darkness. Though it was cool here, my mind flashed memories of warm Temple halls decorated with intricate tapestries.

I raised the bottle to my mouth and took a swig. A drop of flame lit on my other hand, and I juggled it between my knuckles as I walked.

"Elián," a deep voice called behind me, and I held back a wince. But I stopped, and turned around to face the one who had followed me out of the common room. I extinguished the flame.

I'd hoped he would grow uninterested, but Danner seemed determined to get me in his bed again. "Danner," I greeted. His pale skin was lightly flushed, and his light hair was almost as long as mine now was. His deep chocolate eyes almost reminded me of *hers*, and I ground my teeth at the realization.

He was dressed in an easy, white tunic and tight leather trousers, and perhaps it was the alcohol or the months since I'd returned, but I could remember why I'd been drawn to him throughout the years. He was just slightly shorter than me, his lean but strong frame eager to take anything I gave him.

But I hadn't touched anyone else since *her*, and I had barely even felt my own hand. It all felt so pointless and empty.

Even now with heat plain in his stare as he stopped very close in front of me, I felt no desire whatsoever.

"I've been trying to get your attention, if you haven't noticed." He smirked at me, point of his right fang showing, and I let him inch another step closer.

"I know," I said as I looked down at him. He smelled of grass fields and fresh-tilled earth. It was once a smell that reminded me of a place not far from my father's home. When Papá, Leandro, and I would leave the Well to stay at his house, we would sometimes take a basket of food to eat in the sprawling meadow. My twin brother and I used to catch the grasshoppers and examine them before they jumped out of our palms.

Danner stepped closer to me, and my head tilted, considering. Maybe it was time to feel this again. The physical exertion of teaching and training on my own did distract me for that stretch of time. But even the liquor didn't adequately quiet my thoughts, the ruminating.

He raised a hand and rested it on my chest. I'd actually dressed in something besides training clothing or leathers, and the embroidered, high-collared Zonoran vest left most of my torso bare. Danner's hand was callused and dry on my skin, but it was almost as warm as my own. He applied a bit of pressure, and I let him push me back into the wall of the corridor.

A pair of Shadows walked lazily up the hall, probably headed for the common room, but they barely even glanced our way as they passed.

Danner's thin lips wasted no time lunging for mine, and I pressed my mouth back onto his. His other hand twined in my hair, untucking it from behind my ear. His kiss made my lower belly stir slightly, and I focused on that feeling, trying to make it take me over.

He prodded his tongue at the seam of my lips, and I let him in. My hands were still down at my sides, one still clutching the bottle of brown liquor, but Danner clung to me with his entire body. His chest pressed against mine, hips grinding as we kissed.

He detached from my mouth, only to make his way down my jaw to latch himself at my neck. Danner's hands were now on my hips, and I met the iron press of his cock with my half-hard one. I looked, unseeing, at the wall across from us while he licked and nibbled. Before, when he and I would sometimes fuck, this touch from him would leave me shoving him into the nearest empty room and demanding he take his clothes off.

But now, the lust didn't rise. My body halfheartedly stirred, and I again tried to focus on the parts of me that did respond to Danner's familiar touch. He never demanded I talk or that I share anything other than flesh.

I reached a hand between us—maybe touching him would help. He moaned into my throat while I palmed his cock, feeling it jerk. I sent more warmth into my grasp, and moved my hand against him, still focusing my gaze on the wall opposite.

If I closed my eyes, I'd only see her.

"I need you so badly," he rasped before shoving his hands in my loose trousers. I leaned my head back against the wall and let Danner work my body to respond.

He brought me in for another long kiss before dropping to his knees.

I watched him, concentrating on filling my mind with only this. He unfastened my trousers easily enough, and once my cock was out, he gave it a few jerks that made my hips buck involuntarily.

When he finally took me in his mouth, I didn't have to feign the grunt of pleasure. Danner sucked and licked in a way that my body remembered, responding even when my mind was somewhere else.

"Oh for the love of—"

I heard Tomás's grating voice and turned my head in the direction of the common room. He and Noruh were leaving together, and they didn't stop walking. But judgement filled their eyes as they watched me get my cock sucked in the middle of the corridor. I couldn't bring myself to care. The acolytes weren't permitted in this part of the Well, and I had certainly witnessed those two in similar positions many times.

I raised a brow at them as they passed and took another swig from my bottle. They quickly turned down a corner, and I was left alone again. My best friend had been trying to goad me into leaving my room for something other than my duties for months, and now he wanted to tell me how to do it. He'd told me to search for *her*, and I just kept returning to the Well without catching even a glimpse. For nearly six months, I returned to the Well empty-handed. Again and again.

Then, Tomás told me to try moving on, so that's what I was doing.

Danner's slurping and moaning were nearing obscene, and I

felt the release barreling down my shaft. I watched him fist his own cock while his head bobbed over mine, and for a second, for a moment, I was lost in it. I grunted as I fisted his hair and thrust faster and faster into his mouth until my lids clenched closed. My toes curled, and my cock went almost painfully stiff before it shot down his throat.

My head craned back to the wall while I caught my breath, and when my eyes opened to stare at the ceiling, that sinking feeling in my chest came back with renewed weight. It was even fucking heavier.

Danner groaned with his own release, his seed splattering on the floor between us. I glanced down and saw him wipe it up with a rag he pulled from his pocket, and I grunted.

We didn't speak to each other—we usually didn't afterward—and quickly sorted our clothes out before parting. Though my limbs felt less tense, my mind was still dark, perhaps even more so than before.

My room was a quick walk two floors higher. I quickly fished my key out of my pocket and shut myself in my own solitude. I breathed in and out, and after reaching for my necklace out of sheer habit, I ran a frustrated hand through my hair.

I was taken again with how sparse it was in here. When I'd been in her home, in her childhood bedroom, it was neat, but there had been so many *things*. Some from cities that I had recognized, some not. Books and artwork and drawings of the people that she'd encountered and loved.

Had that wall of drawings in Versillia been destroyed with the rest of the estate?

I sat down before my small hearth and let flames erupt from my hands. The firewood I'd replenished after my morning lessons caught quickly, but I didn't pull my left hand away as the fire transferred. The palm with my brother's name stayed in the flames, and I wondered if he could feel it, wherever he was.

The cut in my soul, the wound that existed since Leandro

died, had healed. Or, at least, I thought it had until I returned to the Well when she'd told me to go.

I'd grieved my father and twin fiercely and for a long time. But at a certain point, I pulled myself out of it. Got back to working, training. It felt like the days had purpose. But now, it was like everything was tedious. The alcohol softened the edges of it, but it never really disappeared.

I stared at the flames enveloping my fingers, my wrist. They lapped at my skin, and try as I might, I couldn't help but remember how her darkness felt on my body. It cooled the edge of my heat and allowed for the brightest, purest parts of it to shine. To blaze.

At some point, as I sat there, my eyes began to fill and spill over. This had become a nightly ritual as well. Throughout the day, I focused on teaching the young fighters their forms and exercises, then I trained by myself or with whichever Shadow was available. I ran the forest outside. I trained again until my body finally felt tired enough to stop.

And when there was nothing left to do for the day, I retreated here, and the thoughts of all I'd lost would barrel through my mind.

Another pull from the bottle, and the memories became watery, less tangible. My twin and his jokes, my father and his easy nature, my mother and her steady guidance, and—

A silent sob wracked my body, and I set the bottle on the stone next to me. I pulled my hand out of the fire and scrubbed both over my face.

What else was there?

Tom and Noruh were staying around the Well for me. I knew they were. But soon they would realize that their attempts couldn't pull me out of this.

I—I wasn't sure anything could pull me out of this.

And, eventually I would be able to take contracts again. They would leave, and I would venture out, but I *knew* that the hollowness would follow me.

And I still loved her.

So, here, alone, I hugged my knees to my chest, and hummed to myself. My favorite song that my mother would sing to me played in my head, and then, voice cracking, I picked up the somber melody. The lilting scales still soothed the deepest part of me, and when the words ended, I picked up another song while staring at the fire I made with the power the Goddess had given me.

Chapter Three
Elián

One year after her

My mark wasn't even able to struggle in my grip before I slit their throat. Their blood was a curious, dark shade of green. Their gray skin was cooler than most other beings I had come into contact with, but they bled and died all the same.

They slumped against my hold as their life drained down their front, staining and saturating their simple yet neat clothing. A gurgling sound bubbled up as they tried to speak or breathe, but there was no use, of course. Before I let them fall to the ground, I snatched my proof of kill from their belt.

The little chittering creature that hired me for this particular contract had not paid all that much, but I was eager to take anything and everything to keep myself busy.

The bejeweled rapier I was instructed to bring back was very fine. If it had not been me, I was sure my mark would have gotten killed and robbed for it since they insisted carrying it around like this for all to see. The streets of Banfas were not dangerous, necessarily, but anyone with sense wouldn't walk these dark streets boasting a useless, expensive ornament like this.

I was beginning to think more and more that my employer had no other reason to wish this person dead aside from stealing the weapon and assuring they wouldn't come looking for it. The hilt was obscene with gaudy rubies and gold pommel and cross-guard. It was almost embarrassing for me to carry it at all.

The rapier was an irritating weight in the long pack slung over my shoulders, but I would be rid of it come tomorrow. My mark, I left slumped against the stone wall of one of the buildings that made up the alley. Someone would find them in the morning soon enough.

I looked up to the sky and bent my neck from side to side, stretching it and waiting. A few Banfians passed by up ahead, and I waited in the shadows for an opportunity to slip out unseen. Not that I was that worried about being caught, but the caution was engrained in me.

When all was clear, I slunk out down pale paved streets. The air was blessedly warm and dry, and a large part of me felt easier here. It wasn't Zonoras, but it was the closest I'd ever get.

The city was tremendously old, and the structures I passed had obviously weathered many sandstorms. They were spaced to maximize precious airflow, and while the pale stone blended with the sprawling desert just outside of the city, the Banfian people decorated their shopfronts, porches, and bodies with richly colored tapestries and fabrics. Oranges, reds, and purples brightened what would have been a dull sight as I made my way to our—my apartment.

It was far from the city center, but luckily my mark had been headed that way anyway. It was less busy here, away from the main markets and royal palace.

I slunk down another alleyway and entered the side door to the nondescript building. The ground floor held a vacant office space now, though businesses had cycled through over the centuries.

It was only three stories, and when I reached the top of the old steps, mine was the last of six doors in the corridor. The last person to rent a room had been a few decades ago, as far as I knew. My father had purchased the building before Leandro and I were born, and when they died, ownership transferred to me. I did not care to promote the vacancies, so I had the whole structure to myself these days. Not that I stayed here much.

Once inside, I began my routine of checking the lofted space, though I'd known I was alone when I'd entered the building.

When we'd been sworn in as Shadows, Leandro and I had chosen this apartment for the high ceiling and large window that overlooked the street. It wasn't the most practical for a Shadow —we'd admittedly been too excited at the prospect of having our first space that was *ours* and the idea of jumping from the upper level with our beds to the main floor below was too enticing to pass up.

Now, I threw my pack down on the long sofa that faced the wall of window. My father had insisted on purchasing and installing glass that would obstruct any outside view within while allowing a clear view from inside the apartment. And for our own short-sightedness, my father made us pay for the modification out of our first few contracts. That had taken at least a year, but we did not care.

When I'd arrived yesterday, I had to sweep and dust away about three years of no one entering the space at all, but I didn't keep much in here anymore. The first time I'd drummed up the courage to return after Leandro and Papá were killed, I'd sold most of it and packed away the smaller things that held memories. They were now in a trunk that sat in the corner of the room, and I looked at it now as I flopped down on the sofa.

I didn't bother lighting the hearth or the candles around the room, and there were no lamps or magic lights in here. We'd never needed them, and the moonlight and activity outside illuminated the space fine enough.

I sat there for a while, staring at the trunk, before shaking myself out of my rumination and retreating into the bathing room to wash. About two hundred years ago, we'd had it renovated to include a large tiled shower that was only slightly less expensive than the window. Luckily, we had more money to fund the project at that point.

The rust-colored tiles were cool under my feet, the water scalding, and I washed quickly, lest the thoughts come through as they always did in my idle moments. Once I emerged and dressed in loose undershorts, I brushed through my hair. Before I could avoid looking at myself in the mirror, I remarked how much I looked like my father this way. He had always worn his brown hair longer, well past his shoulders. Maybe that was why I had hesitated and given up each time I reached for shears to cut it.

I had kept the beds upstairs, where Leandro and I used to sleep when we stayed here, but nowadays I made do with the sofa. Reaching in my pack past the rapier I'd be rid of tomorrow, I retrieved a bundle of spiced, dried meat and my skin of water. Feeding had been one of my travel preparation tasks before leaving the Well one week ago so that I wouldn't have to seek out blood while I was here.

The sun wouldn't rise for some time. My mark had been laughably easy to find, and just to prolong the hunt, before I killed him, I'd diverted and tried to… look for her.

My punishment for killing Jones had ended six months ago, and though I'd given up for a short time, after starting up contracts, I could not help but try to seek her out everywhere I went. I tried to pick up her scent, to look down every street to catch a glimpse. I lingered in the taverns and backrooms where we solicited work, willing for her to just walk through the door with her daggers on her thighs and her plaits trailing down her back.

But it never happened. I took contracts in a new city every time, sometimes traveling for weeks on end, but to no avail.

I tore through a piece of meat and chewed perfunctorily while mentally crossing Banfas off of my list. The water in the skin had warmed from being in my pack all day and night, but it helped clear the tough meat. And I couldn't—I knew that I could not keep drinking to numb my mind. Though Tomás had belabored that point for weeks, *months*, I eventually came to the decision on my own.

Even when I passed out on my bed at the Well, body exhausted from constant training and stomach empty except for the sloshing liquid I'd been consuming since ending my duties for the day, thoughts of her never truly left. The disorientation just made it worse.

One night when I stumbled around my room, I'd thought for a moment that she *was* there. But I'd been in the half-asleep state, forgetting that I was dreaming, and when I did fully wake, I had descended into frustrated tears and shoved over my wardrobe until it crashed onto the floor. The next morning, when I was sober, I looked around at the mess I'd made and sighed in resignation.

No, I knew that I wouldn't be able to continue on like that. The first few nights without ending my day in a drunken slumber were more difficult than I thought they would be. But… it did make me feel better. If at the very least because Tom and Noruh stopped looking at me with that frustrated pity. And the more I just accepted the thoughts and the pain, let them wash over me, it became easier to breathe.

I looked out on the outskirts of Banfas, and I thought of Mamá. She had not liked the bustling cities, but she took Leandro and me to Banfas sometimes for theatre performances, festivals, and to shop the markets. When Zonoras fell, Papá used the building for somewhere to stay when my brother and I longed for the dry desert heat. It was the closest we could lay our heads when we wanted to be close to her.

And now they were all gone.

The dried beef and water filled my stomach easily enough, and I felt my body request the rest of sleep. There was no doubt that I would dream of her. I had every night since leaving the witches' cottage. Sometimes it was just her voice, sometimes the sensation of her Death curling around me, or it was swirling flashes of my memories with her.

My fingers twisted in my hair, gathering it at the base of my skull and braiding it over my shoulder in the way the golden witch taught me. One of my first nights away from the Well after my punishment ended, I'd tried to plait my hair all the way down my scalp like *she* wore it. But it was infuriatingly difficult to do on myself, so I quickly gave up.

Few people were out at this time of night, but I watched a group of adolescents laugh and run down the darkened streets. My lips turned up as I remembered Leandro, Noruh, Tomás, and I behaving similarly when they would visit. When things felt so much easier.

I retrieved a thin strap of leather from my pack and tied off the tight braid. The sofa was comfortable enough, and I pulled on one of the blankets Papá had made for us when we were born. He'd added to it over the years as we grew, and the patched look and feel of it always made it my favorite, even when he gifted us finer blankets and quilts later.

I'd long ago brought it from the Well to live here, in this place that was mine and my twin's. Perhaps one day I would move everything to Papá's old house by the river, but that was for another time. As I lay my head down on the old pillow I retrieved from the loft, I counted the number of cities I'd searched for her. Where I'd taken contracts to try and revive my older self. Banfas was number five, and though I was dreading the next one, I felt a bit… steadier now.

My mind was clear, and as I closed my eyes, I still saw the lights from the city behind my lids. I rehearsed the words in my mind, what I would say to her when I finally saw her. And after I ran through them over and over, my trailing thoughts ran to the Zonoran lullabies, as they always did.

I would retrieve my payment and get rid of the ghastly rapier. And then I would proceed to the next place to look for her. Across another sea, away from Savya to the land many of my kind called home. To Eryva.

To Nethras.

Chapter Four
Tomás

Thryx, give me the wherewithal to withstand this grumbling, I chanted to myself. Not that They would really care about this particular situation, but I found myself praying to the Godyx every time I had to deal with him and this rubbish.

The closer we got to his female's apartment, he became more and more of a complete arse. Granted, he was a complete arse a lot of the time. But this past year had been a nightmare to witness. I hated to admit that I was truly afraid there for a moment. The lingering stench of drink and self-loathing had been like a cloud around his body, to the point that the others hadn't wanted to be around him.

For the entire time I'd known him, my best mate was a quiet and respected member of our little group. Some were wary of him and his Fire, but if I was still walking around and not a smoldering pile of ash yet, they had nothing to fear.

But while he'd been despairing over *her*, he had scared me.

I shook my head and cleared *those* thoughts. Nethras was an all right city—reminded me a bit of where I'd lived before being swept up into the Shadows, actually. The towering brick buildings close together, the mix of races walking past us in varying dress and speaking several languages settled something inside of me.

Those at the Well had been born all over, and though we could mostly dress however we liked there, we'd all been around each other too long. The same corridors with the same people could be so banal. I could never understand why my best mate chose to stay there more often than not. After I'd been sworn in and could buy my own apartment back in Sjatas, I couldn't pack my things fast enough.

Not that I didn't like being a Shadow. I glanced over at him, and yeah, he was looking forward and making that face again. The one where he ground his jaw to try and keep the emotions and flames at bay.

Nah, I'd probably have a crude blade buried in my gut and body tossed in an alley a few hundred times over if I hadn't joined the Shadows. And it was a life that gave me adventure and the ability to do everything I wanted. Well, almost everything. I could go the rest of my immortal life without having to teach the squeaking acolytes. But, it was a small price to pay.

"You sure you want to do this, mate?" I asked quietly as we reached a café that was closed for the evening and rounded the corner.

"Yes." I huffed at his response. Wasn't quite sure why he was torturing himself like this. Obviously, the female did not want to be found. At least by him. And she would be incredibly stupid, if she *was* in hiding, to return to her own godyx-damned apartment.

But I didn't say that to him. He'd groused enough when I demanded to come on this contract with him. I'd used the guise of needing to get out of the Well, but we both knew I could leave at any time. That I had stuck around and stayed at my room there to keep an eye on him.

I also knew that he'd been looking for her in each of the cities he visited, but when I asked him where he was off to next, I saw that this place was going to be different. Though, not until we'd walked past the stone city gates and dispatched his mark did he tell me that he wasn't just going to look for her. He was going to her apartment.

We reached a side door, and he pulled a key from his pocket. "If you can't smell her now, Nogón, I doubt that she—" my head snapped to the street. There it was again. That prickling feeling on the back of my neck. "We're being followed," I hissed at him as he unlocked the door and stepped in.

After re-locking the entrance, he began to ascend the steps and shrugged. "Let them follow." I scoffed and rolled my eyes. *I* was supposed to be the reckless one.

But whoever it was, they weren't close enough to be a problem. Yet. It was a certainty that I felt in my gut, but I had too much training and had seen too many years to write it off as nothing. Since we'd finished up with his contract and joined the crowds walking in the mild summer evening, I kept getting pangs of this certainty. We weren't in Shadow clothing anymore, but I knew we had an air about us. Usually it worked to our advantage, but it also made us stick out if you looked too close.

We reached the top floor and stood before one of the four apartments. Elián's hair was knotted at the back of his head, though, right now, he ran a hand to clear the few strands that always seemed to escape. I watched as he made a point to straighten himself and unlock her door, but I caught the slight tremble in his fingers while he fiddled with a different key that let him open the door.

As soon as the air from inside was released, I knew that she hadn't been here. It was too stale in there. But I didn't say anything. If this was what he needed to do, I'd keep my mouth shut.

He seemed to realize it, though, because his shoulders sagged a bit. He took a deep breath and stepped forward. And when I made to follow him, I had a harder time, forcing my way through the old barrier that left a sweet lavender taste in my mouth and felt like fingernails scratching at my skin and the inside of my mind. Bloody magic.

Whoever had made the barrier was strong, but years without reinforcing had left it penetrable to someone determined enough. And once I'd crossed the threshold, the uncomfortable sensations began to clear.

And then we were in her home.

It was… smaller than I thought it would be. Not that I was one to want to live in a palace or anything, but this was not what I envisioned the home of a de facto queen would look like.

Though, when I looked closer, I could see the fineness in some of the dust-covered things. When I walked further inside, I saw that the large sofa was expertly built, and when I reached my hand out, I found the fabric soft and no doubt expensive.

The table near the kitchen was of sturdy, dark wood, and the wall of hundreds of books before me surely cost a pretty coin. The drapes covering the large window looked soft and luxurious.

I whistled low. "She's got good taste." And I had been about to say more, but I clamped my mouth shut when I focused on him.

He was just standing there, between the sofa and dining area. Glowing eyes moving around, searching, but everything else about him was still. It was almost like he wasn't breathing.

Though I'd had many trysts and lovers in my two hundred and forty years, I hadn't been in love like *that*. I'd never been heartbroken like he was.

I wasn't stupid enough to offer kind words or a comforting embrace, though I would have given it if he'd asked. But nogón needed me to keep him moving. To bear witness to this while also not make him think I saw him as weak. And, yeah, okay, I'd laid it on a bit thick when he was drinking himself sick every night.

But tonight, he was as sober as I was. He was making himself feel this, and I wasn't going to stop it.

We stood in silence while I let him sort this out. Let him work through the emotions surely surging through him like a hurricane while I listened to the steady noise of the Nethran people outside. After a long time, though, wherein he still hadn't moved, I cleared my throat and tried, "Is there anything that I should be looking for?"

He flinched but collected himself almost instantly. His eyes had startled me the first time we met. Even as a children, I could sense the enormity of his power, and though he could hide almost everything else, there was no denying *those*. Now, they were shining miserably in the darkness of the apartment. Where her spicy scent that somehow had the faint saltiness of sea air was stagnant and heavy. We could both tell that she hadn't been here for years.

But if he wanted to turn the whole place upside-down, I'd help him empty her cabinets and flip back the sofa cushions. I'd search the page of all the books if he needed.

"No. I..." he swallowed and shook his head before fiddling with one of the golden rings in his ears.

I shrugged easily, "Well, let's have a look to see if we find anything useful. I can take in here if you want the bedroom?" Because I knew that he needed a moment to himself. And while I wasn't going to leave him completely alone, I could give him that. Not to mention, I knew he wouldn't want me in there, anyway.

Elián nodded and crossed to the closed double doors, but I didn't miss the look of gratefulness that swept his face before all emotion was erased.

We wouldn't find anything.

At least, anything that would point us to where she went. I could scent the various lands she'd traveled to on the little trinkets on her bookshelves. There was even a little Sjatan puzzle cube sitting amongst the books. I smiled to myself as I worked the little silver toy between my fingers, twisting and shuffling until each of the differently textured pieces all stood on their same sides. These little things were tricky, but I'd made enough wagers on—well, okay, everything—my ability to solve them with almost impossible speed.

I put the solved puzzle back on the shelf and bided my time by slowly walking around the large room that was like three in one. There was a vase full of long dead… begonias? Is that what they were called? I tried to think back to visiting Noruh's little cottage and her going on and on about her flower garden. Yeah, I think that's what they were.

For some reason, I swept up the fallen petals in my hand and dumped them in the waste basket I found in the kitchen.

The cabinets were fairly bare already, though she did have a few canisters of tea leaves just above multiple shelves of mugs and teacups. Some were delicately crafted and painted, others were made of thick ceramic with rich color and heavy handles.

I stopped before a framed drawing above her stove. Her, I knew. She was the one on the end, looking like she was trying to temper her amusement at the other three. They, all smiles, were no doubt having a good time. I chuckled softly. Most of what I learned about her proved more and more why she infuriated him. Though markedly different, they were so similar in other ways.

The one next to her, I assumed, was that witch Elián had mentioned. She looked like she could be the queen's sister. And that would mean the other two… were those the ones that the Vyrkos had killed?

After he'd cleaned himself up, Elián spoke about her a bit more. Each time he'd dropped a bit of information, I acted like nothing was out of the ordinary, lest he catch himself and refuse to say more. And a month ago, he mentioned that she'd returned to Versillia because her friends had been murdered. I'd put good money on that being them. Shame.

I made my way back toward the front door at the same time he came back out of her bedroom. His face was locked down, but I noticed that the pockets of his trousers looked a bit heavier.

I didn't comment on it, though. "What else?"

He shook his head, and more of his hair fell out of the knot. I was glad for my own locked hair—those slippery strands of his would irritate the shit out of me. "We can go, now."

I nodded, and on our way out of her apartment, I clapped my friend, my silver rings undoubtably heavy, on the back. I couldn't resist trying to offer a bit more comfort, and he was in need of it by the way he didn't stiffen at all.

When we walked back out onto the city streets, there was a clamoring of some summer festival a few streets away, so we made our way in the opposite direction. That prickling feeling was stronger now, but I kept my gait easy, lazy smile on my face. Elián didn't show alarm—he was probably itching for someone to attack so he'd have an excuse to take out some of his frustration.

"Shall we go find something to eat?" I called over the noise.

He nodded, and when I pointed out a restaurant on the other side of the upcoming intersection, he nodded again.

But just as we were about to cross, I shot out my arm behind us and grabbed a handful of fabric. There was a surprised squeak, and I turned into an alley just beside us.

A few around us definitely saw, but they did nothing, which was expected for a city of this size. Elián followed without protest, and I dragged our pursuer into the darkness while they tried to dig their heels into the ground.

When we were safe to question the idiot, I shoved them against the brick wall and crossed my arms. A glance to my left, and I saw Elián doing the same thing, miserable longing gone from his gaze. The shifting colors now revealed something... amused? And annoyed.

"Why have you been following us, boyo?"

Chapter Five
Tomás

What the fuck?

"What the fuck?" I hissed at Elián who was crouching to look the little sneak in the eyes. Some gangly kid who had been following us and finally got close enough to snatch.

He tilted his head and looked the kid up and down. "Out with it." Though his words were short, I caught the tinge of gentleness in them.

The kid didn't, though. His skin was a few shades lighter than Elián's, but it paled a couple shades more now being confronted by the both of us. His dark green eyes were wide, and his mouth was parted to reveal a few missing teeth. Why the hell was this child following us, and why was Elián acting like he knew him? Though I was aware he enjoyed teaching the acolytes, for reasons I'd never understand, it wasn't like he made a habit of interacting with them or *any* children outside of that. Right?

"I—I saw you earlier today. And I w-wanted t-to…"

I rolled my eyes and sunk down to crouch beside Elián. The lad did look like he was going to piss his too-short trousers. With both of us at eye level, he relaxed a fraction, but my hand fisting the front of his tunic didn't loosen.

"To what?" Elián pressed.

The boy took a breath and opened his mouth to respond, but at the last moment, he swept a questioning glance over the both of us and blurted, "Where are your swords?"

My eyes narrowed at the boy. He'd met Elián when he was working, then. "Gone. Now explain yourself, Marco." He knew the boy by *name*?

His little hands tried to pry mine away from him, but I wasn't going to budge. If this was some sort of trap, the boy some sort of lure, I was going to hold onto him for collateral. Though, he was looking at the both of us with a sort of awe that made me embarrassed for him. His little heart was beating fast, but not as quickly as I'd expect if he was truly terrified. I loosened my grip. Just a little.

"O-okay. Um, um, I j-just, saw you walking down the st-street," he took a breath, and the air whistled in the gaps of his lost teeth, "and I thought… you know…"

I shook his chest, just a bit, and he clamped his mouth shut, looking at me. "You thought what? I'm growing impatient, boy."

Now he was afraid. At least of me. Which was laughable because Elián was definitively the more dangerous of the two of us.

He sucked in a quick breath. "I was going to ask to be a Sh-Shadow."

My stomach dipped.

Elián's brows rose quickly, and the boy looked frantically back at him. He stammered, "Master Elián, I-I've been keeping up on my training like you told me, and I w-want to be a fighter like you."

I was stunned, but my friend tsked at the boy. "You don't want to be a Shadow, boyo."

The lad puffed his chest and looked at him defiantly. So, he did have a bit of fire in him. "Why? Because y-you kill people?"

Now *my* brows flew to my hairline. Yeah, he definitely had fight in him. His heart had calmed considerably, and faced with this denial, it looked like he was prepared to prove himself. I dangled my hand over my crouched leg. "That's right. Kill and steal and protect. We're not soldiers, boy. You want to learn to fight and save damsels? Go talk to a city guard or something." Not that they were useful at all. But no one would ever call a Shadow 'noble.'

"I don't want to be a city guard. They're useless." The boy all but spat on the ground, and I felt myself softening even more toward him.

"But you know nothing about being a Shadow," Elián cut in.

He righted his clothing and lifted his chin. "Then tell me. I've already heard a lot, and it hasn't changed my mind." How old was this kid? Five years or something? He looked gangly, his clothes too small for his body. Did the lad not have enough money for clothes? I glanced at him again, and he seemed clean. A bit more color had returned to his face, and he looked healthy. But there was a wariness under his large eyes. One that sent a curious pang through my chest.

"No," Elián said, and the boy's face fell. I clenched my jaw as I saw the sadness on his face while Elián and I stood.

"Perhaps the boy can have supper with us." What the fuck— what was I even saying. "We were heading that way anyway."

He looked at me with a bit of hope, and my chest tightened again. Elián shot a questioning glance at me before he reluctantly gave a nod.

"Yeah, yeah, tha-that would be great! Thank you!" The kid gave a full, gap-toothed grin, and I rolled my eyes to keep from returning the favor. I didn't know what came over me when I'd blurted the invitation, but there was no taking it back now.

Elián was sneaking confused glances at me while we exited the alley, the kid chattering all the way. Now that we'd agreed to at least sit with him for a bit, he seemed to want to tell us all sort of random anecdotes about his life in Nethras and pester us with questions about fighting and weapons. And we had only been walking for two fucking minutes.

We surely looked a strange trio, and we were seated quickly and efficiently at the small restaurant. Elián and I wordlessly chose a seats in the far corner and sat beside each other, backs to the wall. The boy was practically jumping out of his seat before us, and that just made me feel even… softer toward him.

"Have you talked to Lady Em? Is that why you're here?"

We both stilled. Elián had been nodding along to the boy's incessant chattering, but he became stone at the question. Not only had he not told me about this child he knew in Nethras, but he hadn't mentioned that the child knew his female. He still wouldn't even say her *name*, for godyx's sake.

Though he'd seemed innocently curious when he'd asked the question, the boy quickly caught on that it wasn't the right thing to say. I snuck a glance at Elián beside me, and he remained frozen with his hand around a frosty mug of ale. I'd almost protested him ordering one but decided quickly to drop it. Even before the boy's blunder, he'd been taking small, non-indulgent sips.

I cut in, "Have you?"

The boy looked at me gratefully and took a drink from his cup of water before responding, "Yes—" I winced, and the boy continued more cautiously— "well…Whitley has anyway."

He seemed to shrink a little, his shoulders turning inward when he snuck a look at Elián.

"And Whitley is…?"

"My caregiver. They run the children's home where I live." I nodded, putting another piece of this fucked-up puzzle together.

"And Lady—what has she been speaking with Whitley about?"

The little boy heaved a sigh that held weariness well beyond his years. "Just two letters. Checking in about Francie." When I gave him another questioning look, he added, "Whitley's mate. One of my other caregivers."

"So, your Lady Em," I couldn't help glance at Elián who was still sitting as motionless as a statue, "has been in communication with this Whitley about your missing caregiver. And you've convinced yourself that you want to become an assassin. Have I got the right of it?" I crossed my arms and settled back in my seat while our server placed our food on the table.

Nogón and I ordered roasted chicken, and the boy had followed suit, though I suspected that he'd wanted something else when he began to order one thing but stammered out the name of the dish when it was his turn to order.

I began to dig into my food, uncaring that the two rainclouds with me were leaving their suppers untouched. Someone had to keep us moving, after all.

Though I was a quick eater, there was a long stretch of silence that ended with my plate half-finished and Elián's low voice. "Has she said anything else to you?" Sure, we had a child, barely old enough to walk, demanding that we make him a Shadow, but all he could focus on was the female he'd had and lost. It was taking all of my effort to not hunt her down to berate her for making him descend into this place.

The boy finally picked up his fork and began shuffling around the vegetables on his plate, probably to avoid Elián's unsettling gaze. "Um… no. She just wrote to Whitley that she'd hoped we were all doing okay, considering. And that she thought of us often."

I couldn't help my sardonic chuckle at that one. If she thought about them so much, why hadn't she visited? If she cared about Nogón, why could he not find her?

Elián leaned forward, finally taking a bite of his food. That had been another part of this whole ordeal. When he was upset, my best mate drank to excess and didn't eat nearly enough. Even when Leandro and Emmett had gotten killed, he hadn't been in as bad of a way as when he'd returned to the Well. The only thing that kept him feeding regularly was the impending threat of Frenzy always lingering. He could starve or drink himself to death, but, luckily, the thought of going on a bloodthirsty rampage to quench that need was enough of a deterrent.

"So… would you reconsider?" Our table had grown quiet again, save for our chewing, but the boy tried his best to be nonchalant and quiet in his request. At least he wasn't shouting in this very public space about what we were.

"Reconsider what?" I asked just because it made him squirm.

Before the boy could say anything, Elián grunted and contributed, "To be like us, Marco, is a very large decision to make. One that should be done carefully and with the consent of one's parents or caregivers. Have you spoken to Whitley or Lydia about this?"

Elián's comment made the boy fidget in his seat, almost like he'd wet himself or something. Oh, godyx, had he not grown out of that yet?

I knew that if Elián was going to refuse the boy, he wouldn't be talking to him as he was. He probably wouldn't have agreed to this meal at all. And I had to admit that… okay, yeah, there was a soft spot in my heart for the lad's predicament.

Godyx knew that I had been in his place once upon a time.

But none of us at the Well would want to take care of a babe that still wet his shorts, that was for sure.

"Um… well, Whitley doesn't exactly know that I'm speaking with you."

"And do they know that you are wanting this life? To take this oath?" Elián said after swallowing a gigantic mouthful of food.

"And just as importantly," I cut in, "are you even old enough?"

The boy glared at me, clearly upset at my insinuation. "I'm almost eleven years now!" My head tilted as I considered and tried to remember how old I'd been when Nogón, his twin, and their father had found me on the streets of Thalas. I sucked my teeth at the realization—nine years, if I was recalling correctly. "And Whitley will go for it! So will Lydia!"

Elián asked sternly, "How can you even be sure, boyo? Most would not be happy with their child becoming a blade for hire. Nor would they want them to leave their home for the foreseeable future for training."

The boy was pouting now, dear Godyx, "They have enough on their hands now, anyway. And you both did it! I already train and… I don't want to be at the children's home anymore. I want to train. And be a great fighter."

"The choice was easier for us, lad," I chimed in. "What with this one being born to a Shadow father and me being a street rat with nowhere else to go. You seem to have a home and people who care for you here. If you're accepted, there's no going back."

He nodded and took a quick mouthful of the roasted carrots on his plate. I noticed that he was picking around the chicken and had barely touched it. "I know that. I have no parents, and Whitley and Lydia know that I want to be a Shadow. So it won't be a surprise."

Elián heaved a sigh, and I knew it wasn't from his stomach being full, though his plate was nearly licked clean now,. After many, many decades, we really were like brothers, blood be damned, and I knew his tells as much as he knew mine. The particular tone of this sigh was one of capitulation. Neither of us had outright denied the boy yet, but I hadn't been persuaded so much by his words to just give in like that.

I ran my eyes over Elián's face while he examined the lad who seemed perceptive enough to know to keep his mouth shut and concentrate on eating. Half of Nogón's hair had fallen down his shoulders, now, and his brow was tightened in contemplation.

As if he could feel my gaze, he cut his eyes to me without turning his head. The color in his eyes was a rich, dark orange, and my shoulders dropped a little in defeat. His face was still hard, his posture still guarded, but I knew where to look to read him. He had a soft spot for the boy. And though he was a full-grown adult, his expression reminded me so much of him as a boy on that rainy day in Thalas.

When he'd taken a long look at me while his brother and I haggled away over some stolen trinkets I was trying to sell. Their father had stood back, watching the exchange, until Elián walked over to him. They'd talked in hushed tones, but I was too busy trying to convince Leandro into buying a finer puzzle cube than the one he'd originally eyed.

When he eventually did, they'd left, and I used the coin to buy a hot meal and a night in an actual bed and saved the rest. They came back to my corner the next day, though. And the next, and the next. Leandro had been jovial, and sometimes he'd buy something, and the other times, we'd joke back and forth. I'd never had a friend before—life on the streets was about survival and competition, not camaraderie—so I wasn't sure if that was it. But it'd felt nice.

Elián had been quiet, never really speaking, but he would stand beside his twin. Leandro would include his brother in all of his jokes and stories, and when Elián made a grunting noise or tugged at his brother's sleeve, Leandro would share a look with him and then speak for them both.

I remembered thinking it was so strange. I'd seen my best mate whisper with their father that first day, so I didn't think he was mute, but he never spoke around me.

The fourth day, the three of them came back mid-afternoon. I never admitted it to any of them, but I'd been waiting all morning for them to show up. Their father would have been intimidating in his black leathers, but his kind blue eyes and smile put me at ease. Even at nine years, I'd learned to identify when someone actually meant me harm.

For some reason, my eyes kept falling on Elián when the three of them spoke with me that day. Their father crouched, long hair shifting over his shoulders, and explained what he was. What they were. That he'd been watching me, seen that I was quick, smart. He'd said that his sons had vouched for me, saying that I'd be a good acolyte. Leandro had looked at me with hope in his glowing, happy eyes, but it was Elián's serious ones that convinced me.

Yeah, a place to call home was the main draw, and I could tell that the silent twin wasn't easily swayed. But sometime in the course of the few hours we'd spent together, he'd softened toward me.

My best mate was acting that way toward the lad now. And the silent glance we shared was its own conversation. He'd eventually spoken to me when I'd been accepted as an acolyte, many weeks after our first encounters in Thalas. Even after that, though, he much preferred nonverbal communication, which I soon learned could be just as effective.

In Zonoran, I asked, *"Are you sure about this, Nogón? We'll be the ones responsible for him. At least until he's sworn in."*

"I'm sure."

I rolled my eyes. "Fuck, just great." I didn't know who I was more irritated with. This boy who was now derailing my entire life, at least for the next few decades, my best friend for being swayed by a *child*, or myself for going along with the whole damn thing.

The boy's face fell, and I just couldn't take the pouting anymore. If we were going to keep him, we had to get this Whitley and Lydia to agree. Then cart his arse all the way back to the Well. He really better have been toilet trained, because I sure as shit wasn't changing nappies. If he really was almost eleven years, he should have been, but with his round, innocent face, I wasn't completely sure.

I shoved up from the table and left a small pile of coin from my pocket on the table. Elián stood more slowly. As we turned toward the entrance, it seemed he wanted me to explain to the boy who looked one second away from bursting into tears.

Fuck me.

"Come on, lad. Show us to this children's home. You can explain your decision to your caregivers, and *if* they consent to it, we have a long journey ahead of us. I won't have any shit coming down on us for snatching you away without word."

It took him a moment to process through my words, but once he had, his face broke into a shining grin. He jumped up from his seat and started spewing a bunch of excited thanks, and I rolled my eyes.

Elián led the way toward the door, but I caught the almost-smile on his face before he turned his back for us to follow. He was a bastard, but it was the first time I'd seen him crack any kind of positive expression in a year. So if we needed to practically adopt an orphan to make it happen again, I'd do it.

The boy touched my hand like he'd been about to hold it, but he dropped his arm to his side like I'd burned him when I glared. He gave me an apologetic glance then continued to grin like I'd given him a pile of sweets and toys for his birthday. I huffed and shook my head while my chest made compressed with a strange, aching sensation. The Well wasn't a place for that childish shit, but it had been the start of a new life for me. A new beginning that was far better than the sorry life I'd been saddled with at first. Swords and blood and darkness had been the best gift for me. Maybe they would be that for this boy, too.

Chapter Six

Meline

A lifetime after him

I breathed in the scent of Death. The taste of it, the thrum of darkness pulsing through my fingertips. The crimson, hot and wet, stained my leather-wrapped hands.

And the screams. Goddess, the screams were sweet enough to pierce the thick veil that'd settled over me.

The body below me was releasing faint grunts and gurgles while I dug my knee into his chest. The ebony blade, its touch now more familiar than any other, was embedded in his throat. The last guard, defending the man whose life we came to claim, fought till the very end. While we cut down every single one that lined the carpeted halls.

A nobleman's son, given everything in the realm he could ever need. Home equipped with guards armed to the teeth, felled by two females with fewer than five weapons between them.

I sighed, the guard beneath me no longer twitching, and pulled my blade from his throat.

Settling on my haunches, I dragged my tongue against the

flat of the dagger and hummed at the rich taste. The robust, earthy flavor coated my tastebuds as I licked my blade clean.

When the screams continued, however, I huffed and looked over to the overstuffed bed and the two forms writhing amongst the blankets and furs. The chill outside was all but a whisper in the extravagant home, and the nobleman's son, we found, slept in the nude while piled under extravagance.

"Some might say the gift of a killing blow is an honor," I called over but, from my position on the floor, could only see the edge of her profile. Her black leathers and hood that matched my own.

"I had a better idea," she giggled, and though I groaned, something akin to excitement bubbled in my stomach. A mirage that I limped toward as I stood.

Blood fell across his palms and down to his wrists that were strung to the posts of the bed. Muffled plunks rang as Tana worked on another finger.

She rested on his stomach, thighs restraining his convulsing torso. The cloth she'd stuffed in his mouth barely muffled the volume of his wailing.

The bed was high enough for me to lean a hip against it and watch my cousin work. The contract specifically required his death, a few fingers as proof of kill. "Those could've been removed after, you know. So we would be spared his whingeing."

Tana made a quick, swift cut at the knuckle of a meaty thumb, and, proving my point, released a torrent of his tears and the foul smell of urine. I straightened and watched a pool grow beneath the man marked for death. And a little round of torture, it seemed.

She removed three, and after collecting the digits in her own gloved hand, Tana sprang from her perch and stood back with me. Admired her handiwork.

The light cutting in from the moon washed the room in silver, and I saw the pride in her emerald eyes. The hunger for blood in a way she'd never felt before, now sated. Her staff, lined with delicate etchings from the nomadic Savyan people she bought it from, held remnants of her magic's light. A dazzling white manifestation of aether that withstood strike after strike as we fought our way through the manor.

"How much would you like to wager that his wife is awake right now?"

I thought it over, cataloguing again her absence in their marital bed. Of course, our employer had stated they'd make sure of that part. At the time, we'd assumed it meant there would be no one in the home besides our mark and his guards.

The cluster that'd been protecting another bedroom proved wrong that theory. We'd cut them down too, but left that door closed and continued until we ended up here.

Upon Tana's question, the man took up his noises again, mumbling something, fighting through his own agony. Whatever he was asserting, he said again, head lifting from the pillow soaking in blood, staring right at us.

With a shrug, I stepped closer to pull the fabric from his mouth to hear what he was so intent to tell us. If Tana was insistent on dragging this out, so be it.

Wasn't like I had anything else to do. Anything to look forward to.

"P-please. Please. Take them both. I can give you c-c-coin. More than you'd know what to do with."

I scoffed, regretting my decision immediately, and gagged him once more.

Tana was already walking away, throwing open the heavy door and prowling up the silent hallway. I listened as another door opened—urgent murmurings, quiet crying and confusion.

I stood, stock-still and staring past the man lying in his own piss. The beat between battle, between blood and blade, was… a fog. Outside of myself, I watched my body stand on the ruined wool rug, breathing and humming the melancholy lilts of an unknown but faithful song. The same I would sing while weeping on the banks of the Ralthan river.

My eyes cut to the door as Tana reentered, this time with two new people. One who barely glimpsed at the figure on the bed and started wailing.

Wincing, I looked to my cousin for any indication what the fuck was the purpose of bringing the child and future widower into the room. But, she gazed at me worriedly instead of following through with whatever plan she had in mind.

I sighed and pulled back my hood, revealing my face to the midnight light. Wasn't as if there was true concern for concealing my identity in this human village on the far reach of the continent.

"P-please," the wife croaked, dry voice breaking. The child, just over the line of adolescence if I had to guess, remained silent, staring at their father lying in his own waste. Fingerless hands pointed toward the ceiling.

"He will die tonight. Whatever words you would like to say, now is the time."

Dressed in a flowing pink nightgown, the wife gaped at me, then Tana. Tried to hide the child behind her while she sobbed.

"*Please* don't hurt them. They cannot speak. T-take me."

Oh, for the love of—I sighed. "We are not here for either of you. Just him. Do you have any goodbyes before I end him?"

Reason flickered in the wife's swollen eyes as she looked between us. Her shoulders relaxed infinitesimally, her lip trembled. At least the overwhelming scent of fear began to wane. The man in question still reeked of it, mumbling pleas, releasing fat tears as he stared at his family. That couldn't be helped, though.

The wife remained a trembling statue, expression shifting and hands shaking as she held onto her child. Now that she knew we weren't here to harm them, though, she didn't seem inclined to stop us. Very well, then.

I removed the spare dagger I had sheathed to my thigh, blade shining under the moonlight. One plunge into the heart would be sufficient.

As I turned to the bed, an urgent hum reached my awareness, and I hesitated. The child came forward, long braid swishing against their back, dressed in night tunic and trousers. They couldn't speak, but their intention was clear when they pointed to my weapon.

The wife protested but stayed rooted in place, probably motivated by Tana at her back, as I flipped the pommel toward the child. Watched the resolve shine in their brown eyes.

Instead of taking my kill, I stood beside the head of the bed and pulled the gag from his mouth once again.

Pleas fell. "Please, princess. G-go get help. I need to be here for your mum and you. Grandpa will know what to do, how to help. Run along now and get someone to h-help!"

But the child was already climbing on the bed, mouth set.

The man's screams came after the first plunge of the dagger. After that, it was a flurry of blood, the woman's wailing. The child's determined grunt as they stabbed the man's groin. Over and over and over.

Red splattered on their face, ruined their tunic. Even then they kept on, seeking their revenge I wouldn't dream of taking from them. It wasn't until they let the dagger fall to the soaked mattress, panting with burning stare, that I approached them again.

But they were still with us, still present and not retreating into their mind or the memories that probably haunted them.

The man was barely hanging on. Passed out from shock, most likely, so I ended him swiftly. The blade I conjured plunged between his ribs like sinking toes in sand. The death infected his heart quickly, released a puddle of blood beneath my fist.

Unlike the guard, I let his life force go to waste.

The child, I helped climb off of the bed. They clung to me a moment, when their bare feet met the carpet, holding onto my arms.

The memories threatened to wash me away, then. Made me suck in gasps and blink back tears while this child stared up at me like I was their savior when they'd saved themself.

It was a little wobbly with my stomach tossing and empty, but I managed a smile down at our employer. Kissed their brow.

In their ear, I whispered, "Be well, little one. I know that you will thrive." This country, luckily, did not mandate a woman marry after losing her husband. Their mother could inherit the wealth, pass it to this child who I would wager was the stronger of the two.

With the proof of my killing blow still clinging to my skin, I dragged my fingertips over their forehead, leaving a warrior's mark.

"I suppose we don't need these now," Tana mused, and the child and I both looked to her. The fingers rolled in her palm like chopped carrots.

The wife watched her child with renewed tears, shocked. She hadn't known that the child wrote to us. Had been a victim of his cruel words and strikes since before they were born. If they'd told us otherwise, she would be lying beside the corpse, joining him in whatever afterlife awaited humans.

She reached for the child, ignoring the blood and filth, and pulled them into her arms. She muttered apologies, swayed as they clung to each other.

And I tried not to break. I fought like hell to keep the jagged pieces of me together. To not fall to the floor and demand that they burn me with the rest of the bodies. Or turn my own blade on myself.

Tana took a moment while they had theirs, and she ran her palm up and down my spine. Breathed with me. She hadn't removed her hood, but I held onto her stare. The jade that reminded that I hadn't lost *everything*. Everyone.

I blew a concentrated breath from puckered lips. Felt the weight of her touch and my feet beneath me again. I nodded at my cousin. A gesture she returned with a sad crinkle of skin beside her eyes.

Grounding myself into our last tasks was harder. Floating in and out now that the carnage was done. We stepped over bodies and directed the wife and child back to the bedroom. Instructed them to change and wash while we took their soiled clothing—evidence—with us to burn elsewhere.

Freshly bathed and in a clean tunic and trousers, the child stopped us before we could leave and thrust a coin purse into Tana's hands. When she and I both refused payment, they huffed, stomped their foot to remind us that though they'd known the horrors of life, they were still a child. That they knew what they were about, which was honorable.

So, we sighed and took our payment for ridding this monster from their lives. We instructed them both to barricade furniture against the door once we left so that when reinforcements came, they had a story to tell.

And Tana and I went once again to the forest, taking to the shadows all the way to the inn where we stayed. Her first, then me, we slipped through the window, boots thumping on the dusty wood floor.

We were still working our way up, replenishing our pockets since we had no access to our accounts this far away from Nethras. Not like I was touching that coin, anyway.

That life...one of friends and fighting in rings for a laugh. It belonged to a person who died a while ago. All that connected me to the old Meline was standing in front of me, slowly removing her weapons and leathers.

The smirk I released was genuine as I watched her upend the coin purse and begin to count our haul. It'd been quite a surprise to bid for the contract, only to meet an employer that was little older than a babe. But as we'd argued in a back alley, going back and forth over the words they furiously scribbled, my cousin and I elected to take it. In the room we now stood in, Tana and I had decided to reject payment.

But, the pile of gold coin was a pretty sight. One that kept this life going. And going.

"What do you think they'll do with them?" Tana began to pull clean sleeping clothes from her pack. I headed to the small fire that was reduced to smoldering embers when we returned. After prodding until it roared around fresh logs, I tossed our employer's blood soaked clothes and their mother's splattered nightgown into the flames.

Whipping around until the heat sighed at my back, I focused on her question. "Keep them in a jar? Make a necklace?"

Tana clucked, turning toward the door. We'd taken the risk and paid extra for the adjoining bathing room, since we knew we'd probably return in an incriminating state. Before she turned the knob, she mused, "Just hope they don't get caught."

"They won't."

She nodded, and with her face revealed, I saw the concern she wore every day. The heavy heart as the witness to my destruction, fatigued muscles as she shouldered her own ghosts.

I swallowed. "You did great. I...I'm glad to be adventuring with you."

Her nose wrinkled as she smiled, true and cheerful even with flakes of blood caught in her golden brow. "I'm glad, too."

She left the door cracked as she began drawing a bath. It would be a while before my turn, but I couldn't bring myself to relax into this time alone.

My feet stayed planted in the middle of the room, refusing to look at the fire but letting it provide false warmth all the while. Faint splashes came from the bathing room while Tana washed away the evening, our first contract of this magnitude as a duo. I reflected on the wisps of pride I felt as I caught a glimpse of her cutting down guard after guard, using her staff and dagger with a poise and grace I couldn't even take credit for. Everything she did had a finesse, a delicate nature.

For me, it was just cold instinct. A dark tunnel I retreated into until bodies lined the path like cobblestones. Killing was easy. As simple as breathing to strike here, twist there. To sense a pulse and drain it dry until the beating is a sighing echo.

When that was gone? When Tana wasn't filling my ears with pleasant chatter or questions or reassurance?

I started humming the notes, the melody that drowned out the silence that was wrong, wrong—

A sob caught me off guard, choking my soothing until I hunched over, arms crossed over my middle, as I tried to keep it all in. The words I wanted so desperately to take back, the one I cursed Rhaea for snatching away from me.

I didn't hear Tana jump out of her bath. Didn't remember falling to the floor in a heap of tears. But I'd ended up there, somehow, whimpering and shaking, thinking about all that'd slipped through my fingers. Her naked, wet limbs held me tight. She whispered assurances into my cropped curls. Spouting fierce reminders that she knew. She was there, and I didn't have to shoulder all of this on my own. That we needed to share it.

That all was not lost.

Chapter Seven
Tomás

"You can't be serious." Nor looked between the three of us. Me, Nogón, and the boy who was practically wiggling with excitement. He was obedient enough, not running around or *touching* anything, but he might as well have been. His energy was like an irritating buzzing, Elián's depressed calm making it even worse.

I tried to look at the Well with fresh eyes. Remembering how it felt to be standing here for the first time. It certainly looked bigger back then, but it wasn't *small*. An imposing estate constructed of dark stone and iron. Ancient ivy covered much of it, breathing life within the aether swimming over the estate.

Of course, with the magic that cloaked it, any non-Shadow would just see more of the expansive forest in the northeast of Eryva. But with us, the boy had been able to pass through the protective measures. Where now the few members training or lounging outside were visible, as well as the stifling freedom of the Shadow Well. The grounds were militantly maintained, the paths leading to and around the place always swept and cleared. I hoped the boy was ready for that bloody boring task. I'd made it a point to never again touch a pair of hedging shears once I took the oath.

Noruh had been stretching in the manicured garden when we walked up with the babe after the weeks-long journey. Our faces should've conveyed that we were as serious as an arrow to the throat, but she was still looking at us like we'd lost our minds.

Sure felt like we had. Neither of us had brought a prospective acolyte to the Well before.

"Hello!" The lad put his fist to his chest and bowed quickly. I shot Nogón a tired glare. Wonder where the hell the boy had learned that. "I'm Marco."

Noruh put her pale hands on her hips, but her pursed lips were trembling, already becoming charmed by the boy. She looked to us. "Thought you went out to find a queen. Not bring home a tiny Shadow."

"The lad hasn't been accepted yet, so don't get ahead of yourself," I grumbled. "And you can blame the other one for this."

Elián ran a hand through his hair, frowning but not apologizing. After leading the conversation with the boy's caregivers, he'd been his usual laconic self since. But the boy seemed content with his own thoughts, taking in the sights, or talking to both and neither of us at the same time. After seeing how many children they had to divert their attention for, I would wager that he had to entertain himself more often than not.

The boy had been watching our Shadow siblings who were either minding their business or giving curious glances toward us, but Nor's words had him straightening and looking toward her once again. "You do know that being an acolyte is a years-long commitment. And it's no easy feat."

He nodded quickly, jostling his red curls. "Yes… um. What is your name?"

And then, because apparently we were all insane, she gave him the Shadow salute and smirked. "Noruh. Though, that's Master Noruh to you."

"Thank you, Master Noruh! Are you all friends?" As we let the boy pack his things before we left Nethras, I couldn't help notice that the longest goodbyes came from Whitley and Lydia.

The children waved and gave quick hugs, but nothing that lingered. The two adult Lylithans that ran the home had been a bit hesitant, but they were aware of the lad's goals and ultimately gave their blessing.

The other motivation for the visit with the caregivers was more information on Elián's queen. They'd even given him the two letters she'd sent, though he hadn't asked for them. And when I caught him reaching in his pocket, no doubt to feel the thick paper between his fingers—or reading the female's words to himself when he thought we weren't paying him any attention—I hadn't said a word. Noruh should give me a fucking award for how much restraint I was exerting.

"Oh, since we were wee acolytes trying to stay out of trouble." She flicked one last glance at Elián and me. "You both are sponsoring him?"

He nodded, short and sure, and I sighed before doing the same. If this would help him heal, give him something besides fruitless journeys and the bottle to focus on, then I'd be all for it. Really, we wouldn't have to spend much time with the lad outside of our training responsibilities.

Nor wasn't lying—the life of an acolyte was hard. Thank fuck I'd long ago earned my leathers.

"All right." She waved us behind her. The lad skipped along while we followed at a slower pace. "We'll get you to your room for now. Luckily for you, we just had an acolyte graduate to full rank. I'll send out a message to the rest of the Elders."

The Shadow Well halls were dark and familiar, both home and not. But with the lad's excitement, I couldn't help feel the surge of gratitude for what it provided me. Now and then, when I'd been younger than him.

Somewhere along our journey through the Well, Marco clutched onto Elián's tunic, betraying the nerves that he'd expressed before through jabbering. But the ancient halls seemed to even intimidate him into silence. What I saw now as my default, a home I no longer bothered thinking about because it was always *there*, was clearly salvation to him.

I tried again to imagine myself in the lad's place. As Noruh launched into a brief explanation of acolyte life in her light brogue, I traced the steps I took with Elián and Leandro when Emmett provided the same introduction to me.

Instead of sneaking my hand into that of the twins' father, though, I'd kept mine in my pockets, eyes swiveling and senses taking in everything. At once accepting the gift but also seeking out the sharp edges that may slice me later.

Now, little fingers squeezed mine as we came to a stop in the acolyte wing. Another set of wards protected it should we be under attack, and the metallic taste of it brushed along my tongue.

"This will be your room for now." Nor gestured to the closed door before knocking.

Through our joined hands, I felt Marco stiffen further. His fist tightened in Elián's tunic, but neither of us attempted to shake the boy away. Nogón had an uncharacteristic affection for him, and I wasn't fucking cruel. Many days of travel provided reassurance that he knew how to wash his hands, at least.

A quick scuffling sounded from behind the door before it swung open.

I'd no idea the name of the acolyte assigned to this room, and she remembered herself, bowing her head, arms down by her sides, and feet planted evenly on the floor. The gray, woolen tunic and trousers were slightly rumpled, as if she'd been relaxing before we'd interrupted.

A gray braid hung toward the floor as her lashes of the same color fluttered wildly. Her breaths were quick. "Masters Noruh, Tomás, and Elián. Good afternoon. T-to what do I owe this honor?"

Noruh clucked her tongue. "Calm yourself, Briar." The acolyte gasped, straightened even further, when Nor used her name. "We have a new prospective acolyte, and he needs a room."

The boy's fingers squeezed mine a little tighter, holding on for his life while buzzing with excitement. "Hello," he whispered and tugged at Nogón's tunic, shifting the embroidered fabric. "My name is Marco."

Briar relaxed a bit, lifting her head. The hard look in her silver eyes forced a healthy roll from mine. "Hello."

These damn acolytes took everything way too seriously. It wasn't as if The Shadows limited the numbers on purpose. Well, we did, but when half the Lylithan race was dead, there weren't exactly droves knocking on the doorstep. To be an acolyte was to undergo a selective process. Sponsorship from a current Shadow was rare, but it wasn't this cutthroat competition either.

"I will clear the other side of the room for you. Then we will get you proper clothing." Briar gave the boy's travel-worn tunic and trousers a disdainful up and down, and I didn't like it one bit.

"The boy hasn't been accepted yet, so his clothes will do for now. And I trust that you will be kind and a true representative of The Shadows."

Nor and Elián gave me a funny look, but they should've known that I could—and would—pull rank when I needed. The boy needed discipline and to see the reality outside of childlike dreams, but I wouldn't hear of Briar or anyone else being unto-ward. That would be in terribly bad taste.

The young acolyte's shoulders stiffened right back up at my thinly veiled threat.

The acolytes had their own community, customs. There were so few of them, and their positions so unique, how could they not? Perhaps Nogón, Noruh, Leandro, and I would've been friends otherwise, but spending every waking hour with them scrubbing floors, training, and whispering in the shadows forged a bond that I still felt, even with one of us dead and gone.

The greatest gift the Shadows had given me wasn't my

freedom from Sjatas. No, it'd been the two idiots who were my family in every way but birth. When he was tired down to his fingernails, the boy would need to lean on himself and acolytes like Briar the most.

"Yes, Master Tomás."

I grunted and started to unravel my fingers from the lad's, let him go off and have Briar help him get his bearings.

But he let go of Nogón and doubled his hold on me. He stared with wide eyes and his red curls bouncing around his brow. "Will…" his lip started quivering, eyes swimming, but a shuffling of passersby at the top of the hall pulled him out of the emotions about to brim over, thank godyx. He cleared his throat and dropped his hands to clutch at his front. "Will I be able to see and speak with you?"

Why in the world was he asking me? I scoffed, "Lad, this is The Shadow Well, not a prison. Keep up your training, take no shit, and you'll be fine."

An elbow caught me in the middle of my spine, and I glared over my shoulder. My brother's expression was impassive, aside from that damned brow I wanted to pluck clean out of his skin.

I huffed and swiveled back to the newest Shadow-in-training, should everything go well. "We'll be in and out, what with contracts and travels. But one of us is usually around. And quite literally anyone else here should help you, what with the oaths of kinship and all that."

He continued staring at me for a few more beats before thanking Nor and Elián. And after one last look at us, he followed Briar into his new room, his new home.

As we walked back up the hall, Noruh cut a glance at me. "Marco seems to be quite taken with you, Tom." I grunted, taking a note from my silent brother to my right. In unspoken agreement, we ascended to the Masters' level of the Well. Activity quieted, and we passed bedrooms, vacant as their occupants were elsewhere.

The large windows of Noruh's overlooked a cloak of misty

fog hanging over the deep green forest surrounding the Well. I remembered the day she'd selected this one, admitting shyly to me that it reminded her of home in the Trylan mountains. I sank onto the cushion and mounds of pillows set against the glass.

"How long do you think it will take the boy to start calling you Papa?" My eyes sprang open to glare at her across the room. Noruh leaned against the door while Elián sat before the unlit hearth to my right. He didn't even try to hide the snort at our sister's comment.

"Hush." I wiggled my road-dusty body into the clean fabric. "There will be no such thing."

"Not sure, Tom. He's imprinted on you like a newly hatched chick."

"I didn't ask for that!" My head began to pound at the thought. "It wasn't even my idea to make a Shadow out of the boy. He knew *this one*," I pointed at Elián, "and pouted until he got us both to agree. Never in my immortal life will I want some brat to worry about."

Noruh tsked and sat on the ornate carpet between my brother and me. She could be a pain in my rear, but Nor had fantastic taste. "Your aversion to responsibility is unbecoming of someone of your advanced age."

"Just because I don't want to adopt a child, informally or otherwise, does not mean I am afraid of commitment. I've been loyal to you lot for centuries. Now, if you don't want my muddy boots on your furniture, stop pestering me."

"And what about you?" She directed her words to Elián, blonde hair brushing across her shoulders. "Are you prepared for the commitment of sponsoring an acolyte? You don't seem the type to drop him off and leave him be."

My brother rested his ankle on his thigh, elbow propped on the arm of his seat. He appeared stoic, pensive, but the twitch of his lip wasn't fucking fooling me. "I do not share Tom's reservations."

A familiar few beats of silence coursed around us, wherein I planned the rest of my evening. A fragrant bath in my quarters, supper in the common room before prowling for someone to relieve the fucking tension in my shoulders.

Noruh broke through my reverie with a hesitant whisper. "And your queen?"

So much for daydreaming.

The hint of amusement on Elián's face disappeared in an instant, and the stoney despair fell back into place. He'd had something to focus on while we traveled across the continent to get the lad here. While he answered a litany of questions or concentrated on the path home.

What were we to do now? "We did not find her." His voice pressed flat the agony that I knew tore at his heart. On second thought, I would spend the evening with him, ensuring that he didn't get lost to his sorrows. His tendency to drown it in silence or the bottle wasn't happening under my watch.

Nor looked to me, blue-green stare asking for help, but I didn't have any words that would make this better for him. When he'd lost his mother, he'd leaned on Leandro and Emmett. When he'd lost *them*, it was *decades* of this. Even now, their deaths had changed something vital about him. Holding everyone else at arm's-length, even Nor and me.

"So we go and look again. And again."

Elián's gaze searched me while my body frozen in disbelief. I was even shocked at myself for including the 'we.'

My plans for the next…forever, were to take contracts, shed blood, fuck, and do what I wanted. All that could still be done while searching for this female who had his heart.

Nogón nodded swiftly. "Will you watch over Marco when we are not here?" he asked Noruh as she drummed her fingers along her silk rug. A hawk flew over the treetops outside, gliding past the window in silky arcs before diving into the branches.

"Yes. And I'll draft a message to send to the others who are away so that we can make this vote quickly. The sooner he's given his grays, the sooner you will be able to resume your search."

"That is, if Varus doesn't try to put a stop to it," I grumbled, and Elián grunted in agreement. We were technically equals, but the old male never did like us.

Noruh stood, running a hand through her hair. "I'll personally vouch for the boy as well. Hopefully that will ensure things go smoothly—"

"Or maybe put a target on his back," my brother groused. It was sudden, the change in tone with the subject of the Elders, but not without merit. Nogón's punishment for killing Jones was utter hogwash, but at least it'd given him time to sober up some.

"I won't let that happen. Trenton and Yara have always been friendly, and the rest are reasonable. It'll be fine."

But Nogón still ground his jaw. He released a flame between his fingers and watched it flicker. "It only takes one bad seed to spoil the lot."

"Well, I take offense to that," Noruh huffed. "Besides, one cantankerous Shadow doesn't upend a millennia of tradition. You two go get used to the beauty of parenthood while I write a few letters."

We both grumbled, but there was no use in going back and forth with her. Sure, I'd fallen into the role of a mentor of sorts, but that could easily fit into my lifetime plans, too.

II
LIFE

Chapter Eight
Meline

The water before me roared. Glowed.

The sand beneath me and between my toes was warm, so very warm, and the stars overhead were dazzling. Far brighter than I remembered.

Maman once told me a story, of the Mother and how She was woven into all life of our realm. It was a silly tale in a book for children. One with other stories of tree tricksters who wanted to steal your name and animals who could talk and help you find your way in the forest.

"The night, as black as the skin of The Mother, is when she sees us the most. When she can hear your wishes. And the stars in the sky are the freckles on her face."

I'd sat, engrossed and enamored with the musical cadence of my mother's voice. The one she would use to pray and teach. The gentle sound was often the first and last someone heard, and she carried that honor with a grace I had been in awe of as early as I could remember.

Now, as I gazed at the luminescent water, I wanted…I wanted to be there. With her and all those I'd lost. The weight of being here was too much. Too heavy. But how did I take that step? Could I, truly?

Tana would blame herself.

I used the back of my wrist to swat my tears away. The warm breeze tangled in my hair, shuffling it against my naked spine. Maybe I could just stand. Advance a few steps, and then a few more until the choice was taken from me. Where the waves and the Mother could decide my fate. She and Her daughter were heroes, the beings we thanked for giving us life.

But, as I reflected on those nursery books, on the bedtime tales, the innocence of my childhood belief was soured by how *cruel* I now knew them to be.

Sand fell off of me as I stood. It trailed off the backs of my thighs while a silent sob crashed in my chest, and my shoulders relaxed. It could be over. I could be with him. The mere thought elicited the first real smile I'd worn in years, wobbly with tears and so amazing that I took another step. And another.

I was just on the edge, about to meet toe to wave, when something swept across the backs of my ankles. It was enough to startle me, and I jerked to the side, sending up water and thick, wet sand. The darkness was full, stretching as far as I could see in all directions, but with the scattering of bright, white stars, I quickly identified what scared me.

"Fuck!" I backed away from the water as the snake *charged*.

I'd not been bitten by a snake of that size, nor was I certain what effect—if any—its venom would have on me. It was long, far taller than I even with its body wound and slithering toward me.

I retreated a few more steps, trying to weave left or right to get out of its line of vision, but the snake moved with me. Its underside was striped in alternating colors—perhaps black and yellow? Brown and white?

The Rhaestran sea continued to pulse before me, but underneath the peaceful sound of waves crashing, I heard the growl of the serpent.

They were symbols of Rhaea. Of birth, rebirth, healing, transformation, all those things the Rhaean priestesses lusted after as they kneeled and prayed to their precious fucking goddess, but this serpent held no virtue whatsoever.

I had come in contact with snakes of this size throughout my life, but I'd found, or at least had been told, that most were not aggressive, only striking when provoked.

This fucker nipped the skin of my ankle with its fang, sending me falling to the ground in surprise more than anything. I scrambled backward, heart pounding and bearing my own fangs at it. My fingers and toes gripped at sand, gaining little ground as the snake continued to stalk me, and backing me toward the looming rainforest. Away from the peacefulness of the sea. Of oblivion.

My fingers met something hard, something that did not slip through my grasp, and I closed my fist around it.

"Get the fuck away from me!" I yelled at the animal, for some reason unable to pick myself up and run. I lurched backward in a poor imitation of a crab, naked and pathetic under the eyes of the Mother.

The jagged stick I wielded jabbed the serpent in its side, connecting and even piercing its scaly hide. But it kept coming, sending up a roar far louder than it should have been, feigning left then right as I kicked my legs and tried to stab it again. Why couldn't I kill it? Frustrated and terrified tears flowed down my cheeks, and as the serpent wrapped itself around my middle, bringing its beady eyes close to my face, I didn't long for some absent deity in the sky. My lip trembled, and I wanted *my* mother.

Or course, no such luxury was available to me. I was not given that. My stick was forgotten and useless, the serpent tightened its hold around me, and before it could truly strike, fangs sinking into my heart—

I woke up.

Chapter Nine
Tana

The right hook to my jaw sent my head snapping to the side, but I immediately collected myself and twisted around my opponent. I dodged the large male's fists before throwing another combination of jabs and a swift kick to his side. He fell back some, but I swallowed the laugh of triumph that threatened to bubble up my throat.

The tavern wasn't empty, but it wasn't busy either. The high-profile fights would be later tonight, and I was sad that we'd miss them.

"Slippery." My opponent grinned good-naturedly when I evaded him again. I caught sight of my cousin, sitting at a table with her hood pulled over her head. She lounged in the seat she'd snagged in the corner of the room, but her pursed lips and raised brow let me know that I was dragging this out too long. I flicked my eyes around the tavern, and sure enough, we'd lost the interest of much of the room as patrons turned back to their own conversation or drinks.

I had to remind myself that this was training but also wasn't. The point of the ring wasn't to try out all the ways I could dangle my opponent on a hook for a bit of exercise.

But it was so much fun! I'd spent years training with my cousin, so I'd been more than prepared for this sort of thing. Meline was still leaps and bounds more experienced than I was, and I needed to encounter different styles if we were going to take on bigger contracts. And our other goal, of searching for Francie, had led to more and more dead ends. But we needed to keep moving—for more reasons than just that.

I let out a little giggle and shook my head. I was much leaner and shorter than him, but when I dove straight for his middle, he fell over easily. Before he could start any sort of counter-attack, I had my arms around his neck, legs clamped around his thighs, and I had the urge to plant a teasing kiss on the pale blond hair that stuck to his brow. I repressed the urge, though, and just kept holding him tightly. After he tried and failed to throw me a few times, he finally sagged and slapped his hand against the ground in submission.

To my surprise, he chuckled as I was announced the winner. It didn't hold any malice, and when I released him and we both stood, he just dusted himself off and gave me a crooked smile.

"I know when I've been bested." His shoulders were heaving, and there was a happy flush on his face. I felt my own rise underneath my brown skin, but I couldn't blame it on exertion. To a human, this man would probably prove to be more than formidable.

But to a Lylithan?

I shrugged, ready to return to my perch beside Meline, but the man shocked me when he extended a hand. I'd seen the gesture before, of course, but it was so foreign here, where a glob of spit at your opponent's feet was the custom.

Grin rising to match, I brought my hand to his. When his gaze heated, falling on my fangs, my smile darkened at the blatant interest.

The fighting circuits were a collection of loosely-associated taverns, back alleys, and run-down arenas. We'd been making our way through, taking small contracts since the bidding was never too far from the matches.

Before…everything, I would've been loath to admit that at over two-hundred years old, I was fairly sheltered.

Nethras. Versillia. Both were havens for the shrinking Lylithan population, places where our fangs and thirst were common. Not feared, nor particularly commodified.

Now, traveling with Meline, I realized how short our reach truly was.

"Well." I shrugged and made sure to dart my tongue out to touch my fang. Just a bit. "Perhaps I'd let you best me in other ways," I tilted my head and noticed the stuttering of his heartbeat, "or maybe you'd enjoy a round two?" Some private time with the human sounded delicious in more ways than one.

"Tana," a tight voice rang across the room. She didn't even have to raise it.

I groaned, shoulders slumping. Right. We were here for a purpose, not fun.

Honestly, when had we last just had some *fun*?

What a stupid question. I knew exactly when.

Using my strength that more than tripled his, I pulled the human to his feet, and when he stumbled, I planted that kiss on his sweaty cheek. There were several snorts, hoots, and hollers as I pulled away, but he didn't seem to mind. He looked awestruck as he rubbed where my lips had touched his skin.

Meline rose from her seat, and we both proceeded to the back corner of the tavern, weaving around mostly humans. There was little to no magic swirling here, just the innate skill that they were too unaware to tap into. The aether swam around us, still like a calm, never-ending river, and my limbs were buzzing with it.

Maybe that was why I was practically skipping as we neared the others that were already convened in the back room.

Today was the day. Where we would bid for something *big*.

I wound my arm through Leenie's, and though she grumbled, she tightened her hold against mine. "You win one bout, and you're walking on air." I could hear the affectionate eye-roll in her words.

It hadn't been another Lylithan or someone that matched me for strength, but he'd had some tricky techniques that provided enough challenge. I lowered my voice as we settled in the back of what should've been a storage room. Boxes of supplies were pushed to the corners, and in the center was a tall woman with her dark hair arranged in intricate braids. The careful style contrasted extremely with the fighting leathers and weapons strapped all over her waist and thighs.

She read from a ledger, deep voice commanding the room.

"Next is a domestic dispute. Adulterous husband and all that." She waved her hand as chuckles coursed through the room of assassins. "Wife is offering forty gold pieces for the deed." A few hands shot in the air, but the first was from a short man in the front.

She pointed to him while the rest groaned.

Meline and I stayed still, leaning against crates of liquor while contract after contract were read. There was only about fifteen of us, and with a considerable number of jobs presented, a few were doubling up.

And we waited.

Despite this village's size, the company of two dozen mercenaries alluded to the danger of assumptions. This town was small, but it was as dangerous as a crowded city.

There was no magic stirring in this room, sure, but I could feel the dark expertise pulsing. The well-worn and well-kept weapons that were enough to equip a small army. The calculating cuts of our competitions' eyes.

Because that's what my cousin had taught me. They were competition.

And judging from the wary glances in our direction, they saw us as the same.

The moderator whistled while she trailed her finger to the

bottom of a page. "Assassination of the good governor himself, the chief solicitor, and head of the central bank. Clean jobs, the lot of them. Natural causes. Two thousand gold pieces."

I straightened. Surprised by the size of the task, excitement bubbling. It was just the thing. In an instant, my mind flicked through the possibilities. The poison tonic I could concoct for at least one of them. Mottleroot? Its properties caused a slower decline to make the death come on like a seasonal illness. But swift enough to meet our needs. Most of my experience was with healing, but I was fairly certain I could influence the blood enough to trigger a heart attack, at least in a human. That just left the other, but that could be Leenie's choosing, and then we could use those funds to—

"Done." I whirled around, following the point of her finger to someone who was certainly not us. "Next is draining of the reserves from said bank." The moderator went on, describing the particulars of the task, but I focused instead on my cousin.

Her brown and gold eyes stared forward, brow furrowed. She stared across the room.

"A retrieval. Will take you out of town, expenses not paid but final payment is—" Meline's hand went up before the master assassin could finish.

And she didn't, pointing to my cousin who took the job without even knowing with the bloody payment was! And that much travel would definitely incur hefty costs.

The moderator continued through the last contracts, and I nudged Meline with my elbow. "Care to share?"

She angled my way, and I eyed the edges of her tight dark curls that mirrored my lighter ones. We were mistaken for sisters even more now, but the mischievous lightheartedness we once shared was a faint memory of the old Meline.

Before she could answer me, I detected a new presence at my back, one that wasn't focused on the bidding before us. Meline's brown and gold gaze went over my shoulder, holding a note of familiarity that left me turning slowly.

"Fancy meeting you here, lass." A bald male with black skin and gold teeth smiled down at the two of us. Though he was certainly the least human-looking mercenary in the room, no one seemed surprised or interested in his presence.

Aside from my cousin.

"Grimm," she nodded, "you have something you'd like to share?"

His leathers shuddered as he mimicked her posture, arms crossed. But that smile never fell. "Let's go get a drink."

"So, what can a Mind Walker do, exactly?" I sipped from my mug of ale, filing away all my cousin's old friend and mentor deigned to share with us. It was quite fascinating and more evidence about all that I just didn't *know*.

He leaned back heftily in his seat, bulky body making the wood groan. His pointed ears held thickly-gauged rings, and his eyes had no lashes. "Bit of old magic, said to be of this realm but more of the next one over." I frowned in confusion but didn't interrupt. "A taste a' yer blood, and I can search the memories. Sense 'em as if I were there."

"Wow," I breathed. My mind was already whirring with the possibilities a type of power like that could open. "And do you pull on the aether for that? A certain spell?"

The Mind Walker waved his large hand and drained his full mug in three swallows. He licked the residual froth with a swipe of his black tongue and motioned toward the barkeep for another. "No. Like I said, it's a gift from elsewhere. A little glimmer that passed through me da's line."

"Grimm," my cousin cut in tightly, "explain why we had to take that contract."

I straightened, shutting down the list of questions I had for Grimm about his powers. He'd been the reason she bid on the retrieval job?

After the bidding was ended, we'd hung back to gather our individual reports of relevant information from the moderator. It was a lengthy process, the recitation of instruction, proof of deed required, meeting point with employers, et cetera. None of it was written, I'd learned after our first contract, but a good mercenary's memory ran long. The details of our contract, to find and take a merchant by the name of Paschal Von Herron, were already filed away in my thoughts.

"Funny thing, that. When ye wrote me about yer missing friend, I paid her mate a visit. Didn't make much sense, but I was bored." He shrugged. "Poor fellow was willing to try and see what I could find, what with the city guards turning up with nothin'."

Meline and I both sat forward, arms propped on the sticky tabletop. Ever since leaving Ralthas, we had been training and taking contracts, yes, but all the while, we'd been trying to piece together the mystery of Francie's kidnapping. I faintly remembered her from our lives in Versillia before The Killings. Kindhearted and frazzled, she was a bit of a kindred spirit, and her mate Whitley was one of the kindest people I'd met. Their calm fit well with her buzzing energy, but how were they fairing now with her gone this long?

Last Meline had written them, they still had their marks. They described looking down at their hands every other moment, mating marks reminding them that she was still out there. Maybe staring at her marks too.

"The ones that took her, yer friend, are not to be underestimated. Nor are they easy to get hold of. The merchant," Grimm stabbed his finger at the table, "folks in this region speak of him."

The commotion of the tavern was loud, but the hush that befell our group was thick enough to cut with a blade. "Speak of what?" Meline asked.

A barkeep dropped another mug of ale before Grimm, and he

grasped the tankard. "They aren't from here, the ones I smelt in the sad one's mind."

"And? We aren't from here either."

My heart skipped a beat at the familiar snarky tone, but when I glanced at my cousin, she was focused on Grimm. I called no attention to it.

Neither did Grimm, aside from a fondly chastising look. I'd not inquired much of this side of her life, back when Meline and I were living in Nethras. But even then, she'd mentioned a cunning ring-master who'd taken her under his wing for a time.

"*This* side of the continent, your kind with pretty fangs are few, yes?" We both nodded as he took a far daintier swig of his ale. "Don't know for sure, but Mum always said it was purpose-ful. Your kind and theirs staying far from each other. Too alike, my granny used to say."

Meline growled and shot a finger at him. "Grimm, I swear, *enough* of the riddles and smoke. Speak plainly."

He didn't rise to the challenge. Nor did he shoot back a cocky grin this time. He just sighed and shook his head. "They travel here sometimes. Cross the veil to trade or cause trouble, and that's easier to do with the mortals who aren't as keen to put up a fight. Da was human but always spoke of some great-grand or whomever that had dalliance with the Folk, as mum calls them. The Mind Walking, we think, comes from them, but there's no way to be certain. Anywho, yer merchant is known for dealing their goods. You get to 'im, you might get close enough to one of them."

Grimm nodded, satisfied with the end of his tale, but there were—*so* many questions, I could hardly think straight. I cleared my throat. "Um…when you say cross the veil…"

"Bah," he waved that hand again, "nothing to worry yerself over. S'been happening forever."

I wasn't so sure how that was supposed to be reassuring. Looking over at my cousin, I found her chewing at her lip, fang catching the skin. "And you think there's a chance they could have her."

He shrugged. "I know what I scented, and it's the same as in me da's memories, in his recollection of me gran's, and so on. When they'd make sure to lock the doors in case their Neighbors came knockin'." Grimm stood, deciding for us that our meeting had come to an end. Draining his drink once again, he slammed it on the table, causing it to shake and me to jump in surprise. Meline's narrow-eyed gaze didn't waver.

"That's all?"

Now, his humor returned. Grimm barked a laugh, gold teeth shining in the candlelight. "That's all. Be happy that I happened to see ya at the bidding and catch yer eye." He paused a moment, looking between the two of us. "If ya find them, be careful, lass. And don't forget your debt." He smacked his palm on her back a few times, to which my cousin grumbled and glared.

"Just keep it running for me. I'll pay. Eventually."

He snickered again, already heading toward another table filled with fighters hollering for him to join them.

"Ah…" I started but failed to find the words to finish.

Meline sighed and pinched the bridge of her nose, eyes clenched shut. It also didn't escape my notice that she hadn't asked after her Shadow. They were known to grace these spaces with their presence, circling for a good contract with the rest of us, but we'd yet to see him. I noticed my cousin search the back rooms, linger on the telltale luster of black leathers and pulse of Shadow magic. They were never him, and she never approached or inquired if they knew where he was.

When I'd gently asked her once, why she hadn't approached a Shadow male with pale skin and brown hair, she just looked at me dryly. A lie. *"I wouldn't even know what to say."*

"Do you believe him? About this other realm business?"

"I do. He wouldn't lie. But that just brings more questions. Why would they take her? Why haven't we heard of them before? How do we get her back? How can we trust the ones doing business with our mark to give us answers about Francie?" She scoffed again and took to her abandoned ale, froth now calmed.

She was right. So many questions with no answers in sight. But, if there was one thing we *didn't* have a shortage of, it was time. Time to pursue this lead, to at least make some coin. To chase away the dejection and numbness that'd taken over my cousin's soul.

They'd hovered like vultures over these centuries. And with each tragedy, they gained traction until they sunk their talons into her heart. I tried to fight them off as best I could, give her a moment to breathe.

But my cousin seemed content to just let them pick her bones clean and let the sun to turn her to dust.

"That male is watching you." She pulled me out of my musings, drawling without feeling.

I followed her pointed gaze, and the one I'd bested tonight was indeed smirking at us from across the tavern. With an affable wave, he exuded the universal signs of interest. "And if I explored the option?"

Meline hummed, still not looking at me. "Do what you'd like. I need to feed anyway."

I pursed my lips, weighing the choices. Truth be told, a night of fun would be a delightful reprieve and send-off before we explored this Francie trail in earnest. Wasn't nearly the same, but my own journey from death and destruction walked parallel to Meline's. Maybe it was my sheltered upbringing. Or the fact that Death had chosen her as conduit. Whatever the reason, my cousin seemed unable to grow around the loss, as I'd been slowly doing. For her, it razed and salted, ensuring nothing would sprout ever again.

"Go," she huffed. "I'll be back in our room by the time you're done." Without another word, she left the tavern, disappearing to find someone to feed from and probably return to whatever book she'd been reading before we left for the ring.

I watched her go before heading for the male who would hopefully provide an engaging evening. But what churned in my gut wasn't excitement. No, what weighed in my stomach was the ever-present stone of worry.

How did you keep alive someone who was convinced they were already dead?

Chapter Ten
Tomás

My lip curled as I rifled through our employer's wardrobe. I'd been doing this long enough to know that reconnaissance was important for a target of this status, but that did not at all mean that I wanted to be hunched over and going through some tosser's shorts while a perfectly good party was raging just two floors below.

I searched every bit of the grandiose bedroom but found fuck-all. The man had stationed his guards to keep the guests sequestered on the lower levels of his estate. Not that many would be wandering away from the flowing alcohol and food, anyway.

When I crept to the door that led out to the corridor, I stilled to listen for anyone approaching. With a snort, I walked into the hall and, just for good measure, swaggered on silent steps over to the last room I had to check.

The office proved to be loads more useful. A cursory sweep of the massive wooden desk revealed guards' watch schedules, as well as an opened invitation from none other than Paschal Von Herron. Our mark.

To my disappointment, he was not at this soirée, still making his way back to the city, according to the gossipmongers downstairs. This invitation, though, might provide what we needed to get close to him.

I sat in the expensive chair behind the desk and leaned back as I read over everything, committing it to memory. Also appeared that the man who hired us was writing off his shady dealings as revenue earned by his more legitimate businesses.

My tongue clicked beneath my black mask. Rich people were always so predictable. And oblivious.

Shrugging, I straightened and began to put everything back where it was. Even with the lax security, I was bored, not stupid. Though, I did manage to take a few loose coins he had lying around. *They were just right there for the taking!* I argued when my best mate's grumbly voice admonished me in my head. A man this rich wouldn't miss them, surely.

As I circled the space, turning over and replacing everything to make sure that I hadn't missed anything, the sound of a foot shuffling over carpet rang in my ears like a bell. I stiffened as I focused, and—yeah, there it was again. But it wasn't the heavy footfalls of a guard who had no reason to hide. The person coming was trying, and almost succeeding, to walk the corridor silently.

Curiosity made my heart pick up a bit. Maybe this trip wasn't going to be completely boring, then.

I slunk back into the shadows of the room, where the moonlight streaming in from the large windows didn't reach. All but the top half of my face was covered by my black clothing, and centuries of doing this made it as easy as breathing. All the prep work for these contracts—the scouting, snooping, negotiating—that was the dull stuff. We still needed to pick the right time to make our kill as seamless as possible, so I'd thought that I wouldn't get this thrill for a good while yet.

When that creeping person opened the door, I couldn't help my grin.

Magic wasn't ever my method of choice, but I was always thankful for the handful of Shadow spells that I knew. The darkness of my oath, a living entity bound to my soul, bent the aether at my will. I did not need words, just the intention of my thoughts.

The one I used now masked my scent so that I left no trace of myself behind. And it gave me enough of an advantage—some time—to take in the one that also seemed to be on a mission.

It took me a moment, since she looked a bit different from when I'd last seen her. There was a split second before I really took in her scent, and then recognition hit me. She closed the door with another almost-silent movement, but it was nearly deafening in the quiet space. Then she turned around, chartreuse silk shifting over her body.

Shit.

Fuck, fuck, fuck, fuck.

What was *she* doing here?

My teeth ground, and my fingers flexed, touching the pommel of my shamshir sheathed at my hip. She was done up like many of those I'd seen streaming into the party before I'd entered the estate through one of the back windows. The delicate black gloves she wore smoothed down the front of her slinky gown, like running silk over water.

Elián was *not* going to react well to this.

I watched as she began to search the large bookshelf closest to the door. Though she wasn't rushing, she wasted no time going through all the books I'd looked at, lifting a stone bust carved in the likeness of the owner of the estate with a snicker.

My Shadow training wasn't anything I thought about all that much anymore. When she'd saved my arse that night in Vharas, I struggled at first to explain our ways. Trying to put into words what my body just *did* was a bit frustrating.

But when she suddenly stiffened and lifted her nose to the air, eyes narrowed, I felt something akin to panic in my gut. Had I made myself known? No, impossible.

Or… maybe not. She whipped around and looked right at me.

There was still a gigantic desk, a small sofa, and two plush armchairs between us, but the office seemed to shrink in that moment. Elián's female tilted her head to the side as she watched me in a posture that was eerily like his.

Until a smile started curling at her full lips.

"Hello, Shadow," she said conversationally. She took a step forward, this time making no effort to conceal the noise. And then there were black blades in her hands.

This fucking female was making me question all of my abilities—had she been carrying those with her? No, I was positive that she'd entered the room empty-handed. I would definitely have noticed her retrieving them from a concealed place right in front of me.

Fuck this.

I pushed off of the wall and slunk out of my hiding place. For good measure, I pulled down my mask while I unsheathed my scimitar. Wasn't like we hadn't met before, anyway.

Her smile was still pasted on her face, but it very noticeably didn't reach her dark, almost black eyes. She leaned a hip against the side of the desk, resting her arms at her sides with the daggers still in her hands.

"Forgive me, love, but I never got your name?" I turned on my own wry smirk. The one that seemed to lull people into a sense of security. To see me as less threatening than I was.

She pursed her lips and looked me up and down. "You don't know it?" Something about that seemed to bother her more than finding me in here. How the fuck was I supposed to know her name? The contract Noruh, Elián, and Jones took in collaboration with the Lylithan Council had been kept fairly low-profile from the rest of us. And since he'd been back at the Well, he'd never said her name aloud. At least not to me.

I shrugged and twirled my sword absently. "Should I? Thought that was the deal when we first met, love." I sighed and said dryly, "Not that it stopped you from ratting me out to my pedantic brother, but," I waved my free hand lazily, "I suppose it's water under the bridge."

This seemed to interest her, even if she was trying very much to hide it. As soon as the word 'brother' left my mouth, her body couldn't completely suppress the flinch of her shoulders. She scoffed and rolled her eyes, but her fingers twitched on the hilts of her blades. "Yes, I suppose it is. It was years ago, anyway."

"So," I quirked a brow, "what is so interesting up here when it sounds like there's far more interesting things going on down there?"

She narrowed her gaze at me again. "I think I will ask you that same question, Shadow."

"Tomás." I grinned and flashed my fangs at her.

That got a reaction—she snorted and seemed to relax infinitesimally. "All right, Tomás. What are you doing up here?"

I shrugged again. "Working."

The tension that'd left her slight but powerful frame returned in an instant. Her eyes raced over my body, my weapon. Her nostrils flared. "Are you here for me?"

That made me choke out an incredulous laugh. With my hearing, I knew there was still no one else on this floor. The closest guard was meandering uselessly near the foot of stairs leading up this way, and my outburst didn't even make them shift.

"Now, why would *I* be here for you?"

The silver moonlight hit the side of her face, and the flexing of her jaw was illuminated by its glow. Her nostrils flared again. "Get the fuck out of here."

I tsked and rolled my eyes. "Now, love, why would I do that? I couldn't care less about you stealing a bit of coin or some jewels." I winked. "Might even show you where the good stuff is if you're interested." I'd refrained when I found a few priceless items on this floor. Well, mostly.

She sneered. "I'm not—" but then she clamped her mouth shut, thinking better about what she was about to say.

My smile dropped. She was about to say that she wasn't here

for coin or jewels. I really was getting careless, it seemed. Because there were a few gilded items on the bookshelf that she'd looked right past. And to get all the way up here from the party, assuming that she'd entered with the other guests... she'd gone to lengths to sneak up here for something other than riches. There were enough drunk wealthy people downstairs that swiping a ring, a pair of earrings, would have been child's play.

I groaned and swiped a hand over my face. "*Fuck* me, are you —" *Thryx curse me*. I drew a frustrated breath. "Please do not tell me you're here on a contract."

Her silence told me enough, and I let out another groan. "Fucking typical." Seemed like our employers put out multiple contracts for the same mark. While part of me could understand the logic—it *did* help ensure the job got done—it usually caused headaches for us. Planning for and confronting the obstacles to fulfilling the contract were one thing. But to compete with another assassin was just an irritating obstacle instead of an exciting challenge. Most of them were like annoying insects buzzing past my ear, rather than anything actually worth the trouble.

She seethed through her teeth, "You need to back the fuck off, Shadow. This one is ours."

My head jerked back. "*Yours*? We've already claimed this one." I waved a hand toward the door. "Just go back to the party, love. I really don't have time for this."

"Fuck you," she blurted like it was a reflex. Then, much slower, she said too nonchalantly, "Who's 'we'?"

Oh, Aeras, Thryx, and *Mother take me*. No wonder he was still hung up on her. She was about as infuriating as he was. "I think you know who, love." Her jaw ticked again, and I rolled my eyes. "Oh come, now. You both are so painfully obvious. Just talk and make peace with one another. He's been even more of a tetchy bastard since *you*," I jutted a finger at her, "told him to go."

Her lips pulled back in a fanged snarl. "Both of you can go

fuck yourselves. The contract is ours, and I don't appreciate you shifty motherfuckers trying to steal it out from under us."

"Oh, don't get yourself tied in a knot." I started moving toward the window, uncaring about showing her my back. Even when the deadly points of her fangs flashed at me, I knew that she wasn't going to pounce. Plus, mine were sharper, and my weapon was bigger.

I glanced outside to make sure the ground below was just as unguarded as the rest of this part of the giant home. My gloved fingers made no noise as I unlatched the window and opened it. Salt-tinged air hit my face, and it carried the scent of the pine trees that bordered the estate.

She was so upset, she hadn't yet reacted to the steady footsteps starting up the stairs. One of the guards had decided to do a sweep of this floor, most likely.

Over my shoulder, I smirked. "If you're so insistent, seems like we'll just have to see who gets to him first." Before I dropped down to the grounds below, though, I called, "I'll give my brother your regards."

The manicured grass noiselessly met the bottom of my boots, and I was already slinking away when her frustrated curse reached my ears. Took her long enough to realize the guard was coming.

All mirth seeped out of me as I made my way into the trees.

How the fuck was I going to tell him I'd seen her first?

"What the *fuck* do you mean you saw her?" Just as I'd guessed, my best mate was *not* elated to hear that my reconnaissance had included speaking with the female he was still in love with and had been searching for, to no avail, for years.

The male should have been elated, but his possessiveness had already turned to misplaced anger.

I flopped down onto the worn leather sofa of his Morovan

apartment. Well, it was more of a safehouse. There were no personal effects—just the necessary comforts to be a resting place during or between contracts. It wasn't really even meant for two people to stay for longer stretches but, this was a far better option to crowded or expensive inns.

My hands folded underneath my head as I leaned against the back cushions. If I were to receive a tongue lashing from him, I'd at least get good and comfortable for it. "I *mean*, just as I was finishing up, she crept into the room. Thought she was up there for some good old petty thievery, but it would seem that we have some competition."

"*And?*" By how much louder his voice got, I knew that Elián was standing over me, no doubt seething at my lackadaisical attitude. But if I fed more into the thin but very present thread of desperation in his voice, I'd only make things worse. I was certainly not going to get upset over the female.

"*And,*" I drawled, "she told us to back off, and I left."

"*What*—"

My lips pursed, and then I continued, "Well, her exact words were telling us to 'back the *fuck* off.'"

"What else did she say, Tom," he demanded.

I opened my eyes just to roll them. "That's all she said, mate. She seemed miffed that I didn't know her name, though."

Elián ran a hand over his face then brought it up to pull at his hair. "What do you mean she was *miffed*?" He mimicked my accent on that last word, but I decided to ignore it. Noruh had chastised me for coming on too strong with my worrying about him, and after flat-out disagreeing with her at first, I'd slowly begun to realize that my nagging had been getting him nowhere.

I huffed. "She acted like she expected me to know it. And then she tried very hard to not seem interested when I mentioned you."

He slowly lowered himself into the armchair beside me, and I watched his throat bob with his swallow. He rested his elbows on his thighs, eyes gazing down at his hands, and it was a long moment before he spoke much more quietly, "But she didn't say anything else."

I thought back to the way she'd appeared, beneath the snarls and curses. To the stillness that took her over when I mentioned my brother. To the sharp glint of interest.

What sort of interest, though, I wasn't sure.

"She didn't say, no. But…she certainly hung onto my words once I alluded to you."

His fire eyes flickered with an echo of her expression earlier. He stilled, only his lips moving as he asked, "And how did she seem?"

How was I supposed to know? "Not sure. Annoyed. Even conjured up some daggers to threaten me," I scoffed. The more I'd thought about it, the more certain I'd become that she'd used some sort of magic to will the weapons into existence. I'd not personally witnessed it done before, but with a brother who'd been blessed by the Goddess of Strategy and Combat Herself, this development didn't surprise me in the least. My stomach growled. "Didn't even get to take some food," I grumbled. And it'd smelled divine, too.

"*Tom*. Focus."

"I *am* focused." I told him the rest of the information I'd gathered about the contract. The invitation marked for *another* event. This one, though, was at the home of our mark. Surely, Nogón's female would be there, too. "She's obviously still stuck on you in some way. Hopefully the same way you are for her. The way I see it, you have three days to get yourself together and prepare to meet your queen."

My brother sagged into the chair opposite my supine sprawl, gaze going faraway. And I watched him, a bit warily. What if I'd gauged her reaction wrongly and she held nothing but enmity for him? Or was she longing for a fling she intended to pick up and promptly put down again?

Either of those cases would probably be the thing to kill him.

"Did you read the letters Noruh sent?" I reached out and

plucked them from the small table beside the sofa. In her curling script was reassurance that our young acolyte was doing fine. But the other three pages were from the kid, wishing us well, updating us on his training. He'd even drawn a few sketches of the weapons he was learning about.

I snorted at the lightly shaded scimitar and his determination that the curved blade was not among his favorites.

Elián took a while to respond, but eventually, he grunted. "He is thriving."

There was a lot of happiness that coursed through the lad's large but neat scrawl. He even mentioned relieving Briar of some coin after some heated rounds of The Fool. At least someone paid attention when I taught them card games. "I suppose. Good for him that his binding decision seems to be the right one. Would have been irritating should he regret it."

And then Nogón surprised me. "Do you? Regret it." When I rested the letters across my chest and stared widely at him, he ground his jaw and continued. "You were younger than Marco when you took the Acolyte Oath. You had no home and no family, so there were few options that offered the level of opportunity. I know you have felt stifled."

Stifled? Was that what it was?

I continued to stare at him and searched myself. The Shadow Oath coursed within my veins, weaving dark mist along my soul in a bond that would only break in the finality of death. Sure, I'd seen it as dreadfully…well, final, but stifling?

Being in love the way he was—*that* was stifling. A life on the streets with the fear of hunger, Frenzy, or a knife to the back— *that* was suffocating.

Agreeing to follow Nogón, Leandro, and their father to the Well allowed me to *breathe*. Each year as an acolyte was another gulp, each laugh shared between my siblings and me was a deep, sated sigh. Now, I was the predator that walked alleys without a second thought. I had multiple homes in multiple cities and friends I would keep to my grave.

No, when I'd bemoaned the responsibilities of my Oath, I realized, it was not because I was stifled. I was bloody *bored.*

I swept away his worries with a fluttering of my fingers. "No. I don't regret taking the hand you extended, if that's what you're concerned about. Nor do I regret becoming a Shadow. I complain and bemoan, but don't you fucking dare take it personally." My words got harsh at the end, but I didn't soften my tone.

Elián opened and closed his mouth a few times, struggling to find his words. In a flash, I saw him as the small and silent child whose eyes said everything. When his speech was so halting and difficult that he relied on Leandro to voice his thoughts. At least, unless he was singing. Those sort of words always came smoothly.

In Zonoran, my brother whispered, *"Thank you. For doing this with me. All of it."* He glanced down at this palm, at Leandro's name memorialized for as long as Elián continued to live.

I lifted our charge's letters until the drawings and exclamations filled my vision instead. *"Think nothing of it. We are brothers."*

CHAPTER ELEVEN
ELIÁN

THREE YEARS AFTER HER

They did not want us to see their faces.

When Tom and I met with our employers for this contract on the outskirts of Morova. They kept us to a barn, insistent we meet in the middle of the night. The five of them wore cloaks, for goddess's sake, like commissioning the murder of their fellow merchant and biggest rival was some sacred ritual.

Our race was few, as was the Vyrkos, but our rarity was even more apparent in the human lands. Where they were the majority, and most looked at us with fear, lust, or a combination of both. They were interested or disgusted by the unknown, afraid because of tales brought back and twisted. Or, accurate ones as well.

Now, I straightened my collar. The fabric was a deep violet with amber embroidery woven over it and down my shoulders and chest. Using quick fingers, I tightened the belt in the same motif, closing the jacket over me while leaving underneath bare.

We were to close in, tonight, if the moment presented itself.

"This must be treated delicately. With no witnesses and his guards

unaware." The cloaked merchants had instructed my brother and me as if we were stupid. I could feel Tom's eyes rolling in the quiet barn as we faced the men and received the first half of our payment. They had not said who they were, but I recognized the sea salt clinging to them underneath their colognes and perfumed clothing.

Wealthy but still taking voyages. So, not *that* wealthy.

My hair was dry now, after my quick bath, and it shone as I gave it one last comb. The oil left it slick, smooth in the light of the setting sun streaming through the small window near the mirror. My face was freshly shaved, and the rings in my ears were polished.

I gathered up the top third of my hair and tied it back. Shorter strands still escaped, framing my temples, but I just sighed and tucked them behind my ears.

And breathed.

Smoke came with the action, and it took a few more rounds of breath before I got it under my control. Tonight. I, Mother willing, would see my queen. After years of searching, traversing three continents and enduring crossing the seas, I would meet her deep stare. Feel her in my arms and hear her voice, not just in my dreams.

I would not accept any alternative.

I locked eyes with myself in the mirror, pulse thumping visibly in my throat, and marked this moment. I had dressed for the occasion, blending in with Morova's upper class to get closer to Paschal Von Herron. I disguised myself as a sheep for this hunt, but I had also dressed for her. My attire was not the pearlescent sort common among Morova's upper echelon, but the bright Zonoran colors were vibrant and expensive enough.

Would she recognize me? Would she be able to see how I craved her? Loved her?

My throat began to tighten with worry, words unspoken to anyone but myself, and I coughed to clear it. I would not treat her as I had when I was her Shadow. I would share my thoughts, and I would be honest about my emotions. I would not hold back.

And if she still sent me away?

A heavy hand clapped my back, jolting me out of the memory of her screams as I rode away from her. My greatest regret.

"Do you have any more of that oil?" Tom asked, appearing beside me in the smudged glass of the mirror. He was dressed in similar finery, though his jacket was more revealing than mine.

I pointedly eyed his exposed chest. "Is that how we are getting close to Von Herron?" I reached beside the sink and handed him the hair oil I brought with me and used sparingly while away from the Well.

Tom poured some in his palms, rings clacking as he warmed it between his hands. His hair was so different than mine, but the oil had a similar effect, leaving his locs smoothed and glistening. The remnants left on his hands, he rubbed in and patted against his collarbones and down his sternum. "Seems like one of the easiest ways to get him alone. If you stay close, you'll be able to sense when I've got him. We can slip away then."

"And what is my role?" I accepted the small glass bottle and put it back near the faucet.

Tom scoffed and did a few last tugs on his jacket. "You act as if we haven't been Shadows but a day, brother." I was the one to roll my eyes this time, and more quietly, gaze going soft, he added, "You will have your queen to worry about."

My jaw clenched at the mention of her. He did not say her name in my presence. I was not sure if he ever did, but I was grateful for this. Until she was mine again, I did not want to hear her name on another's lips.

"Yes," was all I said, and because my brother knew me better than anyone else, he did not press me for more.

The party was loud.

As all of such events were. As the trained dancers took their final bows, we, the guests, clapped pleasantly. Several, including Tom, murmured to each other about how impressive the entertainment was, and as the young women in fluttering, shimmering skirts walked elegantly away from the raised dais in the ballroom and the quartet began again to play, I assessed the crowd again.

She was not here.

The scent of a Lylithan alone would be distinct enough, but I would know the aroma of *her* anywhere. It was imprinted in my senses, the feel of her hair between my fingers dug into my skin. I resisted the urge to clasp my hands behind my back, like a Shadow on duty, and instead, crossed my arms, leaning slightly backwards as a bored aristocrat.

Slipping uninvited into the reverie was easy, not that our employers were any help. They wanted as little involvement with us as possible, thirsty for power but unwilling to soak their hands with blood.

No matter. The taste of blood was one of the few pleasures I had in these years without my queen.

My brother beside me used his charming smiles more sharply than the curved blade of his shamshir, fangs a bright white that drew the guests like moths to a light. Another talent of his, thankfully, was forgery. In less than an hour, Tom had replicated the invitations to the birthday celebration of Paschal Von Herron, ushering another year while also welcoming him home from his voyage to Savya. I was moderately skilled in this sort of subterfuge, but I much preferred sticking firmly to the shadows. But I would admit this method had its uses.

He was standing near the table laden with Morovan delicacies. Breads of all shades and toppings including white fish spreads, olives, tomatoes and cheeses. A tower of glasses filled with sparkling wine was constantly reconstructed as guests imbibed. A chef, dressed in their own luminescent jacket finer than most common folk who lived in the city owned, carved from a large cut of beef, showcasing the fine and expensive meat.

Tom turned away from me, giving me his back, and I meandered my way through the crowd. I marked the guards, dressed in steel armor and Morovan maroon. The guards surrounding us lacked the Morovan inscription a fluttering hummingbird, on their armor.

Von Herron, as we had suspected, was not alone for a moment, implanting himself in the center of the reverie and greeting guests who huddled around him, hungry for tales or a chance at his riches. Or maybe both. I had done some reconnaissance of my own on Von Herron, finding him to be a largely self-made man. Once an apprentice of one of the very colleagues who conspired against him. Finely woven fabric in rich, jewel-toned colors that had become as synonymous with Morova as the tiny hummingbird.

There was a shine to it. Something in the thread used, or the dye, I was not sure. I had traveled here enough to have my own safehouse, but it was often just a transition point. I held no true interest in this place or its people. Even for this contract, I was passively collecting information as a means to an end.

My spine snapped straight, then. The young man playing the pianoforte rose to a clanging crescendo, or perhaps that was just my blood rushing in my ears.

Pink peppercorns, the wind over the ocean, and a cool, deep darkness. It made me shiver, the knowledge of her presence, and from my corner near the back, where I had been monitoring the guards as they made circuits around the space, I saw her.

Zoko and Mother take me, I *saw* her.

My queen had just crossed the threshold, she and her cousin already swept up in a group of women laughing and reaching for glasses of the Morovan sparkling wine. But, she was *watching* me. Saw me.

The dress, if such a simple word could be used for what she draped her body with, was a deep jade color. The green of the trees surrounding my father's home in the verdant shades of an evening in the summertime. When life was at once full and sated and also happily turning to rest.

White and gold beads made up the middle, hinting at her navel but obscuring at the same time, and more green softly cradled her breasts. Long gloves in the same shade reached up to her elbows, but I knew the delicate sharpness within her touch. Could feel her nails scraping my scalp when I closed my eyes.

And her hair was…gone.

Instead of the twin plaits or the bountiful mass of curls, there was a rippling layer of waves slicked down and small loops meticulously placed by her ears.

My heart felt as if it had punched through my chest, flying straight toward her. My mouth watered, my cock stiffened, and I wasted no time stepping toward her. The reason for my nightmares and the inspiration for my dreams.

My queen…Meline. She watched me as if we were the only two in the room. As if she felt the pull to me as I felt it toward her. I wanted to hold her in my arms. To take the plump flesh of her lip between my teeth. To give her all of my words, my tears, and beg her to let me in. To sink my fangs into her throat and claim her inside and out.

But, as I took another step closer, as I skirted around another group of wealthy partygoers, drunk and cackling as if they were not in the way of my salvation, Meline…ran.

Or, it was a breaking of a trance. Wherein my getting closer brought to reality the moment. She shook, fang biting lip, and set down her glass of wine beside the others. Her fingers twitched at her sides, and she *fled*.

For a moment, as I watched her push past guests much more roughly than I had, I was stunned. My lungs threatened to crack, and my Fire roared to the surface, burning the inside of my throat until—

Until, she glanced over her shoulder. As if she could not bear the searing of my stare on the back of her neck. Watching her walk away this time.

And there, there I saw many things. Desire, twinkling and singing. Frustration in the flare of her nostrils and deepening of color on her cheeks. Goddess, her freckles even spoke to me, and when she whipped back around, shoving through a door leading to the kitchens, a deep, predatory rumble started at the base of my chest.

My queen would learn that there was no more running from me. From us, from *this*. I was hers, and she was *mine*.

∽

MELINE

I ducked through the drunken partygoers, more rich folk without a care in the world while my own had long ago crumbled.

The contract was to be my beacon. Something, at least for now, to focus on instead of the memories. The mistakes and sins that were a series of black marks on my soul until the whole thing was just a sludgy gray.

We were getting closer, and Tana was relying on me to keep my fucking head on, but I—I just needed a moment. Space to *breathe*.

Because he was here.

How was I supposed to think when those fire eyes kept finding me? When the flame and cinnamon scent was a steady rhythm in the air?

How could I resist going to him and falling into his arms?

I shoved my way into a back room, the fabric of my disguise shifting against my heaving breaths. The tight bodice and airy skirt now felt like vises. Cutting off my air.

My gloved hands shuddered against the wood of the countertop, my feet kicked against the odds and ends shoved in this forgotten space as laughter and music filtered through the walls.

The silence of death and my own screams, apricot eyes that wouldn't open. Tana's emerald ones, watery with tears.

Words I didn't understand. A song of hushed, somber microtones. I hummed, rubbing the heel of my hand against my racing, bruised heart. I'd no idea where it came from, but it was a reassurance that worked like a calming spell for upset babes. A bone-deep recognition that transcended language.

"Meline."

I whipped around, and the song stopped. The melody quieted, and I snapped my mask in place. I backed up, pressing against the counter to put as much space between me and him.

"Stop. Whatever you're going to say, just *stop*."

But he ignored me, advancing forward and bringing heat with him.

Elián.

Gone were the Shadow leathers and shades of black. I didn't miss them.

A fine jacket of violet and gold wrapped around his body. His hair, the color of raven's feathers, was half-up and swimming in elegant waves down his back. The gold rings running up and down his ears glinted with the same spark swirling in his irises.

I swallowed a moan, and he came closer. Eyes narrowed and lips set in a determined line, my former Shadow prowled closer until there was no option. Nowhere to go.

I could've escaped. Of course I could have. But, because I was weak, I remained where I was. Underneath my gloves, my power was swirling in giddy anticipation.

Elián—the bastard—closed his hand around my throat. A rival assassin had me alone and cornered, but his touch was far from a threat. Those mango eyes held frustration, rage, finality. Longing.

He bared his fangs at me, curling over my slighter frame until I was bathed in only him.

"You will listen to me, Meline. This ends. Now."

"Fuck you," I whispered. What could I say? Old habits and all that. "We're not handing over the contract to you. Can't handle a little competition?"

Elián smirked, but the expression held not a whiff of mirth. "No." He tightened his hand on my skin, and a puff of air gusted out of my nostrils. "You running from me is ending now."

My fingers tightened on the counter. Hadn't we been in this position before?

"I'm not running." Wasn't I? But that was only recently. My argument, that the past three years were filled with wanting him more than *almost* anything, died before it even made its way to my tongue.

He did not consider my refusal. "No more running. No more denying this."

I swallowed and shifted in his hold. I moved against him, not quite struggling but pushing against him all the same. "Elián, there's nothing to talk about. You'd better get back out there unless you want to give us the upper hand." I chuckled darkly at the thought of winning this contract. That was something I could cling to.

My laughter immediately died as Elián snarled, bringing his fangs, his heat, and those *eyes* closer. He used his hand on my throat to lift me in the air, and I let him. He didn't release me when I plopped onto the counter, nor did he when he hiked my skirts up so that he could stand between my parted thighs.

I let him.

My darkness, the slithering Death, wound up my arm all the way to my throat, where Elián's fire touch was. It remained on my skin, not yet reaching out, but the contact was enough.

He bent to growl in my ear, "No. More."

Ah, yes. We *had* been here before. When Elián was still my Shadow and had silenced my tantrum in Rhaestras by commanding me onto a table and tasting me.

Unlike then, I moved my fingers from gripping the surface he hoisted me onto and fisted the front of his jacket. Felt his heart hammering against his chest.

Elián's soft hair brushed against my cheek while his words were rough. His grip tightened on my throat, and my Death rejoiced. "You are not going to run. You are *not* going to run from me." Air whistled in and out of my nose like a fierce wind. "Do you know why?"

I opened my mouth to answer, but it shut with a click at the first bite of Elián's fangs.

His hand on my throat shifted just before the pain, enough to leave room for him to close his mouth over my flesh. My eyes rolled back in my head, and my legs opened wider for him to settle between them. His chest vibrated under my fingers.

Elián didn't drink from me, but after he released his fangs, he dragged his tongue through my blood. It was erotically presumptuous, giving me such a claiming bite.

I craned my neck as much as I could.

Hot breath at my ear, he licked my lobe. "I am yours. And you are *my* queen. *Mine.*" He reached under my skirts, finding the undergarment—expensive aeran silk, might I add—and tore it away.

The moan that'd been building within me, like the churning of dark clouds, finally escaped. And again with the telltale clink of a belt. The rustling of fabric.

"I will not leave, and neither will you. We will talk. We will listen. And you will not. Run." The words out of his mouth cut like stained glass, and they looped with an accent. The lilts of his Zonoran tongue that left me nodding.

Nodding while he descended into grumbling words in a language I couldn't translate but understood anyway. That he was taking the decision out of my broken hands. That with the press of his cock at my entrance, that he would accept nothing less than me yielding to him.

Goddess, it was enough to bring sweet tears to my eyes.

I pulled at his jacket, back arching as a whimper tore through my lips. Elián's hand moved to hold the back of my neck, his other to my hip.

And my body welcomed him, stretched for him. He was no longer choking me, but it was now when I felt as though I could barely breathe. My heart fluttered, my skin electrified, and I twined my arms around his shoulders while he thrust into me. Took me.

Elián hovered his lips over mine, halting his descent to whisper, "We belong to each other, and no distance, no amount of time will change that." And his hips pushed him the last few inches into me. I groaned in his face, wordlessly begging for him to keep moving. But he didn't. "Do you understand, Meline?"

I glared, facing the swimming fire in his eyes.

"*Do*," thrust, "*you*," thrust, "*understand*?" Was he still speaking in his native tongue? Or was I imagining that?

Either way, I nodded frantically, clamping my legs around his waist and crossing my ankles over the small of his back.

He still wasn't unleashing. I knew it, felt it. "*Say it*," he demanded.

At this point, how could I deny him? Despite my past actions, I never wanted to hurt him. There was enough pain in both of our immortal lives.

"I...I'm yours. I—*fuck*—no more running. No leaving you. Ever." He hadn't said that part, but the assertion left my mouth anyway.

And he growled in triumph as he bit the other side of my throat and came for my soul.

All parts of me yielded to him in a relieved exhale. Elián drank, now, and the whole bloody realm ceased to exist. The pleasure of him inside of me, hitting a spot that undid every one of my shields.

He could've drained me in that moment, fucking me into true death, and I would've thanked him with my last breath.

Instead, he clamped a hand over my mouth and gave me something to scream into. Sink my teeth into while the ecstasy built, spilled over, and coursed again in an incapacitating cycle. I became undone on Elián's fat cock as it pistoned in and out of me, hips stroking sinfully. More tears fell from my eyes as he told me who I belonged to.

And his final shudder became my own. I came again as he spilled his seed inside of me. Something I should've fought. But it was an undeniable stamp on his claim, taking and giving and destroying.

We still held onto each other, as our hearts gradually steadied. Until he brought his lips to mine in a bloody kiss. One that tasted of me and him.

Elián's tongue slipped against mine, his teeth bit at my lips with no attempt at gentleness.

But wasn't that what this was? Him withdrawing his gentle handling of me for a firm one so I couldn't twist and slither away.

"Wherever you go, I will find you. Whatever words you have, I will listen. Whatever tears you have, I will wipe away."

And there they went, falling and testing his promise after all of two breaths. He brushed them away, not with his thumbs but with his tongue.

In these three years, I had enough tears for him to never grow thirsty.

"Meline," he exhaled.

Those eyes, now calmed to smoldering embers, swallowed mine again. I didn't glare. I didn't break his stare as my gloved fingers still strangled the front of his jacket.

"I am—I'm *broken*, El."

He didn't even hesitate. "As am I." I gasped, guilt churning. "So, we will rebuild. Together."

Chapter Twelve
Meline

"Rebuild," I repeated, not quite believing what I was hearing.

"Together." My heart started pounding again, and my legs tightened around Elián's waist.

He nodded, like he wasn't shattering every expectation I had for this moment. In those hours in the darkness of my bed, or when my mind would wander just to torture me, I pictured my begging. His admonishment. His broad back as he turned away from me.

How long would Elián claim me after he knew how I'd truly failed?

"Meline. Look at me."

I swallowed, focusing back into the present. The thick, brown muscles of Elián's throat. The glossy black of his hair running against my fingers. The feel of his cock still inside of me.

My stare collided again with his, and the cold, sharp panic came back. "Fucking isn't going to solve everything between us," I whispered.

Elián pursed his lips, and when he pulled away, pulled out of me, I let him go. Despite what he'd said, I would never make him stay with me. Not after what I'd done.

Not after I'd taken a hammer to his already-cracking pieces.

But instead of turning tail and giving me what I deserved, Elián shoved my skirts higher, exposing me to the air. My legs hung off the edge of the counter as he tilted his head to gaze between them.

And he hummed a deep, rolling note. One that reflected the satisfaction flaring on his face. Elián took two long fingers and swiped them where he brutally claimed me, collecting the remnants of him that were undoubtedly running out.

"I know. But it is a start." He raised his glistening fingertips to my lips, and fuck me, I opened my mouth. Let him feed our releases back to me. It tasted like home. My salvation. "And I couldn't give you time to let your fear take over."

That had me spitting out his fingers. "I'm not afraid." With a huff, I closed my thighs and hopped down from the counter. Elián took a step back, allowing me to situate my skirts.

That was, until he clutched my chin and tilted my head to his liking. That face. Jaw and brow line strong. In his aristocratic disguise, he looked more like a king.

"I know that you are strong. That you are capable. But you let fear push me away last time. I have…" he paused, thoughts going far away, but I knew where. To the day that I regretted more than any of my misdeeds. Any sin I'd committed—fucked up but true. Nothing compared to how much I hated myself for telling him to leave.

Elián refocused on me, gently petting the nape of my neck. Where the length of my curls now ended. "I have had many days to think about this. Years. As I know you have."

It wasn't a question, and the uncertainty wafting off of him shouldn't have been his to bear. I'd put it there. Swallowing, I nodded.

Years, days, minutes. Seconds.

"So. We will go back out there, finish what we came here for. I have an apartment in the city center. You and I will go there and begin to rebuild."

My fingers fiddled with the hem of his jacket. When had they crept up there? "You've gotten bossier," I grumbled without heat.

"Nâ. I have become certain of what I want."

I exhaled, the breath trembling. Could I lean into this? Truly trust it? While I ran over the last few moments, Elián watching and letting me, I recited his commands in my mind.

My eyes narrowed. "We're not bowing out of the contract for you."

And then my knees nearly gave out.

He huffed, like a laugh, and the smirk that shifted his lips caused the magical dip in his cheek. With his jewelry, the bright color of his jacket and the soft sheen of his hair, Elián looked more himself than I'd ever seen. Like he was no longer using the Shadow black as a shield.

Elián nuzzled into my temple, breathing me in while I blinked back tears. "There are many things I want from you, my queen. But you and your cousin handing over the contract to us is not among them."

I cleared the thickness in my throat. "Um. Good."

With a hard press of his lips to my cheek, Elián released me, but his promises—and mine—were still wrapped around us.

"I think this will be fun, my queen."

And he spun on a heel and left.

When I caught up with Tana, drink in hand and laughing lightly at something spoken in the small circle gathered around the host of the event, her blonde brow was a silent inquiry to where I'd been.

Then, her nose twitched, chin tilting subtly in the air. Her eyes widened for a moment before her mask slipped back into place. A serene, airy smile spread her artificially blushed cheeks.

She hooked an arm around mine, demurely excusing us from

the conversation and pulling me away. A few objections rose, urging Tana to hurry back, and if I could feel my feet beneath me, I might've marveled her quick work, charming these people.

My cousin stopped us in a corner of the ballroom, furthest from where most were milling about, socializing and peacocking.

"Tell me."

I opened my mouth, but before I could report what happened, my attention snapped to the left. Catching on his form cutting through the crowd. Gathering information, just like we should have been.

"*Leenie*," Tana hissed, and I whirled around.

"He…I don't know where to begin."

She rolled her eyes and stomped her foot in frustration. Then, leaning in, she spoke low, "How about the fact that I can smell… *him* all over you. See the fang marks healing."

My lips rolled between my teeth, replaying the feeling of Elián inside of me. Kissing me. My power sparked and tingled on my fingertips, knowing we were going to follow his directives. Every last one. "He told me to meet him once we are done here. To spend the night with him."

Tana paused, gaze roving my face, brows drawn in concern. She threw back the rest of her flute of sparkling wine. "Are you okay?"

A crackling laugh escaped my lips. No, I hadn't been okay in three years. But now, maybe there was hope. "I don't know."

My cousin pulled me into her arms for a fast but grounding hug. It was just a breath, but I took it with her, inhaling against her chest, air whooshing out of our noses at the same time.

The tragedies of my actions, of my life, were at least good for two things. One of which brought me closer to Tana. Would anyone else save me the way she had? Watch me collapse, bleed, *die*, and still be here?

No one. Aside from the male whose seed was running down the inside of my thighs.

"Are you going to tell him?" Tana's tentative question, tears already collecting on her lash-line, threatened another sob from me. Would Elián want this teary mess of a person that I now was?

And, because I'd never been a good person, I shoved the answer to Tana's question away. Closed it in the steel vault in the back of my mind, even if the lock had a tendency to break at the slightest provocation.

"Are you going to be okay? If I go with him?"

She frowned, tracking my evasion but throwing away her objection with another roll of her eyes. "Oh, goddess, Leen. After all the offers I've had? I'm going to spend tonight *very* satisfied." I paused, weighing the truth in her words and found it whole.

My shoulders relaxed, and she clucked, kissing my cheek. "I just worry about you. But," she hooked her arm around mine again and pulled us to face the room, "enough of that."

We resumed our act, a pair of wealthy sisters, traveling and enjoying the pleasures of Morova. Tana whispered all she'd learned about our mark who'd remained surrounded the entire night. By suitors, colleagues, other aristocrats.

The tailored fabrics in rich colors and patterns made for a mosaic of cultures. Though I wasn't the most patient when it came to the posturing of the wealthy, the variety of languages spoken in the ballroom pulled on the same desires that sent me to live in Nethras nearly one-hundred years ago.

"And was he among those to offer himself to you?" Our mark was handsome, youthful and possessing a certain confidence that I could see as appealing.

Tana's grin was enough to reveal her fangs, and I tracked the lustful glances she garnered. "Not yet."

I grunted, and we mutually decided to enter the fold once again. The Shadows and other assassins might've operated by a different code, but where I was concerned, seduction was a perfectly acceptable means to the same end—fulfilling our contract.

As Tana rejoined the circle, bringing me with her, we both fought to keep our expressions pleasant. Our postures relaxed and eager.

Elián and his Shadow brother stood, flutes in hand, as they hung on every word of our mark as he gestured widely, spinning a tale of his last travel. I flicked my attention, counting the guards at each entrance to the ballroom, as well as those that circled the room with trained posture. Covert but obvious.

Now, why would a mere merchant, wealthy or not, need twenty guards for a simple party?

Tana stiffened against me, and I returned to those around us. Elián wasn't looking at me, but my senses pulled to him all the same. My hand twitched at my side, wanting to reach out for him. My throat prickled, remembering his fangs piercing my skin.

Would he bite me again? A steady look from Elián had me forcing back a whimper

"Shit," Tana cursed under her breath with a smile on her face.

Lylithans were difficult to kill, but one of those guards could come over, sword in hand and ready to plunge it into my heart, and I wouldn't see it coming.

Elián raised his brow, smug bastard, then pointedly faced our mark. Who was making starry eyes at his Shadow brother.

After the tale of his travels ended, some art collector took up the story, detailing the purchases he made from our host. And anger rose up my throat as Tomás attached himself to our mark, fanged smile on display. His outfit was a bit more daring than Elián's, jacket and embroidered tunic open to his sternum.

Without looking, he handed his flute to Elián so that he could trace a finger down the center of our mark's chest.

"Fuck this," Tana muttered and wove her way over.

Lylithans, and Vyrkos for that matter, were few here. Not quite legend, but our fangs and need for blood were interesting to the humans. Even the smattering of other creatures—an elf, a few witches, and a wolf shifter—snuck a range of glances our way. Most of them wary.

I halfheartedly engaged in a conversation with a woman marveling at my garment, commiserating with her frustration in finding a good tailor these days. "Such a shame," I sighed and watched Tana out of my periphery. With the tightness bracketing Tomás's smile, and the delight on our mark's face, she was making headway.

Truthfully, with my Shadow just a few paces away, I was more than happy to leave the seduction to her. She was far more charming than me, even on my best day.

As the night passed, the guests got drunker, and both Tana and Tomás were now held in our merchant's embrace. With one in each arm, the merchant excused himself, pulling my cousin and Elián's brother with him.

Before they got lost in the crowd, Tana shot me a questioning look over her shoulder. I nodded as a warm body settled behind me.

She needn't worry. Even with all the unspoken, the hidden, I knew I would be safe with him.

Chapter Thirteen
Tomás

Change of fucking plan.

The private sitting room wasn't so far removed from the festivities that I was able to make my move and finish this bloody contract, but it was a step in the right direction.

At least, if I could get rid of *her*.

The poor fool whose days were numbered was turned toward the witch, heavy hand on her thigh.

His other was on mine, but that wouldn't do. I needed her to *go*. Increase my chances of being invited somewhere without the watchful eyes of his guards that were now standing sentry at the door. Their eyes faced forward instead of on our little triad.

Lowering to his throat, I planted open-mouthed kisses on clean, cologned skin. The strong smell made my nose twitch, but I continued.

A groan from him vibrated my lips, and triumph made me chuckle into the hollow of his throat. And when he pulled away to nuzzle into mine? I let the deep, delighted noise escape.

The merchant's hand was still on her, but his body was otherwise angled toward mine, sucking marks into my skin that would fade before I left this room. Earlier, out in the ballroom, after the telltale surge of lust directed my way, Elián and I had quickly shifted our approach. We didn't even have to discuss it, nor did I need him to spell out for me that he wouldn't be joining in.

Shame. With him on the other side of the sofa, we could've done some real damage. Maybe could've gotten an orgasm or two out of it.

But, something told me that this witch would raise hell and make things much more difficult for me if I showed my hand.

If she wanted competition, then fine, the gauntlet had already been thrown. They'd find that we had more tools than blades and shadows to get the job done.

The witch didn't move, but the fury on her face, nearly identical to Elián's queen's, was too delicious to ignore. My arm was slung lazily on the back of the sofa, and behind our mark's back, I shot her my middle finger, sealing it with a kiss blown her way.

The man moved up to my ear, pulling at the silver hoop with his teeth. His breath smelled faintly of rum, but I'd been watching. Unlike the rest of his guests, he'd kept his imbibing to a minimum. "I want you to fuck me," he panted. "While I fuck her."

Hm. Would the witch go so far? *Let us see.* I smirked again, pulling him back just enough to press my lips to his. "Now, darling," I batted my lashes, "I would love nothing more. But you must ask her first. Either way, I'm all yours."

With desire-hazed eyes, he turned back to the witch who, to her credit, was a picture of delicately wrapped promise. Legs crossed but slit revealing flawless skin, bodice situated to push her breasts forward. Typically, I preferred a more masculine figure, but even I could see the appeal.

Our mark moved to her, nuzzling and whispering in her ear. Whispering of how he wanted her too, the picture she'd paint under him with his body between us.

The feigned giggle made me roll my eyes, and when she pulled his hand to palm her breast, I didn't hide my huff of irritation. She was buggering up this whole operation. We would win anyway, so what was the point?

While Von Herron wove filthy fantasies, the queen's cousin glared at me with brown cheeks reddening. Hm.

With a stretching grin, I grabbed our mark's hips, eliciting a groan that he released into her throat. Even if I did intend to fuck the poor bastard, he certainly wouldn't last long. Not with the way lust was rolling off of him.

I scooted over on the sofa, bringing me closer to both of them. Time to call her bluff.

"Do you need my help getting her ready for you, darling? Or maybe you like to watch? We could put on a show for you," the witch glared with almost as much fire as Elián on a calm day, "drive you out of your mind."

"Fuck," he gasped and pulled away from her. "Yes, yes," the merchant groaned, and with a last kiss to her then me, he bolted to the armchair facing us.

Brown hair in disarray and expensive clothing rumpled, he already looked debauched. Was he really that hard up? Poor bloke.

Facing the witch, I found more cracks in her armor, split apart by her frustration. I couldn't relate, of course. I hardly lost, so I was unaccustomed to the feeling.

To most of the world, the Shadows appeared a stoic, impenetrable force. And, well, we were. But our public face was one of black leathers, armed to the teeth, and standing in a corner. Our killing was whispers in the dark, rumors full of truth.

Tales of *what* we did in order to get the kill often died with our target.

I threw my locs over my shoulder and prowled closer to her. "Are you ready for me?" This was a job for both of us, but I'd never taken a partner unwilling. She could fuck me angry all she wanted, but we both knew who was going to truly get to him first.

She flicked a glance over my body—which was flawless—

and though no desire wafted off of her, she was mighty convincing if you didn't know where to look. Throwing her leg over the back of the sofa, she leaned into the arm and bit her lip. "Yes," she turned her stare to our mark, "please."

Well. I grasped the hem of her skirts and began to lift. She had tenacity, I'd give her that.

Just as I was about to descend, revealing what lay between her legs, there was an insistent knock on the door.

We both halted, throwing questioning glances to our mark. Was he the type to want us to keep going? Or to keep this to himself?

As the knocks rang again, he pulled his hand out of his trousers and signaled to the guards to open the door. Another one came forward, whispering in the merchant's ear, which I had no problem hearing. There was a problem in the southern wing; no, it wasn't a threat to his safety, but they needed his attention at once.

I dropped the witch's dress while still hovering over her. What could be the problem? Had Nogón and the queen gotten into trouble? Certainly not…right?

Von Herron reluctantly stood, barely able to drag his eyes away from us. "I'll be back, sweets. But don't stop on my account." He winked and left one guard with us, the rest trailing with him out the door they left ajar.

So much for getting out of touching her.

Instead of reaching under her dress, I bent until my lips were a brush away from hers. I felt the flutter of her lashes in the air between us as I trailed to her ear. The witch rested her hands on my arms as I whispered, "Ready to give up now?"

She snapped her teeth, sharper than she fucking needed to, and caught the shell of my ear. "Not on your fucking life."

I growled in frustration, running the tip of my nose in the hollow of her throat. She trailed her fingertips up and down my spine and wound her hips. Ugh. "Fine. Anything you're uncomfortable with?" She stalled for a moment, and I backed off, bracing on hands that bracketed her shoulders.

Surprise flitted across her features before she replaced it with want. A minute shake of her head, and I dropped my lips to hers. It was methodical, the pressing of our bodies, the peeks of our tongues. And when purposeful footsteps marched toward us, we both kicked up the show. I grasped her hip underneath her skirts, her hands grabbed my arse and pulled me closer.

By scent and ear, I counted the increased reinforcements surrounding our mark. Ten and then the one with us. Goodness, goodness, what *was* this human up to?

Another quick sweep of my senses, and I detected no hint of Elián or the queen nearby. Were they not to blame for this interruption? Had they caused some damage and already fled?

"My apologies, sweets," the human's voice rang over us.

She broke our kiss first, blinking up at him with a pout and everything. He no longer sounded wrecked, and sure enough, when I turned my attention his way, he appeared far from fucking us.

"You are more than welcome to enjoy the festivities. I have more urgent matters to attend to," he said tightly, left, and all of the guards followed. Curious.

As soon as we were alone, the witch and I sprang away from each other.

She could've done without wiping her lips with the back of her hand, but I just shrugged it off. My mouth was amazing, so it was her loss.

With a loud huff, she stared up at the ornately carved ceiling.

I glared at the floor.

There was no use going after him with all those guards swimming about on high alert. Our contract was blatantly clear that the final deed was to have no witnesses. Otherwise, this whole bit would've been much, much easier.

The witch's bare foot rested near my leg, so I nudged it with my thigh. She glanced at me, and I sighed. "Fancy a hunt?"

What else was there to do but find someone to fuck and feed from?

She paused then sat upright, smoothing the back of her slicked curls. We both stood at the same time, tense competition cleared. At least for the moment.

"Fine."

Chapter Fourteen
Elián

I closed the door, flipping the multiple locks and latches. I leaned my back into the wood and took her in.

The deep green dress with embroidered bodice hugged her frame, the skirt hiding what I knew so intimately. The full hips where my hands belonged. The dip of her lower back, where I wanted to dot kisses and soft caresses.

It also didn't escape my notice that she was dressed in Versillian colors.

My queen stood just beyond the threshold, an inch out of my arm's reach. I looked at the apartment with new eyes, and it was simple. There were no personal effects. A front room with a small kitchen, table, two chairs. A bedroom and en suite bathing room to the left.

Still, she stood, the calm expanding of her chest not quite belying the rapid beat of her heart.

"Meline," I said, and she startled. How long had it been since I'd said her name aloud? Now, I couldn't stop myself. I had her. She was *here*.

My queen glanced my way, but it was a fleeting sweep of her gaze. I almost smiled, recalling her denial that she was afraid. By the cross of her arms and tilt of her chin, she was still going with that lie.

As long as she didn't lie to me about *us*.

She remained still, and I waited. Wondered why she wasn't crossing into the room, demanding I get on with it, berating me for doling out commands.

And then it dawned on me.

Could she be waiting for me to check for danger? As I'd done when I was her Shadow?

Meline was not facing me, so she couldn't see the smirk shift my lips now, but she shuddered as I bent to whisper, "Sit down, my queen. Be comfortable here."

Her gloved fingers twisted, clenched, but she didn't remove the leather coverings. Instead, she kicked off her heeled boots, showing her true height which fit perfectly against mine, and crossed the main space.

She did not sit at the table but on it, leaning against the scuffed but sturdy thing.

Deep brown and twinkles of gold watched me warily. How was it she could have changed and been so much the same? The female that haunted and blessed my dreams. The menace that I'd fallen in love with.

Her long, springing curls were all but gone. There was a deeper sadness clinging to her.

But the way she pushed against me earlier. The way she held onto me. It was *her*.

I eliminated the distance between us in an instant. If she did not want to sit, then I wouldn't either.

Her exhale was shaky. "You've got me here, El. So, talk."

Pink peppercorn. The wind over the ocean. I filled myself with her scent and shuddered at the trails of mine still on her. "I...have missed you." Tears immediately started brimming, making the gold flecks brighter. The brown deeper. "Have you missed me?" I dared.

My queen laughed a high-pitched noise. She stared above,

not looking at me and forcing the tears back. "*Fuck*, El." I waited, holding my breath as she swiped at her eyes. "You have n-no idea."

"I think I do."

Meline's expression crumpled, her body shook, but before I could bring her into my chest, she held out a hand to stop me.

Though I'd taken her in that back room, claimed her so that there was no space to question the connection between us, now that she'd agreed to stay with me, I knew I had to be patient.

My queen gasped, shoulders hitching. "Elián, I'm so—there will *never* be enough words for me to convey how sorry I am. For everything."

My skin warmed, and my Fire stirred at the sight of her breaking. It'd almost ruined me, turning away from her that day. With her howls of despair as I rode from the witch house. "Nâ. I —it was unfair of me. To expect you to not be wary of the Shadows. After all you'd been through."

She shook her head again, trying to fight off my words, but she stayed here. She did not flee. "It would be okay if you hated me, you know. I deserve it."

That, I could not stand for. As Tomás had told me long ago, my queen had been hurting. Recovered from the brink of death and contending with the murder of her uncle and her brother's betrayal. She could have responded differently, but I understood her reaction. Not wanting to be connected to a Shadow. Did she still feel that way?

I rested my palm on the nape of her neck, needing *some* connection with her. And she leaned into my touch, ever so slightly. "I do not hate you. I have loved you for a while, now." If we were going to rebuild, I would not hold back from her.

Her eyes widened, mouth dropping open. She gaped, starting and stopping multiple times before she could gather her words. I caressed my thumb against the strands curling behind her ear and marveled at the veins blackening beside my touch. Her power reaching out to me.

"You can't say shit like that to me, El," she whispered.

I hummed, bringing myself even closer to her. "It is a good thing that I am no longer working for you, then. I am no longer compelled to follow your orders."

She chuckled darkly, but still, she was *here*. "I don't think you had that issue before, either."

The struggle between myself and her had been so infuriating back then. Now, I looked upon it fondly. "Maybe not."

"I don't…I missed you so much," she confessed, and another coil of tension relaxed within me. Heat flooded my fingertips as I continued to hold her. Meline whimpered, lashes fluttering unsteadily. "What—how do we rebuild? How can we, after everything?"

I frowned. "As far as I am concerned, we discuss our past as we see fit. We spend time together. That is…if you've forgiven me? For being inconsiderate, for not being supportive, for—"

"What—for fuck's sake, El. There was never anything to forgive. *I* am to blame. I broke what was starting to grow between us. After everything you did for me, *I* fucked it all up. And, and," her chest began heaving, her words breathy, "I know it's unfair, but I'd do anything. *Anything* you asked if that meant I'd get to keep you." And then, in a whispering plea, she added, "Punish me as you see fit, *please*."

I balked, flinching as if she'd struck me. She didn't wait for my words, stammering over my reaction. "You just—you said it once that you would. Whatever you want from me. To do to me. I'll take it. Whatever it is."

I ground my teeth, my stomach dropping. Moving to hold her hands, I searched her hopeless stare. The trembling of her bottom lip. "Meline. I do not want to punish. I do not want revenge. I want you as you are."

She cut off our gazes, shutting her eyes again. "What if I don't know who I am anymore?"

How could life be so cruel? No matter how many years I

lived, no answers to this question ever came. But to see the suffering reflected in what my queen just divulged?

I tugged on her gloves, pulling at the fabric so that I could feel more of her skin against mine.

But her reaction was not one I'd been expecting.

Meline snatched her hand away, ducked out of my embrace, and put space between us. After all she'd just said, the emotions she'd let me see, why did this send her running?

"*Fuck!*" Meline shouted, and when she tried to grab at her face, her hands were shaking too much to manage even that.

"My queen," I was so confused, "what is wrong?"

"I—I have to go. I can't—" And I watched her angle toward the door. Preparing to run away from me, even when she'd *promised.*

I'd not been angry at her for a long time, but now, with her impending flight, the emotion roared to the surface. Flames sparked to life on my fingertips, and I pinned my queen to the wall.

But my power did not burn her, did not char her skin. Just as the black smoke rising from her hands did not carry Death. With her holding my throat, panic and challenge churning around us, her darkness circled around me. Cool and curious, I welcomed it. All that she was.

Did she not understand that?

She started to say something, but I cut her off, begging. "*Enough.* Show me."

Fear wafted off of her, seeped from her pores as she released her hold on my throat. Her hand hovered between us.

With a pinch of two fingers, while my others were still aflame, I reached and pulled on the glove. For all the resistance she gave before, I felt her tug in the opposite direction to assist me. Saw her swallow while I uncovered what she hid.

Meline watched, then let me uncover the other that matched the first.

In the air, held aloft for me to see, were ten fingers, six as black as Rhaea's Temple.

My queen's brown skin, the sharpened nails. Those were the same. But, on the first three digits of each, down almost to where they connected with her palm, was complete darkness.

"I'm sorry." Her whole body was shaking so badly, now. The apology was thickened with a sob, to the point that it was hard to understand. Even the second and third times she said it.

I didn't…I didn't understand. She was no high priestess. How—why had her powers shifted in this way?

I dropped my brow to hers, snuffed the flames of my anger, and steadied her. I touched the backs of her bare hands and rested them on my face. Felt the cool touch of her power.

"I'm sorry," she whispered, clinging to me so tightly, weeping.

What was there to do but hold her? Give her my words of apology until they were a chant between us? Let her see that just as I was demanding she not leave, I would not be leaving either. She was mine, and I was hers.

So, I let my own tears fall. Let her feel the unsteadiness of my own being. Witness how I was broken, too.

Even as I led her to the bed, gently undressed myself while she fumbled with her own clothing, I did not hide. And when she collapsed on the mattress with me, we held each other tightly enough to break bones.

MELINE

Like that morning in Krisla, I awoke alone in a bed that wasn't mine.

My face was tear-swollen, my throat raw, and my nerves were frayed. The previous evening was a wash of desperate words and frantic touches.

I sat up slowly, letting the sheets pool around me. Slowly, I pulled my hands from beneath the covers and laid them open in my lap.

Blackened skin, nails as dark as coal. Ever since that day.

I forced an exhale, puckered my lips. And when the knot still twisted tighter, I beat against the middle of my chest. How was I meant to rebuild when there weren't any pieces of me left? Almost all of them had died with him.

My senses picked up on Elián's presence in the doorway, long before he made a sound. I continued my piss-poor attempt at self-soothing, running slow circles over where my heart lay.

"I have breakfast ready, my queen."

He couldn't—I clenched my teeth, my eyelids, each muscle, everything. When I finally opened my eyes, I had to fight to keep air flowing to my lungs.

Elián's tattoos were on display. Dark like my marks, a written tale of his life. And his hair, *goddess*, it flowed about his shoulders like a gentle river. Like my favorite river near where Tana and I used to live. In Ralthas.

Locking down those memories was something I had much practice doing, but somehow, it was getting harder each time.

Elián watched me as I did, head tilted to the side as he waited. Eventually, I sent him a wan smile. But who was I trying to fool? He'd seen me at my worst. Now, as I'd descended into a mess as he revealed my hands. And then, when he'd had to bathe me while my body healed after Mathieu nearly killed me.

Rebuild.

"Thank you," I spread my smile wider through sheer force of will, "for everything, El."

He grunted, but it was a sound that hit me straight in the belly, warming me and feeling like home. "Come," he said and extended a hand. Asking me to approach. To take that step.

My limbs were tight, but I forced myself from sheets that smelled like us. I crossed the small bedroom on bare feet and put my cursed hand in his. He didn't flinch. Just closed his fingers around it and pulled me along.

The sun was shining through the small window, brightening the safehouse, but there still wasn't much to see. Elián obviously hardly came here. Even his scent was faint, almost as resounding as mine.

What did his true home look like? At the Shadow Well? Or, did he prefer to live somewhere else?

There was so much about him that I didn't know. That I'd denied us by telling him to leave.

I batted away more tears, chastising myself for running over the same shit again and again. You'd think my mind would run out of the energy, but the despair only fueled itself.

"Wha—" I squawked, landing on a pair of thick, steady thighs.

Elián had led us to the table, but instead of breaking apart to sit opposite of each other, he'd pulled me into his lap. His arms were like vises, holding me to him.

Not that I was going to leave.

His skin was hot, not just warm. With his shirt off, and my body clad in my undergarments from last night, the skin contact was probably as close to heaven as I'd ever be.

But, when I imagined what that might feel like, it was this— being held by him.

"Eat." Elián held a fork in front of my mouth. His was set in a determined line, but the color in his irises was swimming, flaring.

I didn't even look at what I was taking a bite of, just opened up and let him place the food on my tongue. The burst of flavor made me gasp. Eggs, but the preparation was nothing like what I was used to.

Some sort of flatbread, crisp and fried, crunched between my teeth, and pops of acidic tomato balanced out the flavors perfectly.

He didn't even need to tell me to take the next bite he held in front of me. I couldn't recall when last I ate, and my empty stomach welcomed this breakfast greedily.

And, of course, there was the expression he held, almost hypnotized by my eating. If I wasn't devouring the food with abandon, I might've preened. Or teased him for taking care of me like this. I wouldn't have believed him capable of this sort of caring, if not for the glimpses I'd caught during our last days together at the witches' house.

I glanced down at the plate, seeing the large serving halfway gone. Was this all the food there was? Well, of course, he probably hadn't expected to have to prepare food for me.

I'd already taken so much from him. After everything, I drew the line at denying him a meal.

The battle to take control of the fork had his eyes flaring, the color growing brighter, but he ultimately relented. Shifting a bit in his lap, I felt the hard reminder of his erection that both of us were ignoring. Directing my attention back to the food, I gathered egg, bread, and tomato sauce in one large morsel.

He too didn't watch the food. No, he was busy looking at me like I was about to disappear into the aether. Like he had to savor every moment of my being here.

I cleared my throat. "Open," I said, and he did. Opened his mouth to the point that I could see his tongue, his fangs.

My navel fluttered, but I ignored that as well while I fed Elián the rest. He kept his arms around me, and we didn't exchange any words.

When the plate was clean, neither of us rose. With the fullness of our bellies and the contentedness in holding each other, there was no rush.

Last night had been like a storm, but this moment was like the next morning, with raindrops still falling from branches as cool wind whipped through the trees. Though the sun was shining, the remnants of thunder were everywhere.

He was the first to call attention to it. "What changed?" He didn't need to specify what he was referring to, but he held my hand in his to emphasize anyway.

He traced his callused fingertip around the black skin, passing it over knuckle, around fingernail, then back down. Over and over.

As much as I wanted to clamp my mouth shut, change the subject or bite at him so he'd drop it, that wasn't the way. He deserved so much better. More.

"That…is a hard question to answer because I'm still parsing through it myself."

"Are your powers different?"

I nodded and leaned further into him. For strength. My temple nuzzled into his cheek, and he accepted it. Accepted me. "Yes. They feel steadier. Easier to control, mostly. I have greater access to them as a result. But, what all that might entail, I'm still unsure."

Echoing last night, he said softly, "Show me."

I gnawed at my lip but nodded because this line of curiosity was safe. Much safer than the other path laden with traps and truths I wasn't ready to share.

Even though Elián deserved to know most of all.

The dagger I conjured was the easiest to show him. Ebony like the halls of the Temple of Rhaea, the hilt and blade were both black, as was the sharp guard. I hadn't consciously designed it, but the grip and rounded pommel fit my hand perfectly. The metal detailing, like royal filigree, was also not purposeful, but it felt right, looking down at it.

I twirled the blade in my hand, so familiar with this type of weapon that it was merely an extension of my hand. Given that it was made from the power woven through my soul, it literally was.

There was no need for a poisoned blade when the whole thing was made of Death.

After showing off a final twirl, I commanded it away, and the blade disappeared, leaving only a tendril of smoke. Like the trails from a snuffed candle.

"How long has it been," Elián resumed his tracing, now that the blade was gone, "since the marks appeared?"

I locked everything away. Down. "Two years, two months, and fifteen days."

"Why?"

I stiffened, but after his response mirrored mine, I forced myself to relax. Bit by bit. He wasn't accusing. Wasn't blaming. I hoped. "Again, I'm unsure. But Rhaea has not been exactly forthcoming with me. Ever. So," I chuckled, "why would She start now?"

Elián grunted again, seemingly satisfied with what I'd given him. The half-truths.

His heart beat a steady song, and it was some breaths later that I realized mine had synced to the rhythm. I'd blame what I said next on that.

"You've fucked, held, and fed me now. What's next?"

Elián pulled away, just enough to be able to look me over, and I almost took the words back until amusement shifted his stoic features. He didn't say anything, just continued to stare and smirk.

He cradled the back of my head, and I shivered at the wash of heat. "Do you hate it?" He raised a brow, like the quirk at the end of a question, and I elaborated. "My hair. Or, lack thereof."

Not that he'd outright said he'd liked it before. But I wasn't stupid.

As if remembering the mass of coils that used to be there, Elián passed his thumb over the mussed curls that were certainly no longer slicked to my scalp in orderly waves.

"No. I do not hate it. I don't think I could hate anything about you, to be honest."

I groaned and rolled my eyes. Huffed in his face for good measure. "Oh goddess, El. You can't keep being nice. It's scaring me."

He sighed ruefully. "I want to be nice to you. And when you give me a reason to put you in your place, I will do that, too. Regardless, we will be together."

"And…" I croaked. "What would you like from me?"

Elián's brow didn't shift. The hard set of his jaw didn't soften. But the bob of his throat hinted at an uncertainty the rest of him didn't. "I want your presence. Your menacing words. Your body against mine. Your love."

Fuck.

I slammed my lips onto his, begged for his Fire to keep worming its way into me.

If someone had asked me at any point before yesterday, I would have told them the likelihood of my current state was nonexistent.

And yet, here I was, holding hands with Elián as we walked down the streets of Morova. It was a port city, and with the pleasant heat of mid-morning, our slow meandering along the docks was nearing on picturesque.

I'd thrown on one of his spare tunics, the smallest pair of leather trousers he had in the safehouse, and tightened a spare belt of his to secure everything in place. My heeled boots and gloves completed the ensemble, but as much as I groused, I would never truly complain about wearing his clothes.

There was no way I was returning to the inn where Tana and I were staying. I wasn't ready to face her questions. Well, the particular one I was still avoiding.

Seagulls squawked overhead, circling ship sails and lining the rope ledge between pier and water. A pair of them fought for whatever food had been dropped on the wooden boards where we walked, but no one paid them any mind. They were too busy barking orders, calling for patrons to come and sample their wares, or loudly enjoying the day.

"Just how many homes do you *have*?" Something about the way he'd casually mentioned another city where he had an apartment left me wondering.

Elián squinted toward the blue sky, as if he was bloody *counting*. Our joined grip swung slightly between us, but my attention caught on the glimpse of bare chest he displayed. So far from the Shadow leathers.

The white tunic matched the one he'd given me to wear, but his was opened to show the edge of two defined pectorals, as well as the top of his hard stomach. Draped over his shoulders and wrapped around his waist, a fabric the color of the sky above. The gold hoops laddered up his ears shone brightly in contrast with his black hair and tattoos.

"I don't consider any one a *home*. More of a place to stay should I need."

I tore my gaze away from his body, only to realize I'd already been caught ogling him. "That wasn't an answer, El."

He snorted, almost *laughing*, Mother take me. "If I count all of them, I believe eleven or twelve. But only a quarter of those would I actually call any sort of home."

I sighed harshly. "So. You've got three homes and nine spares. How much coin does a typical Shadow *earn*?"

He shrugged. "When you work as much as I do, for as long as I have, there isn't a shortage of coin. And one of those is my room at the Shadow Well."

We rounded a corner, then paused to let pass a group of adolescents as they went by us. "And…do you enjoy it there? The Well."

Our path was now clear, but he stood still. Through the tether of his hand, I sensed his muscles stiffening. Underneath my glove, Rhaea's curse twitched, growing antsy as Zoko's Fire flared beneath his skin.

El started moving again, mouth set in a grim line, and while he led us through the crowd, I mourned the pleasant day we'd been having. With each step along the pier, this dream of being *together* drew closer and closer to reality. How could it not? With my hand fitting so perfectly within his? With the easy smirks I drew out of him and the chuckles he surprised out of me?

A café overlooking the waves had a free table, and I followed Elián's lead, gawking at him as he pulled out my chair.

Any cheeky remark about him treating me like a precious maiden was long forgotten at the twist of his lips.

This was it. This was when he'd tell me that being a Shadow was still too important. That he wouldn't leave his family. Having the worst, darkest time of my life happen without him beside me had provided a plethora of perspective, though.

We'll make it work, I resolved. Even if it meant I'd only see him between contracts. Selfishly, I knew that I'd never give up my own work. The thing that exhilarated me.

And, if being a Shadow was his calling, made him happy, I wouldn't demand he leave.

When a server sidled up to our table to take our order, we both gave clipped requests for tea, coffee.

He started once we were alone again, "I…when I returned to the Well. After I left you," he swallowed, "I killed Jones."

That was not what I'd been expecting. My brows shot to my hairline. "You did?"

Elián nodded firmly. "Yes. It appears that he was working with your brother out of his own greed. The hate he felt for the Vyrkos." I waited for him to continue, and once our drinks were left on the wooden table, he did. "We have our own council of senior members that keeps us in line. However, the punishment they gave Jones was too lax, and I gave him what he truly deserved. *I* was then punished for circumventing the proper protocol in settling Shadow conflict."

"I—I never would have wanted you to do that for me, El."

He gave me a long look, wordlessly calling me out for the liar that I was. "I did it for myself as well. He deserved a far more painful death."

Now was probably a bad time for the surge of lust, making me cross my legs. "Okay. Thank you."

He grunted and took a sip of his coffee. I drank some of my tea and quickly added more honey to it. "My punishment was more frustrating than anything. Six months with no contracts, extra training shifts for the acolytes. It left me a lot of time to think. To grieve us and see the error of my ways."

I started to rebut until he raised a hand, silencing my words. "I began working again after that, taking contracts anywhere I could, hoping to find you in the process."

My face heated, and I rested my hand on his arm. "I'm so sorry, El. You have to know that I wasn't running from you. *Please.*"

That piece of truth left his shoulders sagging, like he'd still been unsure. "At the time, I was prepared to find you and leave it all. My Shadow life." I almost snatched my hand away, convinced I hadn't heard him correctly.

And then I realized that he'd used the word 'was.' I chewed my lip. "And now?"

He shifted, shoulders tightening right back up and bracing. "Now, I truly cannot leave." Elián exhaled slowly. "I am sorry."

"I don't know how we'll balance it all, but I am prepared to do so. To try." What did I have to lose? If there truly were members of the Shadows that wanted to kill me, they could stand in line with the rest of the enemies I'd made in my two and a half centuries. But, "What changed? Are they—" rage flared in my chest "—are they *threatening* you? Because of *me*?"

He was already shaking his head, giving soothing passes of his palm. "No. They are not threatening me. At the Master rank, I am mostly free to come and go as I please. Called to return for official ceremonies, meetings, my mandatory training shifts."

I relaxed. "Oh—okay." That wasn't so bad, right? We were busy people anyway. I could manage being apart from him for those sorts of things. And then, the rest? We could go anywhere together.

"You…are alright with this?"

"I mean, I'm willing to compromise. But," I remembered, "you didn't answer my question. What changed? If you were able to leave before—which I'm not demanding of you now—what is making you stay?"

Those papaya-colored eyes weren't looking at me now. Cast on the table between us. For a beat, I almost demanded the truth he held back. What he was hesitating to tell me. But what right did I have?

"It's okay, El. If you don't want to tell me."

Now he was looking at me, but it was with a glare and a petulant growl. "Don't. I am just wary of your reaction." I counted the breaths, reaching five before he grumbled again and admitted, "I have sponsored a new acolyte. The time needed to become fully trained varies, but for the next ten years, at least, I am required to be more involved."

"Oh. *Oh.*" I shrugged. "That's okay. I mean, Tana and I are still working toward this contract, finding Francie. Not that I'm anticipating it taking years, hopefully. But that's fine, El."

He was wincing, though. Shaking his head again, coffee long forgotten.

"What is it?"

Elián ground his jaw and then spoke the name of this new acolyte. The one he'd brought into the Shadows.

Chapter Fifteen
Elián

"You did *what?*"

I winced again as my queen's voice rose several octaves, sending a group of seagulls jumping back and taking to air. She snatched her hands away, and like last night, I saw it in her posture. Her instincts pointing towards *run*.

Well, perhaps after stabbing me with the blades she could now conjure out of nothing.

"Meline," I barked and pulled her arm back to me. She could rage and curse me all she wanted. Cut me with her power. But she would not leave. We would deal with this.

Her breaths were blustering, dark and glittering eyes wild as her mind undoubtedly ran through hundreds of scenarios.

"Marco found Tomás and me on the streets of Nethras. Asked us—"

"What were you doing there?"

"Looking for you," I admitted, and this truth had her mouth slamming shut. "I was looking for you, and the boy found us. He asked to be a Shadow, and after receiving consent from his care-givers, we took him to the Well. He is sponsored by the both of us and is now residing there. He is happy." It was easy to see, what with the eager smiles the little one kept throwing at anything and everything. The Shadows would never be known for tenderness, but acolytes were revered. Protected at all costs.

I told Meline that much, giving soft touches and willing her body and mind to calm. She may accept me keeping my oath to the Shadows, but divesting from all prejudice against us in the name of the young boy she'd once mentored was a different task.

"You had no right to do that," she gritted her teeth, but she'd also settled back into her seat. Her arm rested resolutely on the tabletop, accepting my touch.

"Yes. I did. The boy knew what he wanted, and Whitley and Lydia attested to that."

"This life shouldn't be his, El," she whispered.

"What life? Coming and going as you please? Killing or guarding or stealing for money? You know better than most the perils this world offers. The horrors. You also know the excitement this work provides, dark as it may be. Should you tell him to forsake his own dreams, of doing what *we* do, because you are worried for him? He will be trained well and only released to take contracts when he is ready. Until then, he will live and work at the Well."

She was silent, face hard as my words battered her. Until she grumbled, "That might have been the most I've ever heard you speak." She chewed her lip, and I increased the pressure of my touch on her skin.

The sight of her dressed in my clothing was fanning a low burn in my gut, flames churning and waiting to be let out. We'd decided to leave the safehouse this morning, to see the sun and let what was rekindling between us into the light of day.

I'd been lost in my thoughts about what might come next. Waiting for the words to be done, for now, and the need for physical closeness to take over. I did not regret claiming her last night, being brutal so that she could see reason. Now, though, I wanted to relish her in a way we hadn't ever been able to.

My thoughts had been far away, elsewhere, so I had to ask my queen to repeat her last question. "How long has it been?

Since you brought Marco in. I haven't…I haven't returned to Nethras at all."

That had been apparent when I'd entered her stale apartment. The scent of her and, briefly, me, sealed inside. Encapsulated in the dust motes floating through the air. "About two years now."

Meline rubbed her free hand at her chest, pressing the heel of her palm toward her heart. "And…he's doing well?"

"Yes. He has made great strides in his training. He has made friends. And he is under Tomas's and my protection and responsibility as his sponsors."

"And with you both away from the Well? Who is making sure he's okay?" The appearance of tears made me lean closer, but she waved off my concern, wiping at her eyes in a familiar movement. Using my sleeve to soak up her worry.

I wanted her in my lap again. In my arms. "Noruh has agreed to stay at the Well until one of us is able to return."

I felt the cool, dangerous presence of my queen's power before I saw it. The black vines that transcended the clothing separating her skin from mine. They wrapped around my wrist, reaching toward my elbow.

Meline said she had more control of it. But she didn't seem to be purposefully letting it out now. Not with her own fire alight in her stare. "And what is your relationship with her? Why would she agree to babe-sitting duty for you?"

There were no clouds in the sky, save for sparse wisps that did nothing to block the heat shining down on us. But it was the sort that made me feel comforted, alive. And with her Death wrapping around me? Claiming me in its own way?

I willed Zoko's Flames to manifest on my skin. With all light and no heat, I watched the sensation reach her awareness. Veins of Fire meeting those of Darkness.

"Noruh, Tomás, and I trained as acolytes together. I have known them both since I was younger than Marco. She is my sister."

"So I guess you fuck your sister, then," Meline shot back, and the venom on her tongue shifted my lips to a quick smirk.

There she was.

"I have been with many over the years, my queen. As I know you have. I've lain with them both, yes, as I have with many of my Shadow siblings. Through my travels, I have had no trouble finding release or someone to warm my bed."

"Why the fuck are you telling me this?" Her power was winding up my shoulder, now. Flowing between my shoulder blades. Barely concealed by the clothes I wore.

And under my tunic wrapped around her body, I tasted her flesh through my Flames. Felt the pounding of her heart on my tongue. "Because I want you to know that none of them, *no one*, compares to you. That I know with certainty you are who I want."

Meline licked her lip, swiping her tongue against the plush pillow of her bottom one. I would have it between my teeth before the day was over. Anything less would be unacceptable.

"Were you always this cocksure?"

This time, the smirk, an expression of triumph, settled fully across my face. "Yes." And, just to emphasize my point and claim, I added a pulse of heat to my power before drawing it back to me. Meline's gasp, the widening of her pupils, was satisfaction enough to tide me over.

She glared as she released the hold of her power, until the only touch between us was of corporeal form.

"Um. Should we…go back? Are you done with your coffee?"

I glanced at the forgotten mug, then at hers. "Yes," and without breaking eye contact, I rose my from my seat. With a drop of coin on the table, I led Meline away from the café and back up the pier, the way we'd come.

A greater understanding and anticipation weighed heavily between us. With the way Meline held my arm, her body closer to mine. If I weren't committed to savoring her, I would've simply turned us down a less-populated alleyway. Maybe under the docks.

But, my queen deserved more. What we were deserved more.

This time, she was the one to stop, footsteps skidding to a halt so quickly that mine stopped almost immediately, too.

"What in the hell?" She said under her breath, and I followed her gaze.

Across the way, as bodies wove between us, were Tomás and Tana. Leaning against a stretch of railing, they both devoured some kind of food wrapped in wax paper, while arguing back and forth at each other.

As we drew closer, I was able to fully pick up on what they were discussing. The tone of their argument was snipping with exasperated annoyance more than anything.

"It's not nice to try and steal a bloke's meal right from under him, you know."

Meline's cousin rolled her eyes and swallowed her food. "I'm not nice, and neither are you." But, the statement seemed far from the truth when Tana caught sight of her cousin. Her expression brightened, smile going wide.

It dimmed a bit as she glanced at me. But she was undeterred by my queen still holding onto me. "Leenie!" The witch who'd helped me save Meline's life brought her into a one-armed hug, bringing closer her lavender scent.

Looking between us both, she started tentatively, "So, I take it your evening went well?"

My brother was the one who answered. "Well, considering she's wearing the male's clothes, I would wager it went very well."

I released Meline's arm so that I could wrap mine around her. Her body settled perfectly into my side, and her shiver shook us both.

She looked to me, but when I remained silent, she sighed loudly, waved a dismissive hand at her cousin and my Shadow brother. "I'm more concerned about what *you two* did last night."

They both scoffed, with Tomás taking a frustrated bite into his sandwich while Tana responded, rolling her eyes so far that her irises and pupils disappeared. "A stalemate because we both refused to back down. Then a night of enjoying intrigued humans. We were stumbling out of the merchant's estate at the same time this morning."

Tomás couldn't let that one go. "I don't stumble, love. A nice feed and fuck, and I feel good as new. Prepared to settle this matter of competition, finally."

My queen stood straighter, no longer sinking into me, and I could've ripped his throat out for reminding everyone that we were technically adversaries. At least, until the contract ended.

The Shadow within, tendrils of the guild's magic pulsing through me with every heartbeat, lurched at the idea of continuing the contract. Amplified by the competition my queen and her cousin posed, it was instinctual to rise to the challenge. A contract such as this, one that called for stealth and deadliness, was what made being a Shadow.

Traveling to cities far and different. Feeling the same sun wash over me. The travel and the bloodshed, the road and the blades, this life was one I would have missed should my queen have asked me to leave it.

Could I truly have both? The blood oath I'd taken at the dawn of my adulthood and this queen? While I had enjoyed my time in this realm, it was *more* with Meline. She brought a prismatic eruption of color to a life that had been cast only in the crimson of blood and black of leather.

While Noruh and Tomás found purpose and rhythm elsewhere, I'd remained dedicated to the work. Letting the plunge of my swords refuel me until I'd been approached for a contract. One that would not be compensated in coin but in the possible salvation of our people.

An honor. To, in my own Shadow way, avenge the death of my father and Leandro. Though guarding was never my first choice, I would do it for my people, I'd reasoned. I traveled to

Versillia, only to meet the spoiled, foul-mouthed, *insufferable* mercenary who'd come between me and the successful end of what should've been a simple contract a few months prior. One a seasoned *acolyte* could even handle.

I'd stood behind her as she negotiated with priestesses of Rhaea, an official of the city of Nethras, and the tyrant King of Krisla. Watching how she advocated for our kind *and* the Vyrkos.

And then, after days of biting at each other, the venom between us had twisted until I was drunk—*intoxicated* on her. She was truly a mamba. I'd crossed paths with the deadly animal before, and it was like the electrifying dance of being with her.

She was often turned inward. Some might even say shy. When truly confronted, her instinct was to flee. Oh, but when she needed to, she would rise past her petite height and hiss. Bite relentlessly until death was a mercy.

Fuck.

I loved her.

Beside me, Meline gasped as I pressed a kiss into her hair. Then she kept her face tilted toward me so I could plant more upon her. Like I wanted to do every minute of every day for the rest of my immortal life. Until she became accustomed to the affection. Unsurprised by the unconditional burning I had for her.

"I hate to break up the lovely reunion, but I believe we may have a problem," Tomás cut in, words muffled with foodstuffs as he chewed.

I glared at my brother, who gave back a look drier than the Zonoran desert. In my first language, he droned, "*I am happy for you, Nogón, but your enamoredness will cause us to lose this contract.*" He jutted his chin toward over my shoulder, and I threw my senses in that direction. With a minute swivel of my head, vision casting in my peripheries, nose and ear searching.

"Shit," the witch cursed. From their vantage point, facing the docks and ships behind Meline and me, they more easily noticed what I had not until that moment.

Paschal Von Herron, boarding a vessel and barking orders to a crew that'd been hustling back and forth when my queen and I had come to the harbor. Probably for hours before that.

The intel that we'd been given at the start of our contract had stated that the merchant would be home in Morova for multiple weeks. Enough time for us to find the right moment and descend.

The tumbling of canvas snapped in the air like a clap of thunder. Now that I was focusing, I caught Von Herron shouting to his crew to prepare for departure. To heave the anchor out of the water.

My queen groaned, slapping a gloved palm against her temple.

When I turned back to my brother, both he and Tana were gone, melting into the crowd. What if Von Herron was to be away for months? Did we follow and catch him at his destination? Lay in wait for when he returned? The possibilities churned in my thoughts, calculating, and by the tension in my queen's shoulders, I could almost hear her mind doing the same.

We stood, holding each other and thinking while droves of humans flowed around us like waves splitting around boulders. Until Tana appeared first. She cut her eyes to me, then to my queen. "Not certain how long he'll be away, but based on the destination, I'd wager quite a while. If we have any hope of finishing this thing," her gaze on Meline took on a new depth, "we need to follow."

Tomás appeared then, appearing out of the shadows. "*Vharas. Caught some crew gossip but not much. An agreement fell through that he is to see to personally. We need to go now if we have any hope of catching up.*"

I nodded, running calculations in my mind. "*Are there any other ships going that way?*" Von Herron's was already pulling away from the docks. Not that booking voyage on a merchant ship was covert in the slightest.

Meline shifted in my arms, and I focused back on her. The slight furrow in her brow as she watched Tom and I go back and forth.

Despite what I'd said earlier and the inherent Shadow compulsion to finish what I'd started, to *win*, I imagined taking her back to my apartment. Making love to her for the rest of the day, until the wrinkle I now thumbed and bade to relax was a distant memory. Without this contract between us, we could enjoy the Morovan markets like we had in Rhaestras. Perhaps I would convince her to come to Banfas. Where the air was dry and the streets held the golden shadows of my childhood.

But my queen, she and I, had never been that simple. "Don't even think about it, El. We're doing this. And *we*, Tana and I, will win."

Of course. Because she was a menace and just as ruthless as I was. And yet... I leaned down, brushing my lips against the shell of her ear. I whispered, "You will not. But we will go, and you will sleep in *my* bed."

A slight puff of air punched out of her, and I tightened my fingers in my tunic she wore. Another sign that she was mine.

She swallowed, throat clicking. "Are...are you sure I won't be holding your hair all night while you vomit over side of the deck?"

Mm. I drank up her words, the Fire within me they fed. The last time we had embarked on the water, I'd been holding onto the last vestiges of my sanity. Being in such close quarters while the floor shifted and tilted beneath me. Pacing and grumbling silently to myself, regretting signing up for the assignment.

This time, our days on the water would be different.

CHAPTER SIXTEEN
MELINE

I released my half of our packs on the lumpy mattress as Tana did the same. The small cabin held a moderately sized bed, especially for a ship of this size, and a window that looked out on the darkening sky. Water lapped lazily against the hull, and heavy steps thumped overhead.

"If weather permits, we'll make it to Vharas right on his heels. We need to close in as quickly as possible."

Tana nodded and began to set aside her night clothes, checked her weapons. "Blackwood agreed to meet with us when we disembark, so at least there's that. No telling what he's arranged with the Shadows, though."

Probably something similar. I chewed my lip, fingers fiddling with my unopened bag.

I wouldn't be staying in here. Not really. But what did I even take with me to his room? Would we grow tired of each other on a weeklong journey?

Would he send me away when I finally built up the courage to tell him the whole truth?

I winced, shoving that sorrow away as best I could. I tried instead to focus on the flutter in my chest— something like *life*— at the thought of his arms wrapped around me. Now, within reach, were two things I'd longed for just a few short days ago—my Shadow in my arms again and a path to Francie.

"Fuck," I wiped at my brow with the back of my hand. Whitley was out there, worrying over their lost mate while I was losing my mind over Elián. I was abandoning my cousin so I could spend the night in his bed, as he'd demanded. "I should just stay here. Hopefully this will be over in just a few weeks' time, and then I—"

Tana clamped her hands over my shoulders, giving me a hearty shake. "Leenie. No. Aside from the fact that I am quite looking forward to sprawling out in my own bed for a change, you won't squander this chance by avoiding him. That would be quite stupid of you, and that's something you've never been."

"Who said I'm avoiding him? I—I shouldn't abandon you. After all you've done? All you've sacrificed?"

My cousin pursed her lips a moment, searching my face with a familiarity bred by seeing the ugly insides of me time and time again. "Listen carefully. You are not abandoning me by taking this chance. And I need you to stop using me as a weapon to harm yourself."

I flinched. Indignation rose quickly up my throat, to the tips of my fingers as I shoved her away. "What is *that* — "

Tana's posture remained rigid while her expression swam with sorrow, irritation, and fucking *pity*. She didn't even try to hide it. "I've watched you whither, cousin mine. We train and have fun, yes, but when light comes through," she waved a hand to the small window on the wall, "you turn away. Claiming that you must focus on Francie. On *me*."

I gaped, sputtered. "You're…you're blaming me because I *care* about you? That I'm trying to repay the favor? What sort of bullshit is *that*?"

"See! Right there!" She pointed a finger at me, as if she knew just where the poison was. "It is not a *favor*. *We* both fled Versillia. *We* both decided to not return to Nethras. To train and search for Francie because we want to help her and Whitley. You act as if I'm some lost puppy that's attached herself to your heel."

I'd lost track of what was going on, how to get back on the path I was so accustomed treading with my cousin. We didn't— we didn't *argue*. Bicker and tease sometimes—well, it was mostly her doing it—but that was the extent of our less than pleasant moments. And even then, they ended quickly with a huff from me and a giggle from her.

I narrowed my eyes. "Is there something else you're wanting to tell me? You're not making sense."

She sighed, frustration draining as her shoulders dropped. "Just…please stop using me as the list of reasons why you *can't*. It's nowhere near the truth, and I don't like it."

My lip began to tremble before I sunk my teeth into it, threatening blood. I was still unsure of what this meant. How this morning started with blue skies and ended in the belly of a ship, arguing with the one person I'd been able to depend on more than anyone else.

Tana sighed again and pulled me into her arms. But it felt forced. Was she finally over my shit, then? Was I just employing Elián to manage me now that Tana seemed fatigued with the role?

Before I could retort, burning oak and cinnamon prickled against my awareness a moment before the resounding knocks of a fist on our door.

My heart jumped, beating heavily against my chest, but I didn't have time to refuse. To ask for another moment.

Tana hollered, "Come in," while staring straight at me.

Fuck, his presence filled the room, forcing my back against the reality of what we did to each other. In those days years ago and now, with his mango eyes landing straight on mine. Neither of us had changed as we made the mad dash to book voyage on the only ship leaving Morova and headed for Vharas.

I was still wearing his clothes, and he still…looked like that. Without a word, Elián crossed the few steps to Tana and me. His hair brushed against me as he reached for my packs on the bed. Every last one of them.

All my life, bundled away in five leather bags.

Elián shouldered them as if they were filled with feathers, posture still ramrod straight. I breathed in his scent like the first inhale of a joint at the end of a long day. Heat in my throat, warming the dark crypt within my ribs.

He nodded at Tana, and she turned back to settling in, sending me off with a wave of her hand. Not even a glance.

"My queen?" His voice was the groan of wood breaking under an inferno.

I turned away from my cousin, obeyed her wishes in that regard to leave her be, and focused on my…the male I was still unsure of how to approach. These hours away as Tana and I had strategized left me fumbling.

My mouth opened and closed multiple times, trying to come up with *something*, but he just nodded toward the door, commanding me to follow as he left.

Now that I'd seen him again, felt him again, there was no letting the thread connecting us pull any further. I trailed after Elián with some weak farewell to Tana, something about how we'd meet in the morning to discuss plans, but my thoughts were already with the male carrying my things down the corridor.

We went by other passengers who paid us no mind, too focused on their own journey to do more than a companionable nod.

And then I was in his room. One not unlike the one we'd just left, but reflecting a glimpse of how much coin he had at his disposal. A large bed secured to the floorboards, two windows and a small desk that overlooked the waves.

My throat was bone-dry as I croaked, "Where is your Shadow brother?"

Elián gently dropped my packs to the rug spread beside the bed. His earrings tinkled as he pivoted his head toward me.

"Last I saw of him, he was being invited for supper with the captain."

I choked on a—a laugh, and he echoed the noise, shaking his head. "Wow. He works fast."

"He does. He has the cabin across the corridor and said that he was 'bloody glad to be rid of me' for the next few days."

My lips continued to spread as I watched him. "Rid of you?"

His smirk dimmed, searching the cabin around us. "Yes. He…he took it upon himself to help me these past years. It is more time than we've spent together in decades."

Help him. I swallowed and dared a step closer. Another and another until I could reach out and touch him. "I'm sorry."

Elián killed the remaining space between us, grabbing my hips and pulling me into his chest. He planted his nose in the curls I'd tried my best to set to rights and breathed. My gloved hands met the anchor of his biceps.

"We have already apologized to each other. I would rather focus on this." *This*, he emphasized with a tender kiss on my brow.

What was there to do but lean into his embrace? I quickly abandoned the halfhearted attempt to keep from truly melting into him, releasing an embarrassing noise that some may say was a whimper. Resting in the bare hollow of his throat was more than I deserved. That light Tana had gone on about? I was basking in it. Letting it carve itself in my memories, so when this all ended, I'd be able to run my fingers over the etchings.

"You are thinking loudly, my queen."

Thinking and crying, but I tried my best to hide the evidence of tears in the blue fabric on his chest. Never in my dreams of Elián did I imagine him wearing color. But the blue made the amber and orange of his eyes brighter. Made the picture of him fuller.

"Not a queen anymore. Never was."

He hummed, running his palms against my spine, caressing

each dip and knot. "And yet, you've had me bowing to you since we met."

"Oh, goddess," I groaned and smashed my face further into him so that he could feel the noise in his veins. "Also not true. You broke my arms the first time we met, asshole."

We shook but not with waves or an earthquake. It was the rumble of Elián laughing. "Yes. I did."

The soft, deep noise persisted, reverberated into the cabin, and I enjoyed it. Like lying next to a roaring river. Hearing the breeze race over the sand on a hot day. If anyone bowed to the other, it would be me to him. So that he gave me only what he felt I deserved.

"I am so glad to have you in my arms, Meline," he whispered after some time. And what was I to say to that?

Something stupid. Honest, but stupid. "You're talking so much. And being so nice. I don't know what to do."

This time, he forced me to look at him, pulling back until my chin was trapped in the vise of his hand. The tip of his nose was not far from mine, the strands of his hair falling softly over his shoulders and brushing against mine. "Do not *do*. Just be. With me."

I frowned, and he thumbed my lip that poked out at him. "What in the hell does that mean?"

But in that moment, instead of fighting with me, spitting wrath, Elián curled further over me and dropped the most delicate kiss of my long, long life. One with the calming sweep of his thumb against my jaw, the possessive pressure of his arm around my lower back.

He was going to fucking kill me.

No stranger to death, I sighed into his lips against mine. The warmth of his body around me. And when he separated the contact for a breath, just long enough to return and pull gently at my bottom lip between his, I followed his lead. Parted my lips and kissed him back.

Hollers carried off into the sunset as the ship pulled away

from the docks, setting us off to Vharas, but I was fully lost in Elián, now. His tongue flicked against mine, and I whimpered—*again*—as something like life sparked beneath my skin.

When we'd been together before, the kisses, caresses, and thrusts were harried, or, at the very least, urgent.

Now, with multiple days' sail ahead of us, Elián's tongue licked at mine like he had all the time in the world to pull me apart. Could he truly sort through the pieces and put me back together?

Just as I started to succumb to the flutter below my navel, the first real stirring of desire since the last time he'd touched me, Elián broke the kiss. My lashes fluttered fiercely, glaring at his spit-glistened lips and peek of the white tips of his fangs.

"That. *Being*, with me."

Before I could respond, Elián bent again, this time latching onto the tender skin of my throat. Where he sank his fangs yesterday—*goddess*, was it only yesterday? This time, instead of vicious bites, he nibbled and sucked, continuing to treat me softly.

Not like I was too fragile but as though I was precious. To be cared for.

And like this morning, I felt the way I affected him, the way we affected each other. His cock was hard against my front, answering the growing urgency of my arousal with the confirmation of his.

But as over breakfast and yesterday evening while he held me, Elián made no move to push us there.

I palmed him through his trousers, forcing a groan out of him as well as a sharper nip of his teeth against my neck. He canted his hips, pressing into the friction of my touch.

He'd said he'd lain with many—his Shadow siblings and anyone else he saw fit to share pleasure with during his long life. The flash of possessiveness within me at the moment was twisted, dark and gnarled at the edges. I had no right to ask it, but remnants of the Meline I'd once been, bold and outspoken, bobbed to the surface. Gasping for air.

"And have you been with anyone since me?"

He stilled, which was all the confirmation I needed. A growl bubbled in my throat as I resumed touching him. It was irrational, but if I were to *be* with Elián in this moment, this was how I needed to do it.

Instead of waiting for him to speak, I busied myself with the front of his trousers, unfastening them with determined ministrations. He breathed shallowly against me while I used the snap of my teeth to free my right hand from the leather glove. I needed to *feel* him.

And the steel silk of his shaft against my fingertips further stoked the brazenness of my words. "You say that I am yours, and you are mine." The feel of him was familiar, but the gold piercing on the underside of the shaft was new. A different sort of greediness took over as I forced away the thought of others seeing this before me. "Which means *this* belongs to me." I spat directly on his cock, wrapped my fist around him, and gave a long stroke, twisting at the top and slicking my fingers more with his moisture running from the slit.

Elián fucked into my fist and watched us do it. He still held me, but he gave me the space to take this, too.

"I-If we are going to *be* together. This cock is mine. Your pleasure is mine." The pumps of my fist cast loud, slick sounds. "I don't want to hear ever again about anyone fucking touching what's mine," I whispered, and Elián's cock bucked.

I wouldn't be able to take it. Barely had been able to earlier today. But, I remembered as Elián neared his release, he always brought out this side of me.

A menacing growl rippled through the air when I stopped stroking and tightly held the base of Elián's cock. Foreskin pulled back and head nearly purple, he made a beautiful sight, and I laughed, mean and low, at discombobulating him the way he had been doing to me.

Leave it to Elián to not go along with my game, though. My grip fell away from his cock when my feet left the floor. Now, Elián was not gentle as he tossed me onto the neatly made bed. Nor was he when he ripped through his own clothing on my body.

I shook for him. Craved him more with each tick of time it took for him to disrobe. And when he prowled over my body, naked skin brushing on naked skin, I reached for him.

Elián tossed my other glove off, removing the last of the barriers between us, and gazed down at me like he was determined to ignite every inch of my soul.

With shaking hands, I pulled at the tie holding the top half of his hair away from his face, and as the black fell in giving ripples, I scraped my fingernails against his scalp.

I'd not...I'd not done this with anyone since him. Though I'd long ago asked Tana to research the spell and process necessary to prevent myself falling with child, I'd not made use of the procedure, in these years.

I wasn't truly upset about that difference between us, my El seeking comfort in others while I had spent years turned in to myself. Underneath the selfish need to hold him tight and close and make sure no one tried to snatch what was mine, I could be... hopeful that he'd found some reprieve in the past years, however he could.

"You are a fucking menace," he drawled over me, pulling the admonishment long, letting it stretch until it was filled with a rich fondness. I moaned beneath him, ran my hands over the taut muscles of his neck, his shoulders. And when he smashed us into another kiss, pressing into me while taking care to not smother me under his weight, I convinced myself that I could have this. Welcome it and *be*.

Elián's hands were restless on my body, sweeping over my waist and hips, thumbs flicking over my nipples. Tiny gasps flipped out of me and into him with each tease. Each undulation of his hips that dragged his cock across my front.

And I let my power be. With the change, it was more settled, but with Elián in my arms and caged between my thighs, it was sated in a way inflicting Death never reached. Not the fullness after supper, knowing hunger would come tomorrow, but a deeper, soul rest.

Elián pulled back a moment, gazing down at me with swimming irises a thin ring around his expanded pupils. A line appeared between his brows as he watched me, and I continued touching him. Running my fingertips around the rose on his heart. Trailing my fingernails along the snake on his arm.

Until I was in the air again, flipped and facing the headboard. Elián lay sprawled beneath me, and he wasted no time grasping my hips and pulling me onto his awaiting tongue.

"*Oh*," I whimpered, most certainly this time, and clung to the wood of the bed. Elián spread me open, left me vulnerable and trembling over him.

And I accepted this gift. More than that, I relished in this, winding my body against the greedy laps of his tongue. The vibration of his groans added another level to his unraveling of me.

But his fevered curses when I turned around and sat on his face once more had me knocking on the door of euphoria. I grasped his flushed and leaking cock in my fist once more, Rhaea's mark wrapping around his skin, and descended. His was the only favor I truly tasted in all of these years, aside from tears and blood. His kiss, his skin, the food he made me. The salty weight of his crown where I placed open-mouthed kisses.

To compensate for his height, Elián propped up himself and my lower half, allowing for my throat to take more. And more. Tears streamed down my cheeks while I worked over him, and he worked under me. Giving and taking in equal measure. Elián fucked my throat, and I smothered him.

The waves rocking the ship only added to it, the wind whipping against the window an echoing roar as I crossed the threshold first. Bliss, this particular taste of it, was overwhelming. Almost cruel. I cried out while Elián was buried in my throat, tears and spit pooling on his thighs and the bedspread underneath.

He was not far behind, tongue still darting into me, drawing out the pleasure. His grip tightened on my ass as he shot his seed into my gasping and clenching throat. I swallowed it all and pulled off only enough to place tender kisses as he softened.

The swells of his chest matched the rhythm of the water outside, and my breaths were no better. I blinked, eyes focusing now on the closed door, the neat pile of Elián's packs in the corner. A wooden desk and illuminated lamp stared back at me as I considered how he'd prepared for this, for me. The windows in here were larger than the cabin Tana and I purchased, the covers beneath my palms softer. As far as passenger cabins went, this must've cost a pretty coin, but I also had a feeling he traveled more simply for other contract voyages.

Strong, sure hands twisted me around again, and my front molded to the hard planes of Elián's body. My thighs rested on either sides of his hips.

"You've got something right...everywhere." I mumbled, winding a finger in a circular motion to gesture at his face. He hadn't even bothered to wipe himself on the pillow beneath his head or grab the tattered remains of his tunic he'd let me borrow.

I rested my arms across his chest, then set my chin on the back of my hands. Those molten eyes tracked every movement, heavy lidded as they now were.

Elián thumbed my bottom lip, pushing into the giving skin. He said no words, but the self-satisfied smirk spoke volumes. Cocksure bastard.

I huffed and scrambled off of him to retrieve said ruined tunic, and when I returned, he let me sit on his stomach while I cleaned him. His cock gave a valiant twitch beneath me, so I sent him a withering glance.

"Really? You nearly killed me with that thing, and you want to try again?"

This time, he chuckled, the gesture more movement of his body than sound, and he forced me back to my earlier sprawl. I tossed the tunic over side of the bed.

And we watched each other. So much eye contact couldn't be good for a person, but all our acts of self-preservation had achieved in the past was heartache. Death.

So, we stared. I traced with my thoughts the hard edge of his jaw, the little bump at the bridge of his nose. His touch traced loops and patterns on my lower back, and I wondered what he was thinking. What he saw.

"Tell me something I don't know about you," I whispered, not wanting to break the trance of this moment.

His black lashes beat quickly, as if he was sorting through memories, snippets of him. I'd always reasoned he was far more than a sullen figure cloaked in leathers and scowls. But these past two days with him showed more than I'd expected, and I wanted to know it all.

"I used to have trouble speaking as a child." I cocked my head to the side, asking him to continue. And he did, "A stutter. It was easier to not talk."

I tried to imagine Elián unable to do anything and came up empty, but the sincerity in his words rang true. "Is that why you're so quiet now?"

His shrug shifted my body with it. "Yes. It is habit. But I notice more this way." I hummed, and this time, I didn't have to prompt him to keep going. "My brother did not have that problem, so he would often speak for me. Even though our father said it just kept me from working on it."

A fond, small smile spread across my cheeks. I imagined two tiny versions of Elián in child-sized fighting leathers. One silent and the other chatty to compensate. "And how did you shake it? The stutter."

He closed his eyes a moment, sadness and love shifting. "My mother. I could hardly speak but had no issue when I sang with her. She practiced with me, over and over. And one visit with her, I was telling her of Leandro's growing infatuation with a boy in the village." He returned my expression with a somber smile of his own. "I'd finished the whole story, and only then did she tell me that I hadn't stuttered once while I told it."

Elián's thumb wiped under my eyes, making me realize that I'd started to cry. For him, for her and his father, for his twin brother. "You miss them terribly."

He sighed thickly. "Yes."

This time, I initiated the meeting of our lips. I stretched and kissed him tenderly, but there was no way I could pour everything into the gesture. There was not enough time in this or any other world to tell him how much I wished they were here again, to tell him that I understood.

"Your turn, my queen."

I blurted the third thing that came to mind. "I used to be afraid of the dark."

To that, he chuckled, and if there was anything in this realm that I had left to be proud of, it was causing that dimple to appear. Both, if I was lucky. "You, Death Wielder, afraid of shadows?"

I scoffed. "Well, when you say it like that. Mat and Ajeh would tell stories of murderous Vyrkos hiding under my bed to eat me. At three years, of course I believed them."

He sobered and reached for that spot on my back. Between shoulder blade and spine. "And do you miss him?"

Mathieu. After saving me, I'd not asked Elián *how*, but I knew he ended my brother after Mathieu nearly killed me. The giggles we shared as children, the helping hand he extended as we both learned the world. Those were all tainted by the last images I had of Mathieu. Ordering our uncle's beheading, his sneers as he admitted to murdering those I loved.

"No. I don't."

After more silence, more staring, Elián spoke again. "Even so. I am sorry."

"There's nothing to be sorry for. He was willing to incite

wars, drive more division between our kind and the Vyrkos. Cut down family all for the sake of power. I've done fucked up thing after fucked up thing in my life, but I would never do that. If I ever get to that point, I want you to kill me yourself."

Elián rotated us onto our sides and took my face in hand. "You won't." I held back my arguments to the contrary. I'd been halfway there while living with Cal. To be complicit and support someone so evil was just as poisonous, maybe even more so.

He kissed me again, and we sank into the mattress, the moment. Our legs twined in a messy, languorous heap.

It was awhile before we came up for air, and I rested the black tips of my fingers in his dimples. Elián kept his smile there, soft to match the deep embers that watched me. His callused thumbs flicked the rings in my nipples, sending shocks down to my toes.

"I am looking forward to our time together, Meline."

"Mm," I hummed, "and how much time are you wanting?" I kept my tone teasing but held my breath for his answer.

"All of it. Em and El."

This time, the laugh was genuine as he parroted my ridiculous words from a different lifetime. The twinge of sadness and doubt lurked underneath, but I could dream a bit longer. "Okay. Em and El."

Chapter Seventeen
Meline

The salt air stirred the tiny waves of Elián's hair escaping the knot atop his head. Now far enough for the coasts to be lost in the expansiveness of sea and sky, we floated on dark waters matching the night above. The moon provided just enough light to allude to the creatures lurking below, but the deep red and orange glowing from Elián's eyes looked on brightly in hot disdain.

"Are you sure you're alright?" I asked, lips trembling. After tearing ourselves out of bed, we washed and went in search of food. The small dining room for passengers was full, the air close with a mix of perfumes and aroma of supper.

Elián's golden brown skin churned with an interesting olive hue almost immediately.

Now, with supper abandoned, save for a few hasty bites before following him to the deck, I watched him fight with himself.

He grunted in answer, and I teased, "You know, it's not the ocean's fault. Maybe letting yourself vomit will help?" Elián turned his glower onto me, and I lost the battle with the snickers. I cooed with a few circles of my gloved palm on his back. "I won't think less of you, you know."

"I'm—" He clenched his eyes and jaw, muscle jumping as he took a pointed swallow. I clucked my tongue and continued my soothing. As much as I enjoyed taunting him, I didn't enjoy seeing him so uncomfortable. After a few more moments, our fellow passengers milling about the deck and swaying from the waves or their own libations, Elián managed, "I am not going to vomit."

"Well, you may be able to fool yourself, but I am not that easily deceived."

He looked about to retort, lips parting in a weak sneer, but his stomach had other ideas. Using Lylithan speed, Elián darted to the railing and pitched his breakfast and whatever else overboard. I kept my amusement to myself as I caught up with him, resuming my back rubs. At least his hair was already up.

We drew a few concerned or amused glances from passersby, but the pointed stare over by the bow snagged my attention. They cocked their head, red eyes like drops of rubies under the moonlight.

Elián straightened after spitting spitefully over the sea. This evening, he wore clothing that was another nod to his heritage— the violet tunic with no sleeves exposed the striking tattoos up and down his arms, and the low cut in front once again displayed him from clavicle to sternum.

My own black and maroon blouse seemed quite subdued in comparison. But I liked him like this. The more vibrant of the two of us.

I reached up, caressing his lip as he'd done with me earlier. His expression harkened back to our first encounters, stony and closed down, so I pulled on the back of his neck, lowering him within my reach. I pecked his lips in reassurance—closed-mouth, but still—and he grumbled and huffed.

"And do you feel better?" I already had my answer with the color returning to his face, but I asked anyway.

This Elián, the one who'd shown me he was determined to rebuild in a new way, didn't dismiss or bite my head off. With a sigh, he conceded with a, "Yes," and for the first time in years, I grinned.

He paused, brow bunching slightly in thought. Elián swallowed again, licking his lips as he took my hand. He gave the gloves, matching the leather of my boots, two more breaths of consideration before glancing at me under black lashes. "You are beautiful, my queen."

I blinked. "Oh, ah, thank you. And…" My words were tumbling more clumsily in the face of his earnest compliments than when I'd had his cock in my mouth.

The tight mounds of his arms, the soft loops of the gold in his ears and the waves of his hair. "You are beautiful, too. Otherworldly so," I added that last part on a hoarse, vulnerable whisper.

Those dimples made an appearance, but one that seemed genuinely born from my words, rather than an action to placate me.

He didn't need to do the pulling this time. The sea air was cool, certainly, but the temperature didn't bother me. It was the air kissing my bare shoulders that forced to my awareness the fact his arms weren't around me.

The heat was immediate as I walked into him, hummed into the embrace. Was this what we'd been missing the whole time we'd traveled together as bodyguard and royal charge? How different could the journey to Rhaestras have been if we'd had this?

I would've gotten a lot less reading done, but Elián certainly would've spent less time angrily pacing. The mornings in my mother's homeland could've been spent luxuriating in the heat, naked and panting into each other, sweat-slicked skin joining over and over. Reading companionably by the pool.

"Do you bring any of those picture books?" I asked with a cheek resting on his chest.

"Yes. Two I had not heard of before, the third is the newest Joran installment."

I snickered, pleasant swells of excitement in my stomach. "I'd like to read those with you, while we're in bed."

Elián grumbled, but it was a pleasant, pleased sound. He pulled me even closer. "I would like that, too."

And maybe…maybe we could make plans. Learn more about each other and what we wanted this future to look like. Provided Tana and I won this contract. But even if we didn't, Goddess willing, Elián would be here and so would I.

A scream cut through the night, one that communicated distress—*fear*—and I wrenched my gaze to where I'd seen those red eyes. Of course, the person was gone.

It took a while for the humans on the deck, with their weakened hearing, to notice something was amiss, but by the time confused then worried whispers started rumbling, Elián and I were already descending into the bowels of the ship, seeking out the danger and ready to snuff it out. We flew down the steps, maneuvered around fumbling bodies unaware of or startled by the commotion.

The yells became louder as we got closer, even with the woman trying to console the source of the noise. Hand trembling and running over the man's shoulders, she tried uselessly to shush and soothe him, but he squirmed and resisted.

The corridor was filled with the well-intentioned and nosy alike, but we were easily able to cut through enough to see. She was about my height, young and pretty, and by scent, the other was her brother. His coloring mirrored hers, as did the wide, flustered look in his eyes.

"What in the name of God have you done?"

The woman cast quick glances at all of us. Some older woman tried offering a robe to compensate for the torn front of her chemise undergarment. "Viktor, *please.* Come back inside, and we will talk about this in *private.*"

"No! No," he pointed a shaky finger, "the one who did that is on this fucking ship!" His chest heaved, and the scent of fear turned quickly to anger.

There was no mistaking the sweet scent of her blood, or the crimson drops staining the slippery white fabric she wore. Even with the poor attempt at a bandage she held to her throat.

Fuck.

I glanced at Elián, only to find his jaw clenched. The ship held mostly humans, and a misguided hunt for the culprit would prove annoying at best. Dangerous at worst.

I started slowly pulling away first, and Elián's presence remained beside me. We melted back into the crowd as more humans started asking questions, wondering if someone had seen something, if she'd been attacked.

We stalked on silent steps, but as we approached the section containing our cabins, Elián turned away. "I will go find Tom, and we will meet you back in our cabin."

His absence from my arms was harder to bear this time, but I pushed past it to the cabin I'd rented with Tana. At our knocking pattern of two slow, three quick, and one more, Tana opened the door with a bewildered pout.

"Did you hear that screaming?" she asked after I quickly shut us inside and pinched the bridge of my nose. We were sailing the waters of Nalya and far away from our home continent of Eryva.

In Morova, we'd encountered many who approached us with lust, but there were also many humans who feared our need to drink mortal blood. Here, on this side of the world, there was also trepidation. Hatred, in some cases.

Luckily, Tana and I had not experienced the latter, but the contempt in the man's words was raising my hackles and agitating my powers.

Slaughtering any that came for us would be an effective yet unhelpful solution, but would we be able to staunch the risings of a mob?

By the time Tana and I were pacing in the cabin Elián and I shared, he brought in a frustrated Tomás who kept glancing toward the corridor. "Bloody *awful* timing," he grumbled, and El rolled his eyes. Judging by the half-dressed state of him, Tomás had been making *very* quick work of the ship captain before Elián brought him here.

"They are beginning to search for the one who drank from her."

I cursed under my breath, and Tana froze. There was no hiding our fangs, and we hadn't embarked on the boat with lips closed or hiding in the cargo hold. It had only been a few hours, but if no one calmed them, the humans would eventually make their way to us.

"Well, it must've been that Vyrkos male," Tana mused, echoing my previous thoughts. I'd only caught a glimpse of him, but other than slight surprise, I'd thought nothing of his presence. "Unless you made a stop in her cabin before wherever it was you went." She gestured to Tomás's bare chest.

He crossed his arms, one of which had the same snake tattoo as Elián. "*Please*. The bloke is over there screaming about the loss of his sister's precious virtue. What would I want with a virginal rube with an overprotective *brute* of a brother prone to hysterics?"

Tana mirrored his posture and shrugged. "You don't seem to be all that discerning, so it was a fair possibility."

"Why, you—" he started but threw his hands up. "What are we worrying about? I've been with the captain all evening, these two," he waved a hand at Elián and me, "have been fucking, judging by the smell in here, so all we need to concern ourselves with is accounting for *your* whereabouts."

"*My* whereabouts?" Tana's voice raised to an uncharacteristic pitch, jolting me out of the possibilities running through my mind. "I had supper in my room, took a bath, and have been reading by myself."

I rubbed at my temples, more dread creeping in. "So, people certainly saw you eating," I deduced. We had at least seven days on the water, provided the weather remained forgiving. Holing up in a cabin for the entirety of the journey was not impossible but certainly uncomfortable. Would the commotion die down? "What did the captain say?" I asked Tomás.

"Not much of anything since we were otherwise occupied when Nogón burst in." He swept a mass of locs over his shoulder, and I frowned at the name he directed toward Elián. What did it mean? "One would hope that since he was begging for my own bite, he won't lead the charge brewing, but I have little faith in humans."

"I did not see this Vyrkos, but he must know by now they are looking for him."

We all nodded, quieted to listen for what was happening on the level below us. There were too many to focus long on any one conversation, and the absence of the previous shouting wasn't at all encouraging. There was a definite cluster still convened on the corridor where the human and her brother were located. Were they calming the siblings? Conspiring with him to hunt for blood?

"They hardly know the difference between a Lylithan and a Vyrkos here," Tomás grumbled and sank into the desk chair.

"But really, that does not matter." We all turned to Elián as he spoke. "Even if they were to rightfully name the Vyrkos as the culprit, they will likely not stop at him."

Tana and I silently agreed, foreboding groaning along with the settling of the ship. "So, should we find him? The Vyrkos?"

"The more we know about what's going on, the better." I also wasn't convinced that the woman was attacked. The way she'd pled with her brother to calm down so that she could reason with him was a curious detail. Maybe she simply did not want to cause a ruckus. Or, maybe not.

CHAPTER EIGHTEEN
TANA

Turned out, the Vyrkos male was quite easy to find.

"And why, pray tell, should I be concerned?" He drawled from his bed, feet crossed leisurely at the ankle, hands folded beneath his head.

Unlike the humans with weak senses now convened in the dining room and strategizing like we'd feared, our sense of smell quickly led us to the male who was lounging contentedly in his cabin. It was small, like mine, and was even on the same floor as the woman and her brother who started all of this.

"Because," my cousin put her hands on her hips, standing over him like a bewildered parent, "they are coming to kill you, and then they'll be coming for us, too."

The Vyrkos stared blankly at all of us, red eyes deep like wine. "If they come because I gave that woman what she wanted, then they deserve to die."

A throat cleared. "Sorry, but we have to ask. Did the human truly ask for you to drink from her?"

The exasperated tone of the room evaporated in an instant. The nonchalant response we received as soon as we'd entered the Vyrkos's space had received all of our attention, but our frustration would certainly take on a new color should the Vyrkos allude to forcing himself on the woman.

If that became the case, we'd no longer be competing only in contract but also for who would kill the Vyrkos first.

He sneered but remained reclined. "Would you consider her pulling me into her cabin whilst her brother was away, palming my cock, and asking me to bite while we fucked consent enough? We shared pleasure, and I left."

I released a breath, and I watched my cousin do the same. Her Shadow male remained at her back, glaring at the Vyrkos, but I'd quickly learned in our flight from Versillia years ago that the expression could mean anything.

"Now, is there anything else you need?"

I gaped while my cousin and the Shadows seemed two moments away from grabbing their weapons. "You would deny our help, even if it could mean endangering your life? Ours?"

He turned a dismissive sweep of his red eyes on me. "I'm failing to understand why I should be any of your concern." There was a scar cut across his pale face, one that looked old but spoke of some experience in conflict. The bottom half of his brown hair was shaved, the rest held back by a leather band. "And four Lylithans against a fumbling group of humans should be quick work."

My cousin flicked her gloved hand, already turning away from the male on the bed. "I'm done. This fucker can get thrown overboard." Elián grunted in agreement, and the three of them headed for the door.

I spared the Vyrkos one last look, but it was met with nothing. Clear apathy.

The corridors were eerily quiet as we went the way we'd come, and when we returned to Meline and Elián's cabin, I released a weary sigh. "How long do you think it will take them to begin searching?"

And like I'd spoken the footsteps into existence, a tumble of them stomped up onto our deck.

It was automatic, then. All of us drew our weapons as if they'd always been in hand. With their larger blades packed away, the Shadows wielded a variety of knives, and Meline conjured her daggers.

I twirled my small blade in my grip, feeling its familiar weight. That'd been one of the first lessons from my cousin. To conceal and quickly retrieve your weapon could save your life, Meline had taught me. We were powerful, few other beings a direct match in strength and agility, but we could still be bested.

Confidence is best balanced with pragmatism, she'd said with the Ralthan sun beating down on us as she trained me. *After a few wins, a nice sum of coin in your pocket, you'll feel strong and quick. But don't let that stop you from watching out for a knife to the back.*

While helpful for me to keep in mind, it was a bit of a moot point for my cousin when she could release a fraction of her power and snuff out all life on this ship.

The rumblings of voices, mostly male and aggravated, grew nearer. A knock rang across the corridor, on the door to Tomás's cabin. Of course, there was no answer, so the group turned around, pounded on the barrier that separated *us* from *them.*

I breathed calmly, despite my heart galloping. We'd all agreed that, aside from none of us knowing how to captain a ship, arriving to port with a boat full of bodies—or an absence of such if we pushed them all into the sea—was not wise. Our kind was durable, but The Killings and other losses had proved that we were not invincible.

The voice that called on the other side was familiar—the one that greeted us when we boarded. "This is your captain. One of our passengers has been attacked, and we need to speak with everyone." Just what we'd feared. The tension wound tighter.

Tomás was the one to step forward. He sheathed his dagger at his side, and when he glanced at all of us over his shoulder, he gestured his hand up and down, as if commanding us to calm. The throwing back of his hair and straightening his shoulders alluded to the tactic he was going to employ first.

Our fabricated relaxation, my sitting at the foot of the bed and Meline and Elián leaning against the wall, was the best we could muster. I didn't bother putting away my dagger but rested it on the mattress beside me.

"Why, hello," Tomás purred when he revealed the captain's tense form standing before the threshold. The Shadow leaned against the frame, giving us a view of what we faced.

And the captain's startled expression, complete with a blush visible over top his thick beard. The human faces behind him were a range of scowls and curled lips.

Tomás continued smoothly, "How can we help?"

"Would you and your, ah, friends please come with us?"

So they could murder us in the corridor? I caught Meline's rolling eyes from across the room. Her Shadow remained facing the door, but I saw his body's shift closer to hers.

"You said that someone was attacked. What happened? Are we in danger?" Tomás slightly stiffened his posture but continued to lean in a nonthreatening manner.

"We are not certain. But, given your race... you could see why we'd be concerned."

From the movement of his arm, I gathered Tomás had reached out and was now touching the captain's coat, probably twisting the fabric suggestively. "I'm not sure when this happened, but I've been with you for most of the evening."

"I know—"

"But not all. Not to mention the rest of you," someone shouted from behind the captain.

"Well, my friends and myself make a point of never taking someone unwilling. Which could be said for most of our kind, as well. We can certainly help, but we also don't appreciate being presumed evil beasts."

More disdainful rumblings stirred, and I grasped the hilt of my dagger. Elián and Meline peeled their backs off the wall. By the symphony of hearts beating, the scents flooding through the doorway, nearly one fourth of the passengers and crew were part of this vengeful party. How many of them were armed? I tracked the tensing of muscle in Tomás's back as someone shoved aside the captain. They stood abreast while the big human in fine travel-wear jutted a finger at Tomás. "Shut your weaseling mouth. One of you bloodsuckers assaulted my *sister*."

This time, the deep silk of Tomás's words shifted. Even though I was unable to see his face, it sent a prickle down my spine. The warning of a predator. "You'll do well to never touch me again, boy."

I stood, and a howl of wind crashed against the windows. The waters had remained fairly calm, but perhaps that was about to change as well.

Before he could strike, Meline stepped forward, and Elián frowned harder. She rested a hand on Tomás's shoulder. "None of us are going anywhere, and we certainly don't want any trouble. My cousin and I have some knowledge in healing. Perhaps we can be of assistance in that regard? Is your sister resting all right?"

"Don't you fucking dare—" he started to spit in Meline's face, and Elián was at her back in an instant. She raised a hand to halt his defending her, but it was the captain who spoke next.

The human's swallow was audible, as was the fast beating of his heart. "I believe some rest is best." I could no longer see him, but his voice turned, as if he was now facing the mob of humans. "Our focus should be on young Rebeka, and the guilty party will undoubtedly be turned over to the authorities once we arrive. A night's sleep will benefit us all."

No one took up my cousin's offer to truly help the injured one in this scenario, but that wasn't surprising either. There was a possibility the Vyrkos male had been lying before, about this Rebeka approaching him enthusiastically, but something told me that he was speaking truthfully.

Already, I could tell that this was about honor more than protection.

Gathering a hold of the humans, the captain ushered them

away, making promises to reconvene tomorrow with fresh minds and eyes, but he was a fool if he thought the worst among them wouldn't be plotting past sunrise.

We all remained at the ready until the last of them retreated, but there would most likely be not a wink of sleep between us. Would a bold human or two attempt to attack us unawares? I tapped the pad of my finger against the tip of my blade. It was due a sharpening, and it was looking as though I'd have the time.

Tomás sagged against the door, head tilted toward the wooden ceiling. I sat again on the firm mattress, something other than fear weighing on my shoulders.

We were opposing a group of humans instead of Vyrkos like the war decades past, but it brought up memories all the same. Tales of massacres, whole villages of Lylithan and Vyrkos alike wiped out, and for what? The horrors of The Killings weren't often in my thoughts, but this whole affair was bringing them back up. Hiding, looking over my shoulder.

Hatred for another race killed my father, and where did that get us? At the end of it all, my uncle, aunt, and so many others had been killed because of what?

Nothing. They'd died for nothing.

I blinked back tears of frustration. Though the war between our peoples seemed to be a tale from a faraway place to these humans, it should have been a warning.

But, wasn't that always the way? Blaming others instead of inspecting the true reasons within. Pointing at the differences to fuel the malice until it raged out of control.

"They're going to kill him before we reach the port." The others didn't necessarily ignore me, but they didn't respond either. I pressed on, "We are able to fight off any attack, but if enough of them try, they may succeed."

"And we tried to bring him here. Protect him. But once they realize another blood drinker is on this ship, if they haven't already, he will have to fend for himself."

Meline was right. Of course she was, but her cold acceptance of letting the Vyrkos die didn't sit well with me. Through the training and contracts I'd participated in, I kept waiting for the inclination toward kindness to wither. I could remove the digits from a man who'd never wronged me, slit the throat of another while relieving his home of all valuables available.

And yet, refusing assistance when it was so easy to give—that felt wrong.

"Oh, lovely. We have a bleeding heart in the cabin. Might be best to find another profession, love."

I peeled my lip back and hissed at Tomás while my cheeks flamed. I needn't the reminder that I was the greenest out of everyone here. That if anyone were to blunder in this situation, it was me. But, was it so bad to be sensitive and still kill for money?

My cousin crouched before me and took my hands in hers. A frisson of tension held my muscles stiffer than usual, but I accepted the touch. Our argument earlier, if it could be called that, still felt unresolved. Particularly with her gazing at me like I was a child, experiencing their first cruelty of the world.

"We can't put ourselves in danger for him, Tana. Not when he's unwilling to even accept it."

"I—I'm not saying we lay our lives down when he won't even—b-but it just—" I ground my jaw, fighting the frustrated tears. Was there some action in between that was not forcing him to accept our help but not reclining in the room while they got to him?

Meline leaned forward and kissed my brow. Something I'd done to her countless times, especially in recent years. "If he comes to us, we will help."

The assurance felt final, so I didn't question or add anything else aside from a nod.

CHAPTER NINETEEN
TANA

We didn't emerge from Elián and Meline's cabin much over the majority of our voyage. The first time we'd entered the dining cabins, the wary glances were nearing on oppressive. Same in the corridors and decks. At least up top, there was fresh air and pulsing ocean to drown out the whispers. Wondering when we'd come for them next.

Tomás tried to speak to the captain for us, requesting him to do more to get the humans in line. But, as Tomás told it, the man had sputtered and made excuses, stating that he was in no way able to force the humans to playact nice around us.

I sighed, then tasted salted air as I inhaled. The sun was ascending into a warm day, the clear sky a pleasant, expansive azure. There were several benches for passenger use, and with the calm winds today, we'd claimed a spot away from the few other humans on the ship.

Their stares, I ignored, even when they seared against my senses. Now that I'd been taught to recognize such things, I had trouble turning it off. The three men at my back, smoking as they leaned by the water. The woman and her child to my left, dressed in expensive fabrics and playing a clapping game with their hands.

The babe had smiled at me when they walked past, a greeting I returned with the sunny smile my mother used to coo over me for. Well, until the woman caught sight of my fangs and hastily ushered her child away as far as she could manage.

My smile had dimmed then.

Another sip of my tea, and I resumed my tasks, picking through the jars I carried with me and adding some hyssop sprigs to the small cotton sachet in my lap. The gardens in Versillia were long out of my reach, as was the one I'd started in Ralthas during our extended stay. Though my world, my days, were filled with contracts, training, and brawls, my craft was woven through every breath.

My healing these days did not extend past remedying cuts and weary muscles, but where I could buy herbs and supplies, I did. The solstice was approaching. Meline was not a coven sister, so the celebration would be abbreviated, but some sachets to give us protection, to ask for additional protection for those we cared for, was enough.

I snipped from my diminishing spool of twine and finished off the small pouch I was working on, stuck on who I would speak the protection spell over. Past years, my cousin and I always spoke over each other, and I still would. But, now she had her Shadow, didn't she?

The child screamed, and I raised my gaze, watching as another joined and began running along the deck's edge, chasing the seagulls that hovered overhead. In my mind's eye, I saw myself, wheat-colored plait trailing behind me while Meline gave chase. A couple years older than me, I'd idolized her, talking her ear off about the simple spells I'd been learning, trying and failing to hide giggles while we were supposed to behave during official Versillian events.

I sniffed as my heart clenched, grief for that far simpler time, when our parents were alive and her brother was nothing more than the studious one we bothered with our silly jokes. My fingers felt heavier, clumsier, as I started on another sachet. My cousin and I had gone off to live our own lives, though our reunions always had us settling back into familiar rhythms. We understood one another, perhaps a bit too much. And after snatching her from the edge of death, we'd done more than lean on each other—we were reliant on one another.

She protected me, shielded me, and I was the buttress keeping her from crumbling to the ground. But, sometimes, I found myself getting quieter when I knew she'd speak for me. I noticed her falling without trying, knowing that I would catch her.

The more I thought of it, how much I looked to her and she to me, the less it seemed…sustainable for the both of us.

"What're those for?" The Shadow asked lazily beside me.

My fingers slipped, dropping leaves of sage onto the floor. I cursed and bent, swiping them up before they could flutter away. "The solstice coincides with the next full moon. We'll probably be traveling, but I want to be prepared."

We weren't spending any time alone these days, aside from trips to the communal bathing room on our deck. Talk of the contract we competed for was effectively put to the side. The three of them groused about this sometimes happening, an employer hiring multiple mercenaries for one job, which often caused confusion and animosity. We would already fight once we closed in on Von Herron, competing to snatch him up and take him to Blackwood first. To save us all from even *more* bickering, we decided to pause talk of our current mark for the time being.

So, we were resorted to shallow chatting, and it'd long grown monotonous. I considered myself a fairly sociable person, but even I had my limits.

"And you just hang that around your neck or something?" Tomás had been stretched out beside me, upper half bare and sprawled out. On my other side, Meline and her Shadow read from their respective books, hers a thick novel and his a thinner packet with pictures.

I snorted and plucked some yellow flowers from a jar, stuffing them in the sachet. "No, I burn them. These are for protection."

He mumbled some contemplative sound and turned his face back to the sky. The four of us spent our evening hours in Meline and Elián's cabin, as that was most likely when the humans would get bold, but the daytime hours were marginally calmer. And staying confined belowdeck was only tolerable for so long.

Elián had already turned green on multiple occasions when we sat too long down there. I wouldn't complain about enjoying the warmth on my skin and spray of sea.

Tomás's voice startled me, but I kept my physical response still. "Is this ritual to protect yourself?"

"Yes, but you can make one for anyone you wish and dedicate it to them. Meline and I do so every year."

My cousin flipped her book, keeping her place while she rested it in her lap. "I'll make mine now if you can spare the supplies." Her eyes flicked to me, the request for permission unspoken yet clear. I nodded quickly, closed-lipped smile an attempt to reassure. My frustrations, at her and myself, had bubbled up in our first true disagreement in…decades.

What could you fix, though, when the strain was impending change?

Meline began to pick out her ingredients, no longer needing my instruction after the past three years.

A dark, cool-toned finger jutted in my line of sight. Two thick silver rings shone under the bright sun. "Can I make one, as well?"

Surprised, I pursed my lips and appraised the mouthy male. The usual taunting smirk was wiped clean from his face, so I acquiesced. The herbs were meant to be used, and they were typical enough in most regions, so procuring more was no hardship. And, after centuries of studying, I needed little to harness the aether to my will. Even now, with just water and sky around us, I felt it humming.

"You don't feel confident in your own abilities to protect yourself?" Meline challenged while she worked on two sachets simultaneously. Her Shadow watched.

Tomás scoffed. "I could take down an army with one hand tied behind my back, love. Confidence, I do not lack."

A faint growl carried in the wind, and we all turned to Elián. He was glaring right back at his brother.

"And which part do you disagree with, Nogón?" Tomás took the empty pouch I offered him. "My abilities or the endearment to your intended?"

My eyes grew wide, despite becoming quite accustomed to how much this one teased. Meline froze with sprigs of lavender twisting between her gloved fingers.

"Um…" I grasped at anything to diffuse the tension. "What does that mean? Nogón." I tried to mimic the accent Tomás used, but it didn't come out the same.

Meline shot me a grateful glance, and I nodded. Though she'd feigned giving up on finding him, the life that filled her eyes, now sitting next to the male she'd lost, was impossible to ignore. I'd already made my position known, that to make this life possible with him, she would have to be honest. To tell him *everything*.

While we'd packed our things and made the journey to the port, I vowed to not mention again. By the tightening of her shoulders, she knew.

"It's Zonoran for 'dragon,'" Tomás supplied while the fire in Elián's eyes calmed. At least, as much as it could. "I've been pulling his tail since we were wee lads. Got burned a couple times, but it's always worth it."

Said dragon grumbled, as evidence of the Shadow's point, and my cousin and I chuckled. "And what were you like as a boy? I'm guessing your disposition has not changed."

"No," Elián answered for him. "It has not."

Tomás flashed his fangs and winked. "Came out of the womb a charmer. One of us has to be the interesting one."

"I think he's plenty interesting," Meline qualified, but her trembling mouth revealed how amusing she thought the flat look on Elián's face was.

I pointed Tomás to the ingredients used for the protection ritual, and he handled them with fingers far gentler than I'd anticipated. Carefully, he placed one after another, hunched slightly over his lap as he worked. He shook his head, locked hair running across his shoulders and smiling to himself. "Nor called it, I think."

"What?" I asked.

"Our sister, Noruh. She likes to tease us."

I felt Meline stiffen again beside me, but she did a better job of hiding the grinding of her jaw.

"About?"

Tomás waved his hand, as if mimicking someone else, and his accent changed from the Sjatan cadence to one similar to Grimm's. "'You two are the most insufferable papas. One who lets the boy skirt the rules at every turn, the other a stifling worry wort.'"

My hand landed on Meline's leg beside mine, not even needing to look. I smiled along with the joke, eventually catching on that they had sponsored the young boy from Nethras. I'd only met him once or twice, but he was a sweet soul.

"Frankly, he needs the excitement. Acolyte chores are boring as all hell, and Nogón's grunts don't add very much."

"I think you misunderstand who she was labeling the worrier, Tom."

"What?" he laughed, aghast.

Elián pointed at the protection bundle Tomás was tying off. "Who is that for?"

"Wha—I—it's for you."

"Are all Shadows this bad at lying?" I gave Meline a final pat, worried I'd drawn too much attention to her. She leaned away from me as Elián drew her into his arms, now sneaking wondering glances while she fiddled with the bows she tied in the twine.

Tomás and Elián started going back and forth at each other in what I assumed was Zonoran. It rolled smoothly off their tongues, and though he used far more words than Elián, the quieter male fired back just as quickly at his brother.

Meline and I watched them bicker with each other, and I tried to grin past the twinge in my heart. I'd so quickly snapped into my place, yet again trying to keep my cousin afloat like this ship.

But now, she had her Shadow, didn't she?

The bathing room had been empty, thankfully, and I was able to sneak some time on my own. I scrubbed the salt clinging to my skin, lathered my own blend of moisturizing soap through my hair quickly.

Refreshed and steam chasing, I opened back out into the corridor for our deck, just as the Vyrkos walked purposefully toward the steps. After so much time with assassins, his footfalls seemed loud, uncaring.

The deepened glow of his red eyes, however, made my heart lurch.

I quickly caught up to him and joined in step, bundle of bathing supplies still in tow. "Do not do what you are thinking of doing. We can help."

His brown tunic appeared worse for wear, and his hair was not in the orderly queue from before. The messy strands whipped about his face as he flashed his fangs at me. "Be gone. I won't have you all monitoring my actions. Pompous school-marms, the lot of you."

Before he could start descending the steps, I shoved him into the wall. The lamps lining the corridor flickered as I called the aether to me. No words spoken but the coaxing of an old friend, I called my magic forth, and it glowed a pale violet around the fingertip I pointed right at his arrogant face. "We are trying to *help* you. They are organizing, waiting until we are most vulnerable to pick us off. Do you hold no value for your life?"

Something flickered across the Vyrkos's face, but it was gone faster than a blink. The scar that pulled from lip to cheek tightened, and he tried to intimidate me again, even when I was stronger. Faster. He was clearly entering the stages of hunger where coherent thought became muddy.

"Let. Me. Go."

I ignored his demand and instead tightened my hold. "We have just a few more days," I tried to keep the frustration out of my voice, but the words were still rough, "and after that, you will be able to go about your life. Hunting as you please without being stuck on a ship, outnumbered by humans just as hungry for blood as you are."

He scoffed. *Scoffed.*

"You think of yourself as invincible? They may be weaker physically, but do *not* underestimate the power of hate and fear." I wasn't sure how old he was, but he had enough years behind him to at least *know* of The Killings. Our peoples had engaged in a whole bloody war fueled by similar motivations, and look where we'd ended up.

The male swallowed, reason focusing on me for a moment before the flaring again in his cherry-colored eyes. Vyrkos needed to feed more frequently than us, as their diet consisted of blood and only blood. He hid it well, but—as I studied him, trying to figure out how to make him see this truth I knew was undeniable, I felt the faint tremors beneath my hold. His widened pupils and irregular breathing.

He wasn't just hungry. He was nearing Frenzy.

Softer, I called back my magic and asked, "What is your name?"

His gaze swept left then right, like an animal cornered. "Fenix."

Aside from the beginning signs of Frenzy, he was not

attacking me, he seemed oriented to himself, where we were. He had the wherewithal to insult us earlier. "My name is Tana. Come with me, Fenix. *Please*. We can feed you. Protect you." Our rations were low, but we'd each fed in preparation for the trip. Emotions would run higher with increased hunger, but Frenzy was still far away for all four of us.

Fenix, on the other hand? We'd all suffer if he didn't get what he needed. I hardly knew this male, but I didn't want to have to kill him.

He relaxed beneath the steel bar of my forearm across his chest, and the beginnings of a smile curled at my lips. I'd never been close to Frenzy before, but during my visits to Rhaestras, I'd been educated on how it affected the body. Reducing functions to a survival state that had one goal—feed.

The function of one's mind was diminished to base urges. Breath, defense, and sustenance. Anything else, even your own *name*, was inconsequential. And if it went on long enough, death would come.

The longest recorded instance of this was ten years. But how many feral blood drinkers existed in Frenzy and were never caught?

Fenix and I both felt a presence approaching, a man walking down the steps from a deck above. He was dressed in the clothing of the crew—light tunic, sturdy trousers, and worn boots—and his loaded glance at the male I held against the wall spoke volumes.

We both watched him turn and continue down the steps to a level below, and Fenix stiffened right back up.

"I know how to care for myself. Now, move."

I wanted to roar in his face. Hurt him until he was too injured to resist. "After they come for you, they will come for us," I tried. "Fenix, please."

But he was done engaging with me. It wasn't enough to overpower me, but my frustration had me relenting to the shove he gave.

"Stay away from me."

And I watched him go, my cousin and the Shadows' assertions at war with the drive within me to keep one of our own from being murdered. We were different races, but there was more that connected us than separated us. How could we let him walk into destruction in this way?

While I stood, fighting with myself, pleasured moans reached my ears from below. The scent of freshly shed blood tickled my senses.

"Fuck," I growled under my breath as I ran down the steps, away from the good sense that *I* was rejecting. And into a trap.

Chapter Twenty
Meline

I panted over Elián, hands splayed across his tattooed chest. Little half-moons were already dug into his skin, reddened from the force with which I held onto him.

His breaths were just as ragged, blustering against the tender skin on my throat. "Come for me, Meline," he demanded.

As if I had a choice. Even on his back, El commanded my body, gripping my hips to hold them immobile while he fucked up into me.

I curled over him and dug my fingers to find purchase on his shoulders. The fabric I'd long ago pushed to the side tangled alongside his hair within my grip. Our clothing shuddered as we joined quickly in our bed, taking this precious moment alone.

Days at sea, tensions rising until it was uncomfortable at night to even traverse the decks beyond our cabins. We'd seen little to none of the stubborn Vyrkos and had been keeping in close proximity to my cousin and Elián's Shadow brother.

So much so that we'd tumbled into the cabin whilst Tomás was retrieving food for us and Tana was bathing. Finally, a moment alone.

I clung to the mountainous swells of Elián's shoulders and

dropped my forehead to his. Our lips and tongues touched in something more passionate and desperate to be called a kiss.

My brow scrunched, and I caught his lip between my teeth as he took my cries for encouragement, pummeling me in just that spot that sent me over the edge. The warm and deep taste of his blood sent me even higher as I clenched around him, pushing him to euphoria with me.

Elián's cock twitched and released inside of me, and I shook in his hold, in his arms. And in the face of my desperation, he cherished me, kissing lazily while we came back down.

"I think I tangled up your hair," I breathed.

He grunted, but not with a note of upset or offense. I was learning the different versions of his laconic communication—there was not much to do but sit ready and talk to each other—and I took this one to mean he didn't give a shit about the state of his hair.

I twirled some strands, skin slipping along the black silk. There was enough to wrap in my fist. Doing just that, I tugged gently. "Next time, I'll use this like reins while I ride you."

There. That got him chuckling, though it was a silent, chest-shaking gesture. My dress covered most of my body and where we were still joined, but El's lazy pets felt as nice as if we'd been naked. "You can try."

Something told me that it would incite another battle for dominance. That part of our dynamic was ever-present, even with this 'just *being*' that El had gone on about. I'd have to admit, I was being lulled more and more into giving in. How could I not when it brought us this?

"Well, I don't have any hair for you to pull anymore."

El leaned back into the mattress, appraising me with that brow raised and his persimmon gaze dancing. "I do not need your hair."

Heat flashed inside of me, particularly in one area of my body, and by the darkening of his gaze, El felt it too.

I was robbed of finding out what he could possibly use

instead by an impatient huff on the door. "Please make yourselves decent so that we can all eat."

If I hadn't been watching El's face, I wouldn't have seen the petulant eye roll. Snickering, I slowly crawled off of him, trying my best to keep my thighs closed.

He was having none of that, though, and his firm hand on my hip kept me on the mattress while he got up instead. The knob on the door twitched while he walked toward one of his packs, and he nearly hissed, lip curling to show his fangs. "Do *not* open the door until we tell you."

Before I could add my own quip, Elián returned with a cloth, busied himself beneath my skirt, and wiped away his spend so I wouldn't be uncomfortable. Blinking back tears, I snagged him 'round the back of his head where his hair was a tangled mess. I pressed up into a kiss, grabbing his face with both of my gloveless hands and treating his lips as tenderly as he met all of me.

"Considering your stupid plan to stay together is keeping me from warming the captain's bed, I'm not inclined to be forgiving of you having all of the fun. You reserved the bigger cabin, so it's really all your fault," Tomás groused through the door, to which of us, I wasn't sure.

Elián dropped my gloves beside me, and he growled low in his throat, that sound speaking of mild annoyance. I *was* hungry.

I smacked one last kiss to his stubbly cheek and let him go to the door.

His Shadow brother didn't bother with any pleasantries, plowing forward in his ranting while he set down the tray loaded with our supper. "Honestly, after all I've done for *both* of you. Some consideration for those of us without a lover in this trying time would be appreciated."

Elián glanced at me, a loaded look that made my heart skip a beat. Tomás groaned, now with a bite of bread roll in his mouth. "Oh, godyx, with the looks. It's bad enough that they're planning to kill us before we get to the dock."

I accepted the food El brought to me, and we used the bed as a surface to balance our plates as we dug in. Well, Elián and I did. Tomás took one look at the bed, wrinkled his nose, and commandeered the desk.

"It's a fool's errand on their part."

Tomás and Elián both nodded along. "The confines of this journey have left them irritable. The woman remains in her cabin, but from what I could deduce, she has long stopped trying to calm her brother." El had taken the most recent shift to find out what he could. When we did traverse the ship, the humans brushed past with wide eyes, terse nods, and whispers that followed as soon as they thought us out of earshot. Of course, with their Shadow magic, he and Tomás were the most skilled at hearing more of what was brewing around us. Though Tana and I were able to move stealthily, El and Tomás were able to bend the aether at their will, to become part of the shadows. Especially to humans, they could be invisible.

Picking at a piece of chicken, I ran through the possibilities for the thousandth time.

Rhaea's power felt less of a parasite taking control at my most vulnerable moments and more of an extension of myself, now that it lived on my skin. But as I imagined the humans coming for us as they were intending, it buzzed within my fingertips, wanting to take flight. I could practically taste the death of these humans, how sweet it would be, thirst for blood and for retribution slaked.

I frowned. "If their ineptitude foils their plan and the weather stays on our side, we should be there in two days' time, right? If not, we may have larger problems."

Both Shadows remained silent, but their agreement didn't need vocalizing. One of the first things we'd done as a group was ration the skins of blood we'd brought for the journey. Of course, the fluid didn't keep for long periods of time, and we were on the last dregs, saving it for an emergent situation.

In our defense, most were more receptive to donating to us before this whole business with the woman's brother.

The three of us ate in silence for a while, listening to the whooshing of the waves, but as my plate emptied, I set it to the side and paused, listening. The bathing room wasn't far away, and after parsing through the sounds of other passengers and the ocean around us, I no longer heard Tana in that direction.

"I'll be back."

El frowned as I left, but he didn't try to stop me. He knew I'd come back.

I crept out into the corridor, checking the empty bathing room with my own eyes before finding the lavender scent of my cousin in the air.

Something still felt off between us, even with the time passing since our argument. We'd forgiven each other, maybe? Was there anything for me to forgive?

When the urge to pull away from Elián— to retreat into the safety of her familiarity reared its head—Tana would see it written on my face and give me a sharp look. My apologetic smiles abounded as my former Shadow proved himself to be steady enough for me to cling to.

But when we get off the ship?

I shook my head, following Tana's scent as urgent voices became clearer. I paused on the stack of steps, headed to the next level. Tana's bag was abandoned, toiletries spilling onto to the floor.

My feet carried me before my thoughts caught up, reaching the commotion as five burly men held Tana while they pulled away the Vyrkos male, metal chain wrapped around his throat.

TANA

A trap. One for him that I'd fallen into. The Vyrkos and human he'd drunk from were tucked away in a dark corner of the ship, on a deck designated for storage and crew work, judging by the crates and supplies stored in the rooms I'd passed.

The man, now sneering and shouting curses at the both of us, watched us in sick delight with pupils blown. Someone handed him a rag to staunch the bleeding at his neck.

"You idiot!" I shouted at the Vyrkos as his skin reddened around the jewelry they held him with. Another six were huddled around the male. Someone must've possessed that particular knowledge, that silver was toxic to their kind, and procured the jewelry from one of the passengers. It was dainty, and the delicate charms waved against his throat as they restrained him.

They tried using another bauble on me, haphazardly pressing it into my brow as if the X-shaped thing had any power. When my skin remained unaffected, they dropped it with a huff.

"By the power of Mortos, we compel you to *yield*," one of them shouted, an older man who was holding his own chain and bauble out to us.

The Vyrkos, whose skin was now releasing smoke underneath the necklace and still struggling within the humans' grip, spat on the scuffed floorboards. He hissed, long fangs flashed toward the mob around us.

Of course, we didn't yield, and the telltale press of sharp metal on my neck halted my movements. If they wounded me enough, like cutting my throat, I might be unable to save him.

Before I could twist out of their hold, the Vyrkos roared, eyeing my throat and the weapon now cutting into it.

"Get the fuck off of her!" he yelled until one of them broke off from the rest with a dagger in his fist.

"You violated my sister, you demon," the man spat, and the humans cut the blade further into my neck. More arms held me still, but my focus was on the Vyrkos. He wasn't even paying attention to his own helplessness! "You are both abominations."

The man sunk the blade into the Vyrkos's heart in the same moment my cousin appeared,.

My eyes widened. Was it poisoned? I couldn't tell from here, but by the color of metal, if there was even a trace of silver that entered the Vyrkos's heart and poisoned his blood, there would be no hope for him.

"Enough!" Meline's voice erupted, sharp and rage-filled, and the darkness came first. She, like the Vyrkos had, eyed the blood running down my neck, but her indignation did not manifest in insults. She did not bear her fangs.

Hands raised, Meline released her power, and the black tendrils, like ivy, found their targets. They wrapped around the humans, and *pulled*. Screams abound, more claims of evil and devils, and I exhaled, body released as the mob was pushed to the walls.

Elián and Tomás appeared, weapons in hand, but it was over before it'd truly began. The humans screamed, shouting more cursing prayers to their God, and the Vyrkos slumped to the floor.

"We tried to be respectful and keep to ourselves. If you're so set on determining evil where you don't understand, then I can give you what you seek."

Oh, no. This was what we'd been trying *so hard* to prevent. Elián and I both jerked forward, hands outstretched to stop her. It wasn't taking over her gaze yet, the brown and gold still there, but black was eclipsing her hands like oil, creeping further and further up her arms.

My magic flared in response, distant recognition, but I doubted some healing spells or flashes of light were any match for Rhaea's wrath.

The humans screamed, some even weeping in terror. And my cousin looked on, lip curled back and Death dancing around her.

Until…until her Shadow touched her. Right where the moving vines of darkness reached toward her elbow. He met her darkness, and Meline flinched. Her hold on the humans tightened, releasing another wave of shouts.

Underneath them, though, I could hear his whisper. "Your

cousin is fine, my queen. You see? Revenge will not serve us today."

I felt Meline's sweeping look over my body, cataloguing every inch in the matter of a second before it moved to the Vyrkos—Fenix! I spun, dropping down beside his collapsed form.

"Demons! All of you! You've no right to live and walk among us!" The woman's brother, the one who started all of this, yelled from the wall, but I ignored him as I turned Fenix over. To see his wide eyes stare up at me, at nothing.

My heart slammed against my ribcage, and magic flared brightly in my palms. The dagger was still planted in his chest, so I cupped my touch around it, seeking, searching for the problem within.

"As soon as we arrive in Vharas, you will be *hanged*. Tried and executed to the fulles—" The man's shouts were muffled, and I glanced upward, finding Tomás stuffing a rag in his mouth. Though the rest of us had sheathed our weapons, save for Meline and her power, Tomás wielded a long, curved sword. By the menacing yet lazy sweeps, he would have no trouble cutting one or all of the humans down if need be.

"Meline. Look at me," Elián urged, now. And I chanted, increasing the aether flowing into Fenix's body. Healing magic was a complex, sometimes tricky thing, but where Meline was the expert fighter, I'd had just as many centuries honing *this* craft.

My magic was another sense, almost like all of them at once, and I parsed through what it revealed to me, that the only silver was in the burns on Fenix's throat. Where his body was preoccupied with fighting its spread, too overwhelmed to heal this and the stab to the heart at the same time.

Luckily for him, Vyrkos healing was more advanced than a mortal, and the boon of fresh human blood helped him stay on just this side of his True Death.

"Tomás," I called, "come pull the dagger out."

He was watching my cousin, or rather, the way her power was coiling over Elián now as he held her. The male was completely unafraid of it, letting it wrap around and brush against him as he gingerly pulled Meline into his chest.

"Tom," I urged, and that brought his attention to me and Fenix on the floor. While I resumed chanting, calling for the tissues in Fenix's heart to knit back together, for the flesh of his throat to do the same, Tomás slowly pulled the blade out and away.

He tucked it underneath his belt, and sat back, hands hovering.

"He's going to be okay. Thank you," I assured them both. Myself.

It was always a wondrous sight, watching the shimmer of aether weave through the body like thread, an otherworldly loom commanded by my word. When Fenix's eyes fluttered, his stare no longer faraway, I pulled my touch back and muttered thanks to the aether for heeding my call once again.

"She could kill us all, couldn't she? Without even a thought." Tomás had resumed watching Meline's power with a mix of wariness and awe. I followed his gaze, taking in the blackened tendrils that were still present, yes, but appeared less vicious. No longer a twitch from snuffing out all mortal life on the deck.

Elián was...he was holding her. Arms firmly wrapped around her now, Elián whispered more words, now too low for me to hear, even with the humans quieted to hushed pleas and whimpers.

And my cousin blinked, the tension slowly draining out of her with each word, each caress of Elián's thumb against her side. With each time his nose bumped against the shell of her ear until her hands dropped to her sides. The midnight color of Death lessened to a transparent, quivering gray.

I answered Tomás's forgotten question. "She could." I wanted to say that she wouldn't. That she would never. But if her Shadow had not been here? If his presence hadn't remind her that life, including her own, could be precious?

No, I was not afraid of her, never that. But *for* her?

A raucous cough alerted me once again to Fenix sprawled before me. His body shook, and I returned my hands to him. This time, it was just to soothe. To provide a gentle touch as he searched the ceiling. When he finally found me, he was still trembling, and I let him grab my wrists for anchor.

His grip was strong for his condition yet weak considering how formidable Vyrkos normally were when healthy. I felt the fast beating of his heart, so different than the typical slow cadence for his kind.

"You are okay. You are alive. Breathe slowly for me," I murmured softly.

Dark circles marred the skin under his eyes. There was still an angry, red mark slashed across his neck, a cruel mockery of the silver necklace they'd choked him with. But he breathed. Lips shaking as I demonstrated the action, silently offering him to follow.

And he did. All arrogance was gone, leaving a scared male, clinging to me for comfort, for life. But that was something I was used to as well, the vulnerable nature of those in my care.

I smiled down at him, but it immediately fell when his breaths stuttered. I took extra time getting him back into the rhythm while sweeping my regular senses over him. The scent of panic was abating. The sound of his lungs was strong, and the barest color started returning to his naturally pale cheeks.

"Good. You're doing great, Fenix," I grinned. He really was. There was still the concern of needing to feed, as I'd sensed how hungry he was, but I would personally give him my ration. Find him someone to drink from before we parted ways.

The Vyrkos continued to stare at me, but I was unbothered, relaxing onto my haunches and keeping my hands in his grasp. There was no need for them now, aside from comfort, but that was part of good healing, too.

"*Right*," Tomás drew the word out. "So, what do we do with them?"

Chapter Twenty-One
Elián

Rhaea's power tickled.

It was not the time, nor the place to divulge this to my queen, so I suppressed a shudder as it searched my spine, gliding against my nape and spilling across my shoulders.

My own Goddess power swam under my skin, but I kept it away, focusing all on bringing peace to my queen.

I'd heard what she said. She claimed so easily that she was evil when she was nothing of the sort.

"Tana is safe," I reminder her once again. "I am safe, Tom is safe, *you* are safe." She was accepting my words, my touch, but I hesitated to go further. To drop a kiss to her brow. Would she push me away if I dared?

"*Right*. So, what do we do with them?" my brother asked, and a growl slipped out of me. I did not save these humans for their sakes. Should we have been on dry land, I might have stood back and watched as she dealt them the hand they sought.

But, I risked a press of lips on her brow and was rewarded a quiet sigh, should my queen have killed them all, it would be because they deserved it. Not because of any lack of *goodness* within her.

"Well, we can't leave them to attack us again," Meline surmised, voice no longer reverberating. The last time I had seen her this way, she was terrified, uncontrolled.

Now, as we looked upon the humans while they stared back at us, I felt the ease with which she commanded her gift. The same as when I drew flames.

I grunted and kissed her again, pulling her closer. And as stubborn as she could be, Meline leaned further into my arms, my chest. Low, just for me, she mumbled, "Thank you."

Another brush of Death prickled the backs of my arms, now lighter, quicker. As if it was playing, coaxing. I hummed low in my throat.

"I'll go get the good captain," Tom volunteered, giving a wide berth between himself and my queen and me. He was a blur as he went up the steps, but shortly thereafter, the quick patters of soft feet tumbled down. Chased by heavier ones.

"Viktor!" A woman gasped, *the* woman. A human man tried to pull her back up the steps, but she shoved him away.

Her eyes went wide as she halted, still a few more steps to go. A bandage rested on her neck, but she otherwise appeared well. Unharmed.

Unlike her brother, who had taken up shouting around the fabric stuffed in his mouth, she stopped a moment, observing the scene.

And when she looked to the Vyrkos, still lying before Tana, her face crumpled. Tears shimmered and spilled down her cheeks, and after a few breaths, pointed and long, she threw back her shoulders.

She came down the last few steps and raised her chin. "This has g-gone t-too far, Vik."

He only shouted louder, demanding attention while we all gave it to the little human. She wore a pair of trousers and easily crouched beside the Vyrkos. He flicked between wary and relieved, suspicion and awe. This woman was the one the humans said they were avenging, and Tana was the one who just saved his immortal life.

"I'm…" The woman bit her lip and shook her head. "I don't even know your name," she whispered, tears falling. "I'm so, so sorry."

Meline and I were both still, and I watched all those around us. How the brother and those standing closest to him were scowling. How the others, more passive followers, flicked their confused gazes between their leader and the scene before them.

The man screamed muffled words, but his sister would not have any of it. "No!" the woman screamed. Her face grew flushed. "I *told* you that he didn't hurt me. No matter how many times you try to convince me otherwise." She focused on Tana, wringing her hands at her front. "What…what can I do to help? *Please.*"

Even the human could see that the witch was a healer. The faint purple glow still had not completely faded from her fingertips, and the male was still clinging to her. Watching her as if she was the Goddess Rhaea Herself.

Palms still pressed onto the Vyrkos's chest, her gaze was hard. "He needs to feed to fully heal. And we cannot provide the adequate sustenance." To us, Vyrkos blood was syrupy sweet, and given their former mortal nature, it was enough to sustain us.

It had been one of the many contentions that fueled The Killings, giving some Lylithans false evidence that we were superior because the reverse was not nutritious for the Vyrkos.

Otherwise, having interacted with the witch now and years past, I was certain she would have opened her vein in an instant for him.

Just as I had done for my queen.

I looked down at Meline again, pleased at the way she was curling into my chest. The gray tendrils were keeping the humans at bay, but a new strain was filling her posture. She was leaning further into me than she had been just a moment ago.

The man started screaming again, loud enough to test the limits of the cloth in his mouth, but his sister was unperturbed. Tom and the captain shoved past the sister's keeper still frozen on the stairwell, but they stalled at the sight of goddess power swirling around them.

Meline sagged further into my arms, and the Vyrkos latched onto the woman's wrist while Tana moved her hand to his shoulders.

"You allowed them to attack two innocent people. What are you going to do about this?" The words burned my tongue as I said them. I'd little concern for the Vyrkos, but the sight of dried blood on Tana's throat was unacceptable. The hatred these humans had for us should not stand. But I was nearing three centuries, had seen how trying to convince a closed mind was a fruitless task.

My question left the captain gaping, continuing to stare. More faces appeared behind him, crew members by the looks of them, and still, he remained silent.

I scoffed and so did Tom. He was the one to suggest, "Restrain them since they cannot be trusted not to try and fucking kill us. Let us disembark first when we reach the port, and we will all go on our merry way."

He looked at me from across the room, the slightest uptick of the corner of his mouth communicating multitudes. I nodded, and the wrath smoldering in my chest settled, placated for now.

No, closed minds were not worth convincing. Best to snuff them out.

The captain whirled around, glaring at Tom. "Are you telling me how to run my ship?" He didn't need to glance at his crew for me to understand this was again wounded pride. Was it their short lifespans that left them mercy to the misguiding emotion?

And Tom, cheeky as always, grabbed the captain by his chin, using every bit of the minute height difference between them. He loomed over the captain and whispered in his ear. Low enough the humans couldn't hear. "I'm most definitely doing so.

And then I'm going to plow you into the fucking mattress like the worthless slut you are."

I sighed, unsurprised by my brother's antics nor by the dazed and hungry look on the captain's face.

"Restrain them, now."

The captain was surely in my brother's thrall, heartbeat still quickened as he directed his crew to do what we said. Some of them retreated, to retrieve said restraints, and I pressed my fingers into Meline's back, finding several tense knots.

"Are you able to let them go, my queen?"

She startled and blinked up at me, and I released a breath in relief to find her eyes still their natural color. When they went black, when the power took her over more completely, that was when my queen seemed to lose herself, if my memory served. Had she learned how to control it in these three years?

Her posture didn't change, nor did her breathing, as she called the Death back into herself. From what I could tell, it did not fight her, and the presence on my skin slipped away until it was just Meline.

"You are amazing," I breathed and dropped a kiss between her furrowed, tired brows.

She had enough energy to snort, and when I pulled back her lips were flat, but her eyes held a lightness. Even with the heaviness of lowered lids.

A shuffling of feet and uptick of murmurs called for our attention, and I unsheathed the daggers at my sides. I handed one to Meline as we faced the humans, power pushed away for now.

The three of us, with Tom to my left, stood at the ready as the crew indeed restrained the twenty or so who had meant to kill the Vyrkos and Tana. Then the rest of us at a later time, surely.

Now, most watched us with contrition, perhaps even regret as they avoided our eyes. But there were a few. Like the brother and the others who were most arrogant, who did not bother hiding their contempt. Whether they were angrier at us or the

Vyrkos who'd now drunk enough from the woman to be satisfied, I was not certain.

She was fine, pressing a cloth into her wrist to clot the bleeding from the small fang marks. She didn't move to touch the Vyrkos further, but she gave him a nod and tentative smile before rising.

Outside of Frenzy, Lylithan and Vyrkos kind had an innate sense of when we were taking too much. The pulse would weaken, the blood would slow, and the urge to pull away would swell. In the name of survival, it was far smarter to ensure one's blood source lived to see another day.

By the look of him slumped in Tana's embrace, though, he'd needed more.

Most of the humans accepted their fate without a fight, but some required the threat of our presence to convince them to comply.

Our voyage was almost over, and the sooner I could put feet to steady ground, the better. Then, I would end the ones who watched us with hate-filled gazes as they were led above.

"What are you thinking about?"

Meline's question brought me back into the present, away from images of bloodshed and sating the need for vengeance within. I'd told her that revenge would not serve us today, and that was the truth.

When we disembarked, however.

My brother who was now following the captain, most likely to his cabin, would understand. Though he felt it less often than I, the centuries as Shadow made it difficult to let this sort of call go unanswered.

There was something else within me, though. Some churning within the hearth of my soul that would not truly calm until I slaked the desire.

Mamá used to call it Zoko's Fury. The side of Her flames that needed most taming, as well as respect.

Let it guide you. Protect you. But do not let it scorch all around you. That sort of inferno can quickly slip out of your control.

And yet, I had succumbed to it when first crossing paths with my queen. When I'd let the wall of Flames roll across my senses as I found her employer, a being intent on retrieving the jewelry from a different world.

Was giving in to that side of myself the first step on the path to my queen? Would I have taken the assignment to protect her had I been able to complete the contract I'd been given? Would the spark have ignited between us without the kindling of our animosity?

I refocused on Meline, the female who I wanted to explore… companionship with. No, not explore, not *try*. A small part of me had worried the image of her in my memories was exaggerated by my sorrow. Would the pull I'd spent most of our initial journey fighting still be there?

Dagger in one hand, the other clamping on the back of her neck, I kissed her.

It was more than pull. More than attraction and sparks. It was everything.

"You," I answered. "You."

Chapter Twenty-Two
Meline

My nose wrinkled as we walked through the streets of Vharas. "It stinks here."

Tana hummed and looked over her shoulder. I followed her gaze and found the Vyrkos walking in the opposite direction, simple bag slung over his shoulder. She smiled with nothing but goodness and cheer and raised a hand.

I watched him startle, then raise a tentative one in kind before slinking into the crowd. "Did he ever say why he was traveling here?"

"No, and I didn't ask. I'm just glad he made it."

"Yes," I internally rolled my eyes. So intent on saving that one. Admittedly, what the humans had tried to do was despicable, and I'd every intention to end them all when I'd seen the blade at Tana's throat.

Until El.

He and his Shadow brother were on my right, but the diversion of our thoughts was becoming clear as they engaged in their own conversation in Zonoran, heads bent together.

The contract.

The whole reason we were on the bloody ship to begin with.

Coordinated but not at all planned, we stopped as we

reached the precipice of the heart of Vharas. I'd been here before once, about fifteen years ago, and if memory served, there were several inns to choose from as we formed our plan.

But, I turned, a tender, fragile part of me was mourning the time with Elián. Our shared cabin while sailing from Morova was supposed to be a time of reconnection. And, while I did feel closer to him, less desperate to burrow my way into his chest and hide—so no a soul could tell me I didn't belong—there was still so much to sort out. To know.

For me to tell him.

I startled from the morose turn of my thoughts at Elián's hand clutching my jaw. I shivered all the way down to my toes as he kissed me fiercely, with hot possession as he showed everyone, myself included, that I was his. That he was mine.

"Tom and I have to go take care of something. But I will see you later tonight, yes?"

For once, Tom and Tana remained quiet, any protest from them flattened into the din of the crowd around us. It smelled like sea salt, rotten fish, and piss, and the shouts of the people of Vharas were just as unpleasant. It was a convenient city for ships to restock their supplies, to offload some goods. For people to transfer between ships as they continued to their destination.

One would think this would incentivize the powers that be to spruce up the place. But, it was just as unsightly as the last time I'd been here. Humans who'd not yet discovered the concept of regular bathing milled past, garbage overflowed in receptacles to the point that people just chucked their discarded items in the general direction of the piles. Weathered faces told of long work hours for little pay, and with the moon rising, they would soon turn to raucous entertainment and debauchery to distract from the filth and exhaustion.

My lip jutted out as I processed Elián's implication, but before I could answer, he bit it. His teeth weren't exactly gentle, but he drew no blood.

I clutched my fists into the deep brown tunic clothing his

upper body. It was the darkest color I'd seen him in yet, and still it was more vibrant than anything he wore in my dreams of the past. The deep opening that showed his chest was almost as revealing as the hungry look in his mango eyes.

So, I played. "Have you forgotten? We're enemies again, El. Who says we'll meet tonight?" By some stupidity on our employer's part, we were competing for the same contract, and my feelings for Elián did not eclipse my desire to *win*.

His expression remained impassive, but there was no controlling the flare of red amongst the orange. "We were never enemies. And we will meet tonight because I do not want to sleep in a bed without you."

Dammit. "And if I use the proximity to foil whatever plans you were concocting with your brother to fulfill the contract before us?"

El raised his brow. He ducked closer, stubbled cheek brushing against mine as he whispered in my ear, "You know that I am a better Shadow than that. You should also know that if anyone will be fucked senseless, it will be you, my queen."

My fingertips tingled beneath my leather gloves, and I gasped before I could suck the urge back down. But, just as I was able to draw letters into syllables into words, he was pulling away.

"There is a tavern I frequent when I must come here. It is called The Crow's Nest. We will meet you there for supper."

I threw my hands up in the air, exasperated. "Why does being together again give you free rein to tell me what to do?"

Neither Shadow responded to that. They simply wove off into the crowd. And when I whirled around to Tana, she snorted. "Come on, we'll find an inn that's more...presentable." Then meet with our employer, she left unspoken. Vharas was not a place I wanted to be longer than I had to, and with any luck, we'd be traveling somewhere else by this time tomorrow.

Tana and I started in the direction I remembered being most

promising, hope tentatively beating against my heart and wonder twining with my thoughts.

A few hours later, we found a suitable inn, one where we paid for two separate rooms and settled in with our things. It was not the airy lodging homes of Rhaestras, nor the fashionable rooms of Nethras. But the beds that were ours for the night were clean, and a small bathing room connected to both mine and Tana's rooms. In these three years of starting over—again—a private bathing room was worth its weight in gold coin. And then some.

Our employer made no mention of Elián or Tomás in the letter we received at the designated pharmacy, but we hadn't mentioned them in our last message when we left Morova. Either way, we were *going* to make certain we got to Paschal first. No telling what Blackwood wanted to do with our mark after we delivered the merchant to him.

But, as blades for hire, we weren't concerned with what happened after our contract was ended. No, we just needed some candid moments with Paschal on the journey to the man who wanted him kidnapped.

Tana and I took turns washing the nautical voyage off of our skin, and while I combed the short, wet curls on my head, I ran through the conclusion of our chase. Paschal wasn't hard to find, as wealthy as he was in a town like this, it took nothing but following the whispers of guards and riches. He had his own Vharan apartment, apparently, and if I'd dared to wonder if it was the correct building, the guards out front and back were evidence enough.

After supper with Elián and Tomás, Tana and I would wait until the late hours of the evening, when the most nocturnal of street creatures would be fully engrossed in their debauchery. Then, she would use a sleeping powder, something to incapacitate the guards without drawing the alarm of outright killing them. From the bit we'd observed, they had checked each and every tenant who emerged from and entered the building, and we'd no time to falsify the records.

From there, we would dispatch the guards in the corridor as discreetly as possible. And Paschal, hopefully none the wiser, would fall victim to the same sleeping spell of Tana's, and we would stroll out the back with him wrapped in a rug.

We would then meet Blackwood outside of the city. It would give us space to restrain Von Herron, question him, and hopefully get closer to locating Francie. At least some contact with these 'Folk' who took her.

With the sticky hair cream Tana made for me, I used a smaller brush to tame my curls into neat, swirling rows. There wasn't much to do with hair this short, so I worked quickly to leave it in swimming waves, setting them with a length of silk while I dressed for supper.

And if Von Herron were to offer us a pretty penny and some information in exchange for protection from our employer?

Now, that would be even better.

CHAPTER TWENTY-THREE
TOMÁS

"No, *please*—" The man begged, cries ringing in the darkened alleyway until cutting off into a despairing gurgle. The blade of my shamshir sliced him from clavicle to hip, and the rich scent of blood deepened even more.

The last three, it turned out, had come to us.

Including Viktor, their ringleader, who was now meeting his end at the curved blade of my favorite weapon. He staggered, gaze and movements panicked as his body spilled its contents, tissue and organs, from behind the tatters of his now ruined tunic.

Rounding my sword over my head, I twisted my wrist, as fluid as water, and brought it down again, slashing him in another clean, deep cut that crossed over the other.

He fell then, and I let him. Facedown in a filthy alley in a filthy city.

Nogón's kills were far more simple, quiet, but more than a week on that cramped ship necessitated some exercise. What better than taking out those who'd made the journey insufferable?

"Always the heads with you."

Elián had two of them at his feet, relieved of their bodies by the dripping short swords he now held relaxed at his sides.

Three humans against two Lylithans, the odds were never going to be in their favor, but time to stew further while restrained in the bowels of the ship during our last day was enough to cloud their last bit of reason.

And the humans, citizens of Vharas who milled by during the men's 'attack' and our correction of the problem, let us be. They did not scream, nor did they help the men whose bodies now lay in various heaps.

"Ah," I sighed. "Smells like home."

Elián chortled and shook his head. While he crouched and used one of the dead men's shirt to wipe off his sword, he teased me right back. "You like to show off."

To that, I could only agree. I shrugged and commenced cleaning my own sword. Certainly, a far more common dagger to the heart, a quick slash across the throat, would have been sufficient. But it'd been a while since I'd been able to use my favorite weapon properly.

"And decapitation isn't showboating?"

He shook his head again, but as we left the humans to be found or left to the scavengers, I nudged his shoulder with mine.

My brother had come out of Roza's womb a grouch, but a good vengeful kill always left him in lighter spirits. Now, I watched him walk with relaxed shoulders, hands swinging lazily.

Our destination probably had something to do with it. "You think your female will be mad at us for stealing the fun?" I'd seen her in action once, when she'd saved my hide in this very city. But, that'd been with steel and our own wits.

When she restrained those blokes that came for her cousin and the Vyrkos, she'd used something far darker than I'd seen before. The same stuff, I'd guess, she used to conjure those black daggers of hers.

"Maybe. But I will handle her." The lovesick fool *smirked* at the notion. She hadn't directed those black snakes in my direction, but even walking past them sent every one of my self-preserving senses into an undeniable state of alert.

"*Handle* her when she could steal your soul if you just glance at her wrong?"

Elián growled as we crossed the street, but it wasn't threatening. Fire was something one inherently knew the dangers of—don't touch unless you want to be burned. What in the hell did you do with *whatever* Death flowed through her veins? How was he not dead already?

"She cannot do that. And she would not hurt me."

"You mean she wouldn't hurt you again." The shot left my lips before I'd thought it through—though it was the *truth*—Elián certainly didn't like it.

He stopped us in the middle of the street as drunkards passed. A few paces down, some humans leaned on the facade of a derelict shopfront, scarce clothing showing off their bodies. A quick glance around and I already witnessed two thieves reaching into the pockets of passersby.

Nogón didn't say anything but communicated just as effectively with one look. We'd sparred often, been around each other for centuries, to the point that I knew him like I knew myself.

The way he squared his shoulders, face closing off, had never been turned on me this way before.

I raised my palms and turned back toward the tavern ahead. "All right. Your message has been received." We ignored the propositions shouted our way, scowled to deter those who dared to get close, intentions to steal from us clear. Most in Vharas, especially the central city, were armed in some way, so our weapons weren't the usual deterrent.

"You've never acted like this with anyone," I observed. It was one thing to hear of the hold this female had over him. It was another to see how she…soothed him. He might have been stony on the outside, but that Fire was always threatening to eat him from within.

But, godyx, when he looked at her, I watched the flames cool to a steady glow. They calmed in a way no other had been able to accomplish. Not his various lovers over the centuries, me, Nor, his parents, or even Leandro.

Elián grunted as we came upon the tavern, The Crow's Nest.

And of course, his queen and her cousin were already waiting for us.

Just to shake his confidence a little, I spoke under my breath at him, "Just let me know the date of the mating celebration. I want to make sure my diary is free."

As I took a seat beside the witch, I watched him scowl over the table at me, maybe in a bit of confusion, but I grinned right back. Meline and Tana glanced between us, questions in their eyes.

"Where have you two been?" The witch asked as Elián and his queen stared at each other.

I didn't wait for him to respond, just relaxed into the creaking wooden seat and answered, "Rat hunting."

The tavern was busy, lively with inebriated conversation and brimming with the aroma of hearty food. Humans clothed in sturdy leather and sun-weathered skin signified the clientele that frequented this place.

Our mark, however, was not here. I'd spent enough time with him to catalogue his scent. And the bit of reconnaissance we'd done upon disembarking, checking the various ships docked at port, sneaking into the offices of the customs officers who logged all departures and arrivals, proved he arrived. And with no planned departure for another three days.

"You got them all?" Meline asked, moon eyes all on my brother.

We'd mutually decided to not escalate the events of our voyage to the Vharan city guards. Though most around the realm were shit anyway, these were mostly concerned with the theft of the goods that kept their economy churning. A bit of intimidation and attempted murder of people passing through? They'd probably somehow make it worse.

"Yes."

"A few we hunted down, the nastiest three coming straight to us. A bit of swordplay to work up the appetite. And you lot?"

And the competitive air descended once again as the females shared a beat of silent communication.

Taking care of Von Herron tonight would hopefully lighten the mood. Maybe we could have a bit of fun before the long trek back to more desirable places.

When was the last time I'd visited the beautiful Sjatas? Or the wondrous desert of Banfas? Now, there some cities with good food. Curious little goods abound, like the wooden puzzle sphere Noruh brought for the lad after her trip back home to Trylas. They had such things in Banfas, and he seemed to like those more than the metal trinkets.

"We rented some rooms, bathed the ship air off of us."

Someone stumbled behind our table, jostling my seat in their wake. They were too far gone for a sharp word to matter, so I redirected my annoyance to the far less experienced mercenaries. "Sure. And what about the other hours you had? Care to share?"

Nogón and I had our descent ready to execute for the wee hours of the night. If all went according to our meticulous planning, we would end one more life tonight.

Now, he rested his arm behind his queen, and both of their bodies shifted subtly into each other. Besides the visceral Shadow urge to complete what we'd started, the drive to finish the contract now was mostly an afterthought.

"How about you share what you have planned, oh so impressive Shadows."

The queen's challenge went unanswered by my brother and me, just as they'd done to us, because we were nothing if not competitive. It wasn't even about the coin, at least, not for Nogón and me.

In a corner of the tavern, a bard took up a lively song, accompanied by a few red-cheeked musicians on lute and drum. Not long after, an adolescent came by to take our orders. There wasn't much to pick from the limited selections, but that was to be expected in a place like this where the main draw was a good brew.

Said ale came by quickly, as did a small cauldron of stew with four wooden bowls and spoons. While we took turns scooping out our portions, Tana, seated beside me, kept our conversation on lighter topics.

"Where have you both enjoyed traveling most?"

I used a bright red crab leg to idly stir the steaming contents in my bowl. Nogón paused his devouring of his meal, mentally flitting through all the places he'd been before.

"Zonoras, I think." The desert city had been hidden, just on the other side of a mountain range that bordered the kingdom of Banfas. My brothers' birthplace was small but mighty. Once.

Nogón swallowed his food and sat back. "I do miss it. Very much. I would say that or Ralthas."

I cracked the leg and plucked out the supple white meat from within. Yes, as far as we'd traveled in our years as Shadows, we still spent our days yearning for ghosts.

"Ralthas? Why there?" Meline was intent, leaning even further to hear Elián's answer over the roar of the tavern.

"My father was from Ralthas," he said and continued eating, but his queen looked... surprised. As if there was more to this information than the simple response that it was.

The initial question made rounds to the two females, though their answers felt stilted. I frowned into my meal. It was flavorful, but the curiosities around us grew. Though they had a pull toward one another, there was certainly a great deal more my brother and his queen had to learn about each another.

Aeras and Thryx, let this whole journey have not been in vain.

After the four of us drained the vat of stew, sucked the meat from every crab leg and swallowed every drop of broth, we had another round as the crowd surrounding us loosened.

Leaned into my seat with a full belly, I tapped my foot along to the jaunty tune. The song was poetic yet not overtly so, and several stepped along to the melodies with varying levels of rhythm. It was no comparison to the cool, dry nights underneath the blanket of Zonoran stars. Bodies moving with expert steps around flames swirling in a coordinated dance. Where the food was hot, the flavors were deep, and I was embraced into a family with no question. I'd only visited once, taking my acolyte leave with Leandro and Elián to see their mother and her family.

The next year, all those we'd danced and sung with were dead.

I smiled sadly, listening to the music, and as if our minds had gone to the same place, Elián turned to Meline. "Would you like to dance, my queen?"

After doing a stunning impression of an owl, she twisted in her seat, eyeing the writhing bodies surrounding the source of the music. The lute player's fingers were fierce as the drummer pounded at the instrument nestled between her legs. Fine music to move to.

"Ah…"

I thought for a moment she'd reject my brother's offer, one I knew he did not give lightly. But, eventually, she threw her shoulders back and stood.

The two of them went off, passing by tables until they were amongst the other dancers. The tavern itself wasn't particularly large—just an old wooden structure overlooking the water and ships passing through. Inside, with travelers and citizens packed together in the name of merriment, the energy was an animated thing.

To the witch, I asked, "Will you be going with them? After this?"

Nogón and I were used to this. Spending days or weeks alongside each other, then having months with nothing but written correspondence between us. The life of an active Shadow was a busy one, and though we'd spent these three years working toward the common goal of his healing and finding the love he lost, I was more than prepared to strike out on my own again.

The witch and queen, though, were attached at the hip, from what I gathered.

"I…"

We both faced the crowd, the music, and our companions as they swayed. Their cadence was slower than those around them, more intimate yet somehow also in time.

"I don't think so."

Huh. Though her words suggested ambivalence, they were said with a steady tone.

"Does *she* know that?" Because I'd also gathered that the dependence was not one-sided. Whatever guidance Meline provided, her cousin provided a gentle steadiness. While one was direct, the other provided a warm solace.

"I don't need her permission to go my own way," she bit, and I turned to face her.

"Plucked a nerve, didn't I?"

The witch wouldn't admit to it, but the blush that darkened her brown skin surely did. "We are more like sisters than cousins, joined forever. We do not need to be in each other's presence for her to know that I will always be there for her. When I've needed saving, instruction, she's been there. When she's needed soothing, *support*, as she lost him and everyone, I've been there. Distance will only strengthen that."

I hummed and tipped my tankard back, drinking the last bits of ale.

"*What?*"

As intimidating as she thought she was, the threatening tone was blunted by her bright eyes and golden hair. "I'm not the one to convince of that, love. I've not a care whether you and your sister remain on good terms as you inevitably move on with your lives. She lost him," I nodded toward them on the dance floor, "but she's found him again. Time for a new adventure for both of you."

"I don't mean h—" she immediately fought my assessment but cut herself off. Another bit of tension straightened her spine.

Eyes narrowed, I filed away the apparent slip. "Well. For your sake, I hope you already have your next venture squared away. Because they," I nodded toward Nogón and Meline, "will certainly want time and space to acclimate to a life together once this is over tomorrow."

"You—" she whirled around to me then stood so fast her chair tipped over and crashed to the floor. Which, seemed a bit dramatic for receiving a fair nugget of advice. I thoroughly enjoyed giving my brother a hard time, but even I knew when to pull back. And for them to give their connection a fighting chance, perhaps even a potential mating, they would need more than a few stolen moments together on a cramped ship or on a dance floor.

But, as I tracked the witch shoving her way to my brother and his queen, it seemed the moment would be even shorter lived than I'd thought. Because she grabbed her cousin's arm, jostling her to awareness and clearing the contented haze. I slowly stood, fingers twitching, as I watched them share harsh words, too low for me to hear, and with a narrowed glance at Elián, Meline caressed his chest and darted toward the exit with Tana.

Elián and I met in the middle, both our steps more of a prowl than the lazy strolling we'd had after our kills this eve. My brother seemed far from upset that his dance was interrupted, though.

"They are leaving to get to him first."

CHAPTER TWENTY-FOUR
MELINE

Dancing.

Dancing with Elián.

The notion was ridiculous. Absurd. And yet, his hand was in mine, and his feet were moving along with my march into the center of the crowd. Not too close to the music so that all conversation was lost, but not so far on the edges that we weren't immersed.

If I had to think about it, *allowed* my mind to sift through the vault of memories, I would more clearly visualize when last I'd done this. Danced in a tavern with someone I cared for.

I stopped and took a bracing breath as I finally turned to Elián.

Instead of the scowl I halfway expected from him, he approached me tentatively. Tenderly, with slow steps eliminating the distance between us.

He palmed my lower back, encouraging me closer. And of course, I reacted body, mind, and soul to my all-encompassing need for him. My arms reached up, sifting past his hair to clasp behind his neck.

Elián began to move. It was gradual, a few pulses of each leg, back and forth. But even that was enough to shift the form we created together, swaying us from side to side. Eventually, as the music around us continued on in joyous rhythm, he began to move his hips. Mine followed.

El looked down at me, not hiding a thing as he pulled out this very moment from what I *wished* I'd dreamt of.

When I'd visualized a reunion with my Shadow, I'd envisioned harsh words, punishment. At the very least, more groveling on my part.

But El was…kind. And fun?

"You never told me that you knew how to dance."

"Mm," he hummed while I ran the tips of my fingers along the nape of his neck. "There is much you do not know about me. Nor I you." And if to emphasize his point, he did something with the tension between us, leading my hips in a circle then back to his before resuming our swaying.

"But your brother knows these things," I accused. I'd no right to be jealous of the fact they had a whole language between them that I didn't know. But no one would accuse me of being unflinchingly sensible.

That brow made its familiar climb toward his hairline, and his hands shifted along my spine. "Not everything."

I'd no idea what to say to that, so I kept on glaring while allowing Elián to lead the dance between us, the circles of our hips.

"We can play your game again. Your questions."

My questions? "How many rounds of five questions will it take for me to know everything about you, then?"

Those dimples made an appearance, and his eyes shifted in color, growing a bit richer. "As many times as it takes. And I will do the same for you."

As long as it takes… there it was again. The assurance that this thing was going to last.

I slid my hands around his shoulders, down to his chest, and rested them there. My right held the minuscule pulse of his heart. "How many years were you when you got your fangs?"

"Fourteen years. And you?"

"Twelve." Elián used his grip on me to spin me around, to hold his front to my back. The lights in the tavern were dim but more than bright enough for me to see the reverie around us. The few interested or hungry glances flung our way.

Elián danced us like this, and goddess, I followed, eyelids lowering until I'd almost shut out the world. Anything that wasn't his body or his scent or his voice. I was cloaked in burning oak and cinnamon, and as if the crackle of flame, Elián's question was quiet yet clear as he whispered, "Your favorite food?"

"Um..." I swallowed, and the answer that came out of my mouth was something I hadn't tasted since Maman was alive. "My mother would make a...cake for special occasions. It had fruit soaked in wine and would come out of the oven black as coal." I let my answer hang in the air, twine with the melodies around us, before volleying back, "And yours?"

Elián leaned his cheek against my temple, thinking and dancing with me, until he quietly gave me his answer. "The breakfast I made you. My mother would make it for Leandro and me often."

My breath hitched, but before I could stumble our coordinated steps, El spun me around again, right on beat, until I crashed back into his chest. He held me to him, now both arms wrapped around me.

"What do *you* want from this? From us."

As if he knew *that* particular question would make me stumble, El slowed our bodies down to a sensuous sway, one with our feet planted on the floor.

He'd said he just wanted *me*. No—that and my *love*. How did I make him understand that he was already giving me what I wanted? I bit at my lip before answering as honestly as I could. "You. I want you and..." I dared, voice cracking, "peace."

And hopefully he'd be willing to give it when I told him the secret nearly dripping from my lips.

But I'd withheld it for so long, and I…I wouldn't do that to him here. I needed to find a time, when it was just us and after this contract was finished and we could—

Someone tugged at my arm, and I turned to find my cousin, darting accusing glances at El and pulling me toward her. "They're grabbing him *tonight*. We need to move in before they do, Leen. This is our *chance*."

Those insufferable—I glared back at Elián, and the male somehow kept his face flat and mocking at the same time. It was the light orange and yellow in his eyes that gave it away, that he and his brother indeed had everything together to pull the contract right out from under us.

He didn't reach for me, didn't demand we continue our dance. But these competing contracts were just another dance, weren't they? It was certainly the reason he dropped his arms around me while standing tall, unfazed.

I ran my hand across his chest one last time, down the center that was bare. My gloved fingers spread across tattooed lines. "You're an asshole."

And my cousin and I went off to take Von Herron.

Chapter Twenty-Five
Tana

I walked as casually as I could, right in back of Von Herron's apartment building. Cursing myself for leaving the sleeping powder in our room, I resorted to the next best thing.

The aether I called forth left my hands glowing, something that certainly drew the guards' notice as I drew closer, but I moved past them too quickly for them to react. My palm waving in front of their faces was enough to leave them unconscious, but without the blend of jasmine, valerian, and other herbs, the spell would only last for so long.

Hopefully enough time for us to grab Von Herron and be on our way.

Like we'd planned, they slumped at their post. We didn't want to kill where we didn't need to, and, like in many cities, no Vharans came to their aid. If we could slip past the ones inside without brute force, that would be preferable.

Something told me we wouldn't be so lucky.

I pulled the guards behind the stone fencing bordering the apartment building. It wasn't finessed, nor the most discreet, but we hadn't the time! At least their sprawled forms were partially obscured, and if one was keeping their head down or concentrated on their destination, they'd be none the wiser.

Meline emerged from the shadows of the alleyway, approach smooth and pointed, but my senses noticed another figure, a familiar note of vetiver, coming from behind me.

He approached at the same time as my cousin, but instead of passing by like the rest of the Vharan people were likely to do, he stopped beside me, hands in his pockets.

"Um. I'd like to talk to you if that's all…" he trailed off, and I followed his gaze to the sleeping guards.

Fuck. "Uh, Fenix! That's really not—another time, yeah?"

Meline was already grabbing my arm, pulling us to the door, but he bloody *followed.* "I just, I never properly… apologized. For my behavior on the ship." It sounded like it pained him, admitting that he should've accepted our help. But now was definitely not the time or place!

Meline shoved us through the door, our cover of stealth all but obliterated, and the three of us stumbled inside. There were two sentries stationed on this level, but the bulk would be upstairs. Even from here, I could sense them.

The expert stealth with which we'd entered that duke's home and taken out every one of his guards, him, and left without a soul's detection, was *long* gone.

I wrestled my arm out of Meline's grasp and pivoted around to Fenix. I roughly shoved at his chest, trying to push him back out the door. "Apology accepted, so glad you're alive, almighty thanks be to Rhaea, good*bye.*"

But he didn't relent, and the guards who'd been standing by the bottom of the stairs began walking over to us. Unfortunately, these two seemed intent on doing their jobs.

"For goddess's sake." Meline stalked toward them, shoulders back, and her daggers materialized, straight out of nothing but pure power.

Before the guards dressed in light armor could call for reinforcements or properly draw their weapons, my cousin's daggers were in their hearts.

Meline didn't bother pulling the weapons out of their chests. She just dropped her hands, and they evaporated, damage already done. The guards fell to the carpet on the floor, and I felt Fenix flinch beside me.

Why was he still *here?*

Meline rounded on us—him—and with a flick of her wrist, a flash of night darted at Fenix. I didn't open my mouth to object, nor did I block the attack.

Instead of killing him, though, Meline secured Fenix to the wall and silenced him with a band of darkness around his mouth.

"You better *pray* that I remember to release you before your life is drained." She didn't bother keeping her voice down, now that the rest of the guards were marching toward us.

Over my shoulder, I glared at Fenix, wriggling and panicking while Meline's power held him. I wasn't certain how quickly said draining would occur, and I wasn't sure Meline was either. But my frustrations were clouding my normal kindness. First his refusal of our help, then his mocking, and now this?

I didn't offer help. I didn't beg my cousin to release him.

Thank goddess I'd worn my staff at my side this evening, and I drew it now, willing the aether to fortify it. To infuse power in it to make my strikes hit with impact tenfold.

And we began, my cousin and I. We weren't dressed for this sort of work, but Meline had me train in all sorts of clothing, all sorts of weather and terrain. What we could manage in the short years and with limited supplies, at least.

Two guards approached us with unsteady feet, attention flicking between us and Fenix who was still mumbling frantically on the wall. I wound my staff in arcs, hopping it from hand to hand as they approached.

A few more, five if my quick counting could be trusted, were waiting just at the top of the steps to descend should need be. How many could I take out before Meline?

The two directed their attentions at me first, swords held at the ready, and charged. Over my head, my staff whistled in the air, taking flight as I batted the first blade of steel away and brought it down on an unprotected head with a satisfying crack.

I kept my staff moving, rounded, and swept my other opponent's leg out from under them. As they fell, I brought my weapon around again, swatting at their head as if it were a ball for sport.

Blood sprayed the walls of the stairwell as the body launched backward and toward the floor, a few paces away from their felled comrade.

My cousin elected to use her power as manifested weapons instead of the sinister snakes that could reach in and snuff out life far more quickly. I'd once asked her why, when we first started training and realized her powers had honed greatly. She'd stated that this level of power, of unearned death, scared her. That it exhausted and excited her too much.

When I looked to the stairwell now, she was still making far quicker work than me, already having cut down three guards with her dual blades.

I ran after her, keeping my footfalls swift and light, and joined the fray. She didn't *need* me, but as I butted the end of my staff into the chest of a guard charging forth with a broadsword gripped by two gloved hands, Meline used his stumble to transform her daggers into short swords, increasing her reach. The guard left his middle vulnerable as he tried to regain his footing, and Meline slashed with the left, then right, deep enough to be fatal.

And the fifth guard, stunned and gaping, I ended swiftly with the dagger I now always carried at my hip. A quick plunge to the heart, and the sounds of battle were over.

The body in my arms became dead weight, and I lowered it

to the floor now stained red and littered with a mess we had no intention of cleaning up. The scent of it was a heady cloud.

With a press of the familiar button, I retracted my staff to its more portable size and secured it to my belt. All while we approached Paschal Von Herron's door.

My cousin caught it before I did, what was amiss. Her hesitation was minute, a moment split between seconds, but it sent her expression from focused intensity into *rage*.

I noticed that first, then the same anger mirrored within me. Instead of crouched at the ready, we straightened, nearly stomping as we flung wide the door to Von Herron's apartment.

It opened to a fashionable if not bare sitting area, but our mark *and* the source of our discontent was in the back, toward what we assumed was the bedroom. We'd not used the full extent of our Lylithan speed before, but we used it then. And came to an abrupt stop as Tomás's form stood at the threshold.

"Well, hello, there, loves. Thank you *so* much for dispatching the guards. Made our jobs a whole lot easier."

"You—reprobate!"

His clothing was just the same as it'd been at the tavern, relaxed as ever. "Reprobate," he repeated, unimpressed. "That's the best word you can use, witch?"

"What about motherfucker?" I shot back while Meline shoved. He relented with a cackle, like he wasn't the seasoned assassin he purported himself to be.

My head was halfway turned, ready to verbally spar with him some more, our job be damned, but the glint of candlelight on steel had the words dying in my lungs. Meline froze, too, arms slack at her sides.

We didn't have to argue over Von Herron, spar physically or verbally to determine who would bring him back to Blackwood. We wouldn't get the chance to negotiate a deal with our mark that may work better in our favor, one that led us more directly to Francie.

No, with a plunge of sword into heart, Elián ended all of that.

CHAPTER TWENTY-SIX
MELINE

What. In. The—

"Fuck!"

The word didn't match the screeching in my mind, the incredulity. It came out garbled like choking on soot.

Elián pulled the blade from Von Herron's chest, where the man had been cowering in the corner, and he used the front of our mark's tunic to wipe his blade.

"What have you done?" Tana whispered, just as surprised as me.

My Shadow turned then, sheathing his sword at his back to cross with the other, and the movement stunned me even more.

An inconvenient wistfulness struck, right in the center of my long-broken heart, at seeing him with his swords again. He was not in Shadow leathers, but just the sight of those weapons ignited the pang of longing for those days, for an opportunity to approach our relationship, particularly its ending, differently.

But of course, the asshole wiped that away as quickly as it'd come when he raised *that* brow and gestured toward the body. Of our dead map to Francie. "It seems we won, my queen."

The sharp words were easy to call forth, then. My voice was clearer as I seethed, "Why in the hell did you *kill* him?"

El paused, looked back at the body as if he was missing something, and sent a silent question behind us. To Tomás.

"Because our contract was to kill the bloke, take his head to our employers, and be on our way."

That...that was not right.

I sorted through the details of our agreement in my mind, but the souls beginning to stir in the corridor and downstairs, they were more noise. Now that my powers were easier to control, I was mostly able to ignore the ever-present stirring of the dead who still clung to this realm. But this whole fucking situation had my wits scrambling.

The sound and scent of the tenants in the apartments surrounding us, pointedly ignoring the commotion for fear that the culprits were still in their midst, were even more to ignore.

Tana was able to vocalize the thoughts I still struggled to coalesce. "You...your contract was to *kill* him?"

"Yes," El answered. Without preamble, he pulled the dead Von Herron up by his hair and unceremoniously heated a dagger he retrieved from somewhere on his person. It glowed a bright orange, like straight out of the forge, as he cut through Von Herron's neck like slicing a pat of butter.

The heat of the blade immediately cauterized the cut, leaving a neat, if you could call it that, trophy to bring back to—

"*Who* is your employer?" I watched El toss the head to Tomás who caught it one-handed. He stuffed it into a leather bag at his feet and slung it on his shoulder.

"Few disgruntled competitors back in Morova, from what we gathered. Why?"

Tana slumped into an overstuffed leather chair, head between her legs. If I could've moved, I would've done the same.

But this defeat had a new flavor to it. I'd had contracts interrupted before—hell, I'd had a contract interrupted by *Elián* before. I was a competitive person, yes, but there'd been more than pride and coin at stake. What were we going to *do*?

"I did you both a kindness by not initiating a wager on our

victory, though it would've won us a sweet addition to the payment we're about to receive. How about you just treat us to a farewell meal before we part—"

I cut Tomás's posturing off with a harsh hiss and raised finger. One could hardly *think* when he was always fucking talking, and it was difficult enough to keep myself from throttling both my Shadow and his brother.

Underneath the soft leather coverings, my blackened fingers, the three that marked me as a vehicle for the dark side of Rhaea, tingled with need. Instead of the parasitic curse I'd thought of my powers to be, since the marks appeared, they yielded more to my wishes.

Death Wielder. I had the mark now, similar to the High Priestess of Rhaea, but instead of a peaceful ceremony supported by sisters under the beacon of the moon, I'd won mine through nothing but pain. The sort that scooped out my insides, every minute of every day.

Peace, I'd said. Freedom from all that plagued my heart and mind and leaving...what?

Even before The Killings, or scrounging together a home in Nethras, or finding comfort in the arms of Elián or my sister. True peace was a state I'd never known.

"Give us the head." I focused back on the bag swirling with an invisible cloud of the freshly deceased. It made my skin prickle.

Elián stepped to my right side, but I took as many steps away.

"Well, we aren't giving it to you."

Tomás crossed his arms and whipped his locs over his shoulder. Somewhere in the apartment building, a tenant slowly opened their door before promptly slamming it shut. The Vyrkos I silenced was panicking downstairs, listening to our conversation. I could taste his internal questions as if I was licking them from his lips.

I pointed, giving the dark urge permission.

And Tomás dropped his haughty posture for one of defense. His feet spread into a fighting stance, but against a weapon that transcended the laws of corporeal form, there was no fighting, was there?

The ache behind my eyes grew in intensity, as I held a portion of myself downstairs and here, but I had enough to do this. To take this and not *fail*.

"*Meline*," Elián barked, infusing his voice with command. But now wasn't the time. I pointed another finger at him, this one a warning to stay back, and even with every muscle in his jaw and neck tensing, he obeyed.

Tomás hissed as my power wrapped around the strap of the pack, retrieving it like a faithful pet. The Shadow stumbled a few paces backward, right into the wall, as I pulled his bag and the head back to me.

I rolled my eyes as I situated the leather strap on *my* shoulder. "I did not harm you."

"No, but the threat was fucking there!"

El Joined in, chastising. "Meline, that was—"

"Both of you, shut the fuck up," I snapped and beckoned Tana. "*We* are going." Because whatever piss-poor band of city guards Vharas could scrape up would certainly come at some point.

Thankfully, my cousin did not ask questions. She stood with me.

Tomás remained at the wall, but Elián loomed over us. And though exhaustion was seeping into my bones, I held my head high.

"You are not leaving with our proof of kill."

"I could give a shit about that. I'm trying to right what *you* have now ruined."

His fangs flashed and his palm closed around my throat. *Heat.* "*I* did not ruin. And you will not run." He exerted no external pressure—no, all of that was beneath my skin, swimming in my blood. "You've lost this contract fairly."

"*Our* contract was to retrieve Von Herron and bring him to our employer. *Alive.* This head is our chance to still get the information we need." Blackwood hadn't stated his intentions, but he knew Paschal enough to have some sort of vendetta. Some score to settle. If he didn't know where these Folk were, then maybe he could point us in a clearer direction. I was grasping at seawater, hoping to hold onto enough without drowning under its weight, but I had to *try.*

Elián went still, forcing me to do the same, as he searched me with unflinching intensity. He asked no questions, begged no clarification. And after nine shared breaths, his hold tightened a fraction, then released entirely.

I didn't dally, exiting Von Herron's apartment the way we'd come.

~

ELIÁN

I had yet to make full sense of what my queen told us. Why their contract, to be fulfilled with a live Von Herron to take back to their employer, was so important. What information they needed. But the wildness coming off of Meline was explanation enough.

Truthfully, the contract mattered naught, to me. The coin, I did not need. The honor, I did not crave. It had been a way to pass the time, then a path toward her, then... a way to spend time. With her.

Now, she led us out of the building, skirting around the bodies littering the corridors and entryway.

The Vyrkos Tom and I had seen stalking the streets when we arrived was plastered to the wall, snakes of Death holding him in the air and muffling whatever he was mumbling to himself, to us. He appeared paler than last I had seen him, his lids dropping over his enraged blood-red eyes.

My queen did not even glance at him. She flicked her fingers his way, and the Death released him, dispersing like fog disturbed and slithering along the wall and floor back toward her.

"You—what the *fuck*!" The Vyrkos, Fenix, sputtered, but none of us answered. I could feel my brother's annoyance, Tana's and Meline's determination. So, we ignored him and proceeded onto the street. It was not my instinct, to leave so brazenly, but my queen appeared past caring. With blood on our clothing, we joined the night.

Vharas was a seedy place, grimy in a way few other cities were, and if I had not experienced many of the horrors of the world, I may have been surprised by the apathy with which her people lived. The way they looked past evidence of how dangerous we were and instead reflected hunger for what we could give, what they could take.

We went on like that for some time, following my queen to the outskirts of the main city, then further still. We did not tire, and even Tom knew not to protest. It was then, however, Fenix made himself known *again*.

"I've been talking to you, you entitled *brutes*! You owe me a fucking apology!"

His fussing was louder, now that we were in a quieter area, yet he carried on with volume as if we were in the busy city center. I bared my fangs without turning toward him. His outrage was very low in my order of priorities, with the top being Meline, who held her shoulders high, fingers trembling, and soft, intelligible whispers escaping. Death swam close to the surface, even wafting off of her like smoke from a fire.

"*Hello?* I could have you *hanged* for what I just watched you do. *All of you!*" He yelled as my boots went from paved streets to packed dirt.

My queen spoke up, then. Even angling her head in his direction, to my left. Her voice was smooth, quiet and deadly. "You know now what it feels like to have your life slowly drained from you. Need I acquaint you with snuffing it out before you can blink?"

I held back a groan, grinding my teeth together instead. My thoughts ran to how it felt to hold her to me in the tavern. To sway together and pull her hips into me.

The Vyrkos sputtered, looking to the golden witch, now, but I was watching my queen. Her ass moving left and right as she prowled. Meline glanced at me, and though I kept myself entirely silent, she noticed the surge of lust all the same. Her gaze flicked up and down at me, sending another surge of heat I had to concentrate on cooling.

"Calm your Vyrkos, Tana."

The witch was beside her, and her glare at Fenix intensified, almost matching the depth Meline could access without a second thought. "Go away, Fenix."

"Not until you tell me what the fuck is going on."

"Oh, for Thryx's sake, let *me* kill him. Please."

To his credit, the Vyrkos did not back down. He jutted a finger and dropped his fangs, energy seeming to feed off of his anger toward—who exactly was he upset with? I had heard my queen and her cousin when they told him to leave. His decision to stay had been his own stupidity. If he kept on, I had no issue with relieving him of his head, too.

"No, I don't think I'm going anywhere."

Tana threw up her hands while Meline stopped. The rest of us followed suit, and I swept my senses around. The road was quiet, this far out of the city, and the yellow moon was nearly full overhead. The lights from Vharas were still too close to give a full visual of the stars, but their blanket was more visible here. Where the grass was long, and the road was little more than a beaten path from years of carriages and people walking. There was a thin forest in the distance, some mature trees and bushes swaying in the remnants of sea air, but little else.

Where were we going?

"Where are we going?" Fenix asked.

My queen snickered, but before she could answer, Tomás spoke up. "I'd...like to know as well, actually." If my brother was wary of Meline before, he was most definitely so, now.

She eyed them both, barely holding back a sneer. "*We*," she emphasized by waving a hand between she and Tana, "are going to our employer and trying to rectify this fuck-up." I grumbled, and she huffed. "You lot can come if you want while I decide just how angry I am with you both, but *you*," she pointed at Fenix, "will most certainly *not* be coming with us. I could give a fuck about some piece of shit Vharan guards. You think I won't slaughter every one of them? Kill you like I should have done on that fucking ship and leave your twice-dead corpse to the buzzards?" Her voice rose with every word, and those black veins were creeping up her neck, around the curve of her ears. "We have been trying to find Francie for *years*, and I will be *damned* if some self-important *child* stands in the way of that. Thinking he's owed answers when we. Owe. You. *Nothing*."

If my anger was scorching, Meline's was cold, so devouring that it threatened to consume all of us and her. The gold in her eyes flashed, and the veins beneath them deepened from faintly blue-green to purple, then black.

I felt my brother take a few steps back, something I had seen him so rarely do but now had witnessed more than once around my queen. Fenix finally seemed to understand the danger he was in, swallowing and raising his palms helplessly while retreating a few paces.

I waited, watching Meline's head twitch to the side, her eyes narrowing with predatory focus. Tana moved slowly, as if wanting to reach for her cousin but uncertain if her touch would be welcome.

"I...I just wanted—"

Meline's response was another step. She let the bag containing Von Herron's head fall to the ground. My cock stirred.

"*Are you fucking jesting with me?*" My brother whispered in

Zonoran, urgently and under his breath. But my queen was not attacking. Yet. She was watching, stalking.

I somehow tore my eyes away from her to glance at Tom who was going back and forth between me and Meline. "Do *something*," he urged.

I redirected my attention to Meline, to her cousin who was still hesitating and the Vyrkos who was now cowering. If my queen truly intended to kill him, she would have done so already. This was her…watching. Seeing what he would do. Maybe giving him a chance before she let her Death truly take over.

My mouth watered with interest, to see what she would do as well.

"You would just let her—use whatever she does to k-kill me?" The Vyrkos looked again to Tana, as if she would get between him and her cousin.

"Yes," I said.

It was the first I had spoken since leaving Von Herron's apartment, and the sound of my voice, of that one word, stopped Meline's slow progress toward the Vyrkos. Her face twitched my way, gaze narrowing to thin slits, but after a moment, of deciding what to do with me, they widened to half-mast. Her crouched posture straightened some, and I tasted the swing from anger to lust.

That sort of need, I understood. After that bloodshed and the wrath that needed space to rage, it was common for a Shadow or other mercenary to find someone to satisfy the lust. The jittery, electric feeling that tightened skin over muscle over bone.

But, now was not the time. I had not missed my queen speaking of Francie. Of their quest to find her. Though I'd known this search was in the forefront of her journey, she had not divulged it was tied to the contract for Von Herron.

Without words, I returned the voraciousness directed my way, calling my Flames to the surface, letting her know that I was happy to be devoured by her.

But, not now.

I slowly licked at my bottom lip, and Meline homed in on the movement. "Kill him later, Your Highness." I ignored the gasp from the one who did not matter. "Now, we must find Francie."

She sucked in a breath, smoke swirling. Deciding whether to stay or go. She opened her mouth, tongue touching fang as she made a blatant perusal of my body once again. The darkness continued to retreat, no longer winding around her freckles. "Later," she agreed and demanded at once. That she would not waste any more time on Fenix and wanted me to help her expel what coursed within.

"Later," I agreed.

Chapter Twenty-Seven
Elián

The Vyrkos was *still* following us.

Like a sullen mosquito buzzing around us. The way we tread led directly back to the city, so, unless he was completely helpless, he would not have gotten lost.

We continued to follow my queen as she veered off the main road, taking a thinner path that was slightly overgrown, returning back to the land. Tana spoke in harsh, hushed tones with the Vyrkos as he grumbled back at her, never once breaking off from our procession.

The witch was too kind, but Tom, Meline, and I had also rid ourselves of the responsibility of dealing with him. He could follow and stay out of our way, or his life would be simple to end.

Long reeds swayed, feathery tips fluttering around us. The shushed lapping of fresh water sang with it, and then, the bottoms of my boots met stone. The crumbled remnants of pavement led forward toward a dark, decrepit structure. Bringing into view the hill it sat upon, as well as the small lake below the ruins of a bridge. Stone piers jutted up from the water, alluding to what once stood, but nearest us, at the start of the bridge, sat a millhouse, suspended over the water.

Fenix's and Tana's steps were muted as we went, and I sensed a human, heart rate slightly elevated, pacing within the structure that was older than me.

I took the moment to walk parallel to my queen, glancing at her. Her power had retreated, no longer visible from what I could see, but I would be naïve to assume it was not close to the surface.

I did not feel remorse for killing Von Herron, and perhaps this was a reflection of my own selfishness, the need to win. But I was also aware this moment, this mission, was now completely hers. To find a lost friend.

It was important to her, so it was important to me. Instead of words, I brushed my fingers along the edge of her forearm, where her sleeve billowed as we walked. She did not react, at least outwardly, but I did not miss the smoothing of tension around her mouth.

A stale rank filled the air, and for a moment, I worried it would crumble around us. Old paint was peeling and flaking off the walls, rotten. Silver moonlight peeked through the slats of the millhouse, some boards fallen away completely. Rusted and rotten supplies were pushed to the corners, anything useful pilfered long ago.

We kicked up dust as we entered to face the human with sword drawn.

"What is this?" he asked gruffly through his teeth. His bald head shone smooth in the dim light, and his beard was a full, slate gray. A dark cloak obscured his shoulders but left his leather breastplate visible.

My queen sighed and slowed her approach. "It's fine, Black-wood. They are…well, they're with us and no danger to you."

He did not lower his sword as he chuckled dryly. "Seems as if I've been told that right before being stabbed in the back."

Meline stopped before him, within range of his weapon. I fought my worry for her safety, reminding myself she was more than capable of fighting off any attack that came her way. It was irrational, and I knew she would not appreciate the show of protectiveness.

It did not stop my focused monitoring of this Blackwood's movements, though.

Meline moved slowly, as if to not startle him, and reached in the leather bag. She held up a hand, wordlessly asking for calm and speaking peace. With the other, she pulled out Von Herron's head by his hair.

The man froze then dropped his sword to his side. He jutted a finger at my queen and took a step closer to her. "This wasn't part of your contract."

A glance at my brother revealed him to be just as perplexed as I was. What did this man want with Von Herron alive? And why did he need to hire a mercenary to bring him?

"I fucking know that. *We* didn't kill him." She did not need to point to Tomás and me. The accusation was abundantly clear.

Blackwood processed through what Meline said, watching the rest of us watching him, and I predicted he would become defensive again a few moments before he raised his blade at us. He crouched into a fighting stance. "Then you won't be getting your fucking payment."

Meline dangled the head at her side, jostling it as she argued back with their employer. "I don't care about the payment. We wanted information from Von Herron, and now that we don't have the opportunity, we are asking it of you."

"Why in God's name would I do anything for you?" He shook his head, angling toward the door. Of course, we were blocking the way, and the sweep of his gaze back and forth, calculating his options, revealed his anxiety over that fact.

Tana stepped up, hands waving in a placating rhythm. "Could you tell us what you wanted with him in the first place? Maybe we can help you, even with him dead."

He snorted, hands beginning to tremble. A human against four—*five*—blood drinkers did not provide high likelihood he'd be able to fight us off. "I'm leaving now." He said, and none of us moved.

"Blackwood," Meline growled, "we are trying to find someone. And we believe Von Herron had a way of communicating with those who took this person." The man stiffened, his heart skipping before he tried to bury his reaction.

My queen noticed, and he grew more agitated. "I don't know nothin' you're talking about. Now, back away from the door."

"Just answer their questions, mate."

Blackwood sneered, tensed muscles revealing his intention of charging toward the exit. I stepped in his path, drew my short swords, and batted his weapon away faster than he could track. It clattered to the ground, and I kicked it away. My eyes were sharp enough to watch it slide, partially underneath a decaying wagon, but his mortal senses could not find it. He drew one of the daggers on his belt instead, the sour scent of fear rising.

"You have an idea of who I'm talking about, don't you? Are they part of the reason you needed Von Herron?" Meline edged toward the man who bared his fangless teeth and retreated toward the corner, like a threatened animal. "Do you know where they are? How we can get to them?"

Blackwood scoffed, pointing his weapon that now trembled in his fist. "What do you want with 'em?"

"What do *you* want with them?" Tana asked.

I had no idea who they were talking about, but that predatory focus returned within my queen, and Blackwood was the center of it. Or, the information he held.

"He stole it from me. Needed him to break the deal."

Meline straightened, rolling her eyes and shaking Von Herron's head, which she still held. "Why must everyone speak in riddles. We will help you retrieve what he stole if it means getting closer with 'them'. All right? Can you put your dagger away?"

Blackwood hesitated, lip quivering as he silently spoke to

himself, maybe running through the assurance my queen offered, or assessing the odds of him getting past all of us.

The man heaved a weary sigh, his age showing in the husky sound and the wrinkles beside his eyes. He lowered the dagger while not completely relaxing from his defensive crouch. This Blackwood had a right to be suspicious—I would have thought him stupid had he not been—but he was also smart enough to know when he had little other options.

"Great! Now, what can we help you with?" Tana spoke as if she stood at a counter and was greeting a pharmacy customer, not offering a consolation service for a failed contract.

My queen pinched the bridge of her nose. Perhaps I would feel badly if my actions truly kept them from finding Francie.

"How are you going to do that? Von Herron was supposed to come with me, to rearrange the terms of the deal he cut me out of. Can't quite do that now, can I?" He gestured toward the head Meline had by the hair. My queen lifted it, glancing at Von Herron in his unseeing eyes and tilting her head, as if listening to some silent communication.

And, if by the otherworldly coolness that swept the mill-house, the gentle wafting of black smoke around where she connected with the dead man, she was. Hearing him.

Meline turned, as if following something, and I leaned toward her. To do what, I did not know, but the center of her eyes had turned black and expanded to leave just a thin ring of white around it. Eclipsed, but not entirely.

"You won't just fucking tell us?" she growled then sighed. Meline jerked her head toward the door and rolled her eyes again at the same time a shot of ice ran down my spine. "He probably deserves that," she called to no one and was unbothered or unaware of the confusion on my face, the wide stares from the others.

My queen dropped Von Herron's head, letting it thunk onto the millhouse floor. She swiped her gloved hands together, as if ridding herself of the sensation. With a deep breath, my queen dropped her shoulders and refocused on Blackwood who had slunk further into the corner.

"Apparently, you were not cut out, you were bested before you could do the same to him." Blackwood opened his mouth to retort, but Meline waved his argument away before he could give it. "I could give a shit about that. The important thing is, he so graciously informed me how to convince them to transfer the same arrangement to you."

"Who told you that. No one was talking 'cept for you!"

"Who the fuck else would I have been talking to. Von Herron's spirit was lingering enough to curse your name, tell me what I needed to know, and fuck off to the afterlife."

Of course. Death Wielder.

"Bullshit," the man cursed, and had I not witnessed the might of my queen's powers, I may have had a similar reaction.

"He said verbatim, 'Walt is a jealous old curmudgeon with no tact who I could not *afford* to include in the bargain, lest he offend them and get us both killed.'" The man went red from hairline to throat. "Luckily for you, I have the knowledge of how *you* can secure a deal yourself to…what? Be the one to transport their goods or something? Paschal was too busy chuckling about you being a cuckold, so that's an assumption."

Blackwood spat on the floor while Tana could not contain her giggles, even when she slapped her palms over her mouth.

"That fucker excluded me from a monopoly that made him richer than most of the men on this fucking *continent*. I took in the fucking street rat only to have him double-cross me."

"And fuck your spouse, apparently. Shame, mate."

I reflected on the information I knew of Von Herron, the wealthiest merchant in Morova, the region. They'd not said explicitly, but our employers had wanted him dead for the same reason Blackwood wanted him at his mercy. For greed.

"The Morovan textiles. This somehow is their doing?" I asked. Von Herron had his hand in the textiles now characteristic of Morova, but the iridescent fabric had not always been a staple there. I had traveled long enough to remember a time before such products were available, before even the moderately well-off were able to dress in trappings that glowed and sparkled.

Blackwood's body trembled, though not from fear. His fists tightened at his sides. "His agreement was binding. They wouldn't even consider working with me, pledging all loyalty to him."

Tomás crossed his arms. "And you want to be rich, not just make a living. Fine, are we ready to go?"

"Go where?" the Vyrkos asked, garnering a few glares.

"We will help you secure an agreement with this people who provide *such* wonderful fabric," Meline barely held back her scoff, "and protect you during such proceedings. All we need is a chance to speak with them about our own interests."

"All of us didn't agree to that!"

My queen hushed Tomás while keeping her attention on Blackwood. The muscle over his bearded jaw ticked, and he ran his gaze over all of us. I did not enjoy my Shadow duties that included guarding as much as I did the hunting and killing. But I would gladly participate, for my queen.

"You will guard my back as I make another deal, with no other payment aside from asking them your questions?" Someone grumbled at the 'no payment' part of the agreement, but we otherwise remained silent. The floorboards of the mill-house creaked beneath our feet.

Meline nodded sharply. "Yes."

Chapter Twenty-Eight
Tana

I was nearly jumping out of my skin, bobbing on my toes while we neared the designated coordinates of the fault line, the crack between realms.

I took note of everything I could, the craggy bark of the trees, the forest life grown hushed as we slowed to a stop. Blackwood had minimal knowledge, just how to get to the meeting point, but even that was heaps more than we'd ever *dreamed*.

"It's a bloody forest," Tomás remarked, as begrudging as anyone could be. His demeanor soured the further we trekked, and if I'd known a jaunt through the woods would shut up his usual teases and taunts, I would've suggested it long ago.

Fenix walked beside me, and he gave a grunt of agreement to Tomás's whingeing. It was such a curious thing, his insistence to come with us. After Blackwood agreed to work with us, we'd gone back to Vharas to retrieve our things, store them at Blackwood's house outside of the city, and pack all we might need for…however long we were gone. We could have paid extra to keep our rooms at the inn, but it was already a surprise our packs hadn't been rifled through when we got back. They surely would have been gone if we'd left them unattended for more than twelve hours.

And when we took again to the road leading out of Vharas, a few hours' sleep achieved and a hunt complete to tide us over, Fenix had appeared. Covered from head to toe in tunic, trousers, and a hood. His darkened glasses shielded his eyes, and I was only able to identify him by scent alone.

My cousin had given him a stern word about staying out of our way, but that was that.

It was two hours or so we'd been walking in these woods, slower than our typical gait to accommodate Walter's slower pace. Horses, he'd said, would not be able to come.

Meline hummed, looking again at her compass then the sky above. It was a pleasant enough day, late-afternoon sun descending and the sky a mix of blue and warm colors. Fat, fluffy clouds trailed by as the canopy leaves remained still.

"A forest to a different *world*," I whispered, unsure if these Folk could already hear us. Our guide grunted. Just ahead, a section of flattened earth was encircled by longer, wilder vegetation. The edges were too organic to be purposeful cuts. "Look," I pointed, "that's a good sign, right?"

"Yes, it's here." The other three Lylithans eyed the man skeptically, but I gladly followed him into the circle, approaching the tree in its middle. An ancient oak with deep, thick roots and enough branches and leaves above to block the sun almost entirely. The width of the trunk alone spanned at least three people wide. "You've still got it?" he asked.

Meline rolled her eyes, crossing her arms. "Of course." Elián gestured to the pack slung on his back, just under the swords sheathed at his spine.

"All right." Walter nodded, straightening and looking at the trunk of the tree. "We're here to make a deal."

The words held a weight, and the forest somehow grew more still. No wind nor sound while the air…pulsed.

Connected more than most to the aether, I felt the moment it changed. Rippling like the surface of water disturbed. Meline, Elián, Fenix, and Tomás, the most skeptical of us all, joined

Walter and me at attention, and we all watched, *marveled*, as the surface of the tree itself shifted. It was a subtle change, but where the oak went almost…pliable, a figure emerged.

Their movements were professional…as if they were unsurprised or unimpressed to be called forth, and then there was another. And another.

The figures stepped out of the tree, and I couldn't hold back a delighted laugh as I witnessed a form of magic I'd never seen before. Even the swords at their hips did nothing to deter my excitement.

By all appearances, these Folk looked fairly similar to the elven peoples who were fairly common in our realm. Long limbs, pointed ears. And they dressed similarly to us in simple leathers, though the breastplates of which were covered in interesting etched details, scrolling swirls and symbols.

"And what bargain do you have to offer?" The first one asked quietly, though it boomed between us. At once, it was a regular voice, and at the same time, there was a deep, almost musical note to it. My ears were entranced, curious. But the hair stood up on the back of my neck, and my lips twitched with the instinct to chant.

Walter ignored the question, maintaining a confident posture. But I could hear his heart racing. "Paschal Von Herron is dead. I would like to offer my services as a broker for your goods in his stead."

The leader narrowed his eyes, unimpressed but still interested. Judging by the fact they'd not left or tried to kill us yet. "Who?"

"The man from our world with whom you've settled a trade agreement with."

His black hair was shorn close to his scalp, skin a similar color to Elián's. On his face, however, were thin, pale marks, symmetrically drawn on his brow, cheeks, and chin. The two others behind them showed similar markings on their skin, though their hair and coloring varied. The tunics beneath their armor shone like pearls. "We know this. We felt our deal with him break."

"Who can I speak to in regard to another deal?" Blackwood puffed up his chest, arms crossed, though he was at least a head shorter than the smallest of these Folk.

The male was no longer paying attention to Blackwood, but looking at the rest of us. We formed a semicircle behind our employer, indeed guarding his back. He narrowed his hooded eyes. "Why do you have Raouga with you? Are you their pet?"

I'd never heard the word before, sounding round and full from his lips, but the assumption Blackwood was *ours* in that sense elicited a sudden snort from my throat. I tried to cover the chuckle by coughing, but I felt Fenix's gaze. Saw the tips of Blackwood's ears go red.

"*No*," he said, trying to stand even taller. "They work for me and are traveling with me."

The one in front, who had been speaking, pursed his lips, considering us, but one of the others took a step forward. Her hair was white and fell long down her back. "What do you have to offer for passage?"

Ah, this had also been something Blackwood informed us about! Apparently, he'd been present during the first meeting between Paschal and these Folk, when they'd first been denied entry and come back with gifts.

He swung the leather bag on his shoulder around and unbuckled the flap that fastened it. "Three bottles of mead and five jars of honey from the best beekeepers in the realm." He held the bag out, daring not to step forward uninvited.

The guards of the portal, though, they grew animated, ears twitching and shoulders leaning forward. Their expressions were otherwise impassive, but their interest was evident. Blackwood placed the bag on the ground, on the plush grass, and stepped back, deferring to them.

The one with the white hair crouched and reached inside, inspecting the gifts. When she pulled one of the bottles from the bag, it was an amber yellow. The honey, slightly darker, moved thickly as she tilted it from side to side.

When she stood and stepped back toward the tree, she took the bag with her.

Without needing to consult with the others, the first Folk nodded, and they retreated into the tree.

The five of us turned to each other, unsure of what to say, but Blackwood wasted no time. He walked up to the tree, hesitated, then planted his boot inside the trunk. The bark gave, revealing the portal still open, and then he disappeared like the rest.

My cousin was next to go, and her Shadow quickly followed. I watched, nearly bouncing on my toes, as they disappeared one by one.

"Fuck." I heard Tomás curse as I approached the tree with a finger extended. Like the others, it went into the wood. *Something* was there. Not resistance, nor a pull. It was similar to the barriers I erected whenever I had a room to lay my head down for the night, or when Meline and I had more permanent homes. That sort of magic was simple, then a bit more complicated the stronger or more selective you wanted the protection to be.

This was…

My skin prickled, and it was as if every hair on my body stood at attention. There was no darkness, no long tunnel or fracture of time. It was a doorway that, once my eyes had crossed and were able to see, revealed another forest.

This one was similar to the one we'd just left. The trees, the deepening sunlight as we grew closer to evening.

However.

Now, we stood on a path dug into the ground with trees reaching toward each other on either side of us. The type of growth provided a sort of enclosure, one that was almost suffocating, save for the gaps between branches allowing glimpses of the rays in the same shades of the mead and honey.

The Folk were already disappearing around a bend, with Blackwood not far behind. Meline and Elián were much closer to us, warily eyeing the vegetation around us, probably noticing what I had—that sensation of being watched. The pressure of an unseen presence.

A far more urgent concern, immediately drying my throat and sending a flash of panic through my chest, was the unmistakable severing once Fenix stepped through into this new world —realm. Once he was on this side, the bark hardened, and when I reached out a shaking hand, I felt the first true coolness of fear.

Because the portal was closed, we'd no way of going back without the help of these people we could not trust.

And my connection to the aether was gone.

CHAPTER TWENTY-NINE
TANA

"Um, Leen?" I caught up to my cousin, trying my best to shake out my hands at my side. Ever since I was a young child, I'd made friends with the natural magic of our world. The beating, the *singing* of it. It was inevitable, had always been. Many of us reasoned the aether was a gift from the Mother. To bring us closer to her, to shape our world as we wished.

The absence of it left my stomach churning and sweat breaking out at my temples.

"Hm?" Meline was frowning and assessing our surroundings, no doubt cataloguing everything about this world, so much we were unfamiliar with. She and Elián walked stiffly, his scowl nearly matching hers. Could they feel it?

"I—" I lowered my voice to a whisper, sidling up to her ear "—there is no aether here. I don't have my magic," I admitted, and tears began to prickle behind my eyes. It was like a limb had been removed from my body.

She immediately stopped, and the rest of us did so as well. "You..." she swallowed, glancing at Elián. Blackwood had not yet noticed we weren't right behind him, but no one made to speed up.

Beside her, Elián raised his palm and generated a flame that lapped at his fingers, licking toward the branches above. He furrowed his brow, and the fire grew slightly. I did not realize anything was amiss until he began to tremble. I could hear his quickened heartbeat, as well as those around us, and he bared his teeth.

The fire began to wane, to die.

He hissed, dropping his arm to his side, and the fire extinguished.

"*Shit.*" Meline watched Elián begin to pace. I'd not seen the reticent male display such naked emotion, save for when he held a dying Meline in his arms. His chest swelled and constricted quickly, and he was mumbling urgent words in what I assumed was Zonoran.

My cousin gripped his bare biceps, halting his pacing, and in his stillness, I choked on a gasp.

His irises were no longer glowing in the way I'd grown used to. Nor were they the vibrant shades of flames.

His eyes were a still brown, faintly amber, but that was it.

"What the fuck." Tom noticed, too. "We need to go back. Fuck this."

"I…I don't think we can," I whispered. Without my magic, I was cut off from any senses that could help me decipher how the portal worked. Unless the Folk allowed us, or we found another who had the power to open the door, we were stuck.

My cousin breathed with her Shadow, holding his gaze and wordlessly leading him to calm, but my morose statement caused his grimace to deepen. "It is finite." He spoke it as if it pained him to utter the word.

Finite.

Meline bobbed her head in a shaky rhythm, smoothing her hands up and down her Shadow's arms, but when she looked to me, I saw the fear. Her irises had returned to how they used to be, a deep brown, almost black, and I knew her goddess gift was stoppered, too.

"What does this mean?"

We all flinched. Fenix's coverings made him a mass of fabric, but even his typical sardonic quips were tempered. His deep voice was quiet with uncertainty, unaware of the situation but feeling the gravity all the same.

"Hush, you," Tomás growled then leaned closer to his brother. "Do you otherwise feel healthy?"

The Fire Bringer without his Fire twitched a nod to both Tomás and Meline. She mirrored the affirmation.

"Right. So, we get them to open up the tree again, and we leave Blackwood the choice to stay or come with us."

My instinct was to agree with the Shadow. Though he had no association with the powers of the Godyxes or the gift of the aether, he'd deduced the turmoil. We were trained fighters, them more than Fenix and myself, but to be without the whole of our abilities was more than concerning.

Meline's jaw tightened, and I was perfectly able to decipher her thoughts, the squaring of her shoulders while the corners of her mouth turned down.

I didn't object.

"Tana and I are staying to retrieve Francie. You all can go. You were never bound to this contract to begin with."

Elián growled, taking hold of Meline, and uttering a single word. "Nâ."

"Oh for godyx's sake," Tomás lamented.

I glanced at Fenix, and though I couldn't tell where he was looking, he faced me. "I don't understand what's going on, but you all still have to make some things up to me. I'm staying."

It didn't make sense, and I opened my mouth to tell him so, but footsteps and a harsh bark stopped me. "You! Do your job and *hurry*." Blackwood glowered at us from the mouth of the bend, one of the Folk just beside him.

The leather pack on my back suddenly felt twenty times heavier, the weight of our new circumstances lead around my ankles.

And yet, I went forward. Meline and Elián separated but stayed beside each other as they moved with me. We were without our powers, cut at the knees, and with Tomás and Fenix with us, we went forward anyway.

Wonder and despair warred inside of me, creating a nauseating flutter in my lungs and stomach. My skin warmed and tingled with the foreign feel of *life* in its most naked form, but the sweet scent of it was almost sour in my nostrils.

Water rushed in the distance, becoming a roar the longer we walked, and the silence was almost as deafening. No one spoke —not the Folk nor anyone from our party. Blackwood's mouth was nearly watering, either blinded by his pursuit of riches or mortal senses leaving him disconnected from how such a world felt.

Because with each step, my giddiness dimmed. With each step through this enclosed pathway between trees, my body screamed that I did not belong here.

My cousin and Tomás rested their hands on their weapons, Elián held his clasped behind his back, and Fenix's were stiffly stuffed in his pockets. Blackwood was the only one jauntily swinging his arms as he walked.

The crashing of water, like fountains poured from the Godyxes themselves, became even louder, and the light ahead changed color. From sparkling yellow sprinkling between the branches to white tinged with blues and greens.

I blinked, adjusting my vision as we reached the end of the tunnel of branches. The trodden ground gradually became white stone, and the further we followed the Folk who guarded the entrance between our world and theirs, my heart dropped at the…the magnitude of it.

As if floating between mountains, a kingdom stood amongst waterfalls.

Or, I assumed it was a kingdom. Large structures with long, pointed roofs reached for the pale blue sky above, and smaller buildings dotted around them. I tried to keep my breathing steady as we continued on the narrow wooden bridge that connected the forest and what I assumed was our destination. I squinted, cataloguing the water falling and mist spraying, understanding suddenly. Between the slate gray of mountain rock, this kingdom was built upon trees. Instead of a mass of leaves, there was a civilization.

We kept walking, droplets of water clinging to my skin and hair, wind never letting me feel completely steady. I hoped my face was blank, or one of concentration, but I'd not the energy to focus on it more than that. *Do not show fear*, my cousin taught me within my first lessons, but how could the same unwavering confidence sustain when I was faced with *this*?

"Where in the name of the Mother *are* we?" Fenix said under his breath. He'd stuck close to me, probably because the others hadn't bothered to ask his name.

"The Mother is not here," I whispered back.

Our crossing the bridge was not lengthy, but when we reached the end, I risked a glance over my shoulder. The sinking in my chest deepened as I took in the distance, where the forest was much further away than I'd originally thought. Hoped.

How were we to get home?

"These travelers from Vyrland would like to discuss trade," one of the Folk said to another whose armor was the blue-gray of the mountain. There were four of them, stationed at the end of the bridge with broadswords fastened between their shoulders. Like the other guards, their skin was a variety of colors, but the markings and pointed ears were there.

One with a shock of red tresses jutted their nose in the air, sniffing before focusing on Elián. "You have brought mortal flesh for the Queen?"

Blackwood flinched, but now that they'd said it…

My nostrils flared before my face scrunched. It appeared any spells I had in place were void in this realm, including the simple preservation incantation I'd put over Von Herron's head to delay the decaying process.

No one responded to the question, so Meline spoke with a shrug, "If that will help secure a trade deal, she can have it. Not much meat on him, though."

I detected the seriousness mixed with jest in her words, but the Folk nodded in earnest. "She will be holding court in the morning."

"Fantastic," Tomás groused, and I silently agreed with a frown. Another day in this place was not the best of scenarios. But—I glanced around and upward at what I could see of the city before us. Then, at the smaller areas below. They were also sustained by gigantic tree trunks, but the buildings seemed more…residential?

And, of course, there was the drop into white clouds between. Where birds cut through with ease, but I doubted a steady ground was just beyond the cover of fluffy white. How long would one fall until they splattered to the ground?

"And where are we to stay until then?" Blackwood asked gruffly, not as eager as he'd once been.

A guard with green hair strung in a collection of thin plaits jerked their head behind them. Their accent was thick, cutting the common tongue words stiffly. "We have a place for visitors of other realms. It is not used often, so you will be alone, save from staff."

I had enough sense to stammer, "We appreciate your hospitality," and seal it with an awkward combination of nod and bow. Thankfully, the Folk standing between us and their home returned it coolly.

Blackwood rested the heel of his hand on his sword, and I didn't miss them all focusing on the change in his demeanor. Nor did the widening of their eyes go unnoticed when our employer said, "Yes, thank you." Was such a pleasantry against their customs here? Was it that much different than what I had said?

More questions than answers plagued my thoughts as the portal guards left us in the hands of two of the guards from the bridge. What other worlds were there? Were their ways to access them from our realm, and if this were the case, was this known?

Our arrival to this kingdom in the sky did not go unnoticed. Further from the cloud bridge, we were under tree cover again. This time formed by the homes and shops built into thicker branches. Walkways made of twisted wood and grass allowed for multiple levels to the city and its inhabitants who stared at us with glances ranging from haughty disinterest to caginess.

The perfumes of their scents were itching my nose and the back of my throat, and I noticed a few who were close by wrinkling theirs as we trailed past.

And their clothing of thin, delicate fabric had the pearlescent quality coveted by more and more in our realm. What was almost exclusive to Morova seemed commonplace here. A Folk person in simple tunic and trousers was sweeping in front of what appeared to be a small café, and even their clothing had the pretty, multicolored quality.

If they were able to produce these textiles in such abundance, what did *we* have that they wanted in exchange?

The language of the Folk, somehow more dense and looser than the common tongue, prattled around us, and given the cutting glances we received, they were talking about us.

The city itself was magnificent. Beautiful in the way nature was literally woven into their homes. Butterflies in a variety of pinks and purples fluttered lazily amongst the people, and as we proceeded through even more extravagance, there were...there were some members of the *Folk* who had wings. Beating absently at their spines.

"We are here." Like the rest of the city structures, our place to stay the night was made of twisted and gnarled wood, but it was lighter than the shops and apartments we first saw, as if it'd been bleached by the pale sunlight. Actually, most of this area was. Made up of lighter wood, progressing to the most imposing structure of all. A bit obscured from my vantage point, a castle of white branches awaited at the end of the road.

"We are grateful," I tried, and the Folk confirmed my suspicions with a disinterested yet calm nod before they left us to fend for ourselves.

There was another Folk, with skin a pale fuchsia and dressed in formfitting tunic and trousers who smiled widely at us, the first sign of animation since we'd arrived.

Their fangs were like ours. "Hello! Welcome, weary travelers! We have rooms prepared for you!" They gestured with a flourish, and more Folk appeared from a corridor, elegant hands extended to take our packs.

All of us but Blackwood politely declined.

The staff, all clothed in the cream colors of their uniform, led us up a winding stairwell. The floor, walls, and ceiling of the corridor were all constructed of wood, but the smoothness varied from a gleaming polish beneath our feet to a richly painted motif to our left and right. A grid of carvings hung above our heads.

"You may select as you wish," the kind one stated with that same grin, "but we have one for each of you. Please come downstairs or use the chimes from your homeland should you need anything at all! We hope you enjoy your time with us!"

Blackwood thanked them, causing their ears to twitch and a hungry flush to take over their slender cheeks. And—there. A sharp, predatory shade took over their posture. Their delicate, long fingers, curled in, just a pulse, but it made me wonder how strong they were. We were still woefully unfamiliar and unprepared in dealing with these beings whose flavor of magic was so different than we were used to. Whether its presence itself or just the construction of their realm, the connection to *our* magic was cut.

Our host quickly smoothed their expression, straightening to demureness. Was this or the hungry gleam their true form?

Our employer marched to the room at the end of the corridor, staff member with his packs following silently behind. The five of us remained in the corridor.

"I-I've noticed some things that bear conversing with you all. Perhaps we can wash and reconvene?"

My cousin agreed, as did the three males with us, and we separated. Meline and Elián took the first room, slowly pushing open the white door. Tomás took the one across from them, and Fenix hesitated before opening the door beside it. I swallowed and spared one last glance at the now-empty corridor before retreating into mine.

Chapter Thirty
Elián

My skin was crawling.

This place…it did not feel *right*. The people, at first glance, were not unlike some of those in our world, but there was something about them—the way they carried themselves that was unsettling.

Not to mention the *smell*. Too sweet, too flowery, too much. My irritation that would normally come with the churn of Flames was eerily quiet. There was little heat or power behind it, but I wanted to scream. Attack something.

"Is it later?" My queen asked simply. In this room sporting an opening in the wall that showed another fucking waterfall cascading from above.

The bed was grand, the pillows were overstuffed, and the sheets were a light, iridescent blue. What really had my attention, though, was Meline's question. The promise in it.

"Yes," I said. She was experiencing the same unease as me, cut off from her goddess and the endless well of power we were both gifted since birth. Perhaps she did not feel as I did, given she often saw her Death Wielding as curse. But the way she backed against the door showed that she understood regardless.

I was raised to embrace my Fire, reared by other Por'Noga to respect and revere Zoko's blessing. Without it, I almost did not know who I was.

Meline wasted no time untying the front of my trousers, freeing my cock and giving it a stroke.

And I wasted no time flipping her around and pinning her to the wood with my hand on the back of her neck. She moaned as I hooked my fingers into the waist of her leather trousers and shoved them down. I crowded behind her and dipped my fingers inside her entrance. My queen craned her head back, onto my chest, while arching her spine, waiting for me.

So, I took her, fingers swirling and tapping as I fucked her brutally against the door. Amongst our preparation for entering this realm, I'd not been able to provide this relief to my queen, so in this wretched place, we took advantage of this moment.

My queen's fingernails dug into the white wood and sent flakes raining to the floor as I thrust and eventually spilled inside of her while her cunt tightened around me. Strangled groans of different pitches filled our room. Our muscles quaked.

I pressed a kiss to the back of her neck, below a perfect curl of her dark brown hair, and breathed through my nose. At least in this place, I still had the comfort of her scent.

"How are you feeling, El?"

My lips brushed against her skin with my response. "Angry. Disturbed."

She paused, curling slightly into herself. "I'm sorry."

There was sorrow in her voice, taking on the fault in this world as her doing, my discomfort as her burden to bear. "It is not your fault, my queen." I wrapped my arm around her middle, pulling her further into me. My cock was still inside of her, feeling her heart beat around me, and I nuzzled the bone of my cheek against her ear.

"I'll keep you safe, El."

The promise and the conviction within it made me pause. "We will keep each other safe. You are not alone in this."

My queen did not have an answer. We breathed, joined

together until the intimacy of our position enticed us to go again. Slower, deeper, and I hoped her crying out my name reached the ears of our Goddesses. Far away, back in our realm.

After tucking myself away and watching my seed trickle down the insides of my queen's thighs, we cleaned our bodies as quickly as possible. The rest of our companions, save Blackwood, were in Tana's room which was identical to ours. Her window opening had a view of a rainbow amongst the crashing water, though the colors were different. Softer.

Tana's blonde locks were wet, and her traveling leathers were traded for a flowing dress. The Vyrkos stood sentry beside her, still completely covered to protect him from the sun. But, for all we knew, perhaps the rays in this world would turn him into a murder of crows, exploding into a flurry to peck and pester and shit on all of us.

The air infiltrating my lungs smelled of roses, though no blooms were to be found of my scanning the room. Meline and I took the corner, and I rubbed my fingers between my brows, trying to calm the ache in my mind.

"Glad you could join us," the Vyrkos muttered, arms crossed and chest high. I remained silent, trying to decide just who he was talking to.

"You'll get used to it." My brother waved his hand. "Wait. Why exactly are you here, anyway? What use are you?"

"I can do plenty, you cretin."

"Really. Let's pull back that hood and see what good you can do." Tom faced me and gave that expectant look, demanding I agree with him.

I grunted, and he seemed satisfied. Before the Vyrkos could snap something back at Tomás, I asked Tana, "You said you had some information to share?"

She glanced at the male standing beside her then at me. "Y-Yes. So, as we know, there is no aether here, and judging by the severe reduction in your and Meline's powers, we can assume we are no longer under the guardianship of the Mother or the Godyxes."

It was one thing to feel the dimmed Flames within myself, it was another to hear the grim situation laid out so plainly.

"I haven't actually—um," Meline cut in, and we all watched her try to release her Death. The familiar black tendrils began to curl in the putrid air. Tom and Fenix flinched while Tana and I remained still, but before the snakes could reach more than a foot in length, Meline's arm began to shake. She gritted her teeth hard enough for me to hear them creak, but as she labored, the darkness—dissolved.

I could not keep myself from embracing her from behind. Instead of finding solace in the abyss of her, I attempted to provide as much comfort as I could.

"Well. I suppose that confirms it," she whispered.

Tana twisted her fingers in her lap, wrinkling the gray fabric of her skirt. "I don't know if this is the whole of their population, but it appears we're at the top of a very large...tree. Between mountains. I've not catalogued many differences, but some of these Folk are winged, some are not. They also enjoy honey and...corpses, apparently. I'm not sure why, but they are disquieted by the words, 'Thank you', but not necessarily the sentiment behind the words. We should avoid saying them whilst we're here. We have our weapons and training at our disposal, but we don't know what magic they may have at *their* disposal."

The Vyrkos coughed, and I reluctantly dragged my attention to him. Underneath the cover of his mask, he spoke with hands behind his back. "I haven't had the chance to try, but they smell...I don't think I'll be able to feed from them."

"Oh, *fantastic*. Now we have to worry about the lad starving."

I had not even—I shook my head, trying to clear the forced sluggishness this world was trying to impose. Like every bit of soft light and odorous breath were lulling one into a false state of calm. We all fed before crossing the threshold, and we Lylithans would be fine for another week. The Vyrkos, however…perhaps three days?

"I brought my own reserves, prat. I'll be fine, so long as we don't stay here for more than a week. After that, I may just feed from Blackwood."

"What Fenix is *trying* to tell you all," Tana sent him a smile, and though I could not see his face, I watched his posture relax, "is that they are not mortal. Obviously, we do not know with total certainty, but it's all we have."

A world of immortals.

Though I was one myself, the thought of a place such as this only stirred the panic I was fighting so hard to quiet. We still had no inkling of where or *if* Francie was here. Last night, Meline and Tana had told us more about what they gleaned from the Mind Walker, Grimm, but even that was flimsy. It was not nearly enough to go on when we were somewhere like this. Where danger felt so close yet under a diamond veil.

Would we find a way to go back before Frenzy set in? Blackwood would surely not be able to sustain all of us.

I was lost in my thoughts on the matter, so the cheery knock on the door was more of a surprise than it should have been. Fenix flinched while the rest of us swung our gazes to the door. Tana stood, trying her best to still the wringing of her hands. She took a pointed exhale and twisted the knob, revealing one of the staff. From what I could see in the corridor, there were others at our rooms, each one holding trays with small vases of fucking flowers and pink cloches.

"The finest spring vegetables in all of Pyrestan, along with fresh baked bread topped with a jam made from our fruit, similar to your strawberries."

Tana took the tray, murmuring, "We appreciate it," and the sentiment was met with a shallow bow. The others marched into the room, lining our trays on the sideboard beside Meline and me.

It smelled foul.

The witch was all pleasant grins as the staff left, continuing to give the very specific way to thank them for their hospitality. Once they were gone and out of earshot—hopefully—Tom prowled to the nearest rose-gold cloche and snatched it off.

"Oh fuck," he covered his nose with a ringed finger, "why does it smell like that?"

I mostly tasted leather as I blocked the stench from entering my body, but from what I could still detect, it was like…rotten fruit. Too sweet.

They did not tell us the names of the meat sliced thinly on a ceramic plate, nor the vegetables, but they resembled asparagus, carrots, and radishes if they were unnaturally bright. The bread appeared soft, but I had no desire for any of it.

Tomás was about to cover the food, but Fenix appeared beside him, knocking the cloche away so he could smell it even more. Back turned toward the window and fingers forming a dome around his nose, the Vyrkos pulled down his mask. Just slightly, but enough for him to take a pointed inhale of our supper.

He was the one to cover it before stepping back beside Tana. "Smells fine to me. More appetizing than our mortal food back home, which is…strange."

I watched Tana's gaze swim somewhere between us, running over this new piece of information. Because of their dead state, Vyrkos were removed from their mortal reliance on food to the point that consuming such yielded no nutrition. From the few I'd talked to, they described food as dead, spoiled.

"Do you think that difference has something to do with you being a changed mortal?"

"Ah, I think it's likely." The Vyrkos startled at Tana's attention, clearing his throat and stuffing his hands in his pockets. "Considering our race differences, that seems the likeliest of explanations."

Tomás gave a long eye roll, wherein his irises and pupils disappeared completely. Meline's snort shook us both. "So, they are born immortals and have shit food. We've packed enough dried meat and fruit to last us a week at most. And that's if we are bordering on starving. Unless you want to hunt us their version of a deer," she nudged me gently with the back of her head, "we have that long to find Francie."

"And this schoolmarm could be anywhere," Fenix concluded.

TOMÁS

What a shit place with disgusting food.

The buttery sunlight finally died a few hours after the staff at the lodging house brought that retched supper. I could still taste it in the back of my throat, like they were choking me with it. Or, perhaps that was the cloying aroma permeating every nook and cranny of the city.

Pyrestan, they called it.

Wherever we were, it did not sit well. The tree they constructed their home out of was magnificent, yes, a true feat of engineering. The rich yet airy fabrics they used to dress their tall and slender forms ought to have been painted. Recorded in artwork that would still not capture the celestial beauty of it all.

But I'd been alive long enough to know when I was being presented with lip color slapped on a hog.

"They do a good bit of staring here, don't they?"

"We are from a different world. Would you not be staring?" Now that darkness had descended, the Vyrkos boy did not have to cover himself from head to foot. He waved affably at a set of female Folk, and they giggled in response. They both had wings that fluttered behind them, throwing the light of the lanterns hanging on the shopfronts.

Nogón's queen and her cousin were speaking quietly as we walked, heads together, and my brother was on my other side. We had no true destination, other than to explore and see if we caught a whiff of a Lylithan named Francie. One who another mercenary suspected was kidnapped to this realm.

Instead of cursing myself again for going along with this fool's errand, I sniped back at the Vyrkos. "Perhaps a bit of flirtation would bring us closer to finding her whereabouts, but before you go and fuck one of them, perhaps decide if that will bring *you* closer to *your* end goal."

Elián snickered, or his version thereof, and the Vyrkos turned a curious shade of white tinged with pink. Almost like some of these Folk, here. His fangs dropped like an ill-trained child. "I've no end goal aside from making you gossiping schoolgirls pay for what you did to me."

"Oh, please, spare us." I lowered my voice because I wasn't a complete arse, "You want a taste of the witch there because she saved your hide from meeting the Mother. You'll be getting no apologies from any of us."

He grumbled more insults, more denials, but I quickly lost interest. Music was playing in the streets, some Folk ate outside, drinking honey-colored liquor from elegant glasses. My stomach rumbled, but I pushed my hunger out of my mind. After slyly chucking our supper out the window to join whatever awaited at the bottom of the mountains, we mutually decided to not eat what was given to us.

Of course, upon checking on *their* employer, Meline and Tana found he was retiring early after ingesting all of his supper and his ordered seconds. The Vyrkos boy said to his formerly mortal senses, the food smelled pleasant. To the very mortal Walter Blackwood, that appeared to be the case as well.

Curious.

We proceeded past stores, past places for dancing, but aside from cursory looks, we didn't indulge in what these people had to offer. But I did notice more of the staring. Outside of a tavern where patrons drank and laughed jovially like the plucking of a harp, they also cut glares at us as we walked past. Wrinkled their noses or grimaced before hiding it with a smile or turning away.

Fenix, on the other hand, garnered a different sort of interest.

His way, these Folks' smirks took on a note that could only be labeled as rapacious. They leaned forward, wings tightening. Some even approached, introducing themselves by names such as Clover or Sebastian. Blushing and taking drawing inhales too close than was proper.

To Fenix's credit, he didn't incite a predicament for us by insulting these creatures who may or may not have been powerful enough to pose a threat. But I'd wager those fangs weren't for appearances. Whilst we browsed a small shop, he glanced at the witch with longing glazing his red eyes. At the same moment, a particularly handsy Folk with a gossamer slip of a dress placed a hand on his shoulder. He politely declined their offer of spending time with him, but as he worried about an unaware Tana's reaction, I saw the Folk apply pressure to their hold on him. Their nostrils flared with something other than lust, and their charm slipped. "Well, how about your name, handsome? May I have at least that?"

Fenix's brows furrowed as he used a bit more force to wrench his shoulder out of their grip. He opened his mouth, but I pulled him along with us before he could answer.

"They looked as if they wanted to eat you, mate. And not in a manner that yields release."

He twisted his neck, looking back with no finesse at all, and the Folk waved, eyes crinkling and dimples showing. "I think they were just interested?"

"You don't sound so sure."

He swallowed, knot in his throat bobbing. "No. Bloody strong, though."

We steered even clearer of the Folk, ignoring all offers to come inside because we *just* needed to see the wondrous jewels mined in their very own mountains, or the music that seemed to draw Fenix's feet without his leave. The first time it happened, his drifting toward the sound of lutes and lilting voices coming from a tavern sporting pillar-like branches around the entrance, I'd assumed it was incoordination on his part. Not everyone was trained to become masters of their own body, I knew this, but the third and fourth times it happened, I suspected it was outside of his control.

If this was how he responded to this place, these people, did Blackwood stand a fucking chance of gaining the upper hand in a negotiation? How had our former mark accomplished such a lucrative arrangement?

As I steered the Vyrkos away from yet another musical invitation to imbibe and dance, having to go so far as clamp my hands around his shoulders and push him to follow the queen and witch, for some reason, I thought of the lad back at the Well.

We'd sent a letter to inform him and Nor about where we were going—as if they would be any help in a place like this with the only entrance being a random fucking tree trunk in a forest—after his last was filled with his typical cheery anecdotes. The one addressed to me asked some terribly naïve questions about how to get in someone's good graces, and because I couldn't have him embarrassing himself or me, I'd spent nearly an hour in the Vharan pharmacy drafting a response.

"Oi, when is that summer ritual?"

The witch had already been eyeing me and the Vyrkos, question in her stare that we mutually decided to leave unanswered with all of these fuckers with pointed ears in hearing range. But *my* question had her perking up. She gestured to the pack slung across her front and bumping against her hip by jostling the strap. "It's technically today. I was hoping we could find somewhere suitable to burn these, but if we don't, we can use one of the hearths back at the lodging home?"

She looked to Elián then shook herself, refocusing ahead as we meandered the dark streets. There were some grassy areas, somehow built into godyx-damned tree branches, even recreational areas lined with wooden benches and floating lanterns to light the way.

No idea how the fuckers didn't fly into them, seeing as they barely watched where they were going as it was. More than a few times, a Folk person with wings clipped one of our shoulders or sprinkled some sort of dust over our heads as they flew above.

We walked the length of the city, save for the palace grounds which were heavily guarded, and returned to the lodging house with our pouches of protection still unburned and sealed in Tana's pack. I'd not done the ritual before, obviously, but it seemed a terribly intimate thing. To so blatantly ask the Mother and Her children to protect those you cared for. In front of an audience of Folk, who I was fairly certain wanted to consume Fenix, did not seem the best choice for such a thing, and the witch had agreed.

So, we were back in her room, where the waterfalls that I now knew glowed in faint blues and greens, lit the room. Until, after peering at one of the small orbs hanging beside her bed, the witch caressed it with the curious tip of a finger.

The lantern released a soft, yellow light, casting our faces in a strange mix of shadows and sending sharp cuts of technicolor where it collided with the mist from the waterfall.

My brother went to the hearth, inspecting it with narrowed focus, and released a drop of flame. I'd watched my brother ignite countless fires over our lives. Some necessary, some for fun to see how things would burn, and some to expel the emotions he was experiencing. Those would grow particularly hot, turning white or even blue.

During the years after Roza's death, he and Leandro would disappear into the forest together, returning with the smell of flames choking all who brushed past them. And I followed the twins, once, when they went far, far away from the Well, released their fire on boulders, and *screamed*.

Now, my brother was cut off from his goddess, Zoko who supplied the endless fuel, and when he stood, I tried my best to communicate understanding. Without the ever-changing color in his irises, the Fire that lived inside of him, he was…sunken. Underwater.

"Right, so here are all your pouches." Tana spread them out on the bed, remembering somehow whose was whose when we hadn't labeled them at all. I'd made two, while we were biding our time on the Morovan ship, and she grouped them together nearest the corner of the tightly made bed.

Meline snatched up her two, and my brother took his. Leaving the witch with two as well, but she didn't take them both. Instead, she offered one to Fenix, grinning from ear to ear. "Here, you can use this one."

He began to reach for it, hesitated, then stuffed his hands in his pockets once more. "Nah, I don't even know what…" He shook his head. "It's fine."

But Tana was undeterred. I slumped into one of the white, ornate chairs in the room, already seeing where this was going. Meline and Elián took the other seats, staring at each other with longing and fear and love, and whatever else newly reconnected lovers did. She caressed him, ran her fingers through his hair, and he…let her do it. Opened up for her, showing so vividly the emotions he typically locked down. I could only see the edges, while his attention was on her, but even that was more than I'd seen from him through most of our lives. It was burn rocks, drink, or retreat with him. Without fail.

Now, he let himself be kissed with a care that made my throat tighten. Bloody wood in here was burning with more of that godyx-awful perfume.

"So, where are you from, Fenix?" Tana asked companionably while guiding him through the sprigs and herbs to choose from.

He was perched on the edge of the bed, as if he couldn't bear to be closer to her but also couldn't fathom not taking that inch. "Um, Vharas, actually. That's why I was, uh, on the ship. With you all."

Tana hummed, holding flat her palm for Fenix to give her the leaf and flowers he selected. She met the small instant of skin contact with a genial, reassuring smile, and started talking him through tying the sachet. Her attention was on the twine and the cotton, but I saw the way he melted.

Stubborn, wanting nothing less but needing nothing more.

He hung on every sunny word from her mouth, fumbled his way through tying off the pouch himself, and when she instructed him to think of someone he wanted to speak protection over, I would bet my immortal life savings on who he picked.

"I'm really glad you're here, Fenix," Tana said absently, and it took everything in me not to groan. Instead, I silently slapped my forehead and looked to my brother and his lover. Those brows were raised, while his queen was doing the opposite.

The Vyrkos stammered, so entranced by the witch and her words that he didn't take in our blatant eavesdropping. "Uh-um, thank you." And the bastard even *blushed*. Lad was going to embarrass himself with this witch who saw him as a patient of hers and nothing more.

"How many years are you?"

My sardonic question unraveled whatever spell she was unwittingly putting him under, and his hair swung as he swiveled to me. He clenched the pouch in his fist but not tight enough to crush what was inside. "Thirty years. What's it matter?" The room swelled with silence, even the fire ceased crackling.

And I burst into tears, laughter. Thirty *years*? I figured the lad was young, but he was basically the same age as our *ward*. What did he think he was going to do with a witch who'd been saving lives for centuries before he was even *born*? I wasn't the biggest fan of her and her meddling ways, but what was he, a *child*, going to do with a female like her?

"Well," Tana cleared her throat and finally took up her pouches, "we've all been thirty years, once. You already seem— wiser than I was at that age."

Her poor attempt at pacifying him just made me descend into

more snickers, which made him angrier, like a babe toddling around and throwing tantrums. No wonder he'd thought it a good idea to glom onto a journey with Lylithans he didn't know, all for a chance to be around someone far out of his range. "Oh, godyx, I needed that. Thanks, lad."

"I'm not a *'lad.'*"

"Sure you are. I've got boots older than you. Embrace it." I slapped him on the back as we all stood before the hearth. "Perhaps we'll give you an easier go, now that we all know immaturity is at play."

He mumbled under his breath, something about wondering what our excuses were, but it was all in good fun. Something we desperately needed in this unknown realm. Where we had no clear path to the caregiver our young acolyte had lost.

When we'd gone to the children's home, me and Nogón, Whitley and their sister, Lydia, met with us in the small courtyard outside. The children buzzed about, playing by themselves or being nosy in the way children were, but despite the caregiver's best efforts to care for the children, I smelled the grief in the air. The longing for their mate that Whitley sang with each heartbeat. The life they created with their family, with hands still painted by mating marks.

I'd no opportunity to interact with this Francie, but by the devotion of their mate and the fondness with which Marco spoke of her, she was important. To Meline, the witch, Nogón, the lad, and me because she was important to all of *them*.

"So, you can utter the names aloud if you wish, or you may silently recite them to yourself. Either way, the most important parts are the name, your prayer of well-being, then throwing the sachet on the fire to release it."

No one spoke theirs aloud, but the names coursed around the room nonetheless. Like the breeze flowing from the valley surrounding us. Lost beneath the roar of the water outside that was slowly becoming a dull crashing to my acclimating senses, our prayers were silent mutterings.

Shadow magic was sacred, as my brother liked to remind me, though not nearly as intricate as the sort Tana wielded to drive out sickness or stave off death. But even my slithering, whispering vow was quieted, here. What use this ritual would have when our Mother and Godyxes would not hear it, I was unsure. Could they see us now, in this strange place with these beings of pointed ears and famished beauty? Were they still guiding us with Their all-knowing hands?

I was an adopted child of Zoko but a born follower of Thryx and Aeras. The Twin Godyxes were those of reason, ingenuity, finesse, and craft. They were the most knowledgeable of the five Siblings, if legend were to be believed, but were They aware of this place outside of Their reach?

I felt the pouches in each of my hands, rolling them like the smoothed stones from the Ralthan riverside that I still kept in my room at the Well. The names I selected, the two I wished more protection than for myself, formed a chant in my thoughts as I watched the others toss their pouches in.

Sage, lavender, chamomile, thyme, and other aromas I was familiar with but couldn't name filled the room. For a moment before the scent shifted to the next, and the next, while we all enacted this ritual that was as personal as it was communal.

And rather than berating my comrades to divulge who they cast their spells for, I made another, beseeching prayer to Thryx and Aeras. To the Godyx of Technology and Innovation, I asked for wit, for the lad to have knowledge and continued learning. To take no shit and keep thriving.

And to the Godyx of Love, Art, and Wisdom, I asked for my brother's heart to be protected. For this love to be the safe and nurturing comfort he'd needed all his life. Since his parents were taken from him, since his brother was taken from him.

I asked my Godyxes to protect not only Marco and Nogón's lives but also their spirits.

Chapter Thirty-One
Meline

The five of us formed another wall of protection around Blackwood. Or, the best we could manage in a sea of Folk who were mostly strikingly tall, unwilling to provide us substantial berth as we awaited for the palace guards to open the gates, or trying again to steal the attention of Blackwood and the Vyrkos.

Granted, their attempts were more surreptitious here, hushed and coy instead of the propositions Fenix received the evening before. He was rightfully wary, now, sun protection providing the added benefit of an informal shield.

Our employer, however, was positively gleeful from the attention. When I'd tried to advise him on how to approach this queen, using Von Herron's warnings for tactful negotiation, our employer swiftly disregarded any expertise I may have had on the matter. And now, Blackwood had a full flush spreading on his bald head. His mustache twitched with each guffaw of a man assured he was about to get everything he'd ever wanted.

Now, why was I suspicious this would not be the case?

The guards in white armor, markings on their faces twining in elegant curls instead of the harsh lines of the ones near the portal or at the entrance to the city, stepped back and opened the golden gate. Leaves, roses, and thorns decorated the barrier that was at least four times as tall as Elián. The Folk around us clamored forward, and we tightened our formation behind Blackwood, fulfilling this part of the deal we struck.

What sway Blackwood had with a foreign queen, I doubted immensely. But we *would* be getting answers here. There was no other outcome I was willing to accept. Though they agreed to come, I led the charge to this land. Stripped Elián of his Fire.

If this journey did not end with us entering our realm with Francic in tow, I was liable to use the last dregs of my power to end it. Myself.

I rested my hands on my daggers, feeling the weight of them against my waist since I had no access to the ones I could conjure. There was excited chatter in that language of theirs, rising in pitch and harmony. The palace itself was the same pearl-white as the guards' armor, leaving them like bodiless heads as they stood at attention against the walls. Their swords were marbleized gold, and they wore no helmets.

Upon meeting this morn, Blackwood informed us that he would be making a formal request with the Queen of Pyrestan herself, as this was the original plan when he'd worked with Von Herron years ago. Before the younger man excluded him from negotiations and shut him off of the trade agreement, they were to offer the very honey and mead from the renowned hives of the town they'd both come from.

Eventually, as demand and Von Herron's enterprise grew, he began trading with the Folk jewels or beading made in our realm.

I knew fuck-all about trade and the dealings of merchants, but the sheer amount and demand for Pyrestan fabric I'd witnessed in Morova seemed worth more than some sweet treats and trinkets.

The large doors lining the grand entrance of the palace were closed and guarded, naturally leading us to a space similar to the size of Von Herron's ballroom. Where I reunited with my Shadow.

He was beside me, so close I could flinch and touch him. Dressed in black leathers, now, he was the darkness among so much light. He was the rock to cling to while being assaulted by wind, by rushing water in a current far too strong. Even with his powers gone, the Fire in his eyes dimmed to an amber-brown, he was—I choked and covered it with a clearing of my throat.

He was everything I desired. Everything I would never deserve.

More marble covered the floor, this time in a gold and white checkered pattern, and the view of the mountains was most spectacular, here. The glass on the windows, nearly reaching as high as the cavernous ceiling above, showed not only the edge of the tree the city was constructed upon, but the craggy mountain-side and clouds beyond. Golden sunlight rained down upon the scene, as if whatever deity that created them was looking upon us, now. Figures cut through the fluffy cover of cloud, birds glided over the supple, dense cover of the mother tree, but, as I squinted, I made out those far larger than simple birds.

And they came closer, revealing wings in unnaturally bright colors, even more than the macaws or bluebirds of our world. No, when they bounded closer—but not too close, as if there was an invisible barrier around the palace—I realized they were Folk. Shimmering fabric of their clothing trailing behind them, they flew amongst the animals of the sky.

If this whole place didn't reek, it would be...absolutely splendid.

"All rise, for the royal family and Her Majesty, Sarya, Queen of Pyrestan, Protector of the Arbor, and Leader of Truth."

Behind me, under his breath, Tomás grumbled that we were all standing anyway. Tana harshly commanded him to hush, but that was drowned out, too, as a gilded door, cast in gold lattice-work, drew open. The sound of it rang all the way to the domed ceiling built in geometric patterns of more white and gold.

The first to enter was not the queen. First, was more Folk with wings, these sporting skin varying between golden and brown. Their markings matched each other's, even more elegant and finer than the guards, and the membranes of their wings were liked stained glass. The light streaming through the windows and ceiling filtered through their wings, creating a flood of blues, greens, and lilacs just from their bodies.

To highlight the beauty, most likely, they were also dressed in white. Two in tunic and trouser embellished with gold thread, one in similar motif but in a slim gown of lace. Their eyes were a deep blue, like the morning sky above.

Then, as if they'd been through this countless times before, the Folk quieted to near-silence for their queen. She entered, flanked by guards but creating a force all on her own.

Her features were similar enough to the other members of the royal family, as if they'd been drawn from her. But unlike the white of her children, the Queen of Pyrestan had hair the same shade as mine and a few shades darker than her skin. Plaited along her scalp, the strands were woven in an intricate design with jewels and pearls. Her crown was an array of thin, sharpened bones.

The Queen, Sarya, floated through the quiet room, leaving a train of the fabric Blackwood lusted over trailing behind her, and she took her throne. I could—was it made of winding branches or more bone? Both? It couldn't be comfortable, but she perched demurely all the same. She cast her milky-blue stare on her citizens who were split between watching her, her children seated in smaller thrones, and the door.

I smelled something wild, heard the heavy steps, but I still wondered if it was an illusion when the bear walked into the room.

The wings around me fluttered in excitement, and I gaped as the animal, larger than any bear I'd ever seen, ambled directly to the queen's side, sitting on its haunches and grumbling happily when she sifted her long fingers through its chestnut fur.

But—it was not over? The Queen looked upon her people expectantly, and they still watched the door. Somewhere else in the palace, another door opened far down the corridor, and then…grunting. Far more guttural than the sounds the Queen's pet was making, it sounded like muffled screeches, from the depth of the belly.

My own churned, why, I was not sure, but with each step of the guards' boots, my gut twisted. With each grunt that reached my ears, my pulse ticked higher.

Nothing, *nothing*, could have prepared me for the figure walking through the door. Hands at my back, the steel bands of arms kept my buckling knees from making me collapse altogether. Leather clamped over my mouth, and Elián's silky hair brushed my temples as he pulled me into his chest.

Weak remnants of my Death sifted along the floor of the empty well within me, not even rising past the surface of my skin covered by leather glove.

And that fucking Queen watched. While the Folk chittered gleefully, the Queen with her milky eyes grinned, revealing fangs longer than mine. She reached out for the golden leash, and the guard gave it to her with a bow before stepping back.

Tears stuck Elián's glove to my cheeks, obscuring my vision of the gaunt figure, pale as the room around us. Matted locks fell past a naked waist, fingernails overgrown and curled inward like the talons of birds of prey. They'd tied a leather strap to silence the screaming, but that did nothing to soften the enraged panic. The shifting of their bare, dirty feet.

"Be at ease," the Queen bade us, but I was trembling with rage, no matter how tightly Elián held onto me. No matter the fervent whispers of my cousin in my ear, clogged with the wateriness of her own crying.

Against El's palm, I soundlessly chanted, trying to call out to Francie.

"Welcome, children of Pyrestan," the Queen said with gilded leash wrapped around her fist. "And foreign travelers."

I struggled in El's grip, and his voice joined Tana's, trying to calm me. "Do not be rash. We cannot help her if we are reprimanded or killed, my queen. Please. I am with you."

He was with me, but who was with Francie? Who was with her as she'd been *taken* for three years. Her features were sunken, her back hunched, and her terrified gaze cut to the animals to her left and right. To this queen who'd stolen my friend, the royal retched children who smirked at Francie, and the giant bear who could shred her with one swipe of its claws.

The desperate scent of Frenzy wafted off of her in waves, and I groaned, realization flooding harder than the waterfalls outside. Mother of All, these Folk were born immortals. Their blood would not sustain any Lylithan, nor any Vyrkos. And even if she was able to choke down their rancid food, she was *starving*. For *years*.

In my own depression, I had kissed the edges of Frenzy in self-flagellation, but I had *never* witnessed this. Those of our kind who were for some reason without mortal blood to this extent were immediately taken in to heal or…put out of their misery.

How far gone was Francie's Frenzy? Underneath her body's survival instinct, turning her into *this*, was there still remnant of the person she truly was? Or would I be the one tasked with ending her pain?

These thoughts trampled my rational thought until the droning of this queen of bones made little sense. The petty requests of the Folk, for this and that, were just noise. A chorus underneath my silent screams for my friend, begging her to look, to *know*.

Elián's presence and scent, still of cinnamon and burning oak, were the only things keeping me from storming the dais and plunging a dagger right between the bitch's eyes. Tana's lavender lulled me toward a state somewhere adjacent to calm. The true cool grounding of Rhaea's Death was gone, as if the shadow, the one I'd been born with and had been in-step with all my life, had disappeared. I was here, but my experience of this world was…incomplete.

"Your Majesty." When had Blackwood stepped forward? The rest of us hung back, allowing our employer this moment, as he'd commanded during our meeting. "I come in the stead of Paschal Von Herron. The one you arranged trade with for our world. I wish to seek a similar arrangement. One that benefits the both of us."

It was still unclear whether she was blind or not, but either way, she had no trouble tracking Blackwood's slow advance to the place others had taken to address their queen.

We both flinched, me and Blackwood, when Francie released a scream so loud it transcended the gag over her mouth. She darted, making to leap at Blackwood, to drain him dry. But, of course, the collar around her neck halted her descent, turning her cry of hunger to one of fury and pain.

The queen was unperturbed, not even stirring as she held the leash, and I'd seen more than enough. I twisted, using the shock of the moment to slip out of Elián's grasp. I dropped to a crouch and darted through the crowd.

He was running after me, and so was Tana, but the guards also reacted to my rushing the dais. As fast as any Lylithan or Vyrkos, they formed a wall in front of the royal family, Francie, and the sentient bear, swords pointed right for our throats.

I hissed, daggers drawn. "Francie! We are here for you. We will take you home to your mate."

I heard the shudder of metal on leather, the others drawing their weapons, and I ran over our odds. We were still woefully disadvantaged, unaware of their strengths as well as their weaknesses. Hopefully, they were in a similar position.

I selected the guard I was going to take down first, the one standing directly between me and Francie, but Queen Sarya's calm, commanding voice stopped that, too. "Guards. Fall back. I wish to talk to the Raouga."

They did not hesitate, nor did I relax as I came face-to-face, near eye level, with the queen of this realm. "I came for her." I indicated my kind, sweet friend with a jut of my chin, another crack spider-spreading across my heart to watch her cower and bear her fangs at me. Us. Lylithans who, to her, were standing before the mortal, maybe staking claim on him.

The sharp points of the queen's bone crown arced as she considered me. Her gaze was pinning and expansive at once, and her amusement had a razor edge, as sharp as her fangs. "May I have your name, traveler?"

A creak rang, from the shift of one of the royal children as they leaned forward in interest. The ones beside them looked just as hungry for my answer. With narrowed eyes, I returned the queen's stare and barely held myself back from spitting at her slippered feet. I didn't want such evil to know me at all. For some reason, what came out of my mouth was, "You can call me Em."

One of the children, the one who leaned forward, pouted, and the queen's stained-glass wings fluttered, though her expression did not change. "Em. You travel from your land for my pet. The one who stole from me."

I twirled my blades, and she did not miss the action. "Bullshit."

A cackle bubbled up her throat, one she sent to the ceiling and sky beyond, and just to anger me, she tugged on the leash, pulling Francie by her neck and drawing a whimper from her.

"She has, despite the letter we left at her home. Ninety-four days passed, and I've yet to have what's mine returned."

Ninety—days? What was she on about? The only letter Whitley received, the one Francie's takers left as they forcibly removed her from her *home*, was from *three years* ago.

"That cannot be. She is a teacher of orphaned babes in our world, and you have *stolen her*. Against her will. You are either mistaken or a fucking liar."

Gasps rang all around me, but Sarya silenced them all by

raising her hand. Her voice dropped an octave. Twisted. "You call me liar?"

"Yeah, I'm calling you a liar and a sadistic fucking bitch." I pointed the tip of my dagger right at her heart. "You torture her for *nothing*."

The beating of air was my only warning, the only signal before she was standing right in front of me. Looking down at me whilst our toes were almost touching. I did not show weakness, and there was no fear left.

This queen of bones smelled of the wind through the trees. Icy morning dew. But when she grinned down at me, mouth splitting unnaturally wide through her cheeks, her breath smelled fucking rotten.

"I cannot lie, tiny Raouga. But the rest of your assessment may be quite true."

I was about to jab her in her fucking throat. If I'd had access to my Death, she would be a hollowed husk already, as well as each of her sniveling children. But, no, Rhaea had left me once again.

"And what, pray tell, did a genial caregiver steal from you?"

The Queen raised a finger, one sporting diamonds and pearls, making to caress the edge of my face. She did not make contact with my skin, but it was close enough. I raised my weapon, landing the tip at the low cut of her gown. The blade frayed a few fibers of the fabric, snapping like broken lute strings.

She hummed a pleasant note. "The Royal Bracelet of my mother, Queen Amitola, may she rest among the stars. It was stolen many years ago, and on its way back to me, it was stolen again."

"All—you torture the wrong person, all for a piece of jewelry?"

That grin returned. "Yes."

I cut my eyes around me in the span of a blink, assessing the guards ready to cut me down, my cousin and lover behind me, and Francie cowering against the throne, cerulean blue eyes wide and wary. "You said that you *cannot* lie."

She tilted her head, shifting the braids falling down her back. "Yes."

Could I believe that? What choice did I have? "If I find this bracelet, if I return it to you, will you release my friend to me?"

Her eyes widened, and more of her white teeth showed. The stained-glass wings behind her fluttered. "You wish to make a deal with me, Em?"

Even the shortened form of my name on her lips slid down my spine like sludge. "Yeah. A deal."

"Upon the return of my bracelet, you will have the return of your friend. My pet, here."

The urge to slice open her throat for calling Francie such a word prickled beneath my fingertips. Where my Death should have been keen to enact the fantasy. "Yes."

And the Queen giggled, lightly and musically, a sound that belonged in a choir. The joy removed the grotesque from her beautiful features. Her wings twitched happily, and my stomach turned to stone.

"Yes, tiny Raouga Em. It is a deal."

She was going to have to stop calling me tiny—not all of us were spindly crones. "Then what does this bracelet look like, then. Where was it last seen?"

She hummed again, moving the golden leash in her fist, and I clenched my teeth with all of my strength. We made a deal. "It is about this in width," Sarya placed her thumb and first finger a small distance apart, "gold, with many purple stones of varying size and shade. Sapphires from our mountain."

The stone of my stomach began to sink into the mud she'd been spewing at me. Yes, this could be any fine piece of royal jewelry, but...I had known a piece of that description. *Stolen* a piece just like it just before returning to Nethras and giving Francie the coin I'd won. Had I—had I been followed?

"It was last accounted for on an island in your realm. It was stolen from here, then traded again and again. One of my loyal citizens had gone to retrieve it, but they never came back."

I used everything I had left to keep my face impassive, but the queen of bones saw something within me. My blade still rested upon her sternum, and she brushed the tip of her fingernail along the length of it. "You know of it," she surmised. And then, in a whisper like poison, she accused, "Tiny Raouga thief."

Goddess-damn it all to hell. That trip to Dyna Island. When I'd fought in the rings, stolen the bracelet from the human merchant, and crossed paths with the male now at my back. He murdered my employer who was most likely the Folk she sent to retrieve the bracelet.

The thought of unwittingly working for this cruel female rankled.

Though, not as much with the realization that this was all my fault. Whoever followed me must have mistaken the exchange of money, my giving the coin purse to Francie, as me handing her the bracelet. My attempt at helping her ultimately led her to be taken and tortured. For years.

That almost left me turning my blade on myself.

"I will need time. To go back to our world and retrieve it." To my old apartment, to my bedroom and the drawer where I'd stowed the piece of jewelry I never wore. The home was mine, bought and paid for, but there was no telling if it stood undisturbed. The whole bloody building could have been reduced to rubble by now—I'd not set foot anywhere near Nethras in these years away.

I just made a deal, but what if I was unable to find the bracelet?

"No," Elián's voice blazed through the muck. He stepped up, now shoulder to my shoulder. "There is no need. We will bring it to you now."

I kept my mouth shut, but through whatever bond we shared, I screamed a thousand questions, a thousand curses at him for assuring something like that. What did he even know about the bracelet? When he'd stolen my coin and killed my Folk employer, he'd not been concerned with the item itself. I wasn't even sure he'd ever seen it.

But when Elián glanced at me, eyes dim, he gave the minutest shake of his head. Telling me to not undermine him with incredulity.

The Queen turned her attention to Elián like the twitch of a bird of prey. "And who are you? May I have your name, Raouga?"

I lost the battle with the remainder of my better senses. "*No*."

El did not look at me. "My name does not matter. We can get you what you seek."

She remained still, as if made out of the stone or bone or branch. Then, another puff of air, the sensation of her wings carrying her, and the Queen was perched on her throne as if she'd never left it. "You will come back tomorrow eve for supper. Bring me the bracelet, and I will fulfill my end of our deal." Elián did not bow or nod or thank her, and neither did I.

What I wanted to do was demand she not draw this out, but Blackwood shoved forward, glaring at me while twisting around the pack slung over his shoulder. "As I was *saying*. I have come to talk trade, Your Majesty."

She answered him without looking away from us. "What do you have in that bag?"

He deposited it to the floor, remaining kneeled. "Proof of Von Herron's demise, 'Majesty." Blackwood had better sense than me, keeping his eyes downcast and awaiting her judgement, and I barely held onto the part of our contract that required me to protect him.

The queen twisted the golden links in her fist, keeping Francie close to the side of her throne as she watched Blackwood like a starving cat would a mouse. The trembling of her muscles was evident, making her form unclear, shaky.

One of the guards marched forward, picking up the leather pack and inspecting it with quick professionalism. Even still, they licked at their bottom lip, and their throat bobbed with a hungry swallow.

They deemed Blackwood's offering safe, and extended the black leather to the queen who sat, I was now convinced, on a chair made of bones carved and shaved to resemble the elegant twisting of branches. Queen Sarya pulled Von Herron's head, now turning a greenish gray and deforming. It hardly looked human anymore, but some other thing that had no business in the lap of this otherworldly female dressed in white.

But utter *delight* swept her features, as if she'd been gifted a rare jewel instead of a decomposing head.

When we decided to take Von Herron's head with us, we assumed it would provide the assurance that Blackwood was not offering them a deal the people of Pyrestan would not need. With Von Herron certainly dead, his link between their world and ours was severed, leaving an opening for Blackwood.

What we did not anticipate was Queen Sarya, in this room in front of all her eager people, pulling flesh from Von Herron's cheek like that of tender, slow-cooked meat. The discolored skin between her healthy brown fingertips was almost more unsightly than watching her pop it into her mouth.

She chewed slowly with eyes closed, and I fought back the saliva pooling into my mouth, warning of vomit churning. Her children were watching with rapt attention, as were the Folk behind me. But unlike me and my companions, they clearly wanted a taste.

Tomás's dark skin took on an ashen hue, and though I could not see Fenix's, his shuffling feet were obvious. If this Queen of the Folk enjoyed… eating corpses, the propositions thrown the Vyrkos's way now held a much more sinister tone.

The Queen pulled another morsel off of Von Herron's head before placing it back in the bag and buckling the flap. When she returned her attention to Blackwood who now smelled of fear and disgust, she either could not smell it or was even happier at that fact. "This gift pleases me greatly. You will accompany the Raouga to supper tomorrow eve, and we will speak of trade."

"Y-Yes, Majesty."

She batted her lashes, clicked her fingernails against the bones resting beneath her arms. "And may I have your name, valiant human?"

Von Herron's admonishment of his old employer and business partner shone clearly as the queen's taunting compliment reached his ears. In the face of her compliment, Blackwood looked up, stood tall. "Walter Blackwood, Your Majesty. At your service."

And the splitting grin was back, like the great sharks in the deep waters surrounding Rhaestras. She did not have endless rows of teeth, but the ones she displayed were more than enough.

"Yes, you are."

CHAPTER THIRTY-TWO
MELINE

y the time we exited the palace, the sun had retreated behind the clouds, painting the world in shadows of gray. Even the soft grass beneath my boots appeared dulled as I paced, imagining what horrors Francie was enduring whilst we waited *another* day.

"We have to go get her," I said for the fifth time as we stood beneath a tree, away from these Folk who took no issue with the torture of my friend or their monarch eating a decaying head.

This time, Fenix was the one to object, "I'm not in your line of work, but that still seems unwise."

I clutched my dagger for comfort or to stab him, but Tana stepped between us. Her leathers matched mine, brown and simple, yet equipped with enough weapons to storm that fucking castle. My cousin was more than formidable with her staff alone. And with Elián, Tomás, and even Fenix's help? Surely we could spring her from Queen Sarya's captivity.

"Leen. I know it was horrific to see Francie in that state and to know now the cruelty of these Folk. But we are no help to her if we are dead."

Elián had tried to tell me the same thing in fewer words, but just like then, this was unacceptable. "And leave her starving and afraid? Have any of you been in Frenzy before? To that extent? We have no idea what pain she is in, just that it persists."

I doubted the monster of a queen was keeping Francie in a furnished room filled with smooth sheets and a warm fire. She treated an actual animal with more kindness than what she displayed toward Francie.

"It's awful what they're doing to her, but I'm not storming that palace. Nogón says he has the item you need in exchange for the caregiver, and I like my flesh on my body, thank you very much."

I whirled around, shoulders heaving, and shot my arms wide. "I don't even know why the fuck he said that! How can that *be*?"

In all the time since we reunited, Elián's demeanor was the closest to the laconic Shadow I'd first met three years ago. Now, I remained open as he crossed his arms and jutted *that* brow in *that* way, which only made my anger climb higher. "I said it because it is true."

"How?"

Elián remained a statue, letting the breeze sweeping the small field of green and wild flowers shift his hair like the young branches above. Today, it was tied up at the crown of his head, but, like always, silky strands escaped and framed the hard planes of his face.

"When I searched Nethras. For you." My breath stalled on its way from my throat to my lungs. "We will bring it tomorrow, get Francie, and leave."

I dropped my arms, letting them flop against my sides and was reminded again of how Elián had searched our realm. For me. My failures kept mounting, mocking me with the feel of a still body, the scent of Frenzy. El didn't pull me into him this time, but he held my stare, keeping us locked until I could feel my legs steady beneath me.

Fenix stood with his back against the thick trunk—or, branch of the ancient tree beneath us. He was nearly camouflaged by the weight of his shield against the sun, and his voice did not hold its usual audible sneer. "In that state, she will be hard to restrain. Especially if he is with us." Fenix gestured toward Blackwood who was writing notes in a ledger and warily listening to us. "She will scent and view us as adversaries, competitors in the way of her feeding. We will either have to keep her restrained or strike her unconscious for the journey back." Experience underlined his steady instructions, as if he had made mistakes and was relaying what he'd learned from them. In his short past, had he been the one in Frenzy or the one having to do the restraining? "She will need help...adjusting. Once she is in her right mind again. Might help if you are alive for that part."

Tana crouched, brushing her palms over the land. "Thank you, Fenix. That's really helpful, and I agree completely."

I knew my cousin, and I also knew her words were not a betrayal but her trying to engender a sense of belonging for the Vyrkos. It left a bitterness on my tastebuds all the same.

Someone's stomach growled, but we were all hungry, aside from Blackwood. Like on the ship from Morova, we'd rationed our food from our realm, and we had mutually agreed to not feed from Fenix's reserve, despite him offering.

Blackwood closed his ledger with a snap, regarding us all with disdain as if were in the way of his precious trade deal with this despicable place. "You will keep to the agreement we've entered. I care not what you do afterward, but I do need escort tomorrow and once we leave. After that, we are done."

"If that queen doesn't eat you first, you mean." Tomás's words should have been in jest, but repulsion swelled between us all. Did Queen Sarya share Von Herron's remains with her children? Her subjects? I had little consideration for the man's life, but even I considered it a mercy his soul had left the realm before witnessing such a desecration.

Blackwood sputtered in a way he never would have with the Queen. "She will do no such thing. As we saw, she is a woman of her word."

"Were you in the same room with us just then? Are you that easily fooled by pretty appearances? One can tell the truth and still have no honor." And I had made a deal with her. I wasn't opposed to acting against it, and I would be unsurprised to find Sarya to be the same. "We don't even know if her inability to lie is the truth."

Tana was now absently weaving grass and flower stems together, and she tilted her face toward the sky. "Do you think that extends to all Folk or just her?"

None of us had an answer to that, but the whole idea sounded ludicrous. Would such a thing extend to every single minuscule obfuscation of the truth, or would it only apply to blatant mistruths? What would happen if they tried to tell one?

While we stood in silence and my anger waned, a heavy cloud trailed across the falling sun, leaving us in compounded darkness for a moment, then continuing on its way across the sky. The slivers of sunlight piercing through the clouds reflected against the iridescent polish of the Pyrestan guards' armor. Yesterday, when we'd traipsed through the city, the eyes of the Folk had been on us, but today, after our audience with the Queen, we were being followed. Quite blatantly, too.

"My goal is to bring Francie home to her mate as quickly as we can." I thought of the handkerchief Whitley sent me, when I informed them I would be starting this quest to get their mate back. It lay in my packs, folded neatly and waiting for me to give to Francie. Something to remind her of *home*. "If no one will help me get her now, then we will—we'll get her tomorrow. For now, maybe we should retire to the lodging house." I'd little regard for my own safety, but the others' were actively in jeopardy, especially now.

This time, my suggestion met no objection.

Finding calm within the confines of the lodging house inevitably proved quite difficult. While Fenix slept, as his body naturally craved during the light of day, Blackwood fucked off to do whatever it was he had to do to prepare for negotiations with Queen Sarya. So, that left the four of us to pace and snipe at each other within the overly-decorated walls and nosily helpful staff Folk.

Before they came knocking the first time, asking if we needed anything, we were shouting over a scattered pile of cards, Tomás cursing us for not listening to the rules while Tana and I accused him of cheating. Then, when they'd tried to come around with a mid-day meal of sweet yogurt and berries, we'd been arguing again, this time over the minutiae of our plan of exit from this place. How we would first try to calm and restrain Francie, then how we would incapacitate her as kindly as possible, should we need to.

The third time they'd come to the door, meeting a snarling Tomás who slammed the door in their face, Elián had pulled out the bracelet from a smaller leather pouch hidden in his things. I said nothing as I saw the edge of a flat, golden box I knew to be etched with roses.

And the fourth time, when the staff came around with a putrid-smelling supper, I was the one to pull the door open, only to meet the cheery smile of the one who first greeted us yesterday.

My head throbbed, and I tried my best to breathe through my mouth. "What is your name?"

His wings spread, as if to make himself appear larger. "You may call me Ren."

"Ren. Tha—we appreciate your level of...attentiveness, but to our senses, your food is unappetizing. Please do not bring it again. We will call if we need something."

His smile didn't falter, but he did lower the tray, and I saw the others behind him retreat back up the corridor. "Oh. My apologies. The man you are with has been enjoying it, so we assumed."

"Be that as it may. We do not need anything, so if you'll—"

My cousin sprang up behind me, peering around my shoulder. "Wait! Ren, when we went to the palace, your queen mentioned that she cannot lie. Is that true?"

He cleared his throat, taking a step back but still responding, "This is true."

"Can *you* lie?" Tana pressed.

Ren did not hesitate. "None of us can lie."

Tana hummed pensively, but something about his readiness to answer our questions was suspicious in its own way. I clutched the edge of the doorframe, and leaned towards him. He stepped back once again. "Does that mean you always tell the truth?"

There. The lodging house manager kept his expression and posture level, but the pause was *there*. "We are unable to tell lies, just like our queen. Now, if you'll excuse me." And he was gone, moving as fast as any Lylithan or Vyrkos.

"And with that, I will be sleeping away this hunger and fortifying my mental faculties in preparation for tomorrow. Given what we've just learned, perhaps consider how tightly sealed that deal you made is." Tomás slunk his way past Tana and me, retreating into his room with the click of the door latching.

Suddenly, the room felt too big. Or too small—I wasn't sure. Elián's stare collided with mine as he remained seated near the window. All of us had long changed out of our leathers, and his tunic was another colorful one. The green was of Versillia.

"I—I'll retire as well."

I flinched, but Tana didn't give me time to object before she was gone. Leaving me with Elián. Now, just the two of us, I could no longer shove away the image of him searching my apartment, sifting through my things and taking what reminded him of me. Us.

I closed our door and leaned back against my hands. The sheer curtains danced around him, expanding and constricting. Elián had saved me time and time again, willing like Tana to follow me past the edge of the world. And how had I repaid him?

My loose trousers and tunic shifted softly against my skin as I moved toward him. Our family had provided the best distraction they could, in these hours between the deal I struck and the supper where we would enact it. But, truly, the most effective grounding force I had was this male in front of me.

Someone who had changed me so irrevocably. Who proved to me with every action how much he cared for me.

He sat with legs spread, and I stopped between his parted thighs. Elián let me run my fingers through his hair, and when I scratched his scalp, he hummed a low, satisfied note. "I am so grateful for you, El," I whispered, for fear that if I said it too loud, he would be taken away from me, too.

"And I am grateful for you." His eyes remained closed, his body vibrated as he resumed humming.

And he'd said it so easily. Like I hadn't put him through so much shit and was continuing to do so. I had to—I wanted to do *something*. While we still had time.

Elián's black lashes fanned across the tops of his cheekbones, and as I massaged his scalp, I felt the warm gold of his earrings on the heels of my palms. "Can I take care of you, El? Tonight."

He opened his eyes, then, brows tightened and lips pulled into a confused frown. He brushed the backs of his fingers against the outsides of my thighs. "I am just happy to be with you, my queen."

I bent, kissing him on the border of skin and hair, and spoke into him, "Please."

Elián didn't respond, but that was answer enough, so I took his hands in mine and pulled him to his feet. More obedient than he'd probably ever been with me, he remained still while I slipped each button on his tunic loose. Though his Fire was all but gone, Elián's skin was unnaturally warm, almost too hot, and it was just enough. Perfect.

I pushed the fabric off of his shoulders and set it on the back of the chair. His trousers, I unlaced and carefully pulled down his thick, tattooed thighs. Markings of stark, heavy lines made beautiful patterns, and a healthy dusting of black hair covered his thighs and calves.

His cock was hardening, thickening with every second I was near him, but I ignored it. For now.

I pulled on his wrist, and he followed, still watching but allowing himself to remain pliable. Trusting me.

When I shoved on his chest, Elián understood what I wanted and sat on the too-soft mattress. His body sank into the soft cover, and when I nudged him back onto the pillows, he went, falling into the plush, supple feathers.

It wasn't until I began to climb on after him that he chose to speak. "Take off your clothes as well."

I immediately started to do what he said, caught myself, and huffed. I barely kept from stomping my foot. "You aren't supposed to be doling out orders in this."

"I do not know what *this* is. But whatever it is, I want to see you."

That was not a command, but my navel lurched as if it was. My heart quickened as if it was. As I pulled off my tunic, I told him, "I'm taking them off because I *choose* to. Nothing to do with what you've told me." But when I tossed the garment aside and refocused on him before me, Elián's dimples were showing, and I knew I would do anything he asked for a chance to see them.

My trousers took longer, the buttons small and my throat thick with the sudden urge to cry. He deserved care, someone to protect him and his heart, always. If the sadness he felt was even a fraction of what I carried each day, I wanted to be the one to give him comfort. To hold and kiss him until he could breathe.

"I know that I—I hope you know that I think you're the most amazing person, El." The bones of his lower legs were steady, thick, and below one of his knees was an illustration of a flower. A faint crackle rang throughout the silver-cast room as I brushed my touch up and down his legs.

As I climbed higher, pressing into his outer and inner thighs, now, I felt his muscles jump with sensitivity. I focused there for a few moments, digging the undersides of my knuckles into his brown skin. "You're so strong. Watchful. Ruthless." The last word escaped my throat, rough and low, and it seeped into my Shadow's skin. Elián's eyelids lowered, and his cock hardened more. It rested now, against his tight abdomen and the gold piercing shone under the clear light from the large half moon.

I'd no plan for this moment, just wanting his skin against mine and letting my senses lead my care for Elián. Showing him how precious he really was.

He hissed, fighting to keep his legs still as I licked a stripe from the seam of his sac, over the piercing in his shaft, and to the tip of his cockhead. I swirled my tongue, collecting the moisture his body gave me and dropped another kiss.

I continued up the middle of Elián's belly, then to his chest. His heart thudded strongly, quickly, and I inhaled the warmth of smoke and wood. The subtle sweet of cinnamon. Or was that just my association of sweet things with the spice? How as many choice words we'd shared, as much blood I shed, I'd *always* thought of him in the moments of happiness when we were apart. Cradled in my mind's eye and swaddled, protected and cherished.

Elián groaned, this time, as I swirled my tongue around his flat, brown nipple. Still, he let me do what I pleased, and I treated the other to the same open-mouthed kiss. His collarbones were next, the hollow of his throat and the thumping of his pulse. It made my mouth water, my fangs itch, but I kept the drive to claim him at bay.

This was about him.

Elián's breathing grew heavier, his legs spread to allow the width of my hips between them, and I descended once again, pulling on the foreskin of his cock and taking the head between my lips.

Elián held the back of my head, and because he was still the overbearing bastard he always was, he guided me where it felt the best. "Meline," he gritted as I sucked, taking even more of him into my mouth, my throat. The piercing ran against my tongue, and I swallowed it, too, bobbing my head and saliva trailing into the trimmed hairs at the base.

He groaned in protest when I pulled off, but it turned to one of pleasure as I gently took one of his bollocks into my mouth, tasting and shielding it from my fangs. I went between them both, with Elián holding me down and my fist shuttling with the speed I was learning he liked the most. Lust filled the air around us, mine and his in equal measure. How many times over these years had I imagined this? How many lonely nights had I touched myself, wishing that it was him?

I leaned on my hand and knees, hovering over Elián and tracing the tip of his cock around my nipple, leaving wet trails and a lightning crack of pleasure. Perhaps I wasn't completely selfless, but Elián didn't stop me. He did not stop me as I moved to the other, nor when I swallowed him again, this time all the way to the root.

"*Fuck*," Elián cursed while I breathed only him, and he choked as I constricted my throat around him.

He removed his cock from my mouth with a slick pop, but before I could form the words of protest, he flipped and pulled me up, nestled right into his chest. The scar on my back, where the coldness penetrated deepest, tingled with Elián's heat, his heart pounding against it.

He pulled my legs open, planting my feet and using his thighs to keep me spread and completely bared before the glass across from the bed.

Really, what kind of creatures put the mirror across from the bed like this?

"I saw how wet you were for me, Meline." Goddess, I hadn't —I'd forgotten about the fucking thing while I'd been tending to Elián's body. Providing him an excellent view from the front and behind of what I was doing. "See how wet you are now," he growled, softly bumping his nose against the shell of my ear. This attempt at taking care of him tonight was quickly slipping away from me, but at the first swipe of Elián's fingers, I ceased caring.

His cock was heavy and throbbing behind me, and I begged, wanting to seat myself on him properly, but each time, Elián stopped my protests short. He proved that just as I was quickly learning his body, he was learning mine.

"Watch, Meline. Watch yourself come because of me. How perfectly you fit against me."

I tried to hide my head in the hollow of his throat, fucking myself on his thick digits while his thumb swirled, but he wasn't having that. Elián locked my head, facing forward, where I couldn't hide.

He was truly a shadow behind me, smoldering gaze whispering filth and promise and encouraging me to come apart. Telling me over and over that I belonged with him.

And I made for an obscene sight, bared, slick, and arched as I clambered behind Elián's lead. Tears streaming down the side of my face as it became too much, too big, but he just licked them up, denying his own release and pushing me toward mine.

Well, until I was right there, kissing the precipice of it, mouth dropped and breath held. Then, Elián pinched both of my nipples so hard that I screamed, writhing and sobbing because of sensation lost but swept under by the suggestion of pain, anyway. My hips pumped uselessly, running to and away from what he'd done to me. Not just plucking my body with a skill that rivaled any expert lute player, but burrowing even further into me. Where my soul would decidedly never feel complete without him.

While the pulsing surges of pleasure beneath my skin weakened, Elián took liberty with my body, *again*. I sucked in a gasp as I sank into the edge of the bed, and the air punched out of my nose as Elián's hips filled my vision, my world.

The ornate, frilly thing was the perfect height for him to lean forward, to use the grip on his cock and slap it against my lips. It was all the instruction he gave, but I needed less, licking my lips and opening my mouth for him to plunge inside.

A heavy, hot palm closed around the front of my throat, feeling himself there, and I stopped moving. Bracing myself with fists clenched around Pyrestan fabric, I stared up at my Shadow. My love.

And he thrust. Mouth and throat relaxed, chin dripping, I again let Elián fuck my face. I'd once told him that I hardly gave others the privilege of this level of submission, but with him, *for* him, it was liable to become a regular occurrence. I gagged, but when he let up to give me space, I did not take it. I turned myself over to Elián, let him use my mouth.

He braced his knee on the mattress beside my shoulder, fucking into my throat with intense, long plunges. My mind calmed to a low buzzing, like the lazy chittering of an autumn evening, and like that change in seasons, where Elián's and my body joined was warm. The rest of me melted further into the bed, skin prickling but too sated to do anything about it.

And when Elián came, it was with my name on his lips and his seed shooting into my stomach, bypassing my tastebuds altogether. But in this submission, I felt powerful. Giving him such pleasure that he could not hold himself from release.

He pulled his softened cock from my mouth, and a long, translucent string stretched between us. Elián wiped the end connecting to him, collecting that remnant of me and him, and gently shoved it all back between my lips. A hint of salt and Elián's natural musk, I held the taste as long as I could, making it cover every inch and crevice before swallowing it again.

I twisted slowly, righting my vision of the world, and arched my neck. I was about to lightly snip at him for staring at my ass, or trying to suffocate me with his cock *again*, but his fingers running over my curls silenced me at once. He did so as if he was in worship. As if what I meant to him transcended anything able to be spoken.

"Do you—" my voice came out ragged "—do you want me to braid your hair?" The action used to soothe me but was unavailable to me now.

He already enjoyed my fingers running through the strands. Would this be something he'd like as well?

Elián paused, fingering a curl beside my ear. No doubt I resembled a baby duck, curls no longer orderly but fluffy and askew. But, my Shadow didn't seem to mind. The edge of his thumb made one last caress against my skin, and then he pulled away.

I propped on a hip, tracking his movements as he went to one of his packs and rifled through it with neat efficiency, reflecting the orderliness with which I knew he kept his things.

He returned with a small, dark bottle, a comb, and a few leather ties. Elián dropped them beside me, laying out everything I would need, and then he lowered himself. For me. He sat against the bed, facing the night and ever-present waterfalls that swallowed the sounds of our pleasure earlier.

Now, I ran a hand over Elián's hair supplies, a far simpler regimen than mine, and selected the comb first. He waited patiently, chest rising and falling in a calm, steady rhythm. Where I came from, one's hair was a...deeply personal thing. Something to express yourself, to display your status and vitality, but also something truly shared with only those you were close with. How often had I sat like he was now, listening to my mother's stories of her childhood, crying to her about what worried my innocent mind, or laughing with her about whatever we fancied that day?

Or when I was able to get Tana to sit still long enough to tame her buttercream curls, caring for my younger cousin in a way that seemed outside of time itself?

I started at the bottom of Elián's hair, where it reached just past the middle of his back. About as long as mine used to be. The comb was wooden, plain, and I wielded it deftly as I slowly worked out the tangles and knots.

"What did you see for your future when you were a child?" Elián's question wasn't in contrast with the hypnotic task of combing his hair. It was natural, complementary.

There was a larger snag against the comb, and I set it aside to tease it loose with my fingernails. I used the tactile sense to work my way through it. "I suppose…something akin to what my mother did. Not High Priestess, but the responsibilities of the kingdom. The traveling. The throne was never supposed to be mine, but I expected to always be in its proximity." Did Versillia still stand, now? Had the Lylithan Council dismantled upon my brother and uncle's deaths? "What about you?"

A few strands gave me purchase, and I focused on Elián's answer. "A Shadow like my father. I did not see a life without my family, but other than this, I am doing what I thought I would."

"Fucking rival assassins in a different realm, you mean?"

He twisted, just enough for his pupil to sear into mine. "Not rivals. And…no. I did not expect you."

He turned back around, and I picked the comb back up to get the rest of the knot. My fang caught on the edge of my lip as I dared, "Is that a bad thing?"

"It is the best thing."

I nearly dropped the comb as it slid smoothly through the section I was working on. I could leave his words to trail and disappear in the air. Not beat them into something recognizable. But, alas. "We were together for a few days, then *years* apart filled with loss afterward. How can I be the best thing for you, El?" Never mind the fact he was that for me. He'd given me more than he ever knew. My heart and soul had been ripped from my body and trampled under the heels of fate, but to be with him, I would do it all over again.

"Do not put words in my mouth. Do not use my pain to inflict more onto yourself." I sniffed and swatted away my tears, hopefully before he could sense them. He was right. Tana had been right. But that didn't make it any easier to stop. I apologized to him, and he grunted, accepting it. "You bring life to me." More tears erupted, and I batted those away, too. "With you I feel as though…I can be all parts of me. You challenge me to speak but do not truly push when I need the silence. You match me with a sharpness, something I can grab onto."

I pulled the comb through, testing the work I'd done and was met with a smooth glide, no resistance. The bottle he'd given me was half-full, and I plucked out the stopper and carefully poured a small amount onto my palm. I made sure the bottle was secure and used my own body heat to warm the oil. My fingernails acted as tines, raking the liquid through his pitch-black locks.

"You do that for me. Calm me. Enliven me. I think that's why I argue with you so much."

I poured a few more drops of oil and got to massaging Elián's scalp once more, this time pressing the oil in with each roll of pressure. He grumbled sleepily. "I like to spar with you. But I don't like to fight with you."

"I don't like it either." We were quiet for a while, as I ensured every part of Elián's hair and scalp were touched by the oil. That any tension left was cracked and spilled.

When I used one of the leather ties to pull half of his hair out of the way and neatly portioned three even sections at his hair-line, Elián whispered another question. "Why did you cut your hair?"

I'd not braided anyone else's hair in a long while, but I quickly adapted and started on the plait, securing tightly without drawing too taut. And my answer, like so many, all led to him. "You." He didn't prompt me, and after completing about half of the braid, I found the words to explain further. "I wanted something…drastic. To match the way I felt, the loss. And through the years, I got used to the ease, to cutting it once it reached a certain length. Why did you grow yours? Do you normally keep it this length?" I cast off from his scalp, finishing the rest of the plait quickly.

"No. After leaving you, I neglected myself for many months.

My hair grew, and when I found the energy to cut it, I saw my father each time I looked in the mirror. I could not bear to cut it, save for trimming the ends."

That made me sad, cold and chin quivering. I tied the end of the completed braid and started on the other. "You are very handsome, and it suits you. Did you look very much alike?"

"Leandro and I were always told we inherited more features from our mother. Her coloring, whereas my father's skin was paler. His hair lighter. But, when I smile, which he did often, I see him. When I am sorrowful, I see him. In my anger, I see my mother."

I did not envy anyone who crossed Roza, then. "So, you had two beautiful parents. No wonder you look like this."

This time, Elián accepted my attempt at jest. When it was no longer self-deprecating. From where I sat, thighs bracketing his broad shoulders, I saw the valley of his dimple. The one he inherited from his father.

"And what is your favorite body part of mine, Your Highness?"

That cocksure smirk drew a chuckle from me. "Well, it would be too easy to say your cock or your hands, though they may just make second and third on the list. But, I would say your eyes." He rolled them. They weren't their usual vibrant shade, but they still held the same effect. "You communicate far more with them than you do with your words. That I've irritated you. That I've confounded you. That I'm safe with you. I dreamt about them most nights when we were apart."

"And now? What do you dream about?"

The answer locked at the bottom of my throat. Slamming behind layers and layers of reinforcements. I wouldn't be able to get it out if I tried. Not with the hushed tranquility between us tonight. After…after Francie. If I made it back with them, out of this world and into ours, I would tell him.

For now, I tied off the second plait and responded with, "This and that. Now, when I need your eyes, I need only to turn and find them."

I settled the braids over his shoulders, so they could fall down his chest and he could see them. Elián ran over the bumps of the woven strands, and a gust of wind carried with it fresh dampness and crisp, evening air.

El appeared before me, my favorite part of him staring back at me, hands braced on the bed. He leaned closer, bringing our noses to brush and his breath to skate across my cheek. "El," I whispered.

He took my jaw in hand, tilting me where he wanted. Before he eliminated the last bit of distance between our lips, he said, lower than a whisper, "Thank you, my queen."

In a world where we couldn't say the words, they weren't needed and even that more special. *Elián* was special and too good for me. If there was any chance, any hope, for us, I would have to open myself up to him leaving me again. Hating me.

Rather than descend into the pit of the unavoidable, I kissed him, taking my ability to speak and pouring everything I could not say into him.

I love you.

For what I am hiding from you, I am so, so sorry.

Chapter Thirty-Three
Tana

I halted my descent of the front steps of the lodging house, finding Fenix seated on one of the spindly benches beneath those floating, twinkling lights. The city on the treetop was alive, laughter and music making its way to my ears, and shimmers of their fabrics and wings creating a scene out of a storybook.

"Needed some fresh air?" Fenix glanced at me over his shoulder, and I'd almost forgotten what he'd looked like, without all the layers to protect him from burning to ash. The scar around his neck now matched the one pulling at his cheek.

I approached and sat. My nightgown fell mid-thigh, leaving the rest of my leg to rest on the bench seat. "Not really, what with the windows being just holes in the wall."

"Oh. Right, I well—" He made to stand.

"No! You don't have to leave. If you wanted to be alone, I can just go somewhere else."

"No, you—you're alright. Perfect." He shook his head and scowled at the same time a telltale shout transcended the walls of the lodging house, and I wrinkled my nose in camaraderie.

Really, I was happy for my cousin, but passionate reunions and our sharp hearing did not bode well for a restful night's sleep. Until *they* went to sleep, anyway. A deep groan reached my ears, so I focused on this unexpected addition to our little... whatever we were. "Tell me something about yourself, Fenix." Anything to drown out the noise from the Folk and my cousin with her lover.

He ran a hand over his hair, parting the strands like digging through a flowing stream. The shaved backs and sides were freshly shorn, just a shadow against his scalp. "I, um, up until now, I'd never seen mountains before. At least, not this size."

I remembered how Tomás had teased him for his age. Goddess, what was I even doing at thirty years? Still running after my cousin when I wasn't diving into everything I could learn from the covens or the priestesses, no doubt. Just starting to truly recognize the endless possibilities of such a great gift, magic.

Though my upbringing was exceptionally privileged, being the daughter of the Prince of Versillia, his unfamiliarity with the world was telling. "How old you when you were turned?"

The old Fenix made an appearance, posture growing rigid, and he wasn't looking at me anymore. Fabulous—I'd offended him. After Leen and Elián barely gave him any consideration, and Tomás's teasing, I didn't want—the thought of him coming all this way with us and being treated poorly didn't sit well with me. Even if he'd come under the excuse that he was seeking an apology.

I didn't need my magic to see that he was painfully lonely.

"I'm sorry." I risked a hand on his shoulder, but when he tensed further, I pulled it back with another apology. "Forget I asked."

One evening, during my studies at the Rhaestran Temple, I had lost myself in the library stacks, sitting by candlelight and delving into what happened to the human body when it was changed into a Vyrkos immortal. Weaving an old, old magic that had long grown sentient. It seemed untoward to call it a virus, a sickness, but the way it latched onto the body's faculties and transformed, multiplying until all mortal life was suffocated, operated in a similar way.

And, in many cases, mortal life rejected the assault until a draw in the battle between body and virus resulted in final death.

I'd read many accounts that night, and the sensation of burning and being ripped from the inside out was included in just about every firsthand tale of the changing process. Even for those who'd requested to be changed for the chance of a long, long life, few reported they would make the same decision again if they had been fully aware of the pain.

Then, there were those who were changed against their will.

"I was twenty-three years."

I didn't draw attention to his answer, and I didn't ask for more details. That hushed response felt like more than he'd given anyone in a long, long time, and I recited my gratitude to myself. The more time I spent around Fenix, the more clearly I saw him as more than the acerbic Vyrkos we met on the ship and who refused our help. When he wasn't being actively yelled at or pestered, he was…quiet. Helpful.

"And how many years are you?"

"Two-hundred and thirty-five years." Against his thirty, it seemed…I didn't know, but how had I been judging Fenix's lack of experience when I had many, many more years with not much to show for it? A wealth of knowledge in my chosen field, yes, but my own path? What did that look like?

The same swirl of thoughts with no solution other than *doing* throbbed between my eyes. My cousin was making her own future upstairs, and I was down here, feeling sorry for myself.

"You must have seen quite a lot in that time. And you all are from Morova?"

That was something to hold onto. "No. My cousin and I are from a kingdom called Versillia. It's in eastern Eryva, if you've ever been."

"No. Never. It's a place with a monarch? Like here?"

Oh, Goddess, how did I explain? For a true, clear moment, I almost lied. But Fenix was looking at me again, Vyrkos-red eyes reminding me of the impending need to feed. "Ah, you see…" I huffed, and forced out the rest in one breath. "My uncle was the King of Versillia, so I am technically a Princess of Versillia, if the kingdom still stands."

A nervous, shaking smile matched the turmoil of my insides. I rarely thought of what home was like now. If *Versillia* ever crossed my mind, it was how it once was. When my parents had been alive. When Uncle Hugo and Auntie Liana would afford me far too many leniencies for my age. But, they were all that sort, encouraging boldness, curiosity, learning. Perhaps my cousin's and my habit of running off at the mouth was inevitable. Where she was all brashness and sharp assessments, I spouted unwanted questions and let my search for knowledge lead me…well, lead me to places such as this.

It took a while for Fenix to decipher what I confessed but tried to obscure. I knew exactly when he understood because he started coughing, sputtering on his own saliva. "A—you're a *princess?*"

My cheeks ached with how hard I smiled, trying to force away the discomfort. Just like Meline, I loathed being called by my royal title. Hers, the Warrior Queen, was worse because it was inaccurate but notorious. Mine was very much real, hollow but also filled with expectations.

"Technically. However, Versillia was burning last we were there, so who knows?" A stupid giggle escaped at the end, obfuscating the tragedy of our flight from my homeland.

Fenix's pale cheeks flushed. Not with a complete blush, but the best he could muster, and it made my uncomfortable laughter reverberate that much longer. Oh, Goddess, he would certainly be parting ways with us as soon as we returned to our realm, now.

"Um—how are you feeling? Is your injury healed well?" As if I hadn't checked it before we disembarked in Vharas. At least my cousin was no longer screeching while her Shadow rearranged her insides. If these Folk did not send off every innate defensive sense within my body, I would have sought out some local to provide adequate distraction.

"Oh, yes. Thank you, again. I…I would not be here if not for you."

Such words were common when you practiced healing magic, but it always left me feeling happy, to be appreciated for a craft I'd spent many hours honing. "You're quite welcome, Fenix. Like I said, I'm glad you're here."

He snorted. "Fairly certain you're the only one who feels such a way."

The words rang with something, like the sentiment wasn't limited to just those in our party on this journey. "I hope that's not true, but if it is, I'm more than happy to stand on my own." In this, at least.

Fenix parted his lips to say something else, but before he could, Tomás exited the lodging house, mouth cracked open with a large yawn. Once his jaws were able to snap shut, a sly smile spread on his face, and my irritation took hold. Anxieties aside, Fenix and I were having a perfectly pleasant evening. Or, as much as could be had when the whole of Pyrestan would probably jump at the chance to eat his flesh.

"Well, don't you two make a lovely pair," the Shadow mused, but I was not impressed. Petty schoolground prodding would not get a rise out of me.

Fenix, on the other hand… "Finally grow tired of the show and your right hand?"

Tomás's features screwed in disgust. "That's my brother, you know."

And she was my cousin, but—"Didn't you two have a…past, though?"

"You mean did me and Nogón used to fuck?" Tomás shrugged and sat between Fenix and me. "Of course, but two bossy ones in the bedroom grows *so* tiresome. Wouldn't you say?" He rested his chin on his fist, batting his lashes at Fenix.

I would have to pull him aside and warn him that the best way to deal with Tomás was to not let him pull you into his antics. "Wouldn't I say what?"

"What's your preference, lad? Males, females, other genders? Everyone?" As far as what I'd witnessed spewing from Tomás's mouth, the question was one of the most reasonable I'd heard.

"Like that's any of your concern!"

Tomás tsked. "Lad, we might be dead tomorrow as we attempt to spring a Lylithan in full Frenzy from the clutches of a cannibalistic queen with wings. Talk of sex is one of the few entertainments we have left, aside from fucking each other outright."

I kneaded my knuckle between my brows. If he softened his approach, he would be *much* more likely to spare others from quickly reaching exasperation. But, who was going to teach him an entirely new way of being? Not I.

"For example, I prefer males but have been known to dabble with others when the mood strikes. And you, Tana?"

"I never thought I would say this, but we have that in common, it seems."

"Oh, yes, I remember our hunt. Wild thing, aren't you? What about you, Fenix?"

We both turned to the Vyrkos, and, okay, perhaps I also agreed with Tomás that this was an engaging distraction. Fenix ran another hand through his hair, looking close to biting at Tomás, but he then glanced at me and changed course. He swallowed. "I…"

"Oh, Godyx, are you inexperienced? Or uninterested in sex entirely? I've met a few who are, if that's the—"

"Would you just—I am neither," he said so clearly, deliberately. "I prefer females but—"

"But, what?"

"If you would let me bloody finish a thought! I was *trying* to say that I've not been with any who are not human."

"*Oh*. Well, you aren't poorly looking, as long as you keep your mouth shut. Are you interested in females exclusively? If not, I can show you what it's like to be with someone who you don't have to fear you'll break."

Fenix did more of that sputtering, blushing and scooting further away from us until the armrest of the bench halted his movements. But I'd seen when Tomás was exhibiting *actual* flirtation. His voice would smooth to a predatory point.

This was him keeping the conversation light and teasing, trying to give Meline and Elián privacy while also keeping our thoughts away from the real possibility of casualties tomorrow. If Queen Sarya proved to be as vicious as we suspected.

"I don't mind fucking males, but I do *not* want to fuck *you*."

"Pity." He drawled then angled his body toward me. "What about you, Tana? Care to show Fenix here what sort of tenacious minx you are?"

An outraged squeak slipped through my lips, and all the color drained from Fenix's face. "I think your jesting has gone too far, now."

"Has it? I think I'm being quite selfless, helping you two find someone to warm your bed for the evening while thinking nothing of myself."

I rubbed at my temples, shaking my head. "We do not need your help in such matters, Tom."

"Oh, I know that *you* don't. I saw what you did with those men in Morova. They seemed quite satisfied and all too happy to let you feed from them."

I didn't even bother feeling embarrassed. Sex and hunting and feeding had been such a way of life for me for so long, there was little to be shy about. But that didn't mean we had to subject this newcomer to this...whatever this was. He was clearly uncomfortable. "Stop, Tomás. I think they're done, anyway." I could no longer hear my cousin and Elián's words, but their voices were hushed and intimate. Low enough for me to fall asleep with.

I stood, and stretched my arms overhead. The hour was not late, but with the very limited nutrients we were consuming, rest was important, and it would eat up the hours separating us from getting Francie and returning home.

A resounding thumping reached my ears, and I watched as Tomás slapped Fenix's back in a friendly way as the Vyrkos sat with his head in his hands. Maybe they were able to get along more than they knew. For his sake, I hoped Fenix would start to feel more welcome with us.

"I'm going to bed, and you both should do the same. Tomorrow will be long and tiring."

Tomás grunted, slapping Fenix's spine once more before standing, too. I waited until the latter peeked his eyes open and glanced at me.

I waved him goodbye. "Goodnight, Fenix. Thank you for the company."

"Uh...yep."

Tomás groaned and followed me inside.

CHAPTER THIRTY-FOUR
ELIÁN

Beyond the palace, there were rolling, verdant hills covered in dense, thick forest. Under the cover of night, what would have been magnificent took on a more sinister tinge, but the sight was impressive all the same. Beyond that was snow-capped mountains larger than I'd ever seen. Much of them were cloaked with the heavy cover of clouds, but my thoughts wandered each time I set my sights on the mountains of Pyrestan—were there more Folk who dwelled within the craggy rock overlooking the kingdom?

The clink of silver on ceramic brought my attention back to the royal dining room, where I sat to the right of my queen. The windows, like in the lodging house, held no glass, so the rancid smell from the feast before us mixed with the much milder aroma of the wild.

The Queen Sarya was seated at the head of the ivory table, presiding over all of us with a calm viciousness that stirred the weak licks of Flame I still had access to. She sipped from her crystal glass of honeyed wine while ours remained full. "My children, Princess Sen, Prince Sterling, and Pryncet Sage." They'd not been introduced during our audience with the queen yesterday, and like then, I had no concern for their names or titles.

All three were grown and matched their mother in garb of light blues and gold to complement their wings. Prince Sterling's black hair was cut short and slicked back from his brow, Princess Sen's braided like her mother's. Pryncet Sage kept theirs chopped severely at the shoulder with braids and gold beading woven through it.

Queen Sarya did not wear her crown of bone, but it loomed all the same. Her gown of silk reminded me of the glowing waves of Rhaestras. "And I have here, Captain of the Guard, Wesley, who just returned from your world, actually." The head of her armed force sported white breastplate and long, straight hair of the same shade. "Finally, this is my Master of Coin, Larkin."

The others mumbled pleasantries, about how nice it was to make their acquaintance, and if the Queen detected the emptiness in the words, she did not call attention to it.

I did not speak. I watched, noting every shift the Queen, her children, and her officials made. The guards standing around the perimeter of the room. The breaths from the twenty lining the corridor. The other thirty who stood between us and the gate.

If all went against our primary plan, we would not be going that way. Without our Death, Flames, and magic, so many armed immortals would surely bring our end.

"Does our food not meet your Vyrlandian standards?" Pryncet Sage glared at our full plates, something their mother and the others had already noticed but decided to ignore.

My queen squared her shoulders against the royal Folk, corners of her mouth turning upward pleasantly but with something other than kindness lacing her words. "You will have to forgive us. It appears we are unable to consume Pyrestan food. And one of us does not consume food at all. We do not mean offense."

The Queen leaned forward. "We knew of Raouga but not this detail. Might you know why that is?"

"No. If we could eat here, we would. It…" She looked at the spread of succulent meats, salad and roasted vegetables, whole fish and unnaturally vibrant sauces. "It looks divine."

The Queen gave a smaller, more palatable version of the grin we witnessed yesterday. "You lie, tiny Raouga. But I can forgive you for it, since it was in attempt of nicety."

My queen did not respond, just maintained the milky stare of our opponent who gathered a morsel from her plate and ate.

"Your Majesty," Blackwood cut in, mouth half-full, "would now be an appropriate time to discuss trade? Or perhaps I can speak more privately with the Master of Coin?"

She did not deign him a response at first, continuing to study Meline in a way that left me wanting to breathe flames and burn her where she sat. To leave her a pile of ash for even *thinking* of threatening my queen.

But, Meline could hold her own in this, I knew.

"Walter Blackwood," the Queen finally looked at him, "tell us, are you capable of supplying the same goods as your predecessor?"

The one whose head she consumed in front of the eyes of her citizens? "Yes, Your Majesty. I've a fleet that rivals that of Von Herron's, access to the same channels as well as ownership of the finest apiaries in the world. I've the capacity to bring regular shipments to your location of choice."

Larkin, the Master of Coin, addressed Blackwood this time. "And what of the Vyrlandians?"

"The…" Blackwood pursed his lips, disappearing them beneath the cover of his mustache. "My apologies, I do not follow."

The head of trade flipped lilac hair over their shoulder, brushing against their large wings of similar shade. "We had an agreement with the other human to include a steady stream of

Vyrlandians." They said this slowly, as if Blackwood were daft, and the rest of the Folk regarded him similarly.

The five of us who'd accepted no illusions of geniality understood.

How could *one* merchant from Morova secure the trust of a race far more powerful and older than him? With just sweets in return for their cooperation and priceless fabrics?

"How—"

The Master of Coin drummed their fingers on the table beside their gleaming fork and knife. "We've need for the honey more than Vyrlandians. Typically, the other one would include twenty or so each month. Which…" They tilted their head, as if doing quick calculation. With what we knew of Francie's capture, I already knew the answer. "Is about three years in your world. Surely that gives more than enough time to procure the same amount."

Blackwood sputtered and turned a nauseated eye to the meat on his plate. To which, the Queen chuckled pleasantly and took another bite from hers. "Enough talk of business. Tell me, Raouga, do your kind worship the Mother as well? Or just this God the Vyrlandians sometimes pray to. Mortos, I believe His name is."

Tana, who'd remained calm on my queen's other side, asked, "You know of the Mother?"

The Queen's daughter answered, "Not *your* Mother."

Sarya gave her a censuring glance, one that transcended realms, of mothers everywhere. "What Sen speaks of is our sister creators. We are related, you see. Created by a left hand, while the other, by the right. I've always found it fascinating, the children, though. It seems most confusing. Do you just choose which of Her children to follow? When does your Mother override them?" She shook her head, rattling the beads of bone strung into her curls.

"We—does everyone in Pyrestan worship the same deity, then? Do no others rule over your tree and mountain?"

The Prince chuckled as one would to a child asking a silly, ill-informed question. "What the heathens of the lowlands do is of no concern to us." The lowlands…did that mean—

"Which reminds me, Your Majesty. A messenger from the Aeshí has come bearing the official request for you to attend—"

"Yes, yes." Queen Sarya waved her long, ringed fingers as if swatting away the notion. "You can begin preparations for my attendance to this *blasphemous* coronation." When neither of us reacted, she regarded us conspiratorially. "Really, a mortal becoming queen?" To Larkin, she sneered, "Ready whatever jewels we can spare from the coffers for this Sylveena or whatever her name is. Now, golden Raouga, tell me—"

"Apologies, but I must interrupt." Meline smoothed a hand down her waistcoat. "We brought your mother's bracelet, and I would like to secure my friend in exchange for it before we discuss other matters."

"Ah, yes." Sarya downed the rest of her wine. A shadow in the distance, behind the clouds on the mountain, arced behind her. In the shape of her crown. "Show it to me."

I reached into the breast pocket of my leathers, past the knives I'd hidden there. Against the black of my glove, the slender jewelry shone brightly, despite the many hands that had touched it since it left this land. Meline plucked it from me while giving a thankful brush of her fingers, skin also covered.

"Guards, retrieve the bracelet."

Meline's dagger was in her fist and pointed at the guard who'd stepped forward faster than even I could track. "We had a deal, Sarya. The bracelet for Francie, and I don't see her here."

The Queen bade her guard to halt and wrinkled her nose. "You think I would bring a pet to supper?"

"As the *Leader of Truth*," Meline spat her title, "I expected for you to bring my *friend* so that we may take her home."

The room went silent, save for the howling of the wind swirling from the mountains. I watched the children, how they observed Fenix and Blackwood hungrily, how they smirked as if they had won.

At last, the queen of bones snapped her fingers with a resounding click. A large, carved door opened, and my queen and Sarya continued their staring, their measuring of each other while the thick, oppressiveness of Frenzy swept the room.

Like in the throne room, as soon as Francie set her sights on Blackwood, she let out a guttural scream, this time into a strip of linen tied around her mouth. She was covered this time, in little more than a tattered shift. Her hands were bound behind her back, her feet struggling against the iron grip of the guard who held her arm.

Frenzied starvation made a Lylithan stronger than in their normal state, and even so, as Francie tried and tried to lunge for Blackwood and the blood pumping through his veins, the guard had no trouble keeping her from escaping.

Just how strong were these immortals?

"Your friend, tiny Raouga. Now, my bracelet?"

As we had planned, Tomás, Fenix, and Tana pushed their chairs back and stood. They approached Francie and the guard, and the former hissed at them, seeing them as another threat. Meline and the Queen entered another stare down, and even the mountains watched. Waited.

My queen slid the bracelet, deftly avoiding the platters between she and Queen Sarya, until it landed right before her. At the same time, the Queen nodded, and the guard holding Francie stepped back, allowing for Fenix, Tomás, and Tana to take each of her arms. She bucked, snapping her jaws, kicking her feet and screaming.

Tana did not have her magic here, something the Folk may have suspected but we did not mention, but her knowledge of the body was more than sufficient for her to stand behind Francie and press harshly against the side of her neck. Where the large vein delivering blood between head and body ran thickly. A few seconds, and she slumped between my brother and the Vyrkos, head lolling back into the cradle of Tana's palms.

"Well. Pleasure to make your acquaintance, and we appreciate your hospitality. We will be going, now."

And, really, we had hoped but not trusted our departure would be that simple, which was confirmed by the delighted grin of the Queen of Pyrestan. The satisfaction on her children's faces. "I did not say you could leave, Raouga Em."

"Well." Meline adjusted the cuffs of her blouse, where I knew she had two knives hidden. It was also our signal for this version of our plan. Fleeing *through* the trees. "There are many who call me a queen where I am from. Certainly, you must understand that queens do not take orders from anyone, especially not lying, cannibalistic hags such as yourself. So, if you'll excuse us."

When she stood, the guards inched closer. More entered through the open door. I felt the faint gathering of Death beside me. But if what I had access to was similar to her, it would not be enough.

Before coming to the palace, we'd each snuck off on our own, as best we could, and hidden our packs in the forest beyond the bridge. The guards had watched us, absolutely reporting our movements back to their queen. Perhaps they were still there, in the hiding location I'd chosen as the first to go. Perhaps not.

I assessed the guards again, in a flick of a glance and decided to deviate from our plan. To give us more of a chance of escaping with everyone's lives.

I rose swiftly, rounded the table, and grabbed the Prince of Pyrestan.

The only change in Sarya's demeanor belying her confidence was the tightening of lips. But more of my focus was on the Prince in my hold. His hair in my fist and throat against the tip of my dagger. He thrashed, trying to maneuver away, but a trained Shadow, he was not. I sliced through the membrane of one of his wings, shredding it to the sound of his high-pitched wailing.

Without my needing to command them, the others inched toward the window while I had the attention of the room. Meline faced the Queen and her children who were standing, their knives and glowing palms at the ready.

Slowly, I began to walk toward Tom, Fenix, Tana, and Francie. The Prince was digging his heels in while bleeding all over my leathers. Only the Queen's raised hand kept her children and Captain of the Guard from attacking with their magic and weapons.

Blackwood was still sitting at the table, mouth open and eyes bulging.

"Should we make another deal, Sarya? Our safe passage to our realm for the life of your child? He is the heir apparent, is he not?" He was the one who'd been sitting closest to her in the throne room, so it was an assumption.

One that appeared correct. No one but me and the Prince moved, until we were with the others.

"You understand my new aversion to making deals with Raouga."

"Are you also opposed to the death of your eldest?" I sliced another length of his wing, but his cry of protest was noticeably fainter.

Leaning against the table, murky stare on all of us, the queen smiled. Slow, slight. "Walter Blackwood, you will stay here," she commanded at just the moment he tried to stand. His body threw back into his seat, struggling against an invisible force.

"What is the meaning of this?" He rattled the wood, making it groan.

"You would not survive leaving Tyrgard, anyway. My people have told me how much of our food and drink you've enjoyed. I'll decide what to do with you later."

Only Meline and I remained in the royal dining room, our companions already having escaped through the window and running across the grounds, toward the bridge.

Sarya's shut her eyes, becoming a vision of serenity with her silk gown, beads, and jewels. Meline surreptitiously pushed me toward the window first, and I reached the edge, ready to jump to the trees below with the Prince fighting unconsciousness in my arms.

"I suggest you run quickly, Raouga."

And she whistled.

High, sustained, and echoing across the forest, the valley, and the mountain. Meline and I crashed through the leaves and branches awaiting below, and our feet had barely met the ground before we were running with all the Lylithan speed we possessed. Our paced breaths and the whoosh of the wood around us was not loud enough to drown the piercing, shrill call that seemed to fill the whole realm.

I winced as I ran, carrying the bleeding prince with my queen keeping step beside me. We dodged thick foliage, leapt over anything in our path, and closed the distance between us and our companions.

"We can't get through!" Tana shouted as we neared, standing before nothing but unable to pass all the same. Like the unseen barrier between the flying Folk outside and the throne room, I wagered another guess and crossed the barrier with the Prince.

"Keep contact with him, and we will cross."

Quickly, we did just that, ears popping as we crossed a similar magic to the one that skirted around the Shadow Well. To keep intruders out of the palace grounds.

Another shriek cut through the land, now louder, closer, and we wasted no time, legs pumping as we circumvented the city. Her lights shone through the trees as pinpricks of white, but we kept our focus on the bridge. The howl of wind, in the valley between Pyrestan and the wood housing the entrance to our world.

A wall like rocks and pearls awaited us when we finally broke through onto the cliffside, a few yards away from the bridge. The guards in armor of grays and whites leveled their weapons, and I heard the drawing of bowstrings, arrows aimed at us. I could not hold another weapon with the Prince still in my grip, our only means of bargaining out of this place, but the others were ready.

As a trained fighter, Tom's shamshir reflected the light of the gargantuan moon above as he started cutting down those who charged. My brother immediately pushed himself into battle, cutting through armor and flesh as fluidly as air.

Tana, who balanced her staff between both her hands, moved with expert quickness, whipping away weapons and batting down guards for Tomás to finish them off. And Fenix, with no formal training but speed and strength on his side, carried Francie between them, avoiding blows and keeping her safe.

My queen and I fought, back to back with our weapons and nothing else. The prince did not try to escape me, too shocked by the shredding of his wings to flee, but his howls of pain and outrage joined the battle cries. The clanging of steel against steel.

But we were four fighters amongst an army of immortals just as strong, just as equipped. The scent of Lylithan blood began to mix with that of Folk's, but I had not the time to worry which of us was injured. We tried to press closer to the bridge, to avoid the arrows raining down, but as one grazed my side and a sword nicked my arm, I had the clear, sobering thought that we may not make out of this alive. With no access to my Flames, Tana without her magic, and my queen—

I had looked to her—to help, to savor—and I witnessed Meline take a pointed breath, just one. In the space of time, between inhale and exhale, our eyes said more than we ever could with words. *We will fight. We will get Francie to her mate. I've got you.*

A third, final shriek sounded above the treetops, and my queen and I broke our stare to find a—

A monster. One with wings impossibly large, flying with Queen Sarya grinning wildly on its back.

I may have been imagining the Queen's laughter, but what was assuredly real was the bird larger than what should have been possible. Its wings were extended, broad and straight and faintly blue under the black sky.

We did not wait for it to move any closer. We'd no choice but to continue fighting the guards, to try our best to cross the bridge, and to retreat under the cover of trees on the other side. The only advantage, it seemed, was that this bird seemed no faster than its more natural counterparts.

A pained yelp reached my awareness, one in Tana's voice, and after sinking my blade into the throat of a guard, just between helmet and breastplate, the hair on the back of my neck quivered. Chilled.

Again, I glanced to Meline, but now, my queen had stopped fighting. I watched, terrified, as she lowered her blades and cast a disdainful glare to the sky. With flicks of her wrists, she sheathed her daggers at her belt, raised her arms, and *screamed.*

She did not have enough, she could *not have*, but somehow, she scraped the bottom of her well of power, sending out snaking ivy of Death, a tangle that smelled of cool, quieting decay.

She parted the guards, as if stroking expertly through an ocean wave. And more strands of her power shot behind us, upward to the archers tasked with taking us down from above. Bodies thudded as they fell to the ground, some flying over the edge of the cliff into the pure darkness awaiting.

The others reacted immediately. Fenix, as inexperienced as he was, took his task to heart, darting fearlessly with Francie in his arms, making it over the bridge with Tana behind to protect them. Tomás and me took the opening my queen provided, and I tried my best to not think of the swaying wood beneath my boots.

I looked over my shoulder when Tom made it to the other side where Fenix and Tana waited for my queen and I to cross. Not leaving us.

I'd no time to celebrate my own reunion with steady ground, turning already to ensure Meline was truly behind me.

And she was, but.

She was stopped, less than ten paces from me and facing the white bird, large enough to carry the giant elephants of Banfas in its talons. The Queen cackled, hair flying behind her with no regard for her fallen guards. Her attention was on my queen.

"Meline!" I bellowed. Why was she not coming? Why was she not running with us?

Tana shouted her name as well, begging her to come, but my queen. My queen, she risked one look over her shoulder. Her curls shifted with the breeze, calm like the sigh of the Mother, content in the cycle of lives beginning and ending. As they always had.

Blood trailed from her nostrils, painting her lips a bright red, and my heart stopped. It stopped as Meline looked at me, wordlessly telling me—us—to go.

And my heart shattered as she turned away, black shadows churning around her hands she was now raising toward Queen Sarya diving for her.

No.

The giant bird of prey flexed its talons, opened its beak to reveal rows and rows of sharpened teeth, and I ran away from the forest. I ran toward my queen, and my brother's familiar presence at my side assured me he was here. We did not speak, we had no plan, and yet, we moved fluidly.

Shoving away his fear of my queen and her power, Tomás grabbed Meline by the waist in the same moment I threw the Prince over the bridge.

It was the Queen's turn to scream in the outrage of a mother, low and visceral. I encouraged the monster to ignore us with an arc of flame that lit the night. All remnants of my Flames went into the blast, and it shrieked as its belly burned.

As an extension of her, the beast changed course to fly after the Prince who was already disappeared beneath the clouds. Singed feathers rained down on us, Tomás shouted, a sound of *pain,* and we ran.

I took my queen from him, supported him with his arm slung across my shoulders, and we *ran*.

My muscles burned, my heart lay in pieces with Meline exhausted and bleeding in my arms, and we continued on.

The initial walk to the bridge had felt so long when we'd arrived in this world, with the realization my power was all but gone. Now the journey was short as my feet carried the three of us, meeting Tana, Fenix, and Francie at that confounded tree.

And as planned, taken from his home and bound, the Folk who first stepped through the trunk was glaring at Tana as she held her knife to his throat.

"Open it," she demanded, all kindness gone. In the sharpness of the witch's command, I saw my queen. The one I loved who, just moments ago, had fully intended to leave me.

Chapter Thirty-Five
Elián

None of us spoke, but the moment I pulled my queen and brother through the trunk of the tree, into our world, I felt Zoko's breath. Her touch, my direct line to her infinite power, and I staggered under the weight of it rushing in. Sweat prickled at my temples, and the haze of steam formed around my eyes. Meline moaned, back arching as she sucked in a ragged breath. One filled with dark smoke entering her mouth and nose.

Once we and our packs were all through, Tana plunged her blade in the throat of the Folk who gave us access to pass, ensuring he was unable to race back to the other guards and give us chase. As his blood, the same color as ours, spurted and spilled over her, the tree trunk solidified once again. She kicked it to be sure before dropping the Folk guard to the ground.

None of us looked back.

We walked through the Vharan forest, dark and with a chill in the air, still six but with Blackwood left behind to receive the agreement he sought or to be eaten. Both?

Francie remained unconscious, and at some point along the remembered path, Meline began to squirm in my arms. I did not speak when I let her down, and neither did she as she walked with palpable space between us.

It was just before we reached the main road up ahead, visible through the balding trees, when Tom groaned and tripped over his feet. Immediately, I dropped, lowering him to sit, to catch his breath. He should have been healing—*healed*—enough to walk as slowly as we were.

"Fucker." Then, I noticed his panting, the too-fast beating of his heart.

Black pumped around the hand he had clutched at his side, and my own pulse began to race. "Let me see, Tom." I tried to pull his hand away, but he did not let me. "*Tom,*" I said more loudly, firmly.

His eyes were clenched in agony, his skin cool and drenched in sweat, and when I finally wrestled his hand away to see, a deep gash revealed itself. Tana cursed and dropped to her knees, hands immediately hovering over my brother. My vision swam, reaching uselessly, wanting to help, wanting to beg his body to *heal*.

Purple illuminated underneath Tana's touch, and my brother hissed, kicking his feet in the dirt. I held his shoulders down as the witch worked, brow crumpled as she used her reawakened power to fix my brother.

"What's wrong with him?" The Vyrkos asked quietly.

I could not find the words, running over the events on the bridge in my mind. Meline answered for me, whispering thickly over my head. "It bit him. The monster she was flying." As he was helping *me* protect her. Jumping into the fray without a thought, as he'd done for me time and time again.

"Is he healing?" He had quieted, but the cut of Tana's worried green stare told me everything. The shards of my heart pulverized even more. Tomás would survive this. He *had* to. "What can we do?"

Tana was whispering, pouring water from one of our skins over the wound to clean away the blackened blood. The light of her magic seeped inside the wound, sending him into another bout of weak convulsions.

"Fenix."

The Vyrkos stepped up, still holding Francie. "I hate to ask, but do—would you allow him to feed from you?"

He did not answer, but I heard a shuffling, and raised my head to find him transferring an unconscious Francie into Meline's arms. The Vyrkos crouched and rolled up his sleeve without hesitation, without thought. For my brother.

He dropped his fangs and punctured his own wrist, where the prominent vein flowed. A groaning sounded, this time followed by Francie stirring in Meline's arms. At the first scent of blood she could consume.

I ignored the watering in my own mouth at the sweet aroma, the first source of live nutrition we had encountered in days. Fenix clamped his wrist to Tomás's mouth, and through the pain, his thirst took over. I allowed his hands to move, to grab Fenix's arm as he drank.

"I...I'm going to get Francie to feed. I won't go far." I did not take my eyes off of Tomás. Afraid he would drink too much from the Vyrkos. Afraid of what I would find if I were to meet my queen's stare again.

"That's good, Fenix. It's slowing the spread of the toxin," Tana encouraged while healing Tomás. I watched as the wound slowly closed, flesh knitting against flesh, and once both sides of the wound met, it formed a long, jagged scar in his dark skin. One that cleaved in half the tattoo of Sjatan towers on his side, turning the already deep-toned skin there completely black.

I had to pry Tom's hands off of the Vyrkos, once he reached the line of almost taking too much, and it was my strength combined with the Vyrkos's that kept Tom from fighting both of us to drain Fenix dry.

Fenix and Tana both pulled back while I remained close, touching and ensuring my brother was still here. Still alive. He breathed shallowly, still sweating, but he was no longer writhing. "What is it?"

Tana inspected Fenix's wrist, needlessly healing it with a flash of her power before it could do so on its own. She gave him a quick, friendly embrace and thanked him, to which he denied needing thanks. When she turned to me, her expression had calmed. But it was not happy. "That I am not sure of. I...whatever ails him is still in there, but I've staunched its growth. For now."

"For now?" I asked, touch on his pulse to remind myself it still beat.

"For now," Tana confirmed.

I wordlessly shut us in our room. We'd barely spoken to one another as we crossed back into our realm. Aside from simple directions, noises of agreement or dissent, I'd been unable to get my thoughts to solidify.

Each time I blinked, even for that brief moment, I saw it. My queen standing in the line of the beast. The muted dregs of her power swirling around her, ready to fight, yes.

But the resignation on her face. The long, significant glance she gave me, as if committing my face to memory. As if saying goodbye.

The peace she had asked for, I could not help remembering the glimpse of it, then. When she gave herself over to die.

I fell onto the foot of the bed, not tracking how I'd gotten there. Though there were walls between us, I could hear Tana's quiet steps. The soft pulls of my brother drinking from the Vyrkos who volunteered himself as source.

This was the third time they attempted this. The tandem healing and feeding, but the relief would only last for a few moments, hours at most. Though mortals were ideal, Fenix's blood should have been sufficient nutrition.

My brother's body should have been healing itself. And yet, the sickness came creeping back without fail. He could barely walk on his own.

With Mamá, Leandro, and Papá, each heartbreak came with a sudden explosion. The type to leech all air, all light. No matter how much experience I gleaned from the last, the pain of it never abated. The fall after the carpet was ripped violently beneath my feet.

And yet. Losing another brother, slowly, gruesomely. Loving someone whose despair was also decaying them from the inside out. This was a pain I'd never known. The trials of another world could not compare to this.

My hands were shaking.

"El...I..." she tried. Even that sounded like defeat.

A faint glow of light brightened my view of floorboards, my scuffed, muddy boots. Water swam in my vision as Meline's feet stopped before mine.

"El, *please.*"

Please, what? What could I do anymore? What did she want from me? What did I need to promise her so that she would stay?

There was no reason for her to sacrifice herself on that bridge. No reason for her to offer herself as a diversion. And by her withdrawn glances when we returned to our world, she knew.

Meline's knees thudded to the floor. Something else landed beside her, and then her bare fingers were pulling on mine. Reaching for me.

The contact ushered forth more tears, and I watched them pool onto our skin and seep between where she touched me.

"Elián," her voice cracked, "you're scaring me."

To my ears connected to my fracturing heart, her words sounded like an accusation, and Zoko's Fire used it as the kindling it was so begging for. Anything but this pain. "*You* scared *me.*" Through my fangs, it sounded sharper than my heated sword.

Her flinch further fanned the flames attempting so much to weld the pieces of my soul back together. To prevent further damage until I was one mass of welded parts. "*You* promised no running. No leaving. But you lied."

Meline's nails tightened into my flesh, a reflex to my own version of spitted venom. But the pain was good. Physical was far better than what was intangible.

"I—I'm not running—"

"Nâ! You were not going to fight. You were going to use saving us as an excuse to end yourself. *No. More. Lying.*"

I raised my gaze, now, but her mirrored sorrow made me regret it as soon as our gazes met. The despair was not just mine, it was hers, but she refused to make it *ours*.

I had tried so hard to *talk*, to communicate, and all this time, she would not do the same with me. Not with whatever weighed on her so.

We were both weeping, staring with blustering breaths as my brother struggled to heal in the next room. "El…I…I never wanted to hurt you. I would rather—"

"Do *not* finish that sentence. You hurt me by hiding away. You hurt me with what you did in that stupid place!" We remained joined, my queen and me, but I had felt closer to her in my dreams. There was still something she was hiding, and she would not *tell me*. "*Why*?" Smoke wafted from my nose, my mouth, but I could no longer control it. I'd once thought distance, *words* were the obstacles between us.

This? I did not even know what *this* was.

But there was something. I could taste it in the air, could trace it around the trembling of her lips. "*Why*, Meline?"

The bones in my fingers protested, and I could almost hear them creaking under the strain of how tightly she was holding onto me, now. My focus was on her face, searching for clues, for *answers*, but I could sense her power, too. The way it spilled into the air, confused and searching for a threat.

"El…" The trembling of my muscles were joined by the tremors in hers. Until it was an endless loop. "I *can't.*"

"*Why?*"

Her cheeks were a mess of tears, her words garbled. "Because then you'll truly hate me."

The growl I gave came with more smoke. Meline cracked one of the bones in my fingers, like the snapping of a carrot.

We did not drop our hands.

"*Tell me,*" I begged, demanded, sobbed. "Tell me what would make you think it better for me that you were dead."

Meline flinched again, as if my laying out exactly what she'd done was a strike to her face. Her cheeks darkened with a flush, and when she sucked in a breath, I did not know what to expect. Another denial? Placation?

Whatever I had in mind, I did not anticipate… a name.

It was unclear, through the watery fog of tears. But as if gazing at a figure through sheets of rain, I—I thought I could decipher what she said. What it meant, though, I had no idea.

My stomach turned in anticipation as she opened her mouth again, parting her lips to identify the valley that stood between us. Since she had been back in my arms, *this* was it.

"His name was Soleil."

Another of my fingers snapped, but try as I could to focus on the physical pain, the mental was insistent. "You… have someone else?"

Meline's fang ripped through the surface of her bottom lip as she shook her head. Violently. "No. I," she gasped for a breath, "I have not been with anyone but you in three years. Since the first time you tasted me in Rhaestras. It has been you."

Later, I would be able to examine her assertion. Years, and I would be able to access a sense of possessive satisfaction and also disappointment that I'd been unable to say the same.

But just as my Flames grasped for any spark to ignite and guide me through the labyrinth to my queen, the truth I suspected doused them in an instant.

Four heartbreaks.

"Soleil is the name of our son. Our boy."

Chapter Thirty-Six
Meline

If I'd feared Elián hating me before, it didn't come close to the way I now certainly hated myself. The way Elián's strength, even when he was lamenting what I'd done as we faced down those tricky degenerates, crumpled. His hands went slack between mine, only held up because I kept them.

But, goddess, it felt so devastatingly good to say his name again. Instead of leaving it screamed over the lapping waves of the Ralthan river. Where I scattered the first of his ashes.

"Soleil," Elián whispered after a long moment, countless breaths.

The sound of our son's name, curling from his father's voice. That was more my undoing than admitting the truth. Never, as I'd imagined this moment, had I been able to capture how it would sound from Elián's mouth. It was music.

And the rest of the story tumbled out of me, like a rock slide. "Tana sensed him first. As we traveled." I closed my eyes, continued to let the tears fall as I transported back to those days. When I tried my best to process Mathieu's betrayal and my greatest mistake. "We were in Carthas, then. I worked at a tavern, and Tana sold goods and simple spells at market. We were regrouping and licking our wounds, but then there was *him*.

"I...when my belly grew, there was no room for ignoring it. Even as I still expected the pregnancy to end on its own, we..." a sob hitched my chest. "We went on. He grew, and though my body weakened, though I berated myself every day for telling you to go, I became," I winced, "hopeful. My search for you, for a Shadow who could lead me to you, was fruitless. I still didn't trust the guild as a whole, so I kept my name, my state, and my connection to you a secret. Of course, they wouldn't divulge any information to a nameless female. Wouldn't carry any messages for me.

"T-The strain on my body became too much, and Tana and I were forced to stop in Ralthas. Life slowed, and I turned into myself, turned my dreams of telling you to bringing him to you. Or you finding us."

My grip on Elián became so intense that it was unsteady. My vision was all but completely compromised, but El's sorrowful stare pushed me to finish. To reopen the wound I had been wrapping with dirty bandages. "And then... I—the pains were so intense that I don't remember much of the labor. My throat raw from screaming, my body drenched in sweat as I labored on the floor. Tana's steady instruction. Later, she would tell me that it was twelve hours. Like that. But it felt an eternity condensed in a blink, before he was in—" I clenched my eyes and mouth shut, then. I'd never had to speak this aloud. The only person who knew was Tana, and she'd been there to witness it. Had drenched her hands in my blood to help me bring life into this realm when I'd ended so many.

El didn't say anything. But he didn't have to. *He* permeated my awareness. The Fire confused and disturbed by this loss I'd lain at his feet.

When I'd resolved to give myself over to that flying beast, I regretted it the moment I saw the horror on his face. There was no question that I would die for those I loved. But that instant of time, where the dense fog in my mind and heart cleared to almost nonexistence, I realized that the choice I made was not a selfless one. That by sacrificing myself, I was just transferring my pain to him. To them.

Voice thick, I finished the story for Elián. Gave him the full truth that he deserved. "And he was beautiful. So, so, s-so beautiful." I could see him now, smeared with the parts of me still clinging to his pale brown skin and matting his black curls. "And I chanted his name, whispering and claiming him while he was warm and wriggling in my arms."

I was there now, standing in the corner while I watched myself hold him to my chest. Somberly looking on the moment of joy while Tana helped me deliver the rest that connected my son to my body. Ushering him from the universe within me to the one we were supposed to share together. El's question was spoken as if he stood beside me. Two specters with grim knowledge of what would inevitably come.

"What happened?"

I saw it, the moment I'd realized something was amiss. That as soon as our physical connection was severed, Soleil stopped breathing.

I narrated it for El, as if it was happening, as if he was watching it for the first time with me. In a way, he was, because as many hours I'd sat by the Ralthan River with my swollen belly shrinking, I never revisited the actual moments it'd happened.

"And…" my face was a mess of mucous and tears, my eyes swollen. Yet, my chest was the lightest it'd been since I'd known what it was to be a mother without her child. "And when he took his last breath—what I knew later to be his last breath, these appeared." I twitched the marked fingers, marking a loss so deep that it'd changed me inevitably. Irreversibly. I had started over, time and time again, confronted my own death, and with Soleil, I had given life. If only for a moment.

Then, at last, something I hadn't even told my cousin. I whispered, "His soul did not linger. H-He was in my arms, and I felt the brush of his soul being pulled from them." I'd spent many days being thankful that he knew nothing of this realm but safety within my embrace. And I spent many nights mourning every second of lost time Elián and I could have had. Even enough time with my son's soul to say goodbye.

And now, now I shared that burden with Elián. Maybe even doubled it in his lap because at least I'd gotten to hold Soleil. Name him. My grief already felt like too much to hold. He didn't want me to say I'd rather die than hurt him, but it killed me nonetheless. To feel his agony that was too big for this room. For this world.

I drew a breath. "I am…sorrier than words can express, El. I did not—" my breath hitched "—w-want you to feel this. To know this sorrow."

A hot weight fell on my brow, pressing, and I fluttered my eyes open again, cutting my view of the past.

Mango. Honey. Embers.

His mouth opened several times, closing then starting again. I gave him time, and as he cried, his voice was rougher than I'd ever heard it. "D-D-Do n-n-n-n—" I dropped his hands to grab his face, to caress his jaw that was tensing as he fought for his words.

"It's okay, El. I'm…" I almost told him that I was okay, but we'd gotten to this place because I had run that lie ragged. "I will be okay." The assurance, surprisingly, rang true. I said it again. "I will be okay, and I—I hope you can forgive me one day for not telling you sooner and for preparing to leave you once again. I did not want to add to the ones you'd lost but was willingly putting myself on that list instead. I have…I have had three years to come to terms with our son's death. Please, take the time you need. And I…I will be here." For as long as he needed. If he never came back.

I did not count the breaths, didn't even want to impose that sort of pressure on him. So, I'd only the measure of the uneasiness in my gut. It was a different sort, now that I was on the other side of this fear I'd grown so large in my mind. He was touching me, had allowed me to hold him as I told the whole sad tale. But was this the kindness of a farewell?

Elián stood abruptly, so much so that I had to flinch to avoid colliding with him. I twisted my body where I knelt, tracking him as my sobs shot to the surface. His hands were trembling, and his footfalls were—loud as he went to the door. "I-I-I-I w-wi-*will* be ba-a-a-ack."

And he was gone.

I couldn't bring myself to cry any longer. My worst fear in this was what just happened, me telling Elián about our son who I'd lost and then him leaving. But I clung to his assurance. That hope he would return.

For a while, I used my senses to follow the sound and scent of him as he moved further away from me. Through the corridors, outside, into the woods surrounding until even my hearing was no match for the distance.

I looked down at my hands in my lap, the blackened fingers signaling a closeness with my Goddess gift at the expense of my child. In all the years I'd seen, motherhood had not been a title I felt worthy enough to have. Even as I nurtured my body and babe to the best of my ability, readying myself to live and *be* differently.

What was I now? I still hadn't found the answer to that question. Tana tried to assure me—before I'd wept and told her to stop—that I was still a mother. She'd said a mother did not disappear once her child stopped breathing.

But what if they never opened their eyes?

My knees were aching by the time I rose and stripped. Washed my skin with lukewarm water and harsh soap. I lay my wet head to pillow, eyelids swollen and lips bitten raw. This was a familiar position, too. Curling into myself, arm around the home I'd tried my best to make for him. Soleil. My little sun.

Sleep, surprisingly, came swiftly. Tana, Tomás, and Francie were asleep as well, and the silence was welcome instead of oppressive.

I'd done it. No more secrets impeding my view of Elián. No guilt as I looked into his eyes, imagining the particular shade of Soleil's, had he been able to show them to me.

I dreamt of papayas. Of sitting on the same white sand of Rhaestras where I'd once dreamt of a relentless serpent. Tonight, I sat under the warm rays of the sun as I fed the orange fruit to a child sitting in my lap. I dreamt of kissing a mass of black, silky curls and inhaling a scent that was warm and peppery. Ocean and forest.

Of strong arms hugging me from behind and a different kiss planting on top of my own head. Of deep, lilting microtones carried off into the wind that chased the waves.

The child started to turn, already giggling as they were about to say something up at me, but I blinked awake. About to see my son then blearily taking in the rumpled quilt around me.

But the arms around me, they were still there.

Elián settled the quilt over himself and burrowed closer against me. Holding me. I'd not made a sound, but he knew I was awake.

"Will you…one d-day. Draw him for m-me?"

I wondered where he'd been, how long he'd been gone, but I said I'd give him space. He smelled strongly of smoke and flame

And he kept his promise, that he would come back. I could at least keep mine.

I pressed back into Elián's chest, like I'd done in my dream, and nodded, hair shuddering against the pillowcase. My hands had not wrapped around pencil since those days filled with wary hope. When I drew portrait after portrait of his father for Soleil.

If I could have spoken in that moment, I might've admitted that I'd been too afraid to draw our son. Of what new injury it would cause.

"This...I need to share this p-pain, Meline." His voice sounded so small, cracking and vulnerable.

And I loved him enough to do this. Finally.

"I think," I cleared my throat and admitted into the stillness of our room, "I think I need that, too."

CHAPTER THIRTY-SEVEN
ELIÁN

"You're bloody fucking—" Tomás cut off in a fit of coughing, bags heavy beneath his eyes. I reached for the jug of water by the bed and refilled his cup for him. He glared at me as I extended it, but he accepted all the same. Once he was able to speak, he finished, "A *child?*"

I managed a nod, but my head felt so heavy, it was a struggle to right it back up. "Yes. She named him Soleil."

After retreating into the forest, needing air and space to let my powers and emotions rage, I'd returned with dragging feet to Meline. To share space with the only one who knew exactly how I felt.

I did not want to be alone anymore. After finding a few boulders to burn, to get the urge to ignite *out*, I craved the solace of her.

My brother, even in his illness, watched me as if I was the one close to death. And, with the glimpse of myself as I'd washed and dressed this morning, perhaps the concern was valid.

"Soleil. Your…your fucking *son. Shit.*" Whatever strength he had remaining, Tomás used it to bring me into a tight embrace. Not as strong as he'd usually be able to manage, but the pressure of his arms was welcome. Tana was tentatively optimistic that a regimen of her healing magic and steady feedings would keep him well enough to voyage back to Eryva. I clung to that hope.

Now, as he sat with me, the held-back moisture in my brother's eyes made me feel seen. "And so," he gently plied, "what now?"

I had lain awake all night, asking myself versions of that question. As Meline fell asleep in my arms, I counted her heartbeats. The curls on her scalp. The freckles on her shoulders. And still, I had no answer but to… endure this. To know that she birthed my child and lost him, alone. That we would both go the rest of our lives with this mutual heartbreak.

What I did know, however, was that it would remain shared. That I would hold her as I fell apart, and she would do the same with me.

To my brother, I simply said, "Keep going."

Tom situated the blankets on his lap and searched my face for something. After some time, he shook his head, brow furrowing. "The—it makes sense now. The witch slipped a couple of times. Nothing big, but I…I should've put the pieces together."

I shifted in my seat. During my restless night, I had also reflected on the evidence throughout my reunion with Meline that I should have investigated further. I had been blinded by my excitement and relief, at having her with me again. Convinced that she would soon settle into the safety of us rebuilding *together*.

She had thought I was going to leave. Deny her after she shared what she endured. That was rolled up into this as well— an assessment of my character or a reflection of how little she thought of herself? I was still unsure.

To Tomás, I sighed and shook my head once. "No, you could not have known. She was not ready to speak of it, and her cousin is loyal to her. The witch, she," I swallowed, looking down at my empty hands, "she helped her birth him. Was there to lose him, too."

"Have you…talked to her about where you all go from here?"

To that, I shook my head again. We had not. This morning had been stilted. Every flavor and facet wrapped in sadness. Grief. We washed separately but in the same room, dressed, and went to check on our companions.

But we would talk. The intention was in the long, wary glance she gave me as we parted ways. In the brush of my fingers against hers as I headed for Tomás and she for Francie.

My brother and I moved on to other concerns, perhaps him sensing I had no more words on the matter of my son. I had always taken longer to process things, once I set myself on that path. This was no different.

He had me reach into one of his packs and retrieve a deck of cards. Something to pass the time before we were able to set off. I'd offered multiple times to find him a human or other mortal, to bring them back for him to feed.

But he refused, nose wrinkling as he said that he was not yet so far gone. That he would wait for the Vyrkos should he need to feed. How having someone hunt for you was different than having a willing donor coming to your bedside, I was not sure and did not ask.

At one point, after I had lost at least two gold pieces, Tana came in to check on my brother. She used more hushed words over her glowing hands, focusing primarily on Tom's bare chest. When she eventually pulled back, he was able to sit up a bit straighter, but the smile she offered him was not the bright, carefree ones I'd seen her aim at others.

Tom did not seem to notice. Or he did not let himself dwell on it.

"As soon as Fenix wakes, we'll set off." For Nethras, she meant. From what I could hear, Meline and Francie were not yet back from the hunt my queen led to quench Francie's high need for blood, to help her through the remnants of starvation. Of Frenzy.

Meline and I had woken late, but there were still many hours of daylight yet. Tana decided that we would wait for Fenix to sleep, even though he had the coverings to allow him movement during the daylight hours. My fingers tightened on my hand of cards, at the thought of wasted time. The journey to Nethras was going to be even more time at sea. At least four week's ride. The acrid scent of sickness, as much as Tana's powers staunched its growth, permeated the room. Lylithans so rarely fell ill that the aroma was almost offensive.

I was not sure Tom would survive whatever was poisoning his body.

"Did we receive any letters? From The Well."

As soon as we'd come upon this village a handful of days ago, we found a small pharmacy, just one dusty room, and sent word to the Well that Marco should request some leave time and have an escort bring him to Nethras. There was enough time for them to arrange the journey, and hopefully, we would bring Francie home just as he was arriving.

Only Shadows could send word to The Well, and the letters themselves were warded against any who wasn't Shadow. To open it would yield a blank letter.

Today, Tana had spoken of her intention to replenish her supplies at the local market this morning, as well as promising to bring back any letters addressed to Tom and me. "No, there was only a letter from Whitley."

I grunted and thanked her. After finding my own way back to my queen, I was relieved for the Lylithan to finally be getting their mate back.

But the lack of response from Noruh was…concerning. Or not? Throughout our travels, she or Marco had maintained steady communication with us.

I glanced at Tom who was already frowning. "How long were we in that realm again?"

Tana looked off in the distance, counting and comparing. "We were there for only three days. But here…when I asked around town, they confirmed we were gone *from here* for almost four months."

Tomás cursed, and a dark sense of foreboding creeped further up my spine. When we returned, the weather had changed from the brightening of spring to the darkening of autumn, but hearing definitively the skip in time was more than disconcerting.

Four months and no word from The Well.

A knock announced Meline and Francie's return, and when they pushed open the door, they brought with them an unfamiliar human.

"No," my brother said before they could even open their mouths. Tana sighed, and Francie hung back, watching the rest of us. More color had returned to her face, and though she watched with subdued alert, she was much calmer than she had been just a few short days ago.

Was her body confused by the change? At once being in Frenzy for three months but also three years?

Meline pointed a gloved finger at my brother. "You shut up. Now, this is Daveed. He has agreed to let you feed from him. Fenix needs a break."

Tom shot me an incredulous look, as if I had anything to do with this development.

I *had* spoken my support for this idea, when Meline and I were readying for the day, but I did not tell my brother that. It was best to take the choice out of his hands in this matter.

"You traitor!" Tomás hissed at me as I rose from my seat and extended my hand. He slapped his cards into my palm, grumbling about not needing to be fed like a baby bird, or something of the like.

The human appeared hale with a luster to his skin and a flush creeping up his neck and ears. My own impending hunger was a drying in my stomach, a dulling of my overall energy. But I could go out and hunt later.

Daveed shuffled further into the room, gaze going between

Tom's sullen form on the bed and Meline's encouraging one that guided him forward. He sat slowly, onto the edge of the wooden stool. Without instruction, he scooted it until he was practically in the bed with Tom, and he craned his head to the side, exposing his neck.

"Just the wrist," my brother sniped, flustering the human who cleared his throat and obeyed.

Before I could properly chastise him, the insatiable hunger took over, and Tomás's focus was on the vein pulsing in the man's arm. Through this sickness, Tom had lost much of the strength and speed characteristic of our race. But there must have been some remnants, with the way he snatched and sank his fangs into flesh.

The three of us left at that point, giving Tom privacy to feed and Tana to supervise. In the corridor, with rich sunlight streaming in through the windows at either end, the two females turned to me. They looked nothing alike, other than the caution with which they observed me. For different reasons, of course, but they prompted the same reaction within me. A desire to put them both at ease.

"How are you feeling, Francie?" I asked.

She shrunk a moment, a minute curling inward, like she'd done on the dais in Queen Sarya's throne room. But a quick cut of her eyes to Meline beside her kept her from going into the full defensive crouch of a Lylithan in Frenzy. "I'm…" her voice was still scratchy, unused. "I'm feeling okay. Better. Thank you."

I nodded, trying to give her my attention but failing. "I am glad. I would like to speak privately with Meline, if that is all right."

Francie swept her gaze left and right, as if translating and deciphering my words. My queen's spine went rigid, but she managed to slowly place a hand on her friend's shoulder, giving time should she want to pull away. Francie tensed but ultimately accepted the touch. "Do you need me? Or will you be okay?"

Though she'd been cautious of Meline's gesture, anyone

touching her really, she did visibly relax the longer Meline's hand remained on her shoulder. "Yeah. I'll go nap in my room." She even tried for a wooden smile, one that was all effort.

Meline returned the gesture with one much more organic, but the worry was in the strain around her eyes.

Francie scuttled off to her room, leaving me in the corridor, facing Meline. Alone.

"Um," she cleared her throat, "what is it that you want to talk about?" I gave her a long look, one that needed no words to express my feelings about her question. Meline shook her head and chuckled dryly. "Of course. Ah, sure. Where..." She looked up and down the small area of space around us, between us, at a loss.

But I agreed, this was not exactly private, nor the best place for this conversation. "Walk with me?" I remembered to form it as a question, even with the restlessness in my bones.

I waited, watching, as she fidgeted and bounced slightly from foot to foot, as if readying for an attack. Had I the ability in that moment, I would have laughed. Living as a Shadow for so many years, with the power of Zoko in my veins, I'd long become accustomed to people being afraid of me.

If there was anyone in this realm I wanted to feel completely safe with me, though, it was her.

She agreed wordlessly, after a moment, but her gait was charged as we walked from the inn to the forest surrounding. The leaves forming the thick canopy overhead were no longer a fringe of greens and yellows but now a tapestry of oranges, reds, and purple. Some had made the end of their life cycle, turning to brown, falling and now a soft, crackly cushion under our feet.

Meline was the first to speak as we progressed with no destination in mind. "So...is there something specific you wanted to ask me? To talk about?"

I kept my eyes ahead of us, on the moss clinging to trunks. On dead grass and the insects flitting past. "I would like to discuss..." What did I want to talk about? "Our son."

She sucked in a breath but did not stumble. "W-What—" she cleared her throat and picked up a long stick in our path "—what about him?"

Everything, I wanted to say. But that was not sufficient or specific enough. I wanted to know every detail about him, how she'd prepared for him, how she'd healed physically from him, and how *we* were going to move on with his absence like an ever-present wound in our lives. Instead, I asked, "How do you feel about him? Now." Because as much as I longed to know him, Meline was here.

She began to slowly twirl the wood in her hand. "Now... well, I miss him, obviously. But it is difficult? The grief is...more about what could have been. What," her voice grew thick, "he could have been. Rather than mourning what we had." Quickly, she added, "There is grief over that loss as well. It was the first time I'd properly slowed down." I made a noise of understanding, urging her to continue. She chuckled. "Had I not been forced to, I probably never would. Rest as much as I did in those months." The echo of my own grief that was slippery and ill-defined. All I had to miss was what could have been. A faint outline.

I hesitated with my next question, worried how she would take it, but, "How did you—d-did you bury him?"

The lazy arcs she was making with the stick immediately halted. Her steps did as well, and I stopped, turning back to finally look at her. She faced me, almost as if purposefully challenging herself to. "Tana and I, we..." Her lips trembled, and she brought the heel of her free hand to her chest, rubbing. "It is traditional in Rhaestran culture to cremate, s-so, we wrapped him. And I spread the ashes over the Ralthan River and a meadow where I spent many of my days of rest." Aside from the brief stumble, Meline mechanically recited the words, as if she'd already prepared them for me. Shielding herself from my objection to the way she'd said goodbye to Soleil.

But I was not upset. I was... surprised. Shocked and thankful and suspicious of just how much the Goddesses were involved in our fate. Meline always bemoaned Rhaea in particular, for 'cursing' her with the power of Death with no guidance at best, or purposefully making her suffer at worst.

I did not respond, combing over all she had told me, but my queen stepped closer, twirling the stick again. "Is that—is that not what you would have wanted?" Her fear filtered through my awareness. Not quite the sour scent so common in my line of work. Something softer, deeper.

"Yes. Cremation is my people's custom."

She loosed a breath, and her shoulders inched down from their heightened position near her ears. "I figured, but I had still worried."

"The Ralthan River. A meadow," I repeated. Where she'd returned our child's ashes to the earth of my father's homeland.

Where I'd played as a child myself.

Meline switched hands, winding the stick with her left, now. She nodded. "I didn't have much to do, and the little cottage where Tana and I lived was nearby. Spent a lot of time reading and drawing." Then, much quieter, Meline looked down and admitted, "The meadow was when I first felt him move within me. The river was where I first noticed his scent. The beginnings of it, anyway. I would talk to him quite a bit. About everything, anything. You."

A tear, sudden and unstoppable, dripped out of my eye. I swallowed. "My father was from Ralthas."

She offered me a small smile. "I remember."

Speaking this suspicion out loud felt… strange. "I am uncertain if we are thinking of the same places. B-But I—I spent much of my time with my brother and father playing in a Ralthan meadow. Swimming in the Ralthan River." I almost did not want her to confirm or deny it. Without that, I had room to believe I'd been close to him, to Meline and Soleil. That I'd played on the same soil, splashed in the same waters, if only separated by time.

Was my family caring for him now? Playing with him in whatever afterlife awaited our kind?

The stick snapped within Meline's grip, breaking cleanly in two pieces and falling to the forest floor. She stared up at me with wide eyes, and I did not look away. "Y—I thought you were from Zonoras?"

I liked the sound of my homeland on her lips. "I am. I was born there, and because of our gift, my father agreed to primarily raising Leandro and me in Zonoras. He and Mamá were lovers but not companions. They loved one another but also had their own lives. His primary home away from the Well was in Ralthas."

What piece of information she hung onto, though, I did not expect. "And, do you want that, then? To be like your parents?"

It took me some time to catch up to what she asked, my mind still reeling by yet another unexpected connection we shared. I seldom prayed to Zoko, my mother's piousness never something I'd picked up, but I sent a silent one, now. Quickly but emphatically thanking Her and Her siblings for whatever part they played in bringing Meline and me together. From the beginning.

"To be like..." My parents? I loved Mamá and Papá very much, still to this day. And when they'd reunite, they would embrace and kiss and go off on their own, a testament to the centuries they'd been friends and shared pleasure. But when they had my brother and me, they were older than Meline and I were now. Other than just not being something they wanted in life, I'd never gotten a clear answer as to why they did not want to marry or mate. My brother and I used to tease them, when they shared affection after time apart. But, just as they'd alluded to knowing they wanted to remain untied, free in that way, I'd known even as a boy that should I find someone who looked at me the way Mamá did Papá, I would want them *with* me. "No. I do not. I've told you what I want from you."

Her heart picked up, thumping against the inside of her chest, ringing in my own ears. "You want my love."

"Yes."

"My presence. My words and my body."

Without realizing, I'd stepped closer as Meline repeated my words back to me. "Yes."

My hands reached up, gently brushing her sides, and she whispered, "To *be*. To share pain."

"Yes," I repeated again.

"Even after—after Soleil." Could there be such a thing? He was no longer in this realm, but he was forever marked on our souls. On *us*.

I pulled Meline closer to me, until there was nothing left between us. Using the backs of my fingers, I caressed the edge of her jaw, dusted with a faint cluster of freckles. Twelve of them. "Our son does not change how I feel about you. What I want."

She was crying. Not the thick wails of last night, but a silent release, now that we'd finally reached past the valley and met one another on the other side. "I want that, too." Her voice cracked.

I bent, but before my lips met hers, I spoke into them, "I love you. My queen."

A gust of air swept my skin, and a burst of her peppercorn scent bloomed. Her scent carried a gentle twine of the breeze over waves. And, faintly, a flowery sweetness I had not focused on before. One that was not there three years ago.

Fingers tightened in the front of my tunic, sharp fingernails scraping against the skin above my waist. "I—love you, El."

I kissed her. Pressed my lips to hers. But the way she craned up into me, the way we melted into each other, it was truly more than just a kiss. When I had found my queen, seeing her across the ballroom in Morova, I had thought my search ended. The start of my life with her beginning on that day.

But, as our lips parted and joined, over and over in an unhurried pace, I knew I had been wrong. Surrounded by towering ash trees, sunlight dappling through the crimson autumn leaves,

I knew that *this* was the true end to our journey back to one another. Ushering in a new beginning.

III
New Beginnings

CHAPTER THIRTY-EIGHT
MELINE

"Well. My condolences," Tomás mumbled while the rest of us stood, silently gaping at the sight across the street.

My home, the apartment that'd once been mine for a century, was… gone. Not just that, but the building was no more. The charming café where Shoko, Lee, Tana, and I had met for many meals.

Elián's hand wrapped around mine served as an anchor while I parsed through this newest loss. It'd been years since I had such a space of solace, years since I'd had the inclination to reach out for the trinkets and heirlooms within its walls.

A brush of Maman's. Papa's years-worn tome of Versillian history. The things I'd squirreled away during my initial flight from my family's kingdom. They were gone, too.

In its place, a new structure was being built to replace the last. The frame was almost complete, and supplies from the building crew were left for the light of morning.

"Why in the world would they tear it down?" Tana mused, hands on her hips.

None of us had an answer. Well, except for Elián. "Not torn. Burned." I looked up at him to see his gaze narrowed on the wreckage. His nostrils pulsed with quick, analyzing inhales. He crossed the road, pulling me along, and the others followed until we stood before what used to be my home. Where I'd *thought* to stow our things before bringing Francie to Whitley.

Releasing our hold on each other after another purposeful squeeze, Elián crouched, hand to the ground. "The whole structure burned some time ago. Maybe a year." He stood again, gaze unfocused on the present world and looking to the past. "It started somewhere inside. Somewhere above. The fire was already mature when it reached the foundation."

He continued to assess the ground beneath the construction, scenting and feeling, but after a few moments with people streaming past us in the busy Nethras afternoon, he stood, shaking his head.

I gave his stomach a gentle touch, thanking him for gathering all he could.

Had a small part of me been holding out for this home I'd made years ago? Before I knew Elián, before my brother betrayed and tried to kill me. Before Soleil.

"I'd love to continue standing in the middle of the street, but there are at least two of us who need to get inside."

I flinched and turned behind me, taking in Fenix's fully cloaked form and Tomás's slumped one. The former's face was entirely covered by a low hood and a cloth he had tied around his mouth and nose. His hands were wrapped in gloves like mine, protecting him as much as possible from the light of the sun. He even wore a pair of nearly-opaque glasses, shielding his sensitive eyes as well.

Even still, his gait had been slow, careful to not accidentally expose himself to the sunlight. Tomás had been a bloody fucking terror as we forced him into a chair fitted with large wheels, as soon as we charted our own private ship to the Nethran ports.

Weeks. At sea. With a Vyrkos who begrudgingly traveled with us, even with every opportunity we gave him to leave, a proud Shadow who had not accepted that he was ill, and another Shadow who was chronically nauseated when his feet weren't on steady ground.

My cousin's sunny demeanor had even dimmed, as we reminded each other why it was not wise to pitch ourselves overboard and swim to the nearest shore.

Francie had been the only calm one, which worried me even still. The closer we got to Nethras, away from the human-ruled lands to ones where our kinds were more populous and her mate was waiting, she grew more subdued.

Now, she clutched Whitley's handkerchief, shakily tightening it around her fingers, loosening it, then starting the cycle all over again. She stared off into the distance, an unsettled expression on her face that contrasted sharply with her long, brushed hair and new clothing.

"You wouldn't happen to still have your apartment, would you?" I asked Tana.

She shook her head, dashing that last hope of somewhere familiar for us. "I would highly doubt it. I'd packed the majority of my things when I went back to Versillia to see Dad." She looked down. "They've most certainly cleared the rest and rented it to someone else by now."

Shit, I cursed to myself for the lack of options and for tipping my cousin into a somber place. For so long, she'd been propping me up, helping me through the loss of Elián and the death of my son. So much so that I wasn't used to her displaying any negative emotion outside of mild annoyance.

"That's okay," I tried to reassure her. To Elián, I brought forth an option I knew he would not be keen on. He and Tomás already denied having homes in the city, and traveling to the nearest one either of them owned would take far too long. "How about Tana and I go with Francie to the children's home, and we'll meet you at the lodging house in the arts district?" From what I could recall, it was fairly reasonably priced while sporting comfortable accommodations.

As I'd suspected, Elián frowned, but he thankfully did not

protest. Tomás began another fit of coughing, a sound we'd all grown accustomed to on the long sail here.

His condition had slowly worsened, leaving him unable to walk much longer than from the bed to the toilet. Even the journey back was tenuous.

Hence, the chair he hated.

Elián claimed my chin and dropped a kiss to my lips, quick and firm, before walking to his brother. He grasped the handles at Tomás's back, listening intently as I gave him the directions he probably didn't even need.

Fenix's head followed Tana as she linked an arm through Francie's, but my cousin didn't notice. By the time she glanced at the three males, they were already heading in the opposite direction as we steered Francie toward Tulip Street.

We supported her, Tana and I, standing at either side of Francie and filling the time with supportive silence. Nethras was as busy as ever and would only get busier as the night went on. The Vyrkos would come out of their sleep, restaurants would be full with hungry patrons, and live music would fill the streets.

Other than the brief stop on my initial trip with Elián as my Shadow, I'd not been back here since the death of my friends.

Across the street, a group of three, the merry contrast to our solemn one, laughed while exiting a shop.

My neck twisted as I—that was Lee's shop, wasn't it? Where I'd spent many hours perusing the shelves, sitting in one of the coveted window seats and flying through a stack of novels. Where I leaned over the front counter, bantering back and forth over this new release or that special edition.

A tug on my arm, Tana and Francie pulling me back to the present, whipped my attention back around. Now, when Lee was gone, murdered in a horrible—and successful—ploy to shock me into going home to Versillia.

I'd initially intended to fill our walk with steady, pleasant chatter. Something to soothe Francie's nerves. But my brief descent in the past left my mind reeling, and then we were turning down the quiet, familiar street. Francie's breathing got even harder, body nudging mine as she twisted Whitley's handkerchief in her grip. The fluid bends of her white mating marks flexed with the movement.

Finally, the children's home came into view. The toys scattered in the grass surrounding were a different sort than the last time I was here—a red ball instead of green, small wooden swords amongst the ribbons and fabric animals. The spirit of it was the same, though there would be no cheerful little boy with red curls running straight for me.

From El and Tomás's account, he was now an adolescent, gangly and happy to be living his dream as a Shadow acolyte. Had their letters reached him in time? Was he here?

There was a different adolescent sitting with a book out front, cross-legged and hunched in the grass. Upon our arrival, he glanced up, brows still furrowed from whatever he'd been reading. Francie gasped, clutching the delicate white fabric in her hands tighter.

The child, one I now was starting to recognize, fumbled his book closed and scrambled to his feet. "F-Francie?" he asked, revealing a set of fangs that must've just come in.

Tana and I were both watching Francie, waiting for her to get her bearings. Or would we need to step in?

Her lips trembled, cerulean blue eyes swimming and searching. "Evan," she finally said, and the child ran over. My cousin and I released our hold on Francie's arms so she had room for the bony and firm hug from Evan. She did not hesitate to throw her arms around him as he collapsed into her. "You've gotten s-so *big*. Such a big boy." Francie barely held back sobs as Evan sniffed into her neck, already taller than all three of us.

Evan pulled away, face blotchy and tear-streaked, but he offered a wide smile, pointing to his mouth. "And look!"

More tension bled away from Francie's expression, letting her cry and laugh freely. She thumbed Evan's brown cheek, squeezing his grinning face. "What a handsome set of fangs you have. I missed you."

My heart clenched, as if someone tightened their fist around it, but I fought back my outward reaction.

"Um—I-let me go get Whitley. They—they'll be so happy." Evan started to pull out of their embrace, but they needn't get their other caregiver because as the front door of the townhome opened, Francie's mate took a tentative step over the threshold.

Evan, unaware of the turmoil within Francie, ran to Whitley, expressing how wonderful it was to have her back, wasn't that great?

Whitley shakily nodded, staring and slowly advancing forward. They wore a tunic with the sleeves rolled to elbow and an apron splattered with something brown and orange, the start of supper, most likely. Their white curls were longer than last I'd seen, a few strands dangling in front of their brow, the rest a cloud around their head.

We'd shared scattered letters here and there, and three years, to Lylithans of adult age, were no match for our slow aging. Papa had been nearing five-hundred years when he was killed, and he'd just started sporting handsome lines at the corners of his eyes. From half a millennia of smiling.

Whitley hastily wiped their palms on their apron, now standing right in front of their lost mate. They raised their hands, trembling violently with thin blue swirls decorating the backs and knuckles. Francie's mating marks.

"My—D-Darling," they whispered, barely audible, and the first brush of their skin against Francie's she…collapsed.

Her knees gave way, and she slumped onto the cobblestone street. Before I could dive in to help, Whitley fell with her, pulling their mate into the safety of their chest. They cradled her as she wept, rocking them both and keeping their own weeping quiet. They pressed kiss after kiss into her hair, ran their hands in circles on her back.

The vise around my heart had loosened by then, and I turned

toward my cousin to give them a moment. Tana wiped the back of her sleeve at her eyes, grinning for the first time in a long while.

We didn't say anything to each other, but when she offered her hand, I gladly took it. Joining as witnesses of this moment between mates. Taking in this quest fully realized. We found her. We brought her back home.

Francie and Whitley remained on the ground for a long time, oblivious to the crowd of children that convened out front of the townhome and Lydia quietly ushering them back inside to wait. She mouthed 'thank you' to us multiple times as she pushed the children inside and watched her fellow caregivers with relief and joy.

"I—I don't even know how to thank you both. I am…so, so grateful." Francie was still tucked into Whitley's neck, whimpering softly as they looked up at my cousin and me.

Tana answered for us. "We were happy to help," she said, and I nodded. Truly. When I'd needed help, for them to take a risk on my behalf, they did so without even a thought.

Among the truths shared on our voyage back to Nethras, I'd admitted to Francie my hand in her predicament. How I'd been followed that night I brought payment to the children's home after winning a fight on Dyna Island.

While the ship rocked, I'd steeled myself for her rejection. For her anger. But, because she was still a kind soul through it all, she just hugged me. Reassured me that it was *not* my fault.

Hopefully, once Francie shared this with Whitley, they would come to forgive me as well.

I blinked, looking around and still not seeing the boy I'd become close with during my years volunteering at the home. "Has Marco arrived?"

At the boy's name, Francie peeked out from Whitley's neck, gaze sweeping around. We'd been hoping, but… "No, I haven't heard from him. His last letter was some weeks ago."

It could be nothing. The Shadows certainly were not known

for being easily contacted or found. But I'd watched Elián draft multiple letters to the Well, informing the boy of his caregiver coming home. El and Tomás assured me that acolytes were given limited dispensation to travel for important events such as this. Certainly Marco would want to be here for Francie's return.

Something cold started up my spine, stirring my power and making my fingertips itch. Tana's brow furrowed, mind probably taking the same journey as my thoughts had.

I tried my best to keep my face calm, though. "He might already be on his way. Or needing more time before he's able to get away from his duties."

Whitley's gray stare was longer than I'd hoped, showing they hadn't been completely assured by my words. Eventually, though, they nodded and turned back to their mate. Tentatively, as if knowing how fragile and raw Francie still was, they pressed their lips to hers. We'd not told them about what she endured, respecting Francie's process in sharing *her* tale, but I hoped for her sake that she would do so, sooner rather than putting it off.

So the pain would not be only hers to bear.

Over the weeks we sailed, Francie's body had healed itself. With a steady supply of donor blood, rest, and encouragement from all five of us in our own way, she'd left the vestiges of Frenzy behind.

Her mind, though, I knew would take longer to move on.

That seemed to be put to the side, though, as the reluctant meeting of lips on lips turned languid. Heated. The quiet moans between them weren't obscene, necessarily, but judging the swell of lust in the air, obscenity wasn't far.

The levelheadedness I'd come to associate with Whitley asserted itself. Enough, at the very least, for them to pull away and clear their throat. "Well, we will just be—let's get you inside, my love." Francie didn't resist Whitley pulling her to her feet, but the little shifts of her body as she remained pressed to her mate suggested that she was unable to clear the haze of their passionate reunion as Whitley.

A faint redness was now creeping up Whitley's neck, as well as darkening their cheeks. "Thank you both. Will you be staying for supper? I was just…" They trailed off, looking down at the apron of a meal they'd certainly long forgotten about.

I chuckled, already beginning to angle my and Tana's bodies back up the street. "Perhaps another time. You both deserve any time alone you can manage. We will talk soon?"

Francie nodded emphatically, muttering more words of thanks to join the others she'd given over the weeks since rescuing her from the Folk. Whitley's response was calmer but no less sincere. "Yes. Thank you both again. I am forever in your debt."

Tana and I waved off the assertion, not wanting or needing thanks, let alone a debt from the kind caregiver. "Consider us even," I hollered over my shoulder, but they were already across the grounds and opening the door.

The tension while walking down Tulip Street was all but erased as my cousin and I walked back up toward the city proper. A months-long adventure to save Francie was just…over.

And we were back in Nethras. Where we'd both lived for years before everything went to shit. "So…" I attempted, but the rest of my question wouldn't come. Aside from finding Francie, the conflict with murderous humans, Folk, and Tomás's sickness had occupied most of our conversations. But the impending change of course, on the path both of our lives had tread together for so long, was now in the air.

Was that why our steps became loaded again? Unbalanced? Normally, as different as we were, I'd felt in synchronized step with my cousin. We had shared turmoil and trained so much that a step from her brought forth a coordinating one from me. A goading, good-natured taunt from her would elicit a snipe from me, then a melodic laugh from her throat in return. The annihilation of my sense of self after fleeing Versillia, then slow, wobbly growth after realizing I was with child was met with extensive, unflinching care from my cousin.

I owed her everything.

As I opened my mouth again, though, I took in the tightness of her jaw. The hard edge to her jade eyes.

She'd never looked more like me.

"I was going to inquire with my old coven. See if anyone is available to help with Tomás's healing. There were a handful of proficient healers, but I've not spoken to them since I left."

Her tone was…flat. Without the fluttery lightness I'd associated with her since she was able to speak at all. Even after her mother's passing and the murder of Uncle Hendrik, I'd not…

"Do you need any help? Want me to see who I can find as well?" Never mind the fact I knew no one she wouldn't already be familiar with.

She shook her head as we looked up and down the street before crossing. I had to listen past the commotion around us to focus on her response. "No, I'll check on him now then go alone. I'm sure you'll want some time with Elián."

While that was true, I—did I detect a bite in her tone, along with her assumption? Dark heat unfurled in my chest, but I breathed through it. To be defensive and strike against my cousin was not what I wanted. Not what she deserved. "I would, but we have agreed to…be with each other. We have time, and his brother's recovery is our priority right now. Neither of us are healers such as you, but—" a Nethran with fair violet skin and heavy perfume nearly clipped us as they hurried past "—it's not fair for this to all be on you."

Tana chuckled sardonically as we crossed the informal barrier into the arts district. The buildings sported more colorful facades here, with intricately painted murals instead of blank walls, performers on nearly every corner, and more daring ensembles. Our woolen trousers and tunics in dull colors, functional and clean but drab, suddenly made our presence amongst the crowd as noticeable as it'd been in the human-ruled cities across the continent.

"Did I do something to you?" Try as I did to keep peace, my question was definitely an accusation.

Tana certainly took it that way. "What would you have done to me?"

"I don't *know*." I tried to breathe calmly, to draw a clearing inhale instead of the attention of the gossip hounds I *certainly* knew populated this area of the city. "But I'm sensing that something is amiss, and I—I don't like arguing with you."

She whirled around to glare at me, crossing her arms and planting her boots. A group of Lylithans nearly ran into us, seeing as we were standing very much in the way of foot traffic, but they simply scoffed and kept walking, muttering about being late and missing something.

"I wasn't arguing. I was just pointing out that—that you and your male will want time together, just as Francie and Whitley need time together. I don't need placating statements about helping me."

I couldn't hide the incredulous irritation from my words anymore. This was like when we'd left Morova, where she'd criticized the way I'd been hiding behind her, using her as an excuse. Yes, there was some merit to it, but I also detected that it was only a facet of the truth.

"I—I'm not *placating*. With more help, the faster we may be able to find a remedy for whatever ails Tomás. And then—"

"Then what?" she snapped. Her arms crossed tightly at her chest, and the activity around us had thinned enough for me to hear the whistle of her breaths through her nose. "You or whomever help me heal Tomás, and then..." she curled a hand in the air, flippantly judging any response I deigned to give.

My lip curled back from my fangs instinctually, and hers made an appearance in kind. "Then we decide what we want to do afterward!"

"What *you* want to do!" I jerked, mouth gaping. "*I* heal Tomás, the brother of your lover, and then you decide what happens next."

My stomach dipped into something sour. Another fear realized, maybe? "N-No, but I—"

Tana cut her gaze away, glancing further down the road, where the rumble of a crowd grew loud enough to add pressure to what swelled between my cousin and me. Something so big it threatened to erupt. How long had this been churning—growing—between us? "I will heal him because it is the way, my duty. And then we will go out on our own paths."

She might as well have struck me with the staff secured to her belt. It would have bruised my heart less.

Was that what these years had been? Duty? When she chanted prayers to the aether and encouragement over me as she pulled my babe from my body? When she lay amongst the tall grass of the Ralthan meadow, pressed against my back and crying with me after I scattered Soleil's ashes in the wind?

When she buried with me Elián's medallion in the soil, where I'd felt our son move within me for the first time?

Duty. The way.

"Right. Okay," I croaked, any fight draining out of me faster than I could hold onto it.

More footsteps approached, but I averted my gaze downward, unprepared for Tana or any passersby to see whatever unrest was visible on my face.

These did not skirt around us, but stopped some paces away. Which, in the raw state I found myself in the face of my cousin's words, only made me angry. My head pulsed with the fast pinging between emotions, and I snapped my head toward the ones staring.

Of course, I picked up on the scent right as my mind homed in on the armor of guards surrounding a figure cloaked in flowing fabric.

Instead of the gray steel, however, the yellow glow of lights overhead highlighted the golden plates armoring the six standing before us. Violet jewels adorned the gleaming vambraces and spaulders, and the breastplates were damascened with more gold decoration, in the likeness of scales.

At the front, presumably leading the group, a guard with bronze skin and plaited pink hair moved to the side. The remnants of a name pulled at my memory, but when the center of the procession was revealed, my jaw opened in more shock than when I'd watched a male walk out of a tree.

"Hello, Mamba."

Chapter Thirty-Nine
Tana

"Hello, Mamba."

I'd been shaking, trembling with frustration and barely keeping confused tears at bay. The air I breathed wouldn't fill my lungs, no matter how many inhales I took. From where I stood, unable to look at my cousin any longer without succumbing to the irritation and panic, I'd watched droves of people congregate at the epicenter of the art's district.

At that voice, though, I flinched and turned.

I had not lived on the island, but I visited it plenty in my youth and during my initial training. I would recognize Rhaestran armor anywhere. And I *definitely* recognized that sarcastic voice anywhere.

My cousin, for once, was stunned into silence, which appeared to please Cera to no end. A thick braid ran over her shoulder and between her breasts, and gold beads sprinkled amongst the midnight strands.

She raised a brow, looking between my cousin and I, and drawled, "Is that how you greet your High Priestess?"

The provocation cleared the paralysis of my cousin's shock, and she huffed, very much refusing to salute. I, however, followed the compulsion singing in the aether lingering in my veins, in my soul. After experiencing a world where its familiar song was silent, I'd never again take it for granted.

I bowed deeply, thumb and first two fingers at my brow in the traditional salute of Rhaea. Never mind the last time I'd seen the High Priestess of Rhaea, we'd traded insults over a meal in the bountiful gardens of the Temple.

Cera gave me quick, perfunctory salute back before snarling at my cousin, "Can't bother to greet me after you fucked off without a word? I almost thought you dead, if not for the phantom thorn still poking in my side."

Meline advanced a step, and the guards around Cera tensed, closing more tightly around her. My cousin paid them no mind. "A better question would be why you are terrorizing Nethras and *me* with your presence. Though," she waved a gloved hand, marks from Rhaea now hidden, "I am unsurprised the people of Rhaestras have grown tired of you."

A serpentine smile grew on Cera's face, flashing fang and the delicate gold clipped around them. The grin was vicious, *delighted*, and Cera shot past her guards, exiting their wall of protection. As infuriating as she could be, I could never forget her skill with the blades sheathed at her waist.

Cera crashed into Meline, hugging her fiercely, slapping hard claps on the backs of her shoulders, as if assuring she was whole. Real.

An understanding, my cousin had called it. The resolution of her last encounter with her longstanding rival, stretching back to their childhoods. The way they brought their brows together almost angrily, palms clasped against napes, spoke of more than the tentative truce I'd assumed they reached.

This was—this was sisterhood.

"What happened to you?" It came out as censure, but Cera hadn't pulled away, and neither had Meline.

"I—too much."

The High Priestess stared into my cousin's eyes, unflinching, and in a tone devoid of any jokes or slights, she whispered, "You are changed."

Meline had nothing but a nod in affirmation, and to that, Cera shifted them into another embrace, whispering assurances I couldn't hear. And I watched my cousin's shoulders relax with a speed I'd never been able to elicit. Meline clung to Cera with a fondness I'd never seen between them.

But of course, they shared the power of the first Goddess, didn't they? A connection that, in many ways, surpassed that of blood.

My own path.

I surreptitiously swept the back of my hand under my eye. Yes, I needed to contact my old coven. Maybe then, I would resettle here, where being a Lylithan was neither extraordinary nor dangerous. The supplies for my craft were plenty. And I knew now how to enter the fighting rings, should I want to flex the training I was now so familiar with. As soon as Tomás was—

"Wait—are—we could use your help," I blurted, interrupting this...*understanding.*

Cera and Meline separated, and when they turned to face me, they did so with matching fluidity. Their gazes were cutting in a way I knew I could never replicate. Like they already knew how to eviscerate you, so you might as well get to it.

And their eyes. Meline's were the color of rich chocolate, Cera's were a mix of tawny and pale green, but the otherworldly gold flecks within both were like stars plucked from the sky. I know, that if Meline were take her gloves off, her fingers would be the darker counterpart to Cera's, which were marked with the delicate tattoos of the High Priestess.

Meline blinked, and the muscles in her jaw ticked. To Cera, she elaborated, "We have an injured Lylithan whose body does not respond to the best of healing efforts. It's been over a month."

Cera kept appraising me, and though I wasn't a priestess of Rhaea, I felt...humbled. Like a student before their teacher, admitting they were unable to perform simple mathematics. Auntie Liana had been a healer, too. *The* healer who preceded the High Priestess before Cera. Under Auntie Liana's tutelage, I'd incorporated healing into my magic studies, learning as much as I could, save from entering the priestesshood. And with lessons at the Temple whenever we visited my aunt's homeland, I should have been able to save Tomás. Eliminate the sickness from another world that still rotted inside of him.

But he was still dying.

"How long has he been ill?"

I winced, trying to find an adequate answer. It was a simple question, an expected one in this line of work, but how did I explain the skip in time from that world into this one? "Five weeks," was the best I could provide. "We are heading there now for me to resume, but he does not respond to any medicine I've brewed, nor is he physically able to fight the disease. Pure aether has been the only reprieve, and a steady supply of mortal blood. But he is getting worse," I whispered at the end. I'd not told Tomás or the others this explicitly, but, of course they knew. At least he'd been able to limp along before. But at some point on the sail to Nethras, his legs were unable to hold his weight.

Cera nodded once, lips pursed, and glanced in the direction of the distantly roaring crowd. Festivals and more popular performances were common, particularly in this area of the city, so I thought nothing of them.

"Can you keep him alive for the next few hours? Or is his state more urgent?"

I bristled, though the question wasn't an insult. I thought. "Yes. I am going to him now."

"Can you not come with us? The sooner the better," Meline pressed.

And the old Cera made an appearance, though the beautifully embroidered lilac fabric draped over her shoulder certainly denoted her status, as did the wide, gold cuff on her arm. "Well, I am late for a previous engagement." She nodded toward where a few Nethrans were still heading. Aside from the few openly gaping at Cera and her guards with interest.

Meline made the connection, brows raising. "Will you be dancing for spare coin? Spinning yarns on the street corner?"

Instead of shooting back another insult, Cera snorted. "Feels a bit like that." She waved her hand and rolled her eyes. "I was asked by Roalld to speak to the city healers about improving their methods. However, he insisted on some celebration as this is the first time a High Priestess has visited Nethras in over a century."

Of course, because I had been with the last High Priestess, accompanying my cousin and her family. Then, Isabella had been her protégé, my parents were both alive, and Mathieu had not yet shown his true nature.

"Well, when you decide to grace us with your presence, we'll be at the lodging house on the corner of Fair and Fortune. Maybe you can put your supposed healing prowess to use instead of parading yourself about town." The guards, though stoic, held shadows of unease in their expressions, eyes darting or widening slightly at the gall of someone talking to their High Priestess in such a way.

Cera simply snickered and shrugged. "It's part of my duties to parade. Thankfully, it's not something required very often of me. I will leave as soon as I can to help your friend." Without a goodbye, she marched forward, unconcerned about her guards following. They immediately formed a circle around her, unencumbered by their armor and moving swiftly. As they went, a full procession this time, I faintly heard an exasperated sigh from within the perimeter of gleaming armor.

Meline and I instead turned down Fortune Street, steps purposeful and with more than a wide gap of space between us. Neither of us glanced at the other.

～

"What if something's happened?" Tomás croaked while I pressed my hands to his chest. The flare of purple light was so familiar, it shone in my vision even when my eyes were closed. The feel of Tomás's clammy skin, I now always sensed on my fingertips.

The taste of it, the infection from the monster that bit him, was a rancid, sticky muck that clung to my tastebuds. Wherever I shifted the aether to remove it, more grew back and then some.

A bead of sweat began to run down my temple, and I twitched my head against my shoulder, wiping the moisture off on my collar.

"I will worry about it," Elián responded, as he had been since he returned from the Nethran pharmacy with no letters from the Well. I still didn't understand it, the way Shadows were able to send correspondences. There seemed to be no concern of *which* pharmacy letters were sent to. They were able to access any letter that'd been sent to them. I asked in Wilthas, the smaller port town near Vharas where we chartered our ship, what would happen if I walked in to a pharmacy and stated I was a Shadow, even when I was not. Instead of telling me, because of course he wouldn't just provide an explanation, Tomás challenged me to go into the small pharmacy and attempt it.

So I did. I went with Elián and Meline, leaving Tomás and Fenix in the inn with our baggage, and in front of my cousin and her Shadow, I opened the letter to reveal a blank slip of paper. Which then burst into a black flame and disintegrated before I could drop it to the floor.

When Elián asked for the same letter, as it had been for him in the first place, the clerk somehow supplied the same one that I'd just destroyed. The human who likely had never serviced Shadows in their establishment, looked just as surprised as I did when they retrieved it.

It was a note regarding a property he owned, and Elián had sent a response and then another one, requesting Marco be in Nethras to meet us and see his former caregiver.

That was nearly six weeks ago, now, and there was still no reply from the Well.

"It's gone too long, Nogón. I don't—" Tomás curled up off the bed as a series of coughs wracked his frame. Fenix appeared at my side, holding out a cloth for the Lylithan to use, and I thanked him for his assistance. I still kept my palms to Tomás's chest, doing my best to fight back the sticky tar that was coating the insides of his lungs.

When he settled back onto the mattress, he was sweating more than I was, and he crushed the rag into his fist. But I saw the droplets of black before he was able to hide it away.

Two steaming mugs materialized on the small table beside Tomás's bed, and when I tore my eyes away from him, I saw my cousin retreat back to stand beside her Shadow. His face looked as it always did, but she was rubbing soothing circles on his back, as if comforting him.

"I made that tea you taught me," she said, still not looking at me. I could smell the pungent scent of ginger. The brew was simple yet effective for a myriad of illnesses, and since we did not know exactly what sort of sickness this was, it shouldn't hurt. Nothing seemed to be making Tomás *worse*. Nothing seemed to be making him better, either.

"Thank you."

She nodded, but her attention was on the male beside her. Soleil's father.

The night he was born, I was heavily preoccupied with instructing Meline through the birth, something I'd only done a handful of times, and ensuring she stayed alive.

My inability to save Soleil would be my greatest failure, one that haunted me for the rest of my days. But, I kept that to myself, breathing through the tightening within my own lungs as I tore my eyes away from Elián. Even as a newborn, Soleil had looked strikingly similar to his father.

Fenix helped me reposition Tomás so he was sitting upright and able to drink the brew that would hopefully provide a bit of relief. Were she not afraid of worsening his condition, I would have asked Meline again to try and take my place for a spell. Her cursory knowledge of healing left her able to make the salves and medicines that provided some relief to Tomás's symptoms.

Where was Cera? The view beyond the small window to my left revealed a black night and stars dimmed by the city lights. Surely two hours had passed. At least.

Tomás accepted the teacup extended to him by Fenix with a sneer. Not because he was a Vyrkos, but because he'd assumed Tomás couldn't get it himself. The whole act had grown very tiresome at this point.

Fenix curled his lip right back, dropping his fangs. "I'm only trying to help, you ungrateful imbecile."

"Oh, really? Helping me out of the goodness of your heart?" Tomás asked with brows raised high as he took a small sip from his cup. He smacked his lips and went back in for another.

I monitored his body's reaction through the connection between us, and I detected the settling of his stomach and the minute relaxation of his muscles. The infection remained unaffected.

Fenix grumbled and stood, stomping out of the room before I could thank him again for his help. He'd more than paid us back for saving him on the ship to Vharas, so I was unsure why he had accompanied us this long. To another world and back, at that.

Because we needed him to feed Tomás when we first returned to Vyrland, I'd stopped questioning his intentions.

A knock on the door rang over the back and forth Tomás and Elián resumed, worrying about the lack of response from their sister and ward, beginning to plan a return that Tomás was certainly not well enough for. He needed time to rest before even thinking on embarking on another journey. To wherever the Shadow Well was.

Lemon, rosemary, mint, and jasmine. My shoulders drooped

as I recognized Cera's arrival. "There is a Vyrkos sulking in the corridor," she said to no one in particular.

"Oh, I'm sure he is," Tomás said weakly, voice vibrating against my hands. Somehow, he still maintained the same level of sarcasm as when he'd been well.

"Hm, Master Elián. Hello," Cera purred, and a deep, warning hiss stole my attention.

My cousin bared her fangs and stood purposefully between her Shadow and the High Priestess who was now dressed in less formal garb. Her short top and trousers were those of any other Rhaean priestess. She'd not shed the gold accoutrements, though.

"You are here to heal his brother, not ogle Elián."

"Who said anything about ogling?" Cera asked while giving him an exaggerated once-over.

"He is mine, and you're wasting time," Meline growled while Elián looked down at her with the fire in his stare brightening.

Cera swept further into the room, coming toward Tomás and me. "Yours, you say? That is certainly not new. My congratulations."

"And you are?" Tomás asked, skepticism leeching into the air.

Cera did not rise to match his tone. She simply sat on the edge of the bed, beside me, and fluttered her tattooed fingers before his face. "The High Priestess of Rhaea. Best healer in the realm."

"Well, I was bitten by something not of this realm, so."

I glared, trying to communicate silently for him to shut the fuck up, but he blatantly ignored me in favor of taking his frustration out on the best chance he had of recovering.

As abrasive as I'd known her to be, Cera had undoubtedly dealt with irascible patients. "Explain," she commanded and began to slowly wave an assessing hand over Tomás's form. Her fingers splayed wide, and the markings on her three fingers started to glow the same color as under my palms.

Elián began to weave the tale, keeping the account simple, describing the injury and our narrow escape from the Folk Realm. I concluded with a description of Tomás's symptoms, what I'd detected inside his body. Though we tried to keep it succinct, by the time we were able to tell her everything, my untouched tea had grown cold, and Fenix was back in the room, lingering in the corner.

Cera was palpating Tomás's sides, examining the healed, discolored scar where he'd been bitten. She flicked her gaze to Fenix. "What interesting company you now keep, Mamba. And squaring yourself against the Jakshka with no knowledge and no plan? Why am I not surprised?" She sighed and continued her examination without noticing the stares from each of us.

"Jakshka?" The word was faintly familiar.

"You—the tree tricksters from the nursery books? *Those* Jakshkas?" my cousin asked and finally reminding me of what I'd long forgotten. I had not spent as much time around children as she had, so my memories of the tales were from when my parents or she had read to me as a babe. About mischievous beings that lived in the trees or huts built into mounds in the ground.

"Of course. I've never come across one, but the stories did not appear from nothing."

"Fucking Grimm," Meline groused under her breath, even though the male's information and guidance had been invaluable, if not a bit vague. "Whatever. Can you help him?"

We all turned to Cera, and I didn't miss the hope in Tomás's stare that he tried to temper.

"I will need time. And more priestesses. But I believe so." Not a definitive 'yes', but it was a better prognosis than I had with my limited skills.

Compelled again, from one healer to *the* healer, I saluted her, mumbling thanks along with Tomás who sniffled. Tears streaked down Elián's cheeks, but he was unabashed in his emotionality.

"I will go to the Well. Bring Noruh and Marco here."

Cera stood, this time encouraging Tomás to lay on his back so she could begin. While she did, she raised her hazel and gold eyes, looking between the two Shadows. "About that."

Tomás bristled, refusing to settle onto his back, now. His chest began to move more quickly. "What?"

With gentle yet firm touch, she pushed Tom back onto his pillow and pried the crushed cloth in his fist. She opened it, examined the dark sputum, and refolded the cloth. "Much has changed since you disappeared, Mamba. More since you've been making your way back from the human lands."

My own heart picked up, and Meline moved to loom over Cera. "What's changed."

The High Priestess sighed, situating the blankets around Tom's waist, plumping his pillows. Stalling. "The Council."

"The Council," Meline choked. Two words we'd not spoken in years. When we left all of that behind. "What the fuck about it? Just say what you want to say," Meline spat to hide her concern.

"Cal happened," Cera sat back then faced Elián. Instead of leering, her mouth twisted in...discomfort. Something close to guilt. "I received word from Roalld tonight. Confirmation that he's proceeded despite us voting him down. My visit today was my attempt at strategizing under the guise of pomp and circumstance."

"*In the name of Rhaea*, speak plainly, Cobra."

Cera drew a breath. "He's gotten them. Conspired with enough Elders in their organization. The Shadows still stand, but they work for him, now."

Chapter Forty
Elián

The High Priestess's words took a while to fully settle, for me to fully understand. In no time at all, she had revealed that she could heal my brother, something I'd prayed about to Rhaea and Zoko every single day.

And in the next breath, she made my world crash again.

"Wh—what does that mean, Nogón? What about Marco? Noruh? What's going on?" All of my brother's cocksure or grouchy disposition evaporated. Instead, the confused fear mirrored the terror and rage in my gut.

"Shit," my queen cursed and came back toward me. I was frozen, trying to reason through this information, but however I tried to think about it, all outcomes were negative.

No communication from Noruh or Marco. For over a month.

Meline peeled her gloves off so quickly, they squeaked in protest. Cool abyss landed on my skin, where she cradled the sides of my neck. I felt her power creep onto my flesh, winding up to my jaw and down my shoulders. Caressing, and giving room for the heat churning within.

Touching the backs of her wrists, I let out some of my Flames, providing enough relief for me to think. Black and glowing orange twisted in thin tendrils around us, as I used the anchor my queen so readily extended to me. Her breaths encouraged my breaths, her power encouraging my power.

"Mother of all, thank you for this blessing," Cera gasped. "You are one of the lost children of Zoko."

Meline tilted her head toward the High Priestess without removing her eyes from mine. "Now is not the time, Cobra." She swallowed. "We'll figure it out, El. They'll be all right."

"Interesting company, indeed," Cera whispered.

But my queen was right. We would—we would fix this. Unravel The Shadows from that tyrant's clutches. I nodded at my queen, watched our combined power sparkle and wind around her, too. I sent it to cradle her freckled cheek, and both vines responded, moving at my innate command.

Meline's sucked in a breath, not only feeling the combined cold and hot touch but the way…our power yielded to the other.

"I—there is something I need to tell you all," she whispered, and the bubbling excitement, tangled in all the other emotions I was experiencing, popped. Meline shifted, still holding onto me but nibbling on her lip. "I made a vow…to a dying mother. Fourteen years ago. And it appears I've failed."

My Fire quivered, knowing the damning truth of this tale. During our sail back to Eryva, while naked under covers, she'd told me this last secret.

Meline inhaled, long and bracing. "One of my contracts brought me close to Krisla. As close as I would dare, closer than I'd go if I didn't need the coin. One of the slums outside of the city." The rest of the room was quiet as we all listened to her admission. "And there was a Lylithan there. Staying in the room beside me. With her babe. I heard him crying and detected the scent of…a great amount of Lylithan blood." Meline's gaze unfocused, as if going to that day in her mind. "No one was helping her. And when I broke the lock on the door, I found she—she'd labored in the room next to me, in a disgusting inn with no help.

"The babe was already in her arms, as if she'd used the last of her strength to pull him from her womb. I knew she would not survive, with the way Death hung in the air around her. But she saw me. Maybe she thought me an apparition but…she begged me to take him." Meline ground her jaw. "And keep him away from his father. I failed."

My heart lurched, flaring my Flames brighter and releasing small, white sparks.

She did not need to say it, her meaning already clear to me, but Meline continued, "She died as soon as I vowed to do just that. I knew enough from my time working in Versillia of how to care for babes. At least, long enough to bring us both back to Nethras. Where I'd been living and where I knew just the person I would entrust an orphaned Lylithan newly born."

"The lad," Tomás breathed, and Meline nodded.

Tana spoke next, "And his father…" Meline nodded again. Her face tightened in anguish, and I felt the reflection of it in the connection between us. Unconsciously, I moved the vines of black and orange behind her ears, down the center of her spine. Consoling. Comforting.

"That can't be true," Tomás barked, voice thick.

I gritted my teeth as Meline stiffened and whirled around. Tears collected on her lash line, her fists balled at her sides. "You think I'd fucking joke about this? That boy was supposed to be *protected*. He was safe with Whitley, Francie, and Lydia, and then *you* assured me he would be safe with the Shadows." Though she hollered at my brother, I felt the barb as if it had been aimed at me.

Because we both had assured Marco's caregivers that he would be safe as an acolyte. It *should* have been true. For as long as The Shadows stood, we belonged to no ruler. No kingdom. Our collaboration with the Lylithan Council had been borne out of interest in the continuation of our kind.

Or so I'd thought. Been raised to believe.

I ran through those days in my memory, when I'd been approached as the third Shadow to accompany my queen, her brother, and their uncle. Noruh was an Elder, likely chosen to go as a gesture of goodwill. When Jones and I were chosen, it appeared random, but...

What if it was not? Jones was not the most popular of our ranks, but he'd been a competent Shadow. He was a native of Krisla, where Vyrkos were seen as less than, who had become an acolyte some years after I had. When the prejudices of his upbringing were further engrained than they might have been for a child of younger years.

Was—was this acquisition a plot that had been brewing long ago? Was I chosen not because of my centuries of expertise but the belief my twin and father's murders had radicalized me?

Is that what Noruh believed?

"Don't you dare fucking start questioning our sister, Dragon." Tom called to me from across the room, but how could I not? What if—we'd trusted her to provide additional care to Marco while we were gone. If she wasn't part of this, was she in danger? My experience of the King of Krisla was brief, but even that was too much fucking time. He would use us to eradicate any who dared oppose him, under the guise of the betterment of our people. The kinship I'd sworn myself to with blood and soul would be used as an army to terrorize. This, despite all the questions pummeling my thoughts, I knew for certain.

The floor beneath us was still, but I felt as nauseated as I had during the month at sea.

"She would never go along with this. You know what The Shadows means to her. The boy and *Noruh are in danger. We have to go. Now,"* Tom continued to holler at me in Zonoran.

"Nâ," I said. Much more firmly than how I felt. I turned to the rest of the room, within the embrace of Fire and Death though Meline and I no longer touched physically. "You cannot go, Tom."

"Like hell—" his ranting was cut off by more hacking, and Cera shoved him onto his back. Tana sprang into action, holding his shoulders as the High Priestess began winding three tattooed fingers over his mouth.

I would have said more, arguing about what my brother should have known if he wasn't letting pride and panic rule his better senses. He was in no shape to travel the distance to the Well, and he was in no condition to fight should an altercation arise. No.

But my mouth clamped shut as Tana began chanting, purple light spreading to encompass the upper part of Tom's torso. Cera echoed Tana's words, calling to Rhaea, The Mother, and the aether to assist.

Then the High Priestess pulled. At first, she grasped at nothing but air, her three fingers tightening, drawing back, releasing, then repeating the motion. Tom continued to cough, but the sound of it—it changed. From the base of his chest to the middle, then in his throat until the High Priestess indeed pulled something out of his mouth. Black, like my queen's power, but... tacky. Sludgy with a rancid smell that released like noxious gas into the air. I stared in horror as the healers' prayers increased in volume, and the trail of sickness ended, suspended aloft with Cera's purple light surrounding it.

The priestess peered at it a moment, head tilted in fascination as the substance quivered. Until Tom gave a soft moan. Tana watched Cera with wide eyes while still touching and speaking over my brother.

"Fire Bringer, would you please?" I jolted at the title so seldomly directed my way. As a child, it'd been spouted by those marveling at or afraid of us. Since becoming the only one, I'd only heard two others call me such, and they were in this room.

I came forward and noticed the weariness behind my eyes. What the High Priestess was requesting was simple, what any adolescent Por'Noga could accomplish, but my arm trembled as I raised it to direct my Flames.

Perhaps because what extended forth was not just Fire but Death as well. A combination of us, like braided rope, trailed forth and engulfed the poison that infected my brother.

It burned green.

Whether from the mixture of Death and Fire, or the toxic stuff itself, my power burned it up while…while Meline's absorbed the smoke it released. Removing it from existence entirely.

I shuddered and called back my—our—powers, and they retreated readily. Flames absorbed back into my skin, and Death trailed back to my queen behind me. When I glanced over at her, worried how this use of our powers affected her, her shoulders were slumped and her mouth pinched.

Meline smacked her lips and scowled. "That was… disgusting."

I huffed and shook my head, trying to clear the tiredness worming even further in.

"A miracle, more like." Cera watched us with a different sort of interest. One that didn't raise my hackles but made me feel… dissected.

"Um," Tana's voice was now quiet, her words now timid. "It's growing back." She bit her lip and sniffed while I nearly collapsed. How long could Cera pull out what ailed him until his body…

I could not bear to think it.

Tom was now unconscious, brow furrowed in sleep, but his breathing sounded smooth. No longer crackling with what occluded his lungs and throat. For now.

The High Priestess grimly looked upon my brother. "We will need to repeat the process, extracting as the malignancy matures while attacking the remnants it replicates from. Not impossible, but lengthy. Tiresome for him."

Just as I'd thought. Feared. But as difficult the High Priestess enjoyed being in moments of jest, the peace she'd brought to my brother in this moment was enough to win her my trust. For me to feel solidified in my conviction to leave him in her hands.

"I must go." To the Well. To fulfill my responsibilities to my fellow Shadows, to my brother and sister, and to the young boy who put his trust in us.

Meline appeared at my side, glaring. "*You* must go?"

Did she—I frowned. Only…only members and mates were allowed past the illusion. Mamá had not even set foot in the Well, only traveling so far as the barrier that upon crossing, would turn the trespasser around, skirting the Well completely and into the forest surrounding.

Another cruel twist of fate from the Goddesses. The Well was only a couple of days' ride from Ralthas. A week if one was one foot and traveling swiftly.

Had I been at the Well when she lost Soleil? Drinking myself into a hallucinating, incoherent state? When I had cleared myself of that particular stage of grief, there had been no trace of her in Ralthas, one of the first cities I visited when I resumed searching.

"*El*," Meline brought me back to her rage. "You're just staring at me and scowling. You are *not* facing them alone."

I had been thinking, not angry with her. But she seemed furious with me, barely succeeding in steadying the tremble in her lip. The uncertain searching as she looked at me.

I opened my mouth, trying to choose my words carefully when there were too many to grasp. She waited, growing warier by the second, until I managed, "You will not be able to go into the Well, my queen."

Meline huffed and stood straighter. The others, save for Tom, watched us in intrigued silence. "I don't care. If I have to travel up to the border and stand on the other side while you present Marco to me, healthy and safe, that's what I will do."

"And if all is not that simple?" Cera muttered. "You wish to fight the usurpation alone, Master Elián?"

Meline bristled, and I felt the room chill a few degrees. "No." She pointed a black finger at me. "Not in this realm or any other are we going to be apart again, Elián. Not in any world are we facing a threat of this magnitude without the other. Especially not fucking *Cal*." She nearly spit at her feet, uttering the name of the King of Krisla. Her former lover.

"*Meline*." Censure bled into the way I spoke her name. She

was not Shadow. She had made no vows to us, and at least one Shadow had tried to kill her. I would not lose her again.

"It's settled," Meline declared and faced the room. Now, I was scowling out of anger. Frustration. "El and I will go to the Shadows and pull them from Cal's clutches. Cera will heal Tomás, and Tana will..." she trailed off, hesitant in a way I'd not seen her address her cousin.

The witch filled in the direction of this parting of ways. "I will stay here. Aid in Tomás's recovery under Cera's guidance."

"And what will you do, Vyrkos?"

Fenix sneered at the High Priestess. "I have a name, you witch."

Tana sputtered, lip curling and fists clenching, though the slight was not directed at her. "Show some goddess-damned *respect*, Fenix."

To his credit, the male in love with Tana looked properly chastised. Freezing, retracting his fangs, and staring at his feet in capitulation. His pale jaw tensed enough to shatter glass. "I'll stay. To help."

"With what healing expertise? What use will you be?"

"I can pull my own fucking weight," he murmured tensely. "They helped me, so I'm helping them."

Cera was unrelenting, sensing a weakness and continuing to pick until Fenix was a wound she could revel in. "I'm sure Mamba and her Shadow could use another hand in their crusade to the Shadow Well."

Tana appeared mortified, gaze flicking between the Vyrkos who volunteered to remain close to her and the High Priestess who she begrudgingly respected.

"I—I'll be more help here," Fenix argued weakly.

Cera chuckled, glancing at Tana while my cousin was blinking confusedly at Fenix. "I'm sure you will be."

"*So.* We've all decided. El and I will leave in the morning, and the rest of you will stay here to manage Tomás's recovery. Once one of those is achieved, we will reconvene."

I clasped my hands behind my lower back, drawing calming inhales and using every bit of control to keep smoke from tinging my exhales. Pushing back on my queen now would result in nothing but arguing. Shadow traditions—our training, our sovereignty, our magic, our *home*—they were sacred. My love for Meline could not change this.

"Be that as it may, we will not be staying *here*." Cera glanced around the room and pointedly lifted her nose. She sniffed. "Roalld has been gracious enough to secure a home for me during my stay in Nethras. We will relocate ourselves and the sick Shadow there, and I will call upon more priestesses."

As the logistics of yet another journey began to take form, I fell into the planning. Our packs were largely unopened, horses fairly easy to acquire in a city of this size. There was no time to waste, and I gritted my teeth as my queen and I decided to leave in the morning.

I'd no insight into the state of the Shadows aside from what Cera informed us of. All could be running as it should, our ranks slipping quietly under Cal's thumb. Or, much more likely, the acquisition had resulted in chaos. At least, enough unrest to leave Noruh and Marco too preoccupied to respond to my correspondence.

The Well had not been breeched in two millennia. Not by an army, nor by a determined queen with no care for our way when those she cared for were in danger.

Meline and I went back out onto the streets of Nethras to prepare what we could before morning. Food for the days on the main road between cities and townships, feeding so that our energy would sustain for the length of the journey.

At a livery yard in the business district, I shelled out coin for two horses whose owners had designated them for sale.

"What did you do with Noxe?" Meline asked as we left our two mares for our return tomorrow. I'd been quiet for our errands, and my queen had not been more talkative. We became preoccupied by our thoughts, each in our own way.

Meline's tended to show on her features, or in the twist of her fingers and the restlessness of her limbs. The additional awareness given to me by Zoko detected the unrest within her power as well.

"She is back at the Well," I said. After parting ways with my queen, I'd ridden the black horse all the way to the Well, only stopping occasionally for fear of pushing her past her limits. In the years since, I had taken her with me to some of the places where I searched for Meline.

On our way back to the lodging house, we stopped at a cart smelling of meat. One Nethran, a Vyrkos from what I could tell, was working diligently over a grill, hair tied back and cooking tools flying in a blur. A human, their companion judging by the faded fang marks at the base of their throat, engaged the long line of customers with smiles and efficiency.

My queen asked me if I was hungry, and I grunted in agreement. After feeding, my empty stomach had made itself known, and we took our place in the back of the quickly diminishing queue.

"We should get some for the others," Meline mused, and I gave another sound of agreement. I scanned the large parchment at the front of the stall, listing the menu items. Some of which would hopefully be fine for Tomás to consume. His appetite would come and go, but I suspected it would come roaring back after expelling whatever that was inside of him.

We took a few steps forward, closer to the front, and Meline huffed, facing straight ahead. "Why are you upset with me?"

My spine straightened. Reflexively, I responded quietly, "I am not upset."

"You've barely spoken to me since we decided I would go with you to the Well."

Heat crept up my neck, and I tightened my hands behind my back. "*You* decided that, my queen." I felt her flinch, rather than seeing it myself.

We took another step, now fifth from the front. We were still not looking at each other. "You were going to leave without me," Meline gritted.

"I had not yet determined that part of things, Meline. But you must understand there are *ways* to go about approaching the Well. None of them include outsiders barreling onto the grounds without severe ramifications. Namely, an arrow between the eyes." I swallowed down bile at the thought.

"You brought Marco with you before he took his vows or whatever it is you do. Surely I can arrive in the same manner."

I chuckled dryly, shaking my head. "The boy was a child, and he had already entered into the informal acolyte agreement. You make many assumptions, my queen."

"Oh, and you're the most pragmatic person in the realm," she spat.

We were second in the queue, now, so I did not respond with words. Instead, I looked at her, raising a brow.

Before we stepped forward, Meline mimicked my expression. I did not know whether to be grateful this version of her was coming forth again or aggravated by her. In our time together then and now, I had learned my queen and I were both prone to becoming lost to our emotions. My tendency was to turn inward, lest I burn everything to the ground. But my queen had a tendency to use harsh words and tone as a preemptive shield.

Or was that reserved just for me?

We selected an assortment of lamb and chicken, all grilled on skewers with onions and potatoes. They were wrapped loosely in wax paper, and the human gave us a paper bag to tote our friends' meals the few minutes' walk back to them.

Meline and I picked at our meals while we traversed the lively streets of where she used to call home. I'd not seen that side of her yet, the one in which she was able to truly relax and enjoy an evening traipsing a city and reveling in dancing, imbibing, or a simple meal with good company. Any time we tried, there was always some problem or imminent danger. Perhaps that was why we were both so tense all of the time.

"What do you want to do for the rest of the evening?" I asked. We'd still a few hours before we needed to sleep. I would imagine the others would be preoccupied with their own preparations for moving Tom and getting some rest.

Meline tore through a succulent chunk of lamb, finishing the last of her food as the lodging house came into view. We both stepped onto the street to cross. "What—you'd like to know what I want now?" she grumbled and shoved her way through the entrance.

The front room was empty, the clerk at the front desk had their back turned, and I huffed a puff of smoke out of my nose. I tilted my head from side to side, stretching my neck and grinding my teeth while my queen and I began to climb the steps. Her hips swayed as she ascended, and I nearly reached out to swat her ass.

There would be time for that yet.

CHAPTER FORTY-ONE
MELINE

"El?" I called out but made no further advance into the dark room, bathed in blues and grays. The end of this long day left my eyes and heart heavy. We were back in a familiar place, at one point somewhere I'd called home. Francie was finally back with Whitley, and even Cera's sneers were comforting.

But I'd no idea where I stood with my cousin anymore, and the demon of my past who nearly dragged me to hell with him was back. This time coming for the family El held so dear. I'd suspected the King of Krisla had no idea his desire for having the assassin's guild under his control brought him closer to his son, but all it would take was one look, one inhale of the air between them, and he would know.

With his red curls and green eyes, Marco was the spitting image of the female who'd whispered to me the name she chose for her babe as she begged me to take him away from the shadow of Krisla. Marco was kindhearted, more like Francie, Whitley, and Lydia than he would ever be like Cal. But when he was observing, focusing, his lips would settle in a determined line that threatened to send me careening back in time. When I'd delight in Cal's scheming.

A punch of air left my lungs when my back thudded against the wall. My view of fluttering curtains and moonlight traded for that of El's eyes, the flow of his loose hair.

After delivering food to my cousin and Cera, they'd woken Tom for him to put what little he could bear into his stomach. While I'd been sent out to procure more ingredients for the healers—peppermint, chamomile, glass jars, rags, and matches—Elián stayed behind to calmly explain to Tomás what would be happening next. I'd slipped out, fists balling, while the two of them were arguing in El's mother tongue.

Now, Elián descended upon me, mouth taking mine in a rough, passionate attack of his lips. His body pressed against mine, and I wanted to swallow him whole, direct my frustration and desire to possess him and only him. I wanted to take El into me until we ceased to be apart, and I kissed him with such force. Feeling.

He sunk his teeth into my lower lip, groaning and winding his hips against my belly. With him, everything flooded in. Colors, taste. Now would we have that? No longer on opposite sides of a contract, no longer plagued by the mystery of Francie's whereabouts. She was safe, with her mate and healing.

Now, could I heal? Did I deserve it?

I clung to El as we kissed, sinking into the embrace of the male I loved as he lifted me into his arms. I couldn't see where he was headed, nor could I bring myself to care.

With the softness under my body, I assumed he brought me to the bed. And in the tenderness with which he deposited me onto the blankets, I dared believe that I deserved to heal. Even after our quarreling.

"Mm," I moaned against his lips as he loomed over me. "El —" I gasped as he bit my lip hard enough to break the skin. I bled onto his tongue and darted mine out to meet his. "I'm sorry for earlier, I—"

He cut off my words by clamping his hand over my mouth.

With the other, Elián palmed between my legs, pressing in a way that had me groaning out into his skin.

"Nâ," he growled, light in his eyes flaring. To my hazy mind, his fangs appeared even more deadly. Some of my blood was smeared on one of the tips, and the sight made me groan and move my hips against where touched me. "I know that you are weary and anxious, but you will remember that we are not adversaries."

Instead of waiting for my response to that sharp condemnation, I nodded frantically. His feelings on the matter deserved true consideration, I was just—the thought of him leaving without me, possibly straight into more danger, this time at the hands of those who were supposed to protect him, was too much. Then he'd pressed on the same nerve my argument with Tana had already frayed, and I—I'd snipped at him. And not in the bantering way we could manage without truly hurting one another.

El pulled back, denying me the reassurance of his body against mine, and when I scrambled to brace my hands behind me, I was met with his hard glare. Him, standing at the foot of the bed.

"Take your clothes off." My pulse leapt even higher, and though my gloved fingers were fumbling with the laces at my trousers, I was apparently not moving fast enough. "Faster," Elián demanded, and I risked a glance at him.

My fingers slipped again, and my throat went dry. I swallowed as I shoved my trousers and undergarment down my legs while Elián watched, a dragon in the darkness. With the window at his back, his height and broad shoulders formed a sizable shadow while the fire in his stare glowed as he watched me.

The tunic was far easier to shed, and my toes curled as I lay there, spread naked. But Elián still hadn't moved. His tunic was sleeveless and loosely tied at the front, it was unfair how handsome it made him. I eyed what bits of his flesh I could see in the dark, trembling with how much I wanted to touch.

He crossed his arms, bulging the muscles and flexing the serpent winding up his shoulder. "Your gloves, too, Meline." I obeyed, freeing myself of the last barrier between me and the rest of the world, and flung it to the floor. "Put your first two fingers in your mouth." I shivered, eyelids lowering as Elián's command simultaneously lit something within me and smoothed the edges I'd sharpened over the past few hours. Once my lips met the last knuckles of my fingers, El instructed, voice low and rough, "Suck."

Of their own accord, my legs parted, and I laved my tongue against my own fingers. The sensation electrified my senses, leaving me grinding my hips on the mattress.

"Enough." His brow lowered, as did his chin as he watched me. "Touch yourself."

"Goddess," I cursed hoarsely. Would he—would he keep on without gracing me with his body against mine? I leaned back, heels of my feet and hand planted on the bed, exposing myself for his visual devouring. Warmth bloomed across my cheeks, but I pushed through the shyness trying to creep in. The lust was much stronger. "You mean to punish me?" I whimpered at the first tap of my wet fingers. A pulse of ecstasy flashed up to my lungs, and I watched Elián watch me.

My hips wound forward, intensifying the pleasure wrought from my fingers lightly swirling above where I dripped for him. Elián's tongue swiped at his bottom lip, attention between my legs. "I am not punishing." He paused, witnessing me coming apart at his command, before he muttered, "Fuck yourself with them."

Slowly, I did as he said, now groaning openly, wantonly, as I sank the tips of my fingers into myself. The pleasure doubled as I thrust my fingers back and forth while keeping pressure on the outside with the edge of my palm.

"Harder."

I was leaning on my elbow, now, sprawled and fucking myself as the slick sounds of my ministrations filled the room. I lost sight of Elián before me, the prominent impression of his cock hard against his thick thigh. My back arched while I writhed, imagining it was him spearing into me.

I reopened the wound on my lip, trying and failing to hold my release at bay. The dual sensation as I crooked my fingers to massage deep within me and grind against the friction my palm provided was more than enough to take me away. My mouth opened, slack, as I grunted through the race to the end. Where the pleasure would break.

But my hand was ripped away, as was the other, sending me onto my back once again. A choking scream burned my throat as my climax slipped away. My body shook, and tears trailed down my face and onto the mattress.

"This is me putting you in your place, your highness," El whispered and flipped me onto my front. He trapped my wrists in the cage of his hand, and the sudden pressure of my weight against the bed made me cry out. Under his hold, I rubbed my nipples against the blanket, the added stimulation of my piercings making my eyes roll back in my skull.

El moved behind me, over me, as I disintegrated even more and cursed his name into the bed. "What the fuck is my place then?" I spat while tilting my ass in the air, presenting myself for him to give me my release.

Elián hummed as he brought my wrists behind my back, as Death and Fire brushed together and sent another shiver down my spine. He ignored my question, instead directing, "Hold them."

And my power responded, becoming corporeal ivy that kept my hands where he wanted them as he moved to grab my ass. Well, he more so smacked it, sending sharp reverberations through both cheeks. While they burned, something hard and long rubbed along the crease, and I let loose a muffled mewl, squirming against Elián's naked cock.

I struggled to part my legs, to open myself up again and take him inside of me, but a force yanked my ankles together.

Then my calves while El held my hips steady for him to rut against.

I twisted as much as I could, trying to see what—that was not me, that was—

"Your place, my queen," El spanked me again, making me whimper and press back on him, "is with me. Just as I am with you."

The restraint holding my legs together moved, shifting until my knees were bound as well, and from the edge of my peripheries, from the telltale sensation on my skin, the realization released more tears from my eyes. More anticipation clouded my mind.

He was using the twining of our power, like we'd done before, but this time, both tendrils listened to *him*.

El pried my cheeks apart and spat upon my entrance, letting it trail and run over me, and though I could not see it, the imagined visual of him watching his saliva run over my cunt was enough to push me even higher. I wanted him so badly, needed him so terribly.

But I was still me. So, I whined, "Th-Then let me control your Flames to bind and torture you—*ahh!*" El used a few of his fingers to gently smack my entrance and the bud above it, sending something close to lightning through my entire system. I came like that, without him inside of me, and yet he had total control of my body and soul.

Drool was escaping my lips, my muscles were trembling with residual shocks, and El chuckled as he notched the head of his cock against where my body was pulsing for him. His fingers pressed bruises into my hips. "But you like this, do you not?" He slowly plunged inside of me, easily with how relaxed I now was. "Me putting you at my mercy. Even when you grumble and gripe, you love doing what I tell you."

I opened my mouth again, to tell him based on principle that he was fucking wrong, but what came out was a long, sustained groan as he retreated then pushed further inside. That long glide sank him all the way to the hilt, and I felt my heart pulse around him.

I panted, breaths heavy, and tugged on my restraints. A soft noise released from my throat as I found, again, it was not me doing this. The sense I held within, a communication between Rhaea's power and myself, proved it to be…turned to Elián.

While he held, cock just at the line of what my body could take, I tested the Death seeping from my pores, and the bind at my wrist loosened accordingly.

El noticed, retreating then winding his hips to slam back inside of me. He started an intense, steady pace that dragged his cock against the most sensitive parts within me, and I relinquished control to him again, letting myself completely slip away.

"Remember this, Meline," he growled, "remember this when you let your wicked mouth run rampant." El punctuated yet another demand with a swat on my ass that clapped like thunder. It fucking stung, and I pushed back on him as much as I could.

A puddle of drool formed beneath me as breaths punched out of me, as El fucked me, and a rumble of release, deep and undeniable, threatened to knock me unconscious. If this was his way of reprimanding me, he'd soon find it would have the opposite effect.

But, of course, Elián detected I was about to come, just as I did him. How his power trembled and reveled in this connection and sharing of power.

I had trouble tracking where I was, eyes struggling to open, but El was holding me, hands supporting my rear as he nibbled at my neck. I was shaking, from stimulation—from peace—so I was happy to go. For him to take me.

Until my shoulders pressed against the cold wood of the wall. My eyes flew open, then.

El's face was close to mine, his nose nudging mine. His hair was loose and wild, and my fingers twitched behind my back, wanting to card through the strands. "Raise your arms, my queen," he whispered and darted his tongue to catch my lip, the tip of my fang.

Dammit—I did as he said, trying to catch his lips with mine. Of course, he leaned back, keeping himself just out of reach. I growled with my hands straight above my head, but he just watched me with vicious amusement, the beginnings of his dimples casting faint shadows on either side of his face.

And the motherfucker bit me. Instead of kissing me back, he skirted my lips and sank his fangs into my throat.

I came again, screaming, wanting to hold him to me. But as the wave swept over me, my arms would not lower. It was too much, how was I meant to—

Elián pulled back, removing his fangs, his lips, and his hands, and I squirmed, needing him back, wanting— "*Fuck*," El cursed. Sweat flowed down my temples to mix with my tears and the drops of blood he left on my neck.

My lip trembled in time with my muscles, and when I managed to crack my eyes open, the faint light from the lone candle on the night table cast a glow on his profile. Where he stood before me, eyes of the same color as the candlelight, hazy and blown out while he stroked his slick cock. I moaned, seeing it wet with me. Wanting it back, wanting *him* back.

He gently cupped his sac as he shuttled his fist up and down his shaft. Twisting his wrist, releasing moisture from his cockhead, and dragging it back down. "I think you are a bit of a cockslut, Your Highness."

The indignation didn't even rise. A ghost of it flitted through my thoughts, like something I maybe should probably say to tell him to shut the fuck up, but I was more concerned with the sight of him, touching himself while I couldn't move—

I blinked, trying to clear my mind to—I pulled on my wrists, and they would not budge. My legs remained spread, raised in the air, and something was holding me against the wall, but it was not him.

No, it was glittering black and orange, gray and gold, wrapped around my ankles, my wrists, and connecting them to each other. More supported my ass, saving me from any true pain.

Elián used our powers to suspend me on the wall of our bedroom for the evening as he touched what was mine. "Look at you, Meline," he gasped, and his hips bucked. He was close, I could taste it, and another noise—the most embarrassing so far —escaped. A plaintive whine through my nose. And the bastard chuckled, smirked even. "Beg me for it."

My jaw clenched closed, my nostrils flared, and he laughed again. When he stepped toward me, I loosed a relieved exhale, only to whimper as he swept two fingers at my entrance, dipping inside to collect my wetness and use it to slick his cock more. He threw his head back as he resumed fucking his fist, and I drank up the line of his throat, where I wanted to sink my own fangs. The swelling of his chest where his breaths pushed at his ribs and pectoral muscles. The shifting of granite as his biceps tensed.

"P-Please." I wasn't sure what would happen if he came, making me watch whilst leaving me empty, but it wouldn't be fucking good.

"Please, what?" his question was breathy, and he did not stop.

His sac was drawn up tight underneath his cock, and I started panicking. "Please give it to me. F-Fuck me, Elián."

Those dimples popped again. "Why should I do that, my queen?"

I managed a growl this time, struggling against the restraints he managed while indeed fucking torturing me. "Because that cock is mine, and I demand it, you *asshole*."

My insolence got him to lower his gaze back to me, at least. Though, it also caused his brow to raise and him to click his tongue at me. His face went as hard as his cock that was close to erupting. "Give me the real reason, or you will not have my cock in your cunt *or* your asshole."

El's fist flew even faster, the edge of his jaw ticked as he looked between his cock and where I was spread as wide as possible. He drew his lower lip between his teeth, and I couldn't take it anymore. He was just as stubborn as me and would certainly carry out his threat. I was close to hyperventilation, almost delirious with need, and I blurted, *"Please.* I need your cock, Elián. I need you inside of me."

He didn't slow, just looked at me with those fang tips flashing. "Why?"

My heart hammered within my chest, and I swallowed. On a whisper, I admitted, "Because I'm," I shivered, "your cockslut."

The words, what should have been a lie, earned me a cocksure grin from my Shadow. My love. It was crooked, fully displaying his dimples and the deadly points of his fangs. And thank goddess, he stopped stroking himself and took a step forward.

While holding the base of his cock, El braced his body with a hand beside my head, and we both watched as he slapped his cockhead against my cunt. My hips jerked, trying to take him. "Yes, you are mine." Fire around wide, black pupil, stared up at me through long lashes. "Forever."

I was past fear, now, exhausted and on the edge, completely open to him. I nodded. "Forever."

And without warning, El plunged inside of me. Hands pushing my thighs back and upward, he angled my body with total control and gave me what I'd begged for. He fucked me while I could do nothing but take it.

We gasped against each other, any semblance of kissing obliterated as we took pleasure in each other. Everything was stripped away, at least in that moment. At some point, as another release closed in around me and El groaned over where he'd bitten earlier, he released my wrists, and when they fell, they landed on his shoulders, clinging to him.

I gave into my instinct, and he titled his head even more as he thrust. My fangs sank into Elián's throat, just as he'd done to me, and the rich taste of his blood met my tastebuds, he began to come. A long, sustained growl reverberated against my bones as he poured his seed and kept moving, pounding his hips against mine until I came, too. Holding my Shadow to me, drinking from him solely to take more of Elián inside of me, we came together and settled together.

CHAPTER FORTY-TWO
MELINE

I awoke on Elián's chest.

Burgeoning daylight streamed through the window in lazy waves, and his breathing was slow, steady. He didn't snore, thank goddess for that, but, as I tucked a lock of black silk behind his ear, I realized I wouldn't mind. I would still be here.

My body healed quickly due to my Lylithan blood, but as city sounds trickled through the glass and the other guests of the lodging house began to tend to their morning needs, I still felt the sweet soreness within my muscles because of what we'd done.

After El had released me from the wall, we'd tumbled under the quilt where we lay now, kissing sweetly and falling asleep before we could speak much more.

He was taking me to the Well. With him. Whether I'd be able to set foot near enough to even catch a glimpse of it or not was yet to be determined. What I would not stand for would be any unnecessary distance between us or him facing an unknown danger alone. He'd traveled to another realm, taken on the Jakshka to save *my* friend. He'd traversed the continent in the years we were apart while I'd loved and lost and tried to scrape together the pieces of myself that were broken.

When I'd truly needed my El, my Shadow, he encircled me in his warmth and helped me weld the pieces together.

Elián shifted, nose scrunching so cutely. A wobbly smile spread on my lips. The gesture was so much like Soleil in the brief moments I was able to hold him.

There was still an ache there. Where I could almost see our babe, snuggling on Elián's chest instead of my own palm now lightly tracing the rose over his heart.

But, maybe. Maybe those sort of mornings were yet to be ours. One day.

El moved again, still asleep, and pulled me closer. He dropped a kiss to my brow, where my short curls were tangled. On the ship from Morova, he'd said he didn't mind my longer tresses being gone. That he didn't *need* them.

Of course, I'd not expected him to wield my power—as well as his—to compensate for my shorn hair. My lower belly flipped at the memory, and the dying ache between my legs was replaced with a telltale pulse.

"Nmn," Elián mumbled, and his grip on me tightened even more. Our legs were woven together like one of the colorful garments I was now accustomed to him wearing.

I watched him silently, drinking in the peace of this moment before we rode away to yet another place where danger awaited. My fingernails dragged light paths over his sides, where the muscles remained tense but were still looser than when he was awake. He had a tattoo of a decorated blade, one with fluid, wavy edges like the Ralthan River I could draw with my eyes closed. It was drawn in exquisite detail, stretching from the bottom of his rib to the top of his hip. The ink was black, but as I traced what appeared to be jewels set in a circular pattern on the pommel, I tried to imagine such a blade set with rubies. Or emeralds or sapphires. Something colorful to match the personality and depth of its wearer.

The pad of my finger had wandered to a particularly nasty scar on his hip, decades healed over but large, when I sensed the change in Elián's breathing. It shallowed a bit, and then the possessive hand on my own hip took on new intentionality.

Elián kissed me again, lingering on my scalp as he breathed me in. Brazenly, he palmed my ass and gave a gentle yet knowing squeeze. "Sabos al'dia," he grunted, eyes still closed. I continued to silently circle the scar on his hip, unsure of what he said, though I had an idea.

His lids parted to reveal that light, that warmth, and his dimples popped with his widening smirk. Elián dropped a kiss to my nose this time, and he repeated what he said, this time more clearly. Voice still rumbling and rough, he drawled, "*Sa*-bos ahl-*di*-a."

I repeated the words slowly, heat rising to my cheeks. It was so simple, and in this moment, he was such a far cry from the impenetrable statue he once was with me.

"Sabos al'dia," I said more quickly, and El grinned, showing his fangs. He nodded, hair shuddering against the pillow.

"I'm guessing that means 'good morning.'"

Elián passed his touch lightly over the center of my spine, over the scar that sent a faint shiver over my skin. "Sê. Yes."

"Sê. Sabos al'dia," I recited a few more times, testing the pronunciation. Embarrassingly, my fluency in the languages of our realm was limited to the common tongue and an old dialect of Rhaestran my mother used with me as a child. Through my travels as a member of the royal family, then as a mercenary, I'd picked up countless phrases and could more than survive in most towns the common tongue had yet to touch. But I wanted—needed—to know this one. To be closer to him. I moved my fingernail to the valley in the middle of his chest. "Will you keep teaching me?"

He smiled again, lips closed and nose wrinkling, just a bit. "Sê, mé relanha," he said, rolling the 'R' like a tumbling tide. "Yes, my queen. I will."

I let him feel my own grin as I ducked into his chest, inhaled the scent of him as he did me. It had been quite strange, during my pregnancy, to hold more than one being within myself. More than one scent. But it was beautiful, too, the aroma of fire mixed with ocean waves.

"We should go," Elián whispered after some time. Yes, even in this brief moment of stillness, the morning sun had brightened, illuminating more of the rumpled quilt, two pillows that'd made their way to the floor, and our clothes that were strewn in haphazard heaps.

I rose onto my hip, and spoke over my skipping heart as I gazed down at Elián. "How long of a ride from here to the Well?"

His hand was still on my ass, and he used the other to lightly circle my nipple. Unlike last evening, they were not lustful caresses. Just tender reminders and absent exploration. "Nine, give or take. If we were to move quickly."

I sighed. The prospect of traveling with Elián was more than welcome, yet more time in beds that did not belong to either of us irked. And that was a separate, much smaller concern than Cal essentially taking over the Shadows.

Nibbling on my lip, I shoved away the dreadful inevitability of this particular quest—confronting perhaps the worst of the demons of my past. "Once this whole thing is over, where would you want to live?" After a pause, I added in quiet breath, "Together."

Aside from said demon, I'd not lived with a lover before. My personal experience of companionship was so fucked up it shouldn't even be considered, but with Elián, I had an idea of what it could be like. What Maman and Papa had for centuries, even with the mountains of their responsibilities.

Would Elián want to mate me?

To my relief, he did not see or call attention to the flash of panic that forced a thick swallow in my throat. He tilted his head, contemplating. "I do not know. I have not had a permanent home aside from the Well in...ever." He frowned to himself.

"I don't need a permanent home. From birth, I divided my

time between Versillia and Rhaestras, then as an adult, I enjoyed traveling. Meeting new people and seeing new things."

El sat up, and I missed his proprietary touches until he drew me into a longer kiss, this one with the slight slip of his tongue. He pulled away and rested his brow on mine, but even from here, I could feel his uncertainty. Almost, shyness? "We could—I have—" he growled to himself and pressed closer to me "—Leandro and I selected our first home in Banfas. When we were sworn into the Shadows. It is an apartment, but I inherited the building from my father. It is the closest city to Zonoras. Where it once stood."

My eyes prickled, and I cradled El's face in my hands. My Darkness tingled as I pet the sides of his temples. "I would be honored, Elián. We'll start there."

He exhaled, shoulders relaxing. "Thank you. É vahmo."

Emotion filled those words to the brim, and he needn't tell me what they meant. I swept my thumb in an arc over the hard line of his brow, down the slope into his hairline. "É vahmo."

Tana checked her packs silently, but it was the type of quiet with an edge, a bite. With Francie back home and healing, our contract ended, I hadn't realized this freedom would feel like a death, too.

Death of the time I spent with Tana. With her beside me every moment to guide me away from truly disintegrating. Her jokes and soft embraces. The words we could communicate with just a look. Never had I lived so openly with another person, so truly.

She'd volunteered to stay, but with her posture rigid and the harsh manner in which she stuffed the last of her things in a brown, leather bag, I was at a loss of what to say. How had I fucked this up?

"Um. Thank you. For staying to help Tomás." Elián was with

his brother, in the room on the other side of the wall. I tried my best to focus on Tana and not eavesdrop on the gruff bickering going on between them. Needless to say, Tomás was not in agreement with the plan we'd designed while he slept.

Tana paused, still not looking at me, before sighing. "There is no need to thank me. I have grown…well, affectionate is the wrong word. But, I don't want to see the idiot die. And we've come this far." She shrugged, like she wasn't committing again to helping pull someone back from the crumbling edge of a cliff.

"Cera seems to be capable, though," I said and immediately wanted to stuff the words back in my mouth when she flinched. "I—you've just—I would understand if you wanted to rest. A break. After…after everything."

My cousin's hair was growing out, like mine, and the curls formed a yellow fringe that sprung from the scarf she had tied around the rest of it. She glanced sideways at me. "I know how to make decisions for myself, Leen. I can help, learn again from the priestesses, and reconnect with my coven here in Nethras. I'll inquire about a place to live more permanently, but for now, Cera has offered for me to stay with her."

"Oh." I cracked my knuckles and stuffed my hands in the pockets of my leather trousers. "Well, I'm glad this is where we ended up, then."

Tana buckled and situated her packs on the edge of the small bed she'd remade this morning. Or had she not slept at all? Bags hung under her eyes, but she smelled freshly bathed, and she moved with a professional alertness.

I moved from foot to foot, not knowing what to say next, so I tried at a bit of humor. "And Fenix?"

She pouted her bottom lip, a gesture she typically made when she was confused, and it was then that I finally got her to fully look at me. "What about him?"

I swept my gaze and senses around the room, as if he was somehow hiding in the corner or under the bed when he was most likely sleeping the day away. With his infatuation with

Tana, though, one could never be sure. "You know he's besotted with you, right?"

She froze, slumped, then completely straightened. Her emerald eyes cast side to side while she thought, opening and closing her mouth several times.

"Erm, I suppose you didn't know."

Blood rushed to her cheeks, deepening the brown color there to a bright rust. "I don't—he's not—"

I raised both hands. "All I'm arguing is that he wanted nothing to do with us, but after you saved his life, he followed us to another realm and back and is committed to stay in Nethras when there is absolutely no need. He volunteered to be a blood source from someone who I'm certain he still hates, at least a little bit, because it made your healing easier. Cera is here now and has summoned any nearby Rhaean priestess who can assist in Tom's recovery, so there's truly no need for his help. Fenix could go on his merry way, and yet, he's dug in his heels. You really don't see the way he looks at you?" Like she was the one who'd dug her hands in virgin soil and created the world.

Tana huffed, busying herself with straightening pillows and situating her packs again instead of addressing the obviousness of what Fenix felt for her.

I decided to let the subject lie. "Ah, so, I better get going." I winced at the clumsy attempt at farewell.

A deep wrinkle remained between the light, arched brows on Tana's face, but she pulled me into a quick, heavy embrace. I wanted to linger, to hold her to me, but she stepped back before I could even fully hug her to me. Before I turned, I blinked back tears, met her hard stare. "I love you, Tana. Thank you, for everything." I couldn't leave without saying that, at least.

Something sorrowful filled the air, like weeping rain, but she closed her eyes and shook her head, as if clearing the coming storm. "I love you, too, Leenie. Be safe."

The ringing of what hadn't been said screamed in my ears, but I was grateful for this mutual declaration. That through it all, even with the way I'd leaned on her to the point of taking advantage, she still loved me.

I left the room when Tana rejected my offer of help with her packs. The Rhaestran guards would be here any moment to help move her things, she said, and I honored her wishes, going to Tomás's room and announcing myself to him and Elián with a knock of knuckle on wood.

"Oh, fantastic, your co-conspirator," I heard through the door. When I pushed it open, Tomás was dressed and sitting in the wheelchair, arms crossed in outrage.

Elián dragged his hand over his face, pulling at his cheeks and rolling his eyes at the same time. "For the last time. You are in no condition to come to the Well."

"And what if the boy is in trouble? Danger? She can't even set foot on the grounds, you dolt!"

El said nothing to that, tensing of the muscles in his neck revealing an agreement with that concern. There was some truth to Cera's snide critique of my conviction to accompany Elián, but I liked to think of it as confidence.

"I made a vow, and I intend to do everything I can to keep it. I love him," I pointed to Elián, "and the Shadows are important to him. Let alone the fact that Cal intends to do nothing but be an absolute terror at the expense of everyone involved. I'm going."

Tomás gave me a flat look and huffed as he leaned further in his seat. "What a beautiful proclamation of love." He winced, rubbing at his chest, and I saw the way Elián tensed. "This is bullshit. *Balderdash.*"

Instead of deigning his brother's ranting with a response, El grasped the handles of Tomás's chair and began steering him toward the door. At least the male had the good sense to not plant his heels into the floor.

Elián sent me a weak smile, and I returned it, communicating reassurance I wasn't qualified to give. I followed them both into the corridor, just as Cera came stomping around the corner. Well, she glided while her guards stepped heavily behind her. Like when she'd pulled the sickness from Elián's brother, she was dressed in a mixture of gold and typical priestesswear. This time, she overlayed her cream-colored ensemble with a purple shawl around her shoulders.

"These two rooms for now, please," she directed to the guards who were a mixture of Lylithan, human, and elven, judging by their scents and the characteristic features I could see. They wore identical armor, but the one who was taller than the rest, taller than even Elián, went for Tana's room. The human went for Tomás's things, and the remaining guards stood at Cera's back. "We'll have to return for the Vyrkos." She rolled her eyes, even when Tana emerged with that blush still fierce.

"Have you heard anything else?"

Cera grimaced but kept her answer accordingly vague, for fear of nosy lodging house patrons. "Yes, and it's…not encouraging. More silence from your siblings," she nodded toward El and Tomás, "and tales of negotiations we weren't yet privy to."

Ice crackled over my spine. "Negotiations."

The guards emerged from the now vacant rooms, carrying my cousin's and Tomás's things. Cera chewed at her lip. "We're unsure of with *whom* aside from the separate conversations with Quen. But there's been allusion to more."

"For what?" Tana asked quietly yet loud enough for us to hear.

"'Bolstering the Lylithan stronghold'," Cera quoted, and my stomach dropped. Knowing how he governed Krisla, there was no doubt what such efforts would entail.

War.

"We must go," Elián said, and I nodded resolutely.

First to the Shadow Well. And as our procession left the lodging house on Fair and Fortune, I suspected that my peace with Elián, in his Banfas apartment while we made a life together, was retreating further and further away like a receding wave.

CHAPTER FORTY-THREE
ELIÁN

We walked the Ralthan Forest, hand in hand, while we led our mares along the overgrown path. I knew the way like I knew my name, though I'd not been back to Papá's small home in many years. While I had suggested we spend the night at the inn on the main road, with its hot meals and bustling business, here we were.

I paid someone to check in on the home monthly, cleaning and notifying me of any repairs necessary. I could never bear to lease it out, though.

"This—his house is this way?" Meline whispered, her words mixing with the shuddering of the fiery, balding trees above. One of the things I enjoyed most about Ralthas was the visible change in seasons, marking time and providing distinct experiences, celebrations. Zonoras was different, time stretching as far as the endless stretch of sand and rock.

The forest was temperate, just as the one where my queen and I walked, starting our new beginning.

"Yes. It's not much further." The sun was almost fully set, now, and the barest hint of orange hung over the treetops, lighting the way. A wind coursed around us, rustling the land and the hair near my face. Before I had decided to stop us in

Ralthas, only derailing our journey by an hour or so, I had dressed in one of the shawls my father had woven for me, more than a century ago. It was more decoration than anything, providing additional warmth I did not need. But the vibrant stripes in red, blue, and white filled me with pangs of emotion. Too complex for me to try and put words to, so I just swallowed them, let the feelings settle in my stomach while the knotted fringe along the edges swayed with my steps.

My fingers were not as skilled as Papá's had been, but perhaps I could make one. For my queen.

More of those throat-tightening memories threatened to sweep me under as we drew closer. The faint clops of our horse's steps punctuated the count down until we were there. Standing on the path leading to my father's home.

Moss covered the stone in patches, but the windows had recently been washed. The interior was dark, of course, and the greenery surrounding was a bit overgrown. But Papá had liked that, enjoyed feeling surrounded by nature to the point of almost being suffocated by it. So, I instructed the home's carer, a gentle Lylithan who lived closer to town, to only trim what was necessary.

The cottage consisted of three bedrooms, a living area, and a kitchen. Simple and small, even though it had seemed so large when I was a boy. With what felt like the whole world around it. Zonoras was nothing but flattened desert, now, so I clung to this, my childhood home, as much as my and Leandro's apartment.

I started forward, bringing with me the horse named Saffron, until I noticed an absence at my side. I stood between the mouth of the path and the front door. Meline was gazing to the left, where oak and maple trees cloaked the land beyond.

Her mauve tunic was loose, fluttering in the evening breeze while her leather trousers hugged her thighs. The curls that had been short and slicked to her scalp were now long enough to spring around her ears and temples.

"The house where..." Meline swallowed, and pointed west.

"That way." The Ralthan River was a distant rush, a shudder filling the voice of the forest. Another song that colored my memories, like the howling wind rustling the tent fabric of my mother's home.

I looked where Meline was pointing, fear and the familiar gnawing sadness clawing at the underside of my ribs. "We can set down our things and feed the horses. And you will show me?" Because now, such grief could be shared.

She faced me, eyes shimmering with more than the gold I had grown used to, and nodded.

When I fished out the key to Papá's home and let us inside, stale air filled my lungs like dry cloth, and the protective barrier allowed me and Meline, my guest, to pass. I went to the windows, pushing them open to let out the musty air that had been trapped within since the carer was here last. Then, I went to the freshly cleaned hearth stacked with fresh logs. Releasing fire from my palms provided more relief, like a large sigh in the depths of my soul, and when I stood, I took in not just Papá's home, but my queen within it.

Certainly, my father had others within its walls besides him, Leandro, and me, but I was never present for that. Even Mamá did not visit, electing to remain in the arid lands of Savya, the continent where we'd been born.

Still, there were touches of Zonoras in the very Ralthan home. Heavy wood craftsmanship shown in the table set to the right, beside a large window that overlooked the woods behind the house. The dark floors were clean, as was the Zonoran rug sprawling the length of the living area. Its shades of crimson reflected that of the flames, as did the oranges of the tapestry hanging behind the sofa. Cushions were neatly stacked beside it, accommodating for my brother and me who had picked up the Zonoran custom of sitting on the floor.

"It smells like you in here," Meline whispered reverently, looking around what was so familiar to me. I'd not changed anything when my father and brother were killed, so it was the same as it had been before and yet irreversibly changed. A tomb.

Or, so I had thought for many years. With someone else in it, with *her* in it, it felt more again. Like a home.

"It does?"

She nodded, stepping closer and keeping her movements measured, as if she did not want to disturb anything, even the empty spaces. "Yes. Although," she sniffed purposefully, "it smells more strongly of the oak in your scent. Tilled soil and cool water."

I smiled, let my eyes fill. "That's Papá."

Though mine hadn't, Meline's tears fell into two, faint tracks. She did not try to wipe them away. "What was his name?"

My heart thudded heavily in my chest. "Emmett."

Meline took another step closer to me, now in reaching distance. Her gaze softened. "Emmett and Elián."

My smile was sad. Grateful. For her. "Sê."

She did reach out to me, then. After quickly pulling off her gloves, Meline took my jaw in hand, tugging lightly while pressing up on her toes. She kissed me with closed lips and love pulsing from her into me. "É vahmo, El. Gravas." She kissed me again while I focused on remaining upright.

The first part of our ride to the Well was an amalgamation of silence and stories. Tales of her life, mine, and the one we had lost and were trying to create together.

And lessons in Zonoran, when I would say simple phrases, translate, and practice with her. The language of Ralthas was the common tongue, so the weight of her speaking to me in my first language, of telling me she loved me, was almost too much for me to hold. To contain.

"É vahmo, mé relanha. But you do not need to thank me."

"Yes, I do." But she did not elaborate on what, and I decided I did not need her to. Words were still difficult for me at times, and we both still struggled with not using them as weapons and shields. Sometimes, the absence of them spoke much more clearly. When we would speak our son's name, and the long shared pause, staring ahead, was enough. When we would pant into each other's mouths, eyes locked and bodies joined. When she drew a grin from me and would gift me with one of hers.

We placed our things in the spare room, where I had long ago brought a bed for when I could bring myself to stay here. Papá's room and the one I'd shared with Leandro remained as they'd been since the day they left this realm.

The two of us emerged, walking past Saffron and Amber as they grazed the foliage in front of the house.

The forest was quiet for us, yet lively at the same time. What fauna was awake, scuttled under the dying light of day, and nocturnal predators prowled in the darkness. Wolves, wild cats, and scavengers were common in this area, and my awareness of all of it ran in the background of my thoughts.

After some time, walking along the length of the river that was just hidden from view but audible, Meline stopped us again. This cottage was newer than Papá's, though we were watching it through the shield of mature tree trunks. Someone was in it, evident by the electric lights glowing from within. Papá never had modernized to have them installed in his home. And with Leandro and I around often, he had often stated he had no use for it.

Faintly, I could hear the sounds of a family within its walls. The excited babbling of two children, maybe three. The tired laughs of their parents.

Meline's breaths were fast, and her hand rubbed at the center of her chest. I had no connection to the cottage directly, only with her, but through that, I could feel the pain. The longing. Missing what could have been, she had said. And was that not the most overwhelming shade of grief? Letting go of a nebulous hope?

She did not linger long, though I would have stood all evening with her, should she have needed it. But, she led us away, toward the calm roar of the river.

Meline took us to a cluster of boulders, flat and smoothed

where people had most likely sat for centuries, and the deftness in which she crossed her legs, tucking them toward her, showed she had been one of them.

I took the edge, mimicking her posture and following her gaze to the running water. It was dark, this time of night, lapping obscured by the fading light.

Fabric rustled, and I turned my attention back to her, where Meline was pulling the small, gold box from her pocket I'd since given back to her. Flowers were etched into the surface, and when she opened the clasp, a telltale, pungent scent hit my nostrils.

She took one of the tight rolls, fitting it between her plump lips. Meline flicked a glance to the river as she fished in another pocket, unable to find what she was looking for.

I extended my first finger, calling the drop of flame forth and watched as it illuminated her freckled cheeks. Made her eyes twinkle.

My queen smirked around the joint, not even needing to thank me, and leaned over to light it on my Flame. Smoke wound into the night, reaching toward the branches arcing over us, red flaring with each inhale she took.

She pinched the end between two black fingers, dangled her foot over the water, and extended the joint toward me.

Her eyes widened as she angled her lips to exhale away from us and watched as I took it, brought it to my own lips. The taste was not as bad as I thought it would be, though not as satisfying as the pipes I took to smoking with Mamá. It sent heat down my throat, stoking the Fire that always lived within the depths of me.

"I thought it was a disgusting habit?"

I pushed the smoke smoothly through my nostrils, letting it unfurl around me. Most of the time, I did not like being out of control—lapses of imbibing to excess notwithstanding.

I shrugged and took another drag of the joint, noticing the

minute relaxation of my spine. "You rattled my nerves at the time. Everything you did unsettled me."

Meline tsked and snatched the spent joint from me, taking a frustrated pull before stubbing it out on the stone between us. "You were a testy asshole, you mean." But the admonishment held no malice, and the hash smoothed any barb I would normally lob her way. Maybe, had I accepted the way she affected me and also not been on duty, we would have had moments like this. Companionable, affectionate silence.

That was, until my queen began to hum. Through our recent travels, I caught her making the sound, though when anyone came close enough to hear, she would stifle the song and whatever she had been thinking at the time.

Now, though, she let it wind between us while she sat with eyes closed, wrinkle forming between her brow and humming over the river.

Could one's heart clench and soar at the same time? As if its wings were beating fast and hard? I closed my eyes, too, as my queen went through the fragments of the lullaby.

"*And I am with you. Loving you. For all the days we have and after*," I picked up the end of the chorus. Of one of the many lullabies Mamá would sing to my brother and me, then with us as we grew old enough to join her. When my twin would be loud, and my words would come out smooth.

I fluttered my lashes open as my singing traded for the galloping of her heart, the whistling of her breathing. "El—*how?*"

More slowly, I sang the words to her from the beginning. "*My love, there is no world in which I will not protect you. You can count the grains of sand, and you will still not reach the end of my caring for you. I will be with you always, even when my soul is returned to the air in your lungs. Even when you must dance and sing without me. I am with you. Loving you. For all the days we have and after*." The slow, deep melody lilted with the tones that were characteristic of no other place but Zonoras. Banfian songs came close, but the blend of melancholy and devotion was of my people.

A promise and a prayer I'd sang over my queen every day, every hour, in the time before she awoke with the scar now on her spine.

Again, the last line of the song echoed into the night, over the water where she spread the ashes of our son. Of Soleil. And though I wept, I hoped the words were clear enough to reach him.

"You—" Meline cleared her throat "—you have a *beautiful* voice, El."

I smiled through my tears. "Gravas, mé relanha." I had been told so before, that I had a gift for song like my mother. But the compliment was much more, coming from her.

"And you...I heard it. I'd just not realized it was you." Meline sniffed, rubbing at her eyes and scooting closer to me. I opened my arms, giving space she slotted into perfectly. "I don't understand the words, but I *feel* them. Here." She placed my hand on her heart, then landed hers on mine. Somehow, they beat in time. "And I used to hum it to Soleil. *Every day.*"

I buried my nose in her hair, catching the whiff of him on her. Of the love she felt for him, of the home she created for him.

"I will teach you the words. And we will sing it to him. To each other."

Meline kissed the base of my throat, over where my pulse beat for her in this peaceful moment we were able to steal away. Where we did not have to stand alone in our hurt.

"Sê. Mé Zombro." *My Shadow.*

Epilogue

I didn't bother keeping my steps silent. Not even quiet.

The rain battering the windows and facade of the Well drowned them out, anyway. My own rage, pulsing behind my eyelids, was louder.

Ever since I had been overruled, the quiet darkness of the Well was no longer comforting. It was menacing, with traitors and *fools* lurking in every corner. I'd assured my brothers that the others with seats at the Elders' table were reasonable. Now, I spat on the stone floor, twice for my siblings who blatantly assured me that Varus's proposal would not *stand* then proceeded to vote against me.

The Shadows no longer held sovereignty. The Shadows no longer stood on their own.

My fist banged on the heavy wooden door, painted black for as long as the Well stood.

The chandeliers fitted with small candles lit the room, warded for only sitting Elders and invited Shadows to pass through. The hot taste of my blood bloomed in my mouth as I took in those seated at the long table, constructed from the first tree felled in construction of the Well. Did they want to burn that too? Take an axe to it and set it aflame like the rest of our sacred ways?

I'd run away from the Trylas, from my responsibilities at birth and the dangers awaiting. I'd found a *home*, a family, and a profession that felt truer to me than my own name.

"Master Noruh. Thank you for joining us."

Varus drawled from the head of the table as the senior member of the Elders, a position held by the oldest sitting Shadow on our governing body. And one for head puppeteer, it seemed.

"Who the fuck is this?" I demanded, stopping behind my designated seat and eyeing the two unfamiliar faces. They should not have been permitted to enter, neither of them Shadows and neither of them Elders. Hell, one of them wasn't even Lylithan.

"Watch your tone, Master Noruh."

"And you can go to hell, Varus. All of you." I made a point to meet each and every gaze of my fellow Shadows who voted for this. Trenton. Yara. Forrest. Since that night, all Shadow activity had been halted, all members were called back to the Well, and all communication channels paused until we could assess. It was protocol that had not been enacted in over a century, not since the Killings when we had to protect ourselves and our kind.

"Enough. We vote democratically amongst our peers, and the vote was sound, as you witnessed."

I pointed my finger right between the midnight blue eyes staring back at me from across this surface that was supposed to be *sacred*. "And you've given us over to this tyrant. He should not even *be here*."

"Master Noruh. I assure you that my collaboration with The Shadows will benefit us both tremendously." His posture was straight, relaxed, and his voice was as smooth as poisoned wine. Krisla may have held the largest Lylithan population in the world, and he may have a seat on the Lylithan Council, but I held no illusion this decision would have negative ramifications for generations to come.

I thought of Marco, hidden away in the acolyte wing with the others I would shield from this as best I could. They were the most vulnerable of us all, and if it meant my dying breath, they would be safe. My Shadow vow, a slithering, pulsing companion who had walked with me since my twentieth year, demanded it.

I'd no idea what happened to the others'. How had they corrupted us all?

"I have allies who will ensure our race not only survives but *prospers*." He gestured to the white-haired one beside him with pointed ears. Some sort of elven fellow whose cloying perfume was only making me angrier.

"Sit, Master Noruh," Varus bade me again, indignant flush beginning to bleed into the orange strands at the base of his neck. I'd once took comfort in his presence, his appearance that reminded me of my mother and sister back in the highlands. "We will begin discussing the future of the Shadows and our work with the King of Krisla."

I wanted so badly to scream. To shake my siblings who were convinced that this was the path to take.

But, instead, I drew a breath. Reasoning that I would not be able to fight them if I were thrown from the room. At the table, I could do my best to steer us away from total destruction. Here, I could take as much information as I could and warn my brothers.

My seat, one I'd been *proud* to occupy just a few days ago, scraped against the carpet beneath. And I sat.

Acknowledgments

See? I promised you a Happy For Now ending, and I stuck to it!

Of course, I had to leave you on a teensy cliffhanger, too!

Thank you so much for reading Shadows & Flames! This book was two years in the making, wherein I took a little detour with my paranormal romance series, and coming back to this world was like coming home. Meline is the first character I ever wrote, and she is such a big part of my heart. Elián encapsulates everything I love in a male lead, and I hope you've enjoyed them both as they try to find *peace*.

This book, as much as I love these characters, was really difficult for me to write. A variety of things contributed to that, but I somehow found my way to this point, writing this note to you.

Without these people, there would be no Shadows & Flames:

Bojana. At times, you were more excited about this book than I was! Thank you so much for your encouragement and being, seriously, the best beta reader ever. I so much value your feedback, and I'm a better writer because of it!

Darcy. I still remember opening up and telling you I was writing Twin Blades, and you've stuck with me through all my releases. I'm so grateful we met in Spanish class, and since then, I've truly valued your presence in my life. Thank you for reading my books and taking the time to give me feedback, and thank you for being my friend!

Alexia. I tell you all the time, but thank you for talking me out of anxiety spirals again and again. Who knew a lil conversation about books at work would lead us where we are now! I so much value your friendship and the laughs and dinners we share. I hope this HFN ending put your mind at ease!!!

Zaylee, Heather, and Akilah. Thank you so much for beta reading this book, your feedback, and your readership of my other books!

Avery. Thank you for our ongoing alpha reader exchange! You've read the earliest versions of these chapters, and I can't thank you enough for bearing with my wordiness, disorganization, and gushing over writing!

And to my husband. As always. Thank you for being my biggest supporter, my confidant, and helping me figure out the "rogue shit" in this story. Sorry about the Soleil chapter and making you cry.

WHAT'S NEXT?

So. What's next? In case you're one of the few who reads these lil notes, this is where my writer brain is heading:

How I Became a Succubus's Pet is set to release as a novel this October. I've never done a seasonal release before (aside from my short Valentine's novelette), and since half this book was already written as part of an anthology, it is the perfect Halloween release. Get ready for a Hell reimagining, a bratty subby boi, and a grumpy yet caring succubus Domme.

Wicked is the Night is *hopefully* coming at the end of the year. I'm giving myself some breathing room, should *Succubus* take more out of me than I anticipate, but I'm very excited to return to the beautiful chaos that is Xiomara.

After that, I'm tossing around the idea of a red riding hood retelling. With monsters and the appropriate levels of female rage, of course.

I hope you'll join me!

About the Author

Noelle Upton is an indie author and lover of fantasy, romance, and dark tales. When she's not writing or reading, Noelle enjoys dancing, chatting with friends over good food, and laughing with her husband. Her three series, *Twin Blades*, *A Light in the Dark*, and *Demons & Cryptids* are ongoing, and *Shadows & Flames* is her fifth novel.

www.noelleupton.com

Twin Blades

The Warrior Queen, the Protector of Innocents… fights in seedy taverns and picks pockets for the highest bidder.

But her people have been rebuilding from near eradication. And after a century of running, Meline returns home at the request of the only family she has left. They've built a kingdom from ashes and connected with other leaders to give them all a fresh start, but they are still under attack with the threat of another slaughter on the rise.

So, to atone for her sins, Meline agrees to travel to faraway lands and persuade more to her family's cause. Even if the agreement demands she take a personal guard. But not all is as it seems, and her Shadow is hiding a secret of his own.

Through homecoming and redemption, Meline finds herself leaning on her companion as they face tense negotiations, assassins, and the mysterious powers of a dark Goddess. But will it be enough to confront the person she once was and conquer Death? Or will it lead to the ruin of those she loves most and the future of her people?

In the Light of the Moon

Sylvie, a twenty-eight-year-old undergraduate student, has recently moved to Antler Pointe following the death of her father. She's committed to finally finish her degree in English and to learn her family craft under the tutelage of her grandmother. One night, while closing up at her part-time job, Sylvie stumbles upon an injured man. After helping him on his feet, and watching him shuffle off into the night, Sylvie goes into her last year of college with an enthusiasm to finally set her life back on track. What she doesn't expect, however, is to quite literally run into the man she helped, now fully healed. He's curt and suspicious of her but is committed to settle the debt of her kindness.

Orion is a literature professor who has settled in his hometown after years of trying to find his place. After a disastrous attempt, Orion has resolved himself to live a quiet life on his family's land with nature and books for companions. But once a witch with kind eyes saves him by caring for and generously gifting him with her smiles, he starts to hope that he may not need to remain alone.

However, there is something sinister happening in Antler Pointe, and while they're eager to explore a peaceful life with one another, Sylvie and Orion are quickly swept up in a string of disappearances that culminates in a bloody showdown. *In the Light of the Moon* is a paranormal romance with a fall backdrop where witches and shifters meet, fight, and love. All under the light and shadows of a living forest that calls to both groups with very different songs.

Scars of the Sun

Fresh out of the hospital, **Ramona** has left her apartment and studies to move to the small town of Antler Pointe. Being the non-shifter sister of the local pack Leader is pretty lame, but she throws herself into helping with her brother's kids and working in her sister-in-law's magical garden. Anything at all to keep the dark thoughts at bay. But it's when she locks eyes with a tattooed jaguar shifter that Ramona rethinks what it means to be seen.

Río's days in Antler Pointe have already run out. He's overstayed his usual six months maximum in the little town and should be moving on to the next. After eight years on the run, he's used to the rhythm by now, but he's already put down a few extra roots in this place. And when he keeps stumbling across the non-shifter Wolf girl with long legs and honey eyes, he feels an even stronger pull to stay.

Ramona and Río are both floating through life until they collide in a rich and passionate summer romance. So used to living with no true home, Río is unwilling to let this thing stay temporary, and Ramona is terrified to let her Jaguar go. But a greater threat is looming on the horizon. One that endangers the Antler Pointe Pack and has the potential to blow Ramona and Río apart completely. Will they put their new love before the blood ties of family? How far will they go to protect the ones they care about? And how the hell do they fight a damn shifter mafia?

Scars of the Sun is a paranormal romance standalone novel and book two of the A Light in the Dark series. Prior knowledge of the events of *In the Light of the Moon* is helpful but not required.

Bloom in Darkness

In the small New England town of Antler Pointe, **Delaney Warner** is finally living his dreams. He's in his last year of college for his teaching degree, he has a brand new pack that is *so* much better than his last, and he's got more friends than he ever imagined. After his tragic upbringing, Delaney is now determined to try new things and thrive. So, when his roommate suggests he attend a metal show downtown, he dresses up and wiggles on over. If there's one thing Delaney has found, it's that life is full of surprises, and when the lead singer of the Concrete Executioners calls him beautiful and buys him a drink, he may have found the best surprise of them all!

Tyler Lee has the weight of his family's hopes on his shoulders. After moving away from Antler Pointe in the seventies, he returns as a jaded vampire and takes over his family's funeral home so that his elderly parents can finally retire. Now back in the town his younger self was so determined to escape, he's mentoring his nephew, managing his brother's recovery, and counting down the days until he can live for himself again. That is, until he sees a sweet boy with golden hair and pure soul through the crowd and can't resist spending a night with him.

One night turns into more, and Delaney and Tyler form a bond that feels a little too much like fate. Even still, Tyler worries that his darkness is too much for his boy, and Delaney's past threatens to rip them apart.

Bloom in Darkness is a standalone novel featuring characters from the *A Light in the Dark* series. Prior knowledge from *Scars of the Sun* (ALD #2) is recommended.

Love Always, From Antler Pointe

Welcome back to Antler Pointe, a town filled with humans, shifters, vampires, and faeries. This time, we catch up with Sylvie and Orion for a special moment, Río and Ramona as he tries to make up for some oversights, and Tyler and Delaney as the former showers his mate with an unexpected surprise.

After their own celebrations, the Antler Pointe couples convene for an

"Intimate Palentine's Day Extravaganza." Hosted by one very excited Jaguar and his mate who would do anything to keep that goofy smile on his face.

This Valentine's Day novelette is filled with a few spicy moments, a lot of sweet ones, and a special night for this found, supernatural family.

Prior knowledge of the previous *A Light in the Dark* series books is recommended before reading this story.

Wicked is the Night

Xiomara is the head enforcer of the Serafim Group, the best shifter family business in the world. She gets called in to collect heads or make sure people get with the program, but this new assignment is different. When her father tasks her with taking down their biggest rival from the inside out, Xiomara is all too eager to sign the marriage contract. Her husband turns out to be a stupid workaholic, but the job gets harder the longer she's out from under her father's thumb.

Boone isn't new to this. At one hundred and twenty-five years old, he's been in the business since he was running moonshine in the North Georgia mountains. Benicio Serafim has been a thorn in his side for the last few decades, and when the opportunity arises to get close enough to stab him in the back, Boone doesn't hesitate. His new wife is a ball of chaos, claws, and hidden knives, but he slowly grows used to his kitten.

Will Xiomara be able to end Boone Albright when the time is right? Will Boone be able to take down the Serafim Family? And who the hell is stealing from them all?

Wicked is the Night is a paranormal romance standalone novel and is book three of the A Light in the Dark series. Prior knowledge from the previous books is helpful but not required.

How I Became a Succubus's Pet

Daniel, a college junior who somehow found his way in a History of the Occult class, is trying to keep his scholarship. With a degree he may not even want hanging in the balance, he decides to go all-out for this extra credit paper. But conducting a ritual from an old, forgotten textbook isn't one of his brightest ideas.

Not when it ends up being real.

After summoning a succubus and accidentally binding his soul to hers, Daniel is dragged to Hell where he waits for his demon to find a solution. He works in her shop, meets new friends, and builds a new life for himself while Feronia's allure grows by the day. One that asks him to submit.